Prague Spring

David Del Bourgo

MYSTÉRE PRESS

MYSTÉRE PRESS

ISBN 978-1-442-11987-1

Book design by Kevin Lien

A great crime offends nature, so that the very earth cries out for vengeance: that evil violates a natural harmony which only retribution can restore...

Yosal Rogat

Prague Spring

HISTORICAL DISCLAIMER

My research for *Prague Spring* has included books and articles on the following topics: the Holocaust; Czech history from the late Nineteenth Century through the Soviet invasion of 1968; the *Nokim*; the Gehlen Organization; first-hand accounts of people who lived in Prague during the Thirties and the Nazi occupation; Berkeley in the Sixties; justice; psychopathology; and the psychology of murder in its various forms, including genocide.

I have tried to depict historical events with as much accuracy as the constraints of fiction would allow. Given that I wanted to write a compelling story, however, I purposely altered some historical details for dramatic purposes. For example, I portray the Soviet invasion of Czechoslovakia sometime in late September of 1968, when it actually occurred on August 21, 1968. I have also compressed or somewhat altered the timeline of events that occurred during this invasion. Although the Gehlen Organization did exist, and the CIA actually employed thousands of ex-Nazis and S.S., to my knowledge none of them ever came to the United States to counsel politicians or commit acts of assassination. And although the *Nokim* (Haganah avengers) also existed during the years I have suggested, I doubt that any of them ever came as far as the United States to assassinate anyone. *Nokim* lore does state, though, that its members poisoned loaves of bread destined for a D.P. camp that held Germans. The reader can be assured, however, that my fictional protagonist Simon Wolfe did not take part in that effort.

CHAPTER ONE

San Francisco ~ Spring 1952

I watched from my second-story window as Feiertag left his apartment. I wanted to follow and sit at a table across from him at breakfast. To see him go through his routine one last time, pretending he was just another smiling émigré loyal to his newfound land of freedom under America's all-forgiving God. But exposing myself at the last minute would have been self-indulgence. This job had to be done right, requiring a discretion that had not been necessary with previous targets. I'd have to work like the *Kidon*, not the *Nokim*.

When we *Nokim* assassinated Nazis in Europe, we made no attempt to hide our tracks. We wanted the world to know we'd brought another mass murderer to justice. In Germany we'd disguise ourselves in German uniforms and drive right up to the house of the war criminal. I would ask the wife if her husband were home. Sometimes I'd say he was in danger and we'd come to warn him. Other times I'd simply make up a story about a bureaucratic snafu and say we needed him to come down to headquarters to complete some forms.

Then we took the criminal into the forest where we recited the list of his crimes. Each and every one claimed innocence. You've made a mistake, they'd say. They were not there when twenty Jews were shot and dumped in a ravine or gassed with exhaust in the back of a truck. They had not personally pulled the trigger and they would have done something to stop the murders if they could. Or they would have been killed themselves if they'd disobeyed orders. But that was no excuse. The SS death squads were a voluntary service.

We tied their hands behind their backs and blindfolded them. I put the barrel of a gun above their temples and executed them swiftly, without pain. It was more than they deserved, but it was part of our code. First, we didn't kill anybody without properly establishing their guilt. It was not enough to know they'd been part of the SS. The Haganah needed some evidence of their participation in actual crimes. Torture was also forbidden; we did not want to become sadists like them. After we executed the criminal, we left him by the side of the road, blindfolded with a bullet in his head. Our calling card.

But world politics had changed and I now worked for the Mossad, a more modern organization than the Haganah. They did not want the truth to be suspected. I would kill Feiertag their way—not because I felt such a loyalty to them—it was the only way that offered me the possibility of a future. If I botched this job, I'd have both the Mossad and the San Francisco police after me. Perhaps even the FBI. So it had to look like an accident. If nobody suspected that Feiertag had been murdered, the Mossad might ignore the incident.

I sat on the bed's lumpy mattress to wait for Feiertag's return. I'd kicked off the covers and top sheet during the night. The threadbare lower sheet was gathered under me, exposing the mattress's striped ticking. I wouldn't bother to straighten the bedding. I wasn't coming back. None of us was. And whoever moved into this dump would never guess it had once been a jump-site.

I'd run out of Top Cigarette Tobacco, so I rooted around the ashtray. It hadn't been emptied for days and all the best butts had been rolled by Mara. Mine hardly stayed together during a smoke and almost always fell apart when crushed out. Mara's fingers worked with the grace of dancers, bending and flexing to compress tobacco and stretch paper at the same time. I was impatient and tore the paper half the time. She said my hands were like animals waiting in a dark corner. "Good for ambushes, not rolling cigarettes." Her dimpled smile took the edge off her words.

I lay back on the bed naked except for my boxers. Feiertag wouldn't be back until eleven. I knew his routine. He'd return from breakfast, take off his suit and put on a bathrobe to wear around the apartment; then watch TV until two, when he'd nap.

Lighting the longest of the ashtray's crooked butts, I leaned my head against the wall and looked at the empty place next to me. Where would Mara be now? On the beach? No, it was evening in Haifa. In bed with somebody she'd met that day? She'd say it would be just like me to think she could forget so easily. Besides, the Mossad probably hadn't let her go that quickly. They'd be grilling her about why I hadn't returned as planned.

Mara thought I hadn't warned her I was staying because I didn't love her. In a way I guess that was true. I didn't love anybody. I'm not sure that's why I hadn't confided in her, though. I told myself I was protecting her. But I didn't need to tell myself anything. Both Mara and I knew that people who led secret lives didn't share secrets. We didn't even know each other's last names.

"Always like new strangers in one another's arms," Mara said.

Normally her face was as expectant as an eager child's. But I didn't mind, really, when she looked vacant.

"Only I see your sadness," I said.

"That's because I'm not sad around anyone else." She tilted her head to one side like one of Modigliani's beautiful oval-faced girls with floating blue eyes.

We both had Aryan features. That's why we'd been chosen—to blend in with the enemy.

"I'm not going back with you," I told her our last morning together.

"They'll come after you, Simon." She propped herself on an elbow, exposing a small breast that was half pink nipple.

"If they want to kill me, let them," I said.

"But why?"

"The Mossad isn't interested in the *Nokim*," I said. "And I don't want to go back to Israel to hunt down Arabs."

She leaned in closer. "So let's just go back there and live our own lives. We can set up a home."

"I've never felt comfortable in Israel."

"And you feel at home here?" she asked.

"No, but I'd rather be damaged goods in a place where nobody expects you to belong."

Sunlight seeped through the weave of the apartment's burlap curtains. It was dawn already. Our plane was scheduled to leave that morning.

"You want to be left alone," Mara said, climbing over me to open the window. The sun reflected off rooftops through steaming dew, outlining her silhouette as she dropped her head to look at me under her arm. She still had the body of a girl, but the expression on her face was anything but girlish: *Is this all you ever want of me?*

I rolled away and Mara pressed up close behind me.

"I know we're not children anymore," she said. "And there's nothing we can do to get back those lost years, but we're both still young."

"Speak for yourself," I said.

She took her hands off me. I could still feel the close heat of her.

"No matter what I do or say, it's like I'm always pouring salt on your wounds," she whispered.

I fell back to sleep. When I awoke she was gone and I knew what I had to do. It had to be done fast. I might have three days to a week before they came after me. I wouldn't wait that long. I'd do it as originally planned, Saturday, the day after tomorrow.

And now it was Saturday.

I slipped on my watch. 10:30 a.m. Still too early for Feiertag's return. I'd been observing his apartment for over three months. The man was a remarkable creature of habit. He left each morning between nine and nine-thirty. Walked down Noe Street two blocks to Hill, which he took to Castro. He owned seven suits, three he'd brought over with him and four he'd bought here. He always wore the same suit on the same day of the week. I could have emerged from a month-long coma and known it was Tuesday because Feiertag was in the blue pin-striped double breasted. He had only one hat, though, a gray Homburg, which matched all his suits.

Every weekday he dropped off clothes at a cleaner on the corner of Hill and Castro. After leaving the dirty clothes, he'd go a half block up Castro to a small café run by a German couple. Breakfast was either a short stack or two eggs sunnyside up with a side of bacon. I didn't bother to calculate, but I'd have bet his meals were also on a regular rotation. The important thing was that he took between twenty-five and thirty-five minutes to eat breakfast. The extra ten minutes were spent with the owners when they visited his table.

From the few snatches I caught of their conversations, it sounded like mere pleasantries passed in German. Aside from the common language, the owners shared very little history with Feiertag, at least nothing they'd dare talk about in public. Feiertag was a German from Czechoslovakia's Sudetenland and the couple was the genuine article from Berlin. What went unspoken was where they'd all stood during the war, opinions that would not be well received in their new country. If the couple were to return to Germany they might have gotten away with whispering these views. But if Feiertag went back to Czechoslovakia he would either be killed by his own countrymen or sent to Siberia by the Soviets.

Otherwise Feiertag felt perfectly safe to be himself in his new U.S. home. He didn't even try to hide his real identity. I'm sure he assumed the few people still tracking down Nazis were looking for men with SS tattoos on their arms (or the scars from their removal) and high-ranking German officials who could be identified by survivors. Feiertag wasn't even German. Besides, he'd left no Jews behind to act as witnesses against him.

I would not have known what Feiertag had done if I hadn't accidentally run into a childhood friend after the war. I was on covert assignment in Germany. The Haganah had sent me because I spoke several German dialects, including *Praguer Deutsch* and High German. My friend and I went to a café to catch up. He told me he'd survived the camps and was trying to help other survivors find homes and get restitution. Then he asked how I'd managed to get through the war years.

I'd escaped on the Auschwitz death march and then thought about returning home to Prague, but it was still occupied by the Germans. I'd have been a pariah to anyone who took me in. Even old friends who simply spoke to me would risk death for themselves and their families for not turning me in. I'd heard about a ragtag army of Jews who'd gathered in Lublin, Poland, and were marching across Europe. My friend laughed when I told him I was almost shot hailing this Jewish Brigade, wearing a German uniform I'd stolen off a dead soldier. I marched with the Lublin Group down to Northern Italy, which had been occupied by the British and Americans. There I was approached by the Haganah who asked me to work for them.

When I mentioned I was with the Haganah, my friend did not ask to hear any more about what I was doing. I shouldn't have even told him that much. It was just so good to see somebody from home. When we started talking about what had happened to mutual acquaintances, he told me how Mayor Feiertag had rounded up Sarah Möos with other Jews hiding in his town and burned them in the synagogue. Whatever innocence I had left was consumed by the mention of those flames that had extinguished my Sarah's girlish laughter.

I asked him where Feiertag was. He said the mayor had disappeared after the war in the expulsion of Czech Germans to Germany. He might have escaped through a ratline or possibly the Russians had taken care of him.

I didn't forget about Feiertag after that talk. Later, when I read in a newspaper that his daughter had married an American major she'd met in Munich, I decided to keep tabs on her. I thought she might eventually lead me to her father. Feiertag's daughter was living with her husband in San Francisco when Feiertag joined them in 1950.

She now lived in Sausalito. Her father visited her and her children on Wednesdays and Sundays, taking a cab both ways. On Sundays he left home at three in the afternoon and didn't get back to his apartment until well after dinner, often as late as ten. On Wednesdays he also went for dinner, usually returning before nine. Sometimes when his daughter drove into the City to visit her husband, who was president of a San Francisco bank, she'd stop by and take her father to lunch.

Each weekday Feiertag would walk to a small office on Liberty Street where he edited a Czech-German anticommunist publication funded by an organization called the Captive Nations Committee, which was loosely tied to Radio Free Europe. Every now and then if the weather was nice he'd play hooky, walking the mile or so to Glen Canyon in Diamond Heights for a few games of chess. On Friday nights he might go to the opera. He liked Mozart and Wagner, but passed on Puccini and Verdi. All the time we observed him, Feiertag never went out on Saturday afternoons. We decided that would be our day.

For the first six weeks of the operation, Mara and I had a third person from the Mossad working with us. Even though he had been brought up in Israel, he was too young—perhaps a few years younger than me, 22 or 23—to have been part of the Haganah, which was transformed into the Mossad after Israel became a state. He referred to himself as a *Kidon*, the Mossad's name for assassins. Most *Kidon* were involved in the war with the Arabs. I still thought of myself as part of the *Nokim*. We killed only Nazis.

This *Kidon* went back to Israel for six weeks and was supposed to return to help Mara and me do the job. He would be posted on the street to spot and detain a possible intruder, while Mara ran upstairs to warn me. When the *Kidon* arrived in San Francisco, though, it was not to help us complete our assignment. He said the plan had been abandoned and we were to get out as soon as we could book passage.

***

Feiertag returned at exactly eleven that Saturday morning. I waited until 2:30 before crossing the street to his apartment. He lived in an Edwardian that had been turned into four apartments. I entered the middle of three doors off the front porch. The other two led to the downstairs units. I'd previously tested the bare wooden stairs and knew where to step so they wouldn't creak, mostly on the outer edges. The German woman who owned the house had remodeled it on the cheap. That worked in my favor when I got to Feiertag's door. With a simple penknife I was able to silently pry back the lock's throw.

It was dark inside. Feiertag always kept the heavy drapes closed. But I'd broken into his flat several times before when he hadn't been home, and could've gotten around with my eyes closed. It was fourteen steps from the front door to his bed, if walked directly. I took nineteen, circling the edge of the living room, not taking the chance of being seen until I entered through the bedroom door. He was asleep. Four more paces to the head of the bed.

I stared down at him. Every now and then his upper lip fluttered with his outward breaths causing his pencil-thin moustache to do a little jitterbug. I'd never been able to establish his exact age. Finding birth records became next to impossible after the Sudeten Germans got kicked out of Czechoslovakia. I guessed he was somewhere in his mid-fifties. I felt at such peace I thought I could have remained poised, watching him forever. Feiertag opened his eyes and blinked several times as he focused on me. Then he lay utterly still, as if he'd been expecting my visit.

"Yes?" he said.

I took a .22 caliber Beretta out of my jacket pocket, standard issue for Mossad assassins. It was small and easily concealed, yet just as deadly as a .44 Magnum in the hands of a skilled assassin. I stepped away from the bed and motioned with my head for him to get up. When he was standing I moved within arm's reach, hoping he'd try something foolish and I'd have an excuse for breaking his nose. He kept his arms by his side, eyes lowered.

I took out a silencer and began to screw it onto the pistol as I recited his crimes: "Heydrich Feiertag, you stand before me accused of crimes against humanity. In July of 1944, acting in your official capacity as mayor, you burned innocent people to death in your town's synagogue. I am here to carry out your execution for the murders of Joshua Fried, Isaac Kovner, Sonia Weisbach, Martin Fischl, Erma Weiss, Otto and Herta Krauss, Jakob and Marta Pinsker, Frank Jaeger, Helen Möos and her seventeen-year-old daughter Sarah."

His eyes rose sympathetically to meet mine. "You're making a terrible mistake," he said with a timid smile. "Some people were killed in a synagogue in my town, yes, but it was the SS who committed that crime. I wanted to stop it, but what could I do?"

"Were you not one of the leaders of the Henleins, who invited the Germans and the SS into Czech territory?"

"The Germans, yes, but not the SS. I was as terrified of the SS as everyone else."

I had finished putting the silencer on my pistol.

"And to prove your loyalty to them, you killed twelve Jews."

Feiertag's mouth tightened. "Of course the Jews blamed it on me. They would have preferred we become communists rather than reuniting with the Fatherland."

"Reuniting with the Fatherland," I repeated. It was one of Hitler's favorite sayings, even though the Czech Sudetenland had never been part of Germany. "Why lie now? Wouldn't you rather die with some dignity?"

Feiertag straightened, trying to muster all the courage and honor he could. He put his hands behind his back and lowered himself to his knees.

Picturing Sarah on her knees in the synagogue, succumbing to the smoke and fire, I lifted Feiertag off the floor and threw him against the wall. It was stupid of me. He made a loud thump that somebody could have heard.

"Strip," I said. "Come on, take off all your clothes."

He'd become confused.

"Now!"

He took off his robe and laid it on the bed, folding it lengthwise with the lapels touching.

I thought about putting a bullet in his knee or elbow, but that would have alerted the police. Ballistics would know it came through a silencer and he was killed by a professional. Besides, even though I was now acting on my own, I still felt as if I was part of the *Nokim*, and torture was against the avenger's code.

In his clothes Feiertag had looked fit for a man his age. Naked, his skin was pale, beginning to sag off the bone. I prodded him with my gun into the bathroom and had him draw a bath. I told him he was going to get into the water and to make the temperature comfortable. When the tub was full he climbed in. It would have been much more satisfying to hold him under water while he thrashed for his life. But bruises on his skin and water in his lungs would have been evidence of foul play. I wanted nothing to suggest a suspicious death.

I closed the shower curtain so he wouldn't see what I was doing and told him to be still, then waited just outside the bathroom door. When I heard the shower curtain withdraw, I poked my head through the door. "My orders are to insure there's no undue suffering. But I'd just as soon do it the other way."

Feiertag shut the shower curtain again.

I tiptoed into the kitchen and unplugged the toaster. It was the smallest electrical appliance in the flat that would work. The main fuse would trip within seconds after I dropped it into the water, cutting power to the entire house, including the light over the staircase. It would take thirty seconds to dry the toaster and put it back in place. Then I'd climb down the stairs in the dark. While others in the apartment went out their back doors to check the fuses, I'd walk out the front unseen.

Feiertag's body would not be discovered for hours. Perhaps not even until his daughter missed him on Sunday afternoon. He might be dead a full day by the time anyone found him. There would be nothing to suggest that he hadn't simply had a heart attack while bathing. Nobody would connect his death to the fuse that had blown earlier.

I returned to the bathroom, set the toaster on a glass accessory shelf above the sink, plugged it in and clicked the handle into the locked *on* position. After waiting a few seconds for the heating elements in the bread slots to turn red, I pulled back the shower curtain. Though my body blocked the toaster from his view, Feiertag began sniffing the air with terror. I'd forgotten that burning-metal smell toasters make as they heat up.

Hurrying to grab the toaster before Feiertag became uncontrollable, I heard the front door unlock. At first I thought it came from across the hall, but realized the sound was far too loud. Feiertag heard it too. His eyes darted hopefully in that direction. I hesitated. If I had still worked for the Mossad I'd be under strict orders to abort. A Czech mayor who'd only killed a handful of Jews was not worth the wrath of the Americans.

"Grandpa," a boy's voice called out from the living room.

Only one set of footsteps had come through the front door. The boy was by himself. Why would he have come up alone? His mother might have dropped him off while looking for a parking space. Or maybe she'd given him the keys to the apartment and gone across the street to the small grocery for cigarettes. In either case, I'd have a minute or two.

Time enough to drop the toaster in the water and pull it out before the boy saw me. The fuse would blow and the apartment would go dark. I'd run past the boy, put the toaster back in the kitchen and get out the door. A six-year-old would be the only witness and he might not get a good look at my face. His mother would come up and find her father dead. In her grief, the child's story might sound so confused that nobody would take it seriously. There was still a chance they'd think Feiertag had died of a heart attack.

"Grandpa?"

The boy stood in the bathroom doorway studying our tableau: his *Oppa* in a tub of water and a stranger holding a toaster above him. The child's eyes were filled with curiosity rather than fear.

I can still do this, I thought. Drop the toaster in the water. Everything goes dark. Put the toaster back in place and get away before Feiertag's daughter returns. The boy will be in shock, disoriented. His mother will be beside herself when she finds her father dead in the tub. She won't listen to the rantings of a small boy. She'll call for the ambulance and try to get the boy out of there as fast as possible. The police might never even get involved. And if they did, there was no connection between Feiertag and me. The Mossad had made sure of that. The landlord of my room across the street had never seen me. Somebody else had rented the place for me.

Yes, I could still do this, I thought, looking into the boy's large eyes. Perhaps he was expecting me to turn the toaster upside down, floating two slices of golden manna into grandpa's waiting hands. The child looked as though he were ready to applaud such a delightful outcome. Children that age can imagine almost anything, I thought, perhaps even death. But I knew firsthand that the terrible dread of it can only be planted in a child's mind by seeing the real thing with his own eyes.

I set the toaster back on the shelf above the sink and turned to look at Feiertag one last time. He gave me a small smile. Not a thank you, exactly. But a smile I knew, nonetheless. I'd given it to others who'd granted me another day of life.

I edged past the boy and out the open apartment door. Feiertag's daughter was coming up the stairs. Beautiful: tall, full-busted with a small waist and flowing blond hair. The perfect Aryan specimen of womanhood. Her eyes flitted my way as she passed me on the stairs. I didn't look back as I heard her run the rest of the way, calling out, "Martin? Martin? Dad? Is everything okay?"

I stood on the sidewalk in front of the apartment building, deciding whether to turn right or left. Feiertag's daughter would be discovering him in the bathtub with the toaster on the shelf above the sink. Either Feiertag would explain it to her or he'd make up some story. One thing I was sure of, though: he wouldn't call the police.

CHAPTER TWO

San Francisco ~ Late Summer 1968

It didn't matter if the kid was rich or poor. He'd have been just as dead. He looked as if he'd gone painlessly in a fog of junk, but that didn't matter either. How he'd died, how much or little pain he'd suffered, whether he had a shred of dignity left as he faded, that was all grief for the living now. He was neatly tucked in, as if his mother had folded over the hem of the sheet and kissed him on the cheek before putting him to bed. With his shut lids covering the telltale haze frosting his eyes he almost looked asleep. Just in case, I turned my ear close to his parted lips.

I'd seen men caught by a bullet mid-flight, slumped against a wall, mouths twisted in a grimace. People who'd melted into the mud so the only way to tell them from the earth was their white overbite. And once or twice, those who'd simply folded themselves up, heads bowed, mouths seeking solace in the shape of an *O*. They all looked as if they had something left to say. But I took my ear away from the boy's mouth without hearing it.

I pulled back the bedding. The kid was naked. Smooth skin and good muscle tone. He'd eaten well and gotten plenty of exercise. All in all, one hell of a good-looking kid. No marks on his body. Nothing to suggest a struggle. No tracks on his skin. Only the one needle mark. The spike lying next to him on the nightstand.

"No fixings?" I asked my partner, Inspector Richard Evans.

"Nothing in the trash, either," he said.

I took hold of the dead boy's hand. It was clammy. When I lifted his arm it fell easily back to the bed. Rigor mortis hadn't set in.

"Looks a little blue," I said, bending down to check the corpse's butt, just where it touched the bed. It was brownish where the blood had settled. I pressed my finger against its flesh. The skin turned white when I let up. The blood was still viscous. The room was pretty warm, though, up in the mid-seventies.

"Have you checked the street?" I asked.

"So far, it looks like all the cars belong here," Richard said. "There's a bus stop a few blocks away, Simon. I think it runs pretty late."

I smelled the kid's skin for almond or citrus or some other scent of poisons, looking for any indication it wasn't a simple OD. I pulled back his eyelids. The whites were clear but the pupils were so contracted I could hardly find them. It all pointed to the same thing—some sort of opiate, probably heroin.

A slight air of mustiness surrounded the body: the first whiff of decay rather than the sweeter smell of sex. No traces of semen to suggest sexual activity either. I noticed a high school ring on the boy's finger and lifted his hand to look more closely. It said *Claremont Prep*, a private school in Berkeley. I rolled over his hand so Richard could see.

"Doesn't figure he'd be in a shit hole like this," he said.

I dropped the boy's hand. "Some of these preppies get a kick out of slumming."

When I'd come into the hotel room at three-thirty that morning, Richard had already been there an hour. He'd called headquarters with information from the boy's driver's license. He'd also sent two patrolmen into the streets to question locals, and interrogated the desk clerk who'd said the victim had come in alone. A medium-height blond hooker had followed a little later.

"Usually the chicks rent the rooms themselves," the young, scruffy clerk had said when I interviewed him. "I know most of 'em, so a new one like that'll catch your eye—too classy for a place like this. I mean her getup wasn't anything special, just your standard prick-tease shit—miniskirt, spikes, long leather gloves—but this one had good bones."

I bent over a tech who was dusting the bathroom doorknob.

"There's prints everywhere," he said. "Prints on top of prints."

"Yeah, and I'll bet the blonde kept her gloves on," I said, slipping past him.

The bathroom had a white tile floor with light gray dust balls scattered around its black border. I found a pink residue under the lip of the sink, as if somebody had cleaned the bowl in a hurry. I ran my finger over the porcelain and sniffed the rose scent of makeup; then smelled a face towel that had been used and refolded as neatly as the unused ones. It smelled the same. I called in the forensic officers collecting and logging evidence and asked them to take a sample of the makeup.

Back in the bedroom, Richard pointed out a wallet under a fraying overstuffed chair. I was about to pick it up when the boy's clothes folded over the chair caught my attention: a pair of olive cords, long sleeve shirt and a high school letterman's jacket. Good labels—the kind of stuff you'd expect to find on an Ivy League kid. Even his socks and underwear were laid out neatly, but for some reason the belt had been taken from his pants and draped over the back of the chair. His penny loafers were side by side under the bed.

A boy about to get laid by a good-looking prostitute in a shabby hotel room, you'd figure his clothes would be all over the place, mostly on the floor. And if the kid OD'd on dirty smack—and that's what I was guessing—you'd expect to find him in a pool of vomit or with his head down the toilet. Or some other awkward position you wouldn't want to be caught dead in. Everything was just too damned orderly. I refolded the clothes over the chair.

As I crouched to pick up the wallet, I saw a blond hair hidden between strands of yarn on the brown shag carpet. I ripped a piece of paper out of my notebook and put the hair on it, looking closely at the single strand against the white background. I folded the paper and pocketed the evidence to give to the lab to put under a microscope.

Using a handkerchief I picked up the wallet by its corner—it hadn't been dusted yet—and dropped it to the floor. It fell open several inches in front of the chair. "You sure that's where they found it? Under the chair?"

"We used a tape to measure the spot," Richard said.

One hundred and thirty-seven dollars was inside the billfold—five twenties, three tens, a five and two ones.

"How many whores would've left that behind?"

"They're all a bunch of thieving junkies," Richard said, answering the telephone. "Inspector Evans. Yeah, Lieutenant." I waved my hand to let him know I didn't want to talk. "Inspector Wolfe's here now but he's tied up."

I lifted the wallet's leather flap, exposing plastic sleeves for driver's licenses and other cards. The kid's name was Chris Cantwell, but I was more interested in who he was than what he was called. I found San Francisco and Berkeley library cards, a Social Security card and a free pass to a chain of movie theatres. For a second I considered liberating the pass, but at a buck a pop it would have been stupid to spoil one of my few off-hour pleasures with a guilty conscience. When I finally got to his driver's license, the first thing I noticed was his date of birth: February 8, 1951. He was just seventeen. I looked at the address. A swanky Pacific Heights residence.

Richard hung up the phone.

"You know who I think this is?" I said to him.

"Yeah. They got Fanelli out of bed an hour ago. He wants us to meet him down at the Hall."

***

Lieutenant Fanelli wasn't in when we got to the Hall of Justice. I grabbed the newspaper, delivered every morning to the lieutenant's desk by a rookie patrolman. Even though I knew my boss liked his paper left untouched, I gave Richard the sports section. The front page had a story about the Soviet invasion of Czechoslovakia. I hadn't been back for over twenty-five years. I'm not sure I would've gone if I could have. But with the Russians keeping the Czech borders closed, it wasn't even an issue.

I'd pretty much wiped my childhood city from my mind. Yet with Prague all over the news this spring and summer, it was hard not to think about. The Czech's liberated press was calling their new free expression Prague Spring, but it looked like the Russians weren't going to let it last through summer.

Fanelli came in wearing his best suit. The way it hung off him, he must have lost weight since he bought it. His dark beard was shaved close and his graying black hair oiled straight back, smelling of Vitalis. Everything about him bristled with a forced energy, except his drooping eyes—they always looked world-weary.

I understood why Fanelli seemed edgy when Chief Murray trailed him in, looking as easygoing as Fanelli was jittery. The chief only got directly involved in cases where the department might take outside heat. He was good at delegating that heat while keeping an Irish smile on his face. Everybody knew you only dared smile back when invited with something like a slap on the back. And the redhead slapped hard.

Richard came to attention and said, "Chief." He'd never been involved in a case that had reached the top.

I nodded without speaking. I'd called the chief Ron for so many years when I'd reported to him as the lieutenant of Homicide, I didn't feel comfortable with anything else.

Fanelli dropped into the chair behind his desk as if it was already the end of a long day. "Both the congressman and his wife are pretty torn up about their son's death," he said, shooting me dirty looks as he straightened his newspaper.

"Did Congressman Cantwell know where his son was going last night?" I asked.

"We weren't there to question him," the chief said, filling the doorway with his wide shoulders, making an effort not to rush in and take over Fanelli's office. I wondered how long his restraint would last. "We only went to offer our condolences and tell Allen he could count on us."

"I made arrangements for you two to go by later," Fanelli said. "Take it easy with the congressman. He's more than a little distressed about the circumstances of his son's death."

"Then he knows the boy might have been killed by a prostitute?" I asked.

"That's just speculation," the chief said.

"What do you think?" Fanelli asked Richard.

"It looks like an accidental overdose to me," Richard said. "The big question is whether the hooker had anything to do with it."

"You don't think she brought the stuff and shot him up?" Fanelli asked.

"If it was accidental," I said, "it would have been more haphazard. People don't shoot up lying in bed. They're in the bathroom near a sink, sitting on the john or the edge of the tub."

"It could've taken a while for the drugs to take affect," the chief said.

"Yeah, but why would a scared hooker stick around to wash her face and tuck in a corpse?" I asked.

Fanelli glanced nervously at the chief, who said to me, "I want you to report back to Lieutenant Fanelli as soon as you're done at the Cantwells. Don't talk to anyone about this. If any reporters ask, tell them it looks like the kid died of natural causes. And keep your opinions to yourself when you talk to the congressman. Just take his statement."

Fanelli glanced at his watch. "I told Cantwell you'd be there at 11:30. Check out a squad car. I want this to look official."

"Inspector Evans, right?" Chief Murray said.

"Yes, sir," Richard said.

The chief put his arm around Richard. "Would you mind getting the car while I talk to your partner? He'll meet you downstairs in about fifteen minutes."

Richard walked off proudly, wearing the chief's touch like a medal on his shoulder. After he'd left, the chief motioned toward Fanelli with his head. Fanelli got up from behind his desk and said, "Don't forget to report in the minute you're finished with Cantwell." He closed the door on his way out.

"I'm going to need your help on this one, boyo," the chief said.

He sighed and gave me a look I couldn't turn away from. Like an Escher print, his expressions usually went one way or the other, sucked you in or spit you out.

For me they always led to a dead end.

CHAPTER THREE

I needed to blow off some steam after my little tête-à-tête with the chief. So I took some time to leaf through a stack of phone messages on my desk and saw one from Northern, the district station on Ellis Street near the Tenderloin. A patrolman who'd been working with us at the Fool's Gold the night of Chris Cantwell's death wanted me to interview a hooker the desk clerk had seen that night. When I climbed in the squad car I told Richard to stop by Northern on the way to Cantwell's.

"I don't think that's a good idea," he said. "You heard what Fanelli and the chief said."

Most of the guys on the Force thought Richard and I agreed on everything. And we did have a certain understanding. We'd only been partners two years, but we'd been acquainted nearly twelve. He was married to my cousin Miriam and we lived less than a mile from each other in Oakland. I'd stuck up for him when Miriam's parents said she shouldn't marry a *schvartze*; I argued that we of all people must not judge somebody because of his race. Richard and I had stood side by side at her parents' funerals and spent nearly all the holidays together. I'd vouched for him to get on the SFPD. But at the end of the day Richard went his way and I went mine.

"Fanelli didn't say anything about not interviewing witnesses," I said.

"You know that wasn't the deal."

"If I wanted to make deals for a living I'd be doing something that paid a lot more than a thousand dollars a month," I said.

Richard turned over the engine but waited to put the car in gear. "What did the chief have to say?"

"To keep things in perspective." I lit a cigarette. "You know what that means—little guys stay in the background."

"I don't know why you're always bad-mouthing the chief," Richard said. "The way I heard it he put you on the fast track to inspector when he was in charge of Homicide."

"Office politics is one thing," I said. "But when it comes to the death of a young kid, I won't look the other way. Just take me to Northern,"

I folded my arms the way the chief had when he'd told me to take my cues from Cantwell on how to conduct the investigation.

"It's his son. He'll know best," the chief had said, softening his approach and laying his hand on my wrist, having inferred from my silence I wasn't going to oppose him.

***

Lari Zohn wasn't what I'd call a hooker. Too young, too sharp and too beautiful. She had a Slavic elegance I immediately recognized: long silky black hair, dark eyes and a nose that sloped gracefully down from pencil-thin eyebrows. In a waist-cut denim jacket exposing just the right amount of black leotard, she made a nice package that would support the lifestyle of a top-flight call girl for at least another five years. It could've cost her a few hundred dollars waiting several hours for me in the interrogation room. And her haughtily thrown shoulder let me know she wasn't happy about it.

"Hello, Lari, I'm Inspector Wolfe."

I sat across the table from her.

"My friends call me Lari. You can call me Hillary."

I nodded and offered her a Camel. She took a Benson & Hedges out of her purse and put it between strawberry-glossed lips.

"Kind of out of your neighborhood, aren't you?" I asked as I lit it for her.

She looked nothing like a Tenderloin streetwalker. The patrolmen who'd spotted her in an all-night diner near the Fool's Gold wouldn't have even ID'd her as a prostitute if he hadn't seen her in holding at Richmond Station. But he'd told me she'd never spent a night in jail. "Must keep friends in the right position," he'd said with a sly smile.

Lari took her time before telling me what she was doing in the neighborhood: "Clean men like dirty places."

"You know why you were brought in?"

"I know nobody's booked me for anything."

"A dead kid was found in a hotel room where you were working last night. Can you tell me who you were with?"

"Trust me, you wouldn't want to know," she said. "But I can assure you he was very much alive last time I saw him."

"See anybody else there?"

She took a drag off her cigarette and gave me a well-practiced sneer most men would have gladly mistaken for a smile.

"This was just some innocent young kid," I said.

"What was he doing down there if he was so innocent?"

I heard a knock and turned to see Richard's face in the door's glass window.

I took out my business card. "If you remember anything, I'd really appreciate it."

She folded her hands on the table without taking the card.

"You don't have to come downtown or anything. Just give me a call," I said, placing it in front of her intertwined fingers.

"People call me," she said, plucking a piece of tobacco from her lips.

Richard knocked again, held up his arm and pointed to his watch.

"Your boyfriend's waiting," she said without expression.

"Let's just keep this between ourselves, shall we?" I said, getting up.

"That the heat hauled my ass into Ellis Street? Don't worry."

Richard opened the door and planted himself on the threshold. "Want me to go to Cantwell's without you?"

I shot him a look to keep his mouth shut. When I turned back to Lari I noticed my card was missing.

"If you don't want to call the police station, I'm in the Oakland phone book," I said.

She glanced at Richard, then at me and back down at the table, her hands still folded like a school girl's.

On our way out of the station I told Richard he shouldn't have mentioned Cantwell's name in front of Lari.

"You didn't tell her why you were questioning her?" he asked.

"You didn't give me a chance."

"I'm not getting to Cantwell's late," he said.

"A congressman ought to understand we're homicide inspectors and... She could have been up there in the room with the kid."

"The desk clerk said it was a blonde."

"I think that blond hair I picked up was from a wig. Both ends looked cut."

Richard looked askance at me as if I'd been sandbagging again. "Yeah, but then how often you think that pit gets vacuumed?"

"It was human hair from an expensive wig. Not something you'd find on a twenty-dollar hooker. Plus the kid had enough dough on him for a high-class call girl."

"Then why didn't you hold her?"

"No evidence. Besides, there was something about her I trusted."

"I only had to take one look to tell you she had nothing going for her I'd ever trust," Richard said. "A beautiful white chick that grew up with all the advantages—she's got no fuckin' excuse."

I dropped it. There were some things Richard and I would never agree on. I'd seen normal women—mothers and daughters born with every advantage, who never dreamed their world would one day be turned upside down—selling their once pristine flesh for a slice of bread. But Richard had been born into a world that was already turned on its head. In the Oakland ghetto you started on the bottom and didn't get anywhere unless you clawed your way up. It had been that way since he was a kid and he had no reason to believe it would ever change. There would always be the same violent streets and fire-and-brimstone churches his mother had taken him to. Richard credited the fact that he'd "made it" to her church-going ways. Just as he blamed his dad for his sister Doris's fall from grace. She'd moved across town to live with their estranged father when she was in her mid-teens. Richard said it was his old man's fault that Doris had gotten into drugs and prostitution. But he also admitted she should have known better: "The world's just not that complicated. You're either going up, going down or going nowhere."

***

Fifteen minutes after leaving Northern, we parked in front of an ornate wrought-iron fence surrounding an expansive lawn on a steep hill in Pacific Heights. I climbed out of the car and gazed up at the Queen Anne overlooking the city. One of the few Victorian mansions that had survived the 1906 earthquake, it was now a fashionable painted lady with peach scallops and yellow curlicues, all neatly picture-framed in fresh white trim.

"Kids who live in big houses die of natural causes, not drug overdoses," I said, opening the gate.

"Miriam told me you grew up in a big house," Richard said.

"It was more of a large flat, really. But that didn't stop the Germans from giving it to one of their officers."

We walked up a gravel path lined with rose bushes. The housekeeper answered my knock. As Richard and I took out our IDs, Mrs. Cantwell showed up in an expensively simple black dress, with long blond hair pulled back severely like Grace Kelly.

"I'll take care of this," she said, dismissing the housekeeper.

I'd never met Sylvia Cantwell in person, but I'd seen photos in the Sunday *Chronicle's* society page blurbs about the San Francisco Opera Guild, Junior League and other organizations for women with too much time and money. Judging by her son's age, she must have been in her late 30s, but she didn't look it, either in the photos or in person.

"Come in, please, inspectors," she said, without looking at our faces or IDs. "My husband's in the library. Unfortunately, politics does not stop for personal tragedy."

She didn't seem particularly grief stricken, but then she didn't seem particularly anything. We followed her down a dimly lit hallway with a Persian carpet runner. Eighteenth-century portraits lined the walls, with a realism as cold in their perfection as Mrs. Cantwell. Like the modern abstracts my parents once owned, these paintings looked as though they belonged in a museum. I wondered if my parents' treasures ended up in the house of some respected citizens like the Cantwells.

Mrs. Cantwell led us to the back corner of the house, where she stopped at a wood-paneled door and knocked. "My husband's involved in hush-hush matters. One never knows, there could be an undercover agent in there with him." She spoke in an almost girlish voice that made me suspect she was willing to suffer fools who took her at face value. My suspicions were validated when an attractive thirtyish brunette opened the door, dressed in a chartreuse suit with a blue paisley scarf thrown around her neck. Mrs. Cantwell said with the same coy delivery, "Or on the other hand, it might just be Michelle. Did we interrupt anything important?"

Michelle stepped quickly aside to let Mrs. Cantwell pass.

"It's the police, darling. They're here about our son," Mrs. Cantwell said, striding into the room.

In comparison with his wife's charming guile, Congressman Cantwell appeared to be an open book—the grief-stricken father dressed in a somber black suit custom tailored to his trim figure. The only thing in excess about him was his full head of hair, which he somehow managed to keep just so without a hint of that greasy kid's stuff.

"Thank you for coming so promptly," the congressman said, holding out a hand. "I know the Force is overworked enough without having to accommodate a politician's demanding schedule."

"Whatever we can do to help, sir," Richard said, shaking his hand.

"I want you to know I appreciate it," Cantwell said, glad-handing me next.

At six-feet-one he was only four inches taller than me, but his long manicured fingers made my hand feel like a plumber's. His grasp lingered warmly as he flashed compassionate brown eyes that made people feel handpicked to be a special part of his special world.

"Sit, please," Cantwell said, gesturing to a couple of upholstered wooden chairs from the same era as the house. Everything about the room retained its Victorian character. The library walls were painted antique green above mahogany wainscoting and the bookcases were filled with uncreased leather spines. The congressman and his wife sat on a loveseat that matched our chairs.

"We'll talk later," Michelle said, lowering her long lashes and sidestepping as silently as a ballet dancer to the door.

For the briefest moment the congressman's eyes lit on her as if she offered the only color around, which was literally true. "Tell them I'll try to make it down to campaign headquarters tomorrow afternoon," he said. "If there's a committee meeting scheduled on this Czech business, let me know. Otherwise, I don't want to be bothered."

"We know how difficult this must be for you," I said after Michelle had made a hushed exit.

"Difficult?" Cantwell said. "You have no idea. I watched my platoon get slaughtered on the beaches of Normandy, but losing a son... You can understand how we'd simply like to get this over with."

"Of course," I said. "We just have a few questions today."

Cantwell took a labored breath. "I meant the entire investigation."

"We understand, sir," Richard said. "And we'll do everything we can to wrap it up ASAP."

"I don't think you do understand," Cantwell said, giving us a pained smile. "Mrs. Cantwell and I don't believe there was any foul play."

I glanced over at Mrs. Cantwell, who sat by her husband's side with her hands on her lap. Her son had just died. Something had to be going on underneath that magazine pose.

"What do you believe?" I asked her.

"My son isn't the first person to have made bad choices," the congressman appealed to Richard. "This time they resulted in an unfortunate accident. But there was no homicide involved."

Richard glanced at me, letting me know he was prepared to leave without any further discussion. That's what Cantwell wanted—for us to go back to the office, write up a report downplaying the possibility of any criminal wrongdoing that would necessitate further investigation, and feed the press some cock-and-bull story. Cantwell was running for the U.S. Senate. With the election less than a month away, the last thing he could afford was a scandal.

"You must understand," Mrs. Cantwell said, "it's of primary importance for us to preserve our son's memory."

"We get it," Richard said, getting to his feet. "And we've been instructed to take all necessary precautions to protect your privacy." He looked over at me and gestured toward the door with his eyes.

"You know your son wasn't alone," I said, remaining seated.

Congressman Cantwell stood up, letting us know our interview was over.

I stared at Mrs. Cantwell, who like me had remained seated. She returned the look, and although her expression did not change, I thought she wanted to tell me something. Before she had the chance, though, Richard was by my side with his hand on my shoulder, pulling me up and guiding me out the door.

CHAPTER FOUR

When we got in the car Richard cocked his head in my direction as he cranked over the engine, waiting for me to explain my behavior at Cantwell's. I wasn't ready to talk yet, so I lit a cigarette. Richard looked stony as he drove up the block and down the Fillmore Street hill.

"Did it strike you as odd that Mrs. Cantwell didn't seem all that upset about her son's death?" I finally asked.

"She's a politician's wife. You can't really tell how she felt," Richard said.

"But why wouldn't they wonder who their son was with? Why be so eager to sweep his death under the rug?"

"Can you blame them?" Richard said. "What would you do if your kid OD'd in a cathouse?"

"I think I'd feel I owed it to him to find out what really happened."

"You think, but you don't know because you've never had a kid, and the thing you keep forgetting is that it's *their* son we're talking about."

"Not anymore," I said.

We didn't say anything else all the way to the Hall of Justice. After Richard turned off the ignition, we sat silently in the car for several seconds, waiting to see if anybody was ready to say uncle. Nobody was. So we got out and regarded one another over the top of the car.

"Cantwell's probably already called the mayor and D.A. about backing us off," Richard said. "My guess is Fanelli tells us to wrap it up the minute we get inside."

I nodded and headed away from the Hall toward my Citroen DS. I took a lot of ribbing from other cops about my "frog mobile," but I'd gotten used to driving them in Europe.

"Where the hell you going?" he called out after me.

"If I told you, you'd just have to tell Fanelli."

***

I didn't have to think too hard about where to go next. Aside from Chris's parents, I only had one lead. It took twenty minutes to get to the east side of the Oakland Bay Bridge. I got off the freeway at the Ashby Avenue exit in Berkeley and drove up into the hills to Claremont Avenue. Claremont Prep was in a new, plain-looking, three-story brick building, smack up against the sidewalk, without even a strip of lawn for the rich kids to sit on during their lunch.

I decided to tell the school I was there to investigate a robbery. Since it hadn't hit the papers yet, I didn't want to be the one breaking the news about Chris Cantwell's death. But when I got to the administration office, they already knew. Somebody had called somebody.

"You don't think any of the other students were involved?" the principal said as he led me to Chris's fifth-period class. He was a large pear-shaped man with a whispery voice and baby-thin hair, dressed in a heavy tweed sport coat. When I didn't respond he said, "How did it happen?"

"You didn't hear?" I asked.

"All we know is that he passed. You must understand, of course, I'm concerned about anything that might reflect on the school."

"Of course."

"We have other students to think about."

"And their parents." They were the ones who wrote the fat tuition checks. "Why was Chris going to a school so far from home?"

"His father went here," he said in a rehearsed way that made me think there was more to it. "What kinds of questions will you be asking the students?"

"If you don't want me to talk to them on the premises, we could call their parents and question them at their homes."

"I'm sure that won't be necessary. We wouldn't want to put you to all that trouble."

Inside the classroom, kids were buzzing with the news of Chris's death. I stood in a far corner at the front while the teacher settled things down. I would have positioned myself in the back, out of the way, but I wanted to watch the students' reactions.

The teacher was an angular woman in her early forties with large, sympathetic eyes. She explained that I was there to ask some questions about Chris to help with my police investigation. She repeated what I'd told her to say: "This is purely routine and any student who'd rather not talk to the inspector right now does not have to. If you choose not to, however, he may want to contact your parents to make an appointment to come to your house, or have your parents bring you down to the police station."

I hoped that little bluff would get everyone to cooperate.

The teacher then talked about things we hadn't discussed: "When you talk to Inspector Wolfe, please don't pretend to feel something you don't. However you feel, it's okay... "

I studied the students' faces as they listened. Most of them looked squeamish, as if they couldn't wait to get the hell out of there. Several fought back smiles and snickers. I didn't take that to mean much. I'd seen people laugh hysterically over a corpse, out of shock or panic. Then I noticed one girl sitting in the back row wiping tears off her face.

By the time the teacher was done with her talk, I'd figured out who I wanted to question in depth. If I was lucky, maybe one of the kids would even know something about Chris on the day he died.

I met with students in an empty room across the hall. Almost all of them knew Chris but said they weren't close with him. They seemed to admire him from afar. Several boys told me how Chris had single-handedly won last year's football championship for the school. The girls talked about how cute he was with a wicked smile and fast tongue, but none of them said they'd gone out with him.

I was beginning to wonder if Chris kept up a clean-cut image at school while secretly visiting prostitutes. Then I talked to one of the football players, named Bobby Michaels, who'd been a teammate of Chris's. He said he'd seen Chris at a school dance with the girl I'd seen crying, whose name was Patricia Walker. He told me that Chris and Patricia had sneaked out into the parking lot with a group of kids who were getting drunk. But he hadn't seen them go back into the dance and couldn't remember when they'd left. He'd never seen them together again after that night a few years ago.

When I asked Bobby how the boys on the football team felt about Chris, he said they thought he was a "real kick."

"We'd nicknamed him Motormouth," Bobby said. "He was always cutting up."

"But he was your star player," I said.

Bobby shook his head and laughed. "That's Chris for you."

"He wasn't?"

"Nah, he was just our backup field goal kicker. He probably could've been a first-stringer, if he'd tried. But Chris always had to do things his way."

"Why did everybody tell me he won the championship game for you?"

"He did," Bobby said. "The lucky son-of-a-buck became an overnight hero, and he'd only played in one game."

Bobby went on to tell me how Chris had kicked the winning field goal in the championship game. "Technically he shouldn't have even gotten a letterman's jacket, only playing in one game," Bobby added. "But you know Chris—he talked us guys into supporting him and we all went to coach and said the school would be really upset if they didn't give a letter to the guy who'd won us the championship. So they made an exception. I'll tell you, nobody was more proud of their letter than Chris. I don't think he ever took that jacket off."

"How was it Chris ended up playing in that championship game?" I asked.

"It was just a fluke, really," Bobby said. "Week before the game, Chris and Lonny were practicing together—"

"Lonny's your first-string kicker?"

Bobby nodded. "Chris was holding for Lonny when he slipped and pulled a hamstring."

"How did that happen?"

Bobby shrugged. "Must've held the ball over a wet patch or something."

I asked for Patricia Walker next, but she'd disappeared.

The last kid I questioned was a scrawny boy who introduced himself as Mickey Dodge, sticking his hand way out and pumping mine like a used-car salesman. I'd spotted him sitting in a corner with his head turning every which way, looking to see how everybody else was reacting. When a few of the boys got the giggles he giggled too, but softer so he wouldn't stand out. After the teacher told the kids not to pretend to feel something they didn't, he looked lost, until he saw Patricia Walker crying and began wiping his eyes.

There was also something odd about the way Mickey dressed. His wool slacks belted high on his waist and pin-striped dress shirt were old-fashioned. He had a jacket with white leather sleeves that looked like a letterman's jacket, but it had the wrong colors for the school. Mickey waited until I asked him to sit down, folding his hands in front of him.

"Are you going alphabetically or something?" he asked.

I half lifted my eyes from my notes.

"Sometimes they go backwards," he said, "and Dodge is towards the end."

"No, I picked you last on purpose," I said, flipping through my notes, even though I knew there was nothing in there about him. Nobody had even mentioned his name. It made him nervous, though, so I kept it up.

"Not that it matters to me," he said, forcing a series of small laughs. "'Cept other kids lie sometimes, especially when it comes to me."

"Why don't you set me straight, then?" I said, looking up from my notebook.

"In the first place, no matter what anyone else told you, Chris and I weren't what you'd officially call friends. We haven't been for a long time. I... I... wouldn't do that."

"Do what?"

"Stuff they told me not to," he said, glancing down at the desktop.

I was about to ask him who *they* were, when it occurred to me he might be on probation.

"I'm glad you told me that," I said. "Because it's my responsibility to report everything I hear back to the board."

"I'm clean," he said, holding up his hands. "And like I told everybody else, none of it was my idea."

"I've only heard Chris's version of things." I jotted down some notes, mostly to take my eyes off Mickey and give him space.

"It was his father's fault, really. By the time Mr. Cantwell was done, I ended up getting blamed for everything."

"So you and Chris were old friends," I said, giving him my best-buddy smile.

"Since grammar school, but we never did anything like that before."

I nodded crisply: understood.

"Okay, like I told the court, we blew up cherry bombs in ant holes and tied a squirrel in a pillow case and put it in the dryer, but—"

"He was the brains," I said.

"Well, I got the rope." He didn't want to appear to be a total dupe. "It was in my parent's basement. But, hey, I already copped to that, right?"

I smiled. Mickey wasn't going to tell me anything he hadn't already admitted in court. That would be enough, though.

"Nobody liked that dog, anyway," he blurted out.

"Barked all the time and kept everybody up at night."

"If it had been up to me, I think I would have just poisoned it," he said.

"But you got the rope," I reminded him.

"Chris asked me if I had one." Mickey scrutinized me again. "But like I said all along, the saw with the big teeth was Chris's. His gardener used it to cut down tree limbs."

That saw must have gotten good and bloody cutting up a dog. And it would've been a pretty damning piece of evidence against Chris Cantwell. Yet if Congressman Cantwell had friends on the Force, they could have conveniently lost it.

"But nobody ever produced Chris's saw as evidence in court," I said.

"They all acted like I just made it up. Even my own lawyer." He fidgeted and straightened his collar. "Anyway that was a long time ago, when me and Chris got kicked out of school in San Francisco and our parents transferred us here."

"I appreciate your honesty, Mickey. It's going to go a long way in helping me to help you with the board. But I need to know more about your involvement with Chris and drugs," I said.

"I had nothing to do with that."

"With what?"

"That LSD thing," he said. "Like I told his parents and everybody else, when I got to his house that stupid cat was already running around in circles making funny sounds like—I mean it was more like a baby bird." He caught himself laughing. "I told him it wasn't a very nice thing to do." He shook his head and smacked his lips earnestly.

"I want to get this all down," I said, writing myself a note to check into Chris's drug history. "You know if Chris had a girlfriend?"

"He wasn't hung up on anyone, if that's what you mean." Mickey leaned in close to give me the real dope. "He was kind of weird about chicks, though."

"Weird how?" I whispered, leaning in to meet him.

He backed away. "Just saying weird things, you know. A lot of guys do that, I guess."

"Can you give me an example?" I asked, putting pen to paper to stress the question's importance.

"Like once he told me this girl—Patty Walker, the one you saw crying— was trying to get inside his head. Toy with him—you know—play on his neuroses."

I looked up as I wrote. "Neuroses? Is that your word or his?"

"His!"

"Are you sure?"

"I never got above a 'D' in English," Mickey said proudly.

"Did you ask him where he heard the word?"

Mickey shook his head.

I told him I might want to talk to him again later, and hustled over to the school nurse's office. I found her assembling first aid kits, putting bandages, ointment and aspirins into metal boxes. She was a big woman in her late forties. All business in a starched and pleated white uniform, she didn't look like the type to hand over a kid's medical records on the q.t.

I told her I was investigating Chris Cantwell's death and needed to verify a few things I'd heard interviewing other students and the principal.

"He never had anything serious wrong with him that you knew about?" I asked as I flipped through my notes.

"Not that I knew about," she said, weighing her words, not wanting to say anything she wasn't supposed to.

"That's what I heard," I said, still turning pages. "But I thought maybe he'd sprained an ankle or got bruised playing football and came to you without telling anybody else."

"Uh-uh," she said, shaking her head.

I was about to ask her about drug use, but I'd probably only get one silver bullet and wanted to save it.

"Terrible thing," I said, scanning a page with my finger.

"We're all very upset," she said.

"I guess that's it." I smiled to show my gratitude. "Thank you."

"You're welcome, Inspector."

I gave my notes a final once over, as if I didn't want to forget anything.

"His psychotherapy appointments were on Tuesdays, right?"

"I can't remember. It's been about six months," she said.

I nodded, looking down at my notebook to avoid her eyes.

"That's what I was told by Dr.—" I turned pages as if looking for a name.

"Dr. Meyers," she said.

"Yes. Anyway, that's what he told me when I spoke to him," I said, finally looking up.

"You mean *her*?" she said, eyeing me suspiciously.

CHAPTER FIVE

There was only one female Dr. Meyers in the phone book—Dr. Elaine Meyers. Her office was on the north side of the Berkeley campus on Shattuck Avenue, located in a nondescript stucco storefront, above a children's clothing shop. Her receptionist was a mother-earth type, no makeup, glasses, and frizzy hair pulled back loosely into a bun. Behind a small desk she was reading the *Berkeley Barb*, an underground newspaper handed out in Telegraph Avenue coffee houses.

When I entered, she looked up with a nurturing gaze. I wondered if that was how she tried to make new patients feel at ease.

"How can I help you?" she asked as if she really meant it.

"I'm here to see Dr. Meyers."

"Oh, I'm so sorry, did we goof up an appointment?"

I showed her my ID and explained I was investigating the death of one of Dr. Meyers' patients.

"You don't look very surprised," I said.

"Congressman Cantwell called here earlier," she said, averting her eyes.

"He called here, himself?"

She nodded, her eyes still off to the side.

"What did he say?"

"Only that his son had died and he wanted to talk to Elaine about it."

"Did she talk to him?"

"I don't know. Listen, I'm really not supposed to say anything about patients. You're going to have to talk to her."

"Where is she?"

"She works on campus Monday, Wednesday and Friday afternoons."

"She teach there or something?"

"She runs the Remembrance Project. If you leave now you might be able to catch her."

The ringing phone obscured her next words, which sounded like either 14 or 314 Wheeler Hall.

"Association," she said into the phone. "Sorry, she's not here, can I take a message?"

***

I was somewhat familiar with the Berkeley campus from taking night courses there while getting my Masters in Criminology. I cut through Sproul Plaza to get across campus to Wheeler Hall. The early morning haze had burned off and the day had turned out to be clear and sunny. Shirtless boys hung around a line of card tables set up for all kinds of causes: right-wing, left-wing and religious, which I figured was supposed to cover any-and-every wing. All with nice simple answers, of course, to life's most complex questions.

When I got inside Wheeler Hall I searched for stairs to the basement. (I didn't like being cramped in small spaces with metal doors.) Hidden behind the main stairwell to the upper floors, I found a narrower descending staircase. In the basement I found a drinking fountain, men's and women's bathrooms and a glass-front firebox containing a hose and axe. But no Dr. Meyers. So much for her office being number 14.

Upstairs I passed four office doors before coming to Room 314, which had a business card with Dr. Meyers' name printed on it, folded to fit in a small metal frame. That's the way the university handled people who worked there on temporary grants, getting funded from year to year. They didn't get their names painted on doors the way professors did.

I knocked.

Dr. Meyers opened. She was not some gray-haired sixty-year-old shrink, as I had pictured. She wore a youthful outfit, denim skirt and olive-colored French-cut T-shirt, which complemented her sea-green eyes. Her hair was a thick chestnut, cut short like Jean Seberg in Godard's *Breathless*. Not too many women had the kind of feminine face to pull off such a boyish haircut; both Seberg and Dr. Meyers did. In fact, too much hair would have detracted from her cheeks, which had the intriguing contours of a woman emerging from her full-faced twenties into an age of self-discovery.

"Yes?" she said, becoming prickly the way women do when they're being stared at by strangers. Male strangers, at any rate.

I was about to answer, but was stopped by a gaunt man in his mid-fifties wearing an expensive silk suit. He appeared behind Dr. Meyers and waited for us to make room for him to slip out the door.

"Sorry about the interruption, Mr. Weisman," she said, stepping aside. "I'll see you next week, okay?"

He glanced over and nodded hello as if we might have known each other. After he left, Dr. Meyers turned her attention to me. I resented having to pull out my ID. I would have preferred our first meeting to have been on a more informal basis.

"What can I do for you, Inspector?"

"Do you mind if I come in and talk to you?"

Her narrow office had a desk at the far end in front of two steel casement windows. A table that could crowd three people on each side was butted up against the desk. Books overflowed the floor-to-ceiling shelves on both side walls, so that some were piled on the far end of the table and the back of her desk. Otherwise, everything was neat and orderly.

"What did you want to talk to me about?" she asked.

"Chris Cantwell. He was a patient of yours."

She didn't respond.

"I think you've been informed that he's dead," I said.

I knew how to make the most of awkward silences, when people didn't have words to hide behind. But uncomfortable moments were also her stock and trade.

"His father contacted you, right?" I asked.

"Sit, please." She took her place across the table from me. "How did it happen?"

"I'm not one of your patients," I said. "I'm here to ask the questions."

She nodded as if to say fair enough. "There are certain things I can't talk about, unless of course you already know about them."

Of course, doctor-patient confidentiality was a concern. And with Congressman Cantwell pressuring her, she'd be right to worry about what she divulged. I weighed how much I'd be willing to give before getting anything in return. The story would hit the evening paper, anyway, but how much of the truth would they print? How far could I trust her?

"It's got to stay here between us," I said.

She nodded.

"He died of a drug overdose."

She nodded again, not seeming overly surprised.

"How much do you know about Chris?" she asked.

"I'm beginning to get the picture he wasn't what he appeared," I said.

Her momentary smile said that was an understatement.

"I was hoping you could fill in that picture for me," I said.

"You're from Homicide, right?"

I nodded.

"I see," she said. "Where did this happen?"

"In a seedy hotel in the City. I already know that he'd used drugs before. Can you tell me if it was a recurring problem?"

"As far as I know, he'd never been treated for addiction, if that's what you mean."

"Because if he only used them occasionally, it would make an accidental overdose more likely," I said.

She shrugged.

"Are you sure his father didn't contact you?"

She lowered her eyes. "About what?"

"Threatening to have your license revoked if any dirt leaks out on his kid."

"I see you've met Allen."

There was an ashtray on the table with a few butts in it. I pulled out my pack. "You want one?"

She shook her head.

"Mind if I do?" I lit up before she could answer.

She got up to open a window.

"I've been trying to give it up," she said.

I turned to look at her books. Several of them caught my eye: *Survival in Auschwitz* by Primo Levi; *Night* by Elie Wiesel; *Darkness at Noon* by Arthur Koestler.

"It's difficult, though, because most of the people who come here smoke," she said.

"What is this Remembrance Project?" I asked, still facing the bookcase.

"I interview Holocaust survivors."

I turned to face her. "I'm usually quicker than that."

"Denial?" she said with a smile I might have taken wrong from somebody else.

"How did you know?" I asked.

"Partly your German accent. I don't think an ex-Nazi would risk the visibility of becoming a cop."

I wasn't conscious of crushing out my cigarette or her sitting opposite me again. "Have you ever talked about it with anyone?" she asked.

"About what?"

"Everything. Or anything. It's not only important for the world to hear about. Sharing can also help you put it behind you. You were just a normal kid from a normal family. Then suddenly nothing was normal. It's important for us to remember, even after we're forced to do abnormal things, that we're still human. Sometimes just remembering—"

"I'm too busy taking care of present day injustices I can do something about," I said.

"That's important too," she said. "The same things keep happening in different ways, just new names and faces."

"The names may be different but the faces are always the same," I said.

"We all have things we think can't be shared."

"What things?"

"Come on," she said.

"Come on, yourself," I said, lighting another cigarette. "Do you know if Chris Cantwell ever got into any trouble with the police?"

She shook her head.

"Does that mean you don't know or you can't say? The boy's dead. There's no need to protect his confidentiality any longer."

"People survive the dead. People who still care about them." Her smile now seemed melancholy.

I should have tried pressuring her with more questions, but all of a sudden I felt imprisoned in my own skin. "Call me if you remember anything important you *can* talk about," I said, standing up and handing her my card.

As I was heading out the door, she said, "Inspector Wolfe."

I turned.

She shook her head and gave one last smile. This time bittersweet.

"If you feel differently..." she said, reaching into her top drawer, pulling out a business card. She held onto it for a second or two before extending it to me. "Call me if there's anything important you want to talk about."

I shoved it in my pocket without looking at it.

CHAPTER SIX

I'd left my apartment windows open all day. Since the flat faced east and didn't get the late afternoon sun, I returned to a dusky chill. I took off my jacket and hung it in the bedroom closet. Slung my tie over a peg on the closet door and threw my shirt in the bottom drawer of my bureau where I kept laundry for the cleaners Saturday mornings. I recalled leaving Dr. Meyers' card in the shirt pocket but figured I'd fish it out later when I wasn't trying to get her off my mind.

I laid my belongings on top of the dresser. Billfold and wallet with police ID. Shoulder holster and Smith & Wesson .38 Special. Money clip and change. Keys. Cigarettes and lighter. And finally a tarnished top of a tin can whose sharp edges had been beaten into small folds so they wouldn't rip their cloth enclosure. Just about the size of my palm, it was shaped like a kidney, really, more than a heart. I took off my pants and folded them along the crease before hanging them. In my boxers and T-shirt, the nip from the oncoming evening felt just right against my bare limbs.

I stared out the window. The whisper of dusk had fallen over the front lawn, broken only by the laughter of David and Wiki, the young couple who lived across the hall, strolling up the walkway holding hands. I listened as they reached the top of the stairs and it became quiet again. Except for a breeze rustling a few dried maple leaves upturned like imploring palms in the gutter across the street.

I recalled what Dr. Meyers had said regarding survivors still caring about the dead, and pictured our family's small, overcrowded apartment on Siroka Street, overlooking Prague's Old Jewish Cemetery. When the Germans seized the homes of wealthy Jews, my parents and I had been forced to move into the flat of some distant relatives. I'd stay out all day and slip in like a ghost at sundown, then turn my back on the adults to look out the window. They seemed so old and defeated. Now I was older than any of them and felt as though they were turning their backs on me.

A few weeks after we'd moved into the tenement, my mother changed from one of Prague's most chic women into a frumpy middle-aged matron, her hair becoming gray almost overnight. She claimed she didn't care how she looked because my father had stopped talking to her. He'd stopped talking to me too. He'd stopped talking to everybody when the Germans forced him to give up his factory to one of his Aryan workers.

I preferred to remember my mother the way she was at a party my parents had given less than a year before we were forced to move. She wore a light rayon dress with high padded shoulders, her hair piled on her head like her fashion idol, Ginger Rogers. I can still picture the dress's pattern—bright orange and yellow tropical flowers boldly laid out against a Tahitian-blue background. My father couldn't take his eyes off her as she tangoed, the sheer fabric rippling across her still-girlish limbs.

I couldn't stand to see her at the Siroka Street apartment moping around in her bathrobe. So I stayed out all day. If there had not been a curfew, I probably wouldn't have returned until they were asleep. It wasn't easy finding places to escape during the day. I could no longer go to high school. All the Jewish kids had been expelled. I was taking a chance simply by getting on streetcars, which we were forbidden to ride.

I'd leave early in the morning by foot and get lost in the crowds crossing over the Charles Bridge to the Little Quarter. That way people wouldn't see me get on the streetcar in the Jewish Quarter. I'd carry my book bag so riders on the tram thought I was just another kid going to school. Getting off at the Palacky Bridge I'd cross back to the eastern side of the Vltava River. From there I'd pick up another streetcar south to Padoli.

Although the Nazis prohibited Jews from using public baths and swimming pools, the Padoli pool was large and anonymous. I'd plant myself in a corner and hide behind a book. The other regular patrons were young mothers and old people. Some of them probably guessed why I was there, but most of the Prague Czechs were not anti-Semitic. Besides, they still took a certain pride in defying German orders. Later that year when Heydrich "the Hangman" was appointed by the Germans to be the Czech Protector, everything changed.

I became an avid reader by the Padoli poolside. Among the few possessions my parents had brought to Siroka Street were their books. I plowed through everything in their library: novels, poetry, history, and philosophy. Sometimes even religion. Not the Torah or Talmud, though. We were a modern secular family. I'd never felt like a Jew growing up and I wasn't about to start for the Nazis. Sometimes other young people by the poolside tried to say hello, but I'd bury my face deeper in my book and pretend I hadn't heard them. I didn't want to have to make up stories about who I was and what I was doing there.

I'd managed to avoid talking to anyone for a few months, until one day a girl my age sat down beside me. I kept reading and didn't look up at her. I didn't have to—I knew exactly what she looked like. I used to stare at her when I thought she wouldn't notice. I wasn't stealing looks so much because I thought she was pretty. I had no idea if others would have found her so. Yet each time I saw her I discovered something new.

The first time I noticed her she was taking off her swimming cap. I'd expected straight blond hair to glide softly down her neck. That would have matched the paleness of her complexion. Instead this dark wanton mass escaped, leaping down bare back and shoulders. The way she ran her fingers through that tangle seemed wonderfully shameless.

Now my heart raced to have her only a few feet away. I tried to concentrate on my book but found myself reading the same sentence over and over.

"It's much better in English," she said in Czech, pointing to my German translation of *Tom Sawyer*.

I couldn't believe it. No introductions—no *hellos*—she just spoke to me as if we were friends from school.

"I know," I answered in heavily accented English.

She could tell I was showing off, but thought I was clever anyway. And that made her feel all the smarter for sitting next to me.

"I read it in English first," I said in perfect German.

That was my family's first language, as it was with most wealthy Jews in Prague. The upper classes behaved as though they lived in one of the great cities of Western Europe, not on the outskirts of Slovakia.

I took a chance and looked directly into her face. Maybe she was pretty after all. Yet I felt certain that nobody else would be perceptive enough to see it. Surely they'd be put off by her long angular nose and thin lips. Added to that, there was the problem of her hair, which did not belong with any other part of her. Everything about her seemed a mismatch. And because I felt sympathy for all her awkward contradictions, I allowed myself to become friendlier.

"There's a lot of slang and I wanted to see how they translated it," I said, holding up my copy of Mark Twain's book.

She grabbed it out of my hand without even asking and scanned the German text. "It's better in Czech." She also spoke excellent German. "I bet it would even be better in Yiddish, but I don't think they've translated it."

She tilted her head and pressed her lips together, making them all but disappear. As if swallowing what hadn't been said—she knew I was Jewish and she'd just told me she was too.

"We don't speak much Yiddish," I said in a whisper. But I didn't tell her my family looked down on Jews who did. I didn't have to.

"My mother is a liberal Nationalist," she said, "and we speak Czech at home. I bet your father only learned so he could communicate with his workers."

"My father was born in Vienna. German is his first language," I said almost guiltily. Other Jews had adopted Czech as their first language to show solidarity with the Czech Nationalists. "Almost all the people he does business with speak German."

"I guess you're a snob," she said, scissoring up on bird-like legs without using her hands. "But it's not your fault, so I'll still like you."

I extended my arm to introduce myself, but she said, "No names yet."

That's when I noticed her sparkling hazel eyes. I thought they were terribly brave and could pose all the questions I'd never dared to ask.

CHAPTER SEVEN

I awoke on the sofa to the hiss of the TV's early morning test pattern. I looked at my watch. It was ten minutes to seven. I'd fallen asleep in my underwear. I had a crick in my neck from using the couch's arm as a pillow. As I twisted my head from side to side to release the pain, it spread into a wave of nausea that felt connected to something I couldn't quite put my finger on. I tried to recall what I'd been doing when I fell asleep. I didn't even know what I'd been watching on TV. But I did remember an earlier news broadcast.

Russian tanks had taken up positions in Prague's Wenceslaw Square. Student protesters surrounded the tanks, waving fists and placards at Russian soldiers. The placards were often humorous: *DO NOT FEED THE ANIMALS—THE BIGGER THE TANK THE SMALLER THE BRAIN.* Some of the Russian soldiers even looked amused.

The story included a clip from an interview with Congressman Cantwell, taped before his son had died, commenting on Prague Spring. Because Cantwell was on the Foreign Affairs Committee and also a high-ranking member of the House Committee on Un-American Activities, he'd become an anticommunist hero. In this broadcast he denounced the Russians, saying they should get out of Czechoslovakia and allow the Czechs to determine their own fate. Nobody had the right to interfere with the rule of law, and anybody who tried was no more than a common thug.

"Make no mistake about it," he'd said, "this is not some problem we can ignore simply because it seems remote and isolated. We must join with our NATO allies to staunch this wound in the East, which otherwise will most certainly bleed west across Europe. Then, we'll be facing Russian troops in cities like Rome and Paris."

Hawks like Cantwell kept insisting that the Russians were threatening an invasion of Western Europe. To me it seemed as though the Soviets had enough trouble holding onto nations like Poland, Hungary and Czechoslovakia. I could not have imagined them trying to invade Italy and France, and I wondered where Cantwell was getting his information.

***

After staying away from headquarters most of the previous day, I figured I'd better show up this morning. But first I wanted to drop by Claremont Prep to find the girl who'd disappeared when I talked to the students yesterday. I arrived at the school about fifteen minutes before first period and located her in a hallway with several other girls. She told me she had to get to class and didn't have time to talk. I said it would only take a few minutes and backed her into an empty classroom.

Whatever had caused Patricia Walker to cry the day before had vanished this morning.

"So?" she demanded, sitting down without being asked.

She had straight auburn hair down to her shoulders and thick bangs rounded to cover the tail ends of her eyebrows. Also, quick eyes, despite the fact that they were weighted down with heavy mascara. With a slightly hooked nose, she was just on the interesting side of beautiful—exactly where I thought she preferred to be.

I swung around a student's desk and sat facing her, making an effort to smile. "A couple of your classmates told me you used to date Chris Cantwell."

"Who told you that?" she asked, much more adept at forcing a smile than I was.

"You went to a school dance with him a few years back."

"Who told you that?" she repeated, shaking her head, but still smiling. "You're not going to answer me, are you?"

"So, you dated him a few times?"

"Just once," she said, leaning back and draping a gangly arm nearly to the floor.

"He wasn't my type."

"Why do you think he asked you out?"

"Maybe he thought I was a challenge."

"Were you?" I asked.

A dark look swept over her face, but passed as quickly as it appeared.

"So tell me about that night at the dance," I said, flipping through my notes.

She rolled her eyes.

"Did anything unusual happen?" I asked.

"We might not consider the same things unusual. I'm not a forty-year-old cop and you're not a teenage girl."

"Take a stab at it."

"Unusual?" She reached a bony arm around the back of her neck to scratch the other side of her head. "I went with him, didn't I?"

"Perhaps a girl like you going to a dance with a guy who wasn't your type wouldn't be all that unusual," I said.

"What do you mean a girl like me?"

I smiled.

She flashed one right back, straight white teeth telling me to shove it.

"I'm sure you'd like to get back to whatever you were doing," I said. "And I have police business to attend to."

"I was fifteen and too stupid to decide who I liked on my own, so I let other girls influence me. 'You just couldn't turn down an invitation from a boy as gorgeous as Chris Cantwell,'" she imitated one of her girlfriends.

"Yet you went off with him afterwards."

She broke into a nervous laugh. "Where would we go?"

"Up into the hills to drink?"

"*Drink*-drink?" she said, batting her eyelashes. "I'm underage, Mr. Inspector."

"So were all the other kids in the parking lot."

She held out her hands to be cuffed. "Okay, take me in. I confess. I had a few sips of vodka."

"Just a few?"

She nodded and dropped her hands.

"Because sometimes when girls get intoxicated they do things they wouldn't otherwise do."

Patricia blinked slowly—one, two, three, four times—before saying, "I had a headache and he took me home. That's all there was to it."

I nodded noncommittally and jotted down a note: *Did Patricia Walker have sex with Chris Cantwell the night of the dance?*

"Ask my father if you don't believe me," she said. "Go ahead—call him now. I'll give you his damn number."

That meant her father didn't know or he wasn't going to be talking either. In any event, I didn't have the time or patience to deal with Patricia anymore this morning.

"That's all for now. Thanks." I waved her away as if her entire performance was forgettable. "Unless you have something relevant to tell me."

She stood up, keeping her eyes glued to the top of my head. "Relevant? You bozos don't even know the meaning of the word."

"What's that supposed to mean?"

"You're the detective. You figure it out." She turned and marched out the door.

***

When I arrived at the Hall, I dropped by the Coroner's Office to see what they had on the Cantwell kid. As luck would have it, I bumped into the coroner Matt Wilson and Cantwell. Even if Cantwell hadn't been with him, I wouldn't have tried to get any information out of Wilson. He wouldn't give me the time of day. And the feeling was mutual. In my opinion, he didn't know a damn thing about forensic medicine. But he sure knew how to schmooze the right people to keep his job.

The coroner had his arm around the congressman and was telling him to keep his chin up or whatever men like that say to console one another. Cantwell greeted me with a warm good morning as if we were old friends. Wilson asked me if I had business there. He must have seen me down at the morgue a hundred times and had never before asked what I was doing there.

"Just checking your son's report," I said directly to Cantwell. Why screw around with the middleman?

Wilson answered back, "It doesn't look like a homicide to me."

"Probably sunstroke," I said.

Wilson was about to give me some sharp reply—maybe tell me there wasn't room enough for the both of us at the County Morgue—when I turned away and headed down the hall. He would have come after me, but Cantwell said, "I'll take care of it."

I went down to the basement to talk to Dale Smoot, the coroner's assistant, and found him filling out a death certificate at his desk. As always, he wore a western string tie, with thin blond hair parted down the middle, blunt cut against both sides of his head, exposing his pointed ears. Ichabod

Crane couldn't have looked more at home nestled in this little sleepy hollow. Like him, Dale was a scrawny man with a beaky nose and long bony limbs. He reminded me of a vulture, especially when he was bent over a corpse.

I asked him if he'd begun the autopsy on the Cantwell kid.

"Ain't gonna be one," Dale said. "His father just came in to ID the body."

He picked up a large mug of coffee and savored a long sip. Dale liked good coffee and was very proud of the Melitta brewing system he kept ensconced in a corner of the morgue. Sometimes he offered me a cup, but this wasn't going to be one of those mornings.

"I just saw him with Wilson," I said, employing the slightest hint of a smile I'd picked up from Dale, who always spoke Wilson's name with a touch of sarcasm. "What's going on the death certificate?"

Dale lifted the fountain pen off paper and put it in the inkwell by his right hand. I always meant to ask him why he hadn't changed to ballpoint like the rest of the world. He handed over the certificate. "See for yourself."

"Accidental death from food poisoning?" I said, scanning Dale's chicken scrawl.

He looked upstairs. "That's what the man said."

"You saying somebody injected him with botulism?" I asked.

Dale gave me a droll look. He never laughed outright. "Somebody injected him with sumpin', but that ain't what we're putting on the record."

"Okay," I said. We both knew damn well the kid would have puked his guts out and his corpse would have looked wasted if he'd had food poisoning. "Just one more question and I'll let you get back to work."

Dale's left eyebrow lifted just a fraction of an inch. "Shoot."

"What else did you find in his blood?"

"Enough morphine to kill a horse. If the food poisoning hadn't killed him, that would've done it."

Morphine would have explained the kid's constricted pupils. The corpse also had the blue pallor consistent with lungs having given out from an opiate overdose. But without an autopsy to prove there was no internal hemorrhaging caused by food poisoning, they could call it whatever they wanted.

"You sure it wasn't heroin?" I asked.

"Different chemical composition. None of the other elements you'd expect to see with stuff cut on the street, either. Nope, it was morphine, pure as the driven snow."

"And that's not going on the death certificate at all?"

Dale shook his head and smiled wryly. "Just the facts, ma'am."

"What would a hooker be doing with morphine?" I asked.

"Unless she'd entered some sort of sexual Olympics, she wouldn't be shooting up a john with a depressant," Dale said, dipping his pen into the inkwell to get back to work.

When I got outside the coroner's office the sun had warmed the morning air. I stopped to take in the heady aroma from a nearby coffee manufacturer and exhaust fumes from people going to work. I always felt like I'd just gotten a new lease on life after I stepped out of the morgue.

As I walked through the parking lot toward the Hall of Justice, Cantwell approached. "I admire your tenacity, Inspector."

"Likewise," I said.

"How would you like to get together for a drink later on?"

"Why? You ready to talk about your son's death?"

Cantwell smiled genially. "Below the Cliff House at around four, let's say?"

CHAPTER EIGHT

When I stepped off the elevator onto the fourth floor, Richard grabbed my arm and pulled me back in. "We got a meeting upstairs with the deputy chief."

As we rode up the elevator I wondered who else Cantwell had visited at the Hall of Justice besides Wilson. Probably the chief, who'd relayed Cantwell's message to the deputy chief. I wouldn't have cared so much about the congressman tampering with our command structure if I believed his kid had simply died of an accidental overdose. But Cantwell's intense interest in covering up the circumstances made me all the more curious about what had really happened.

Instead of meeting with the deputy chief in his office, his secretary directed us to a conference room where twenty uniformed patrolmen from various district stations were drinking coffee and joking around.

"What gives?" I asked Richard.

"Beats me. Fanelli just told me to find you."

A captain who reported to the deputy chief stepped up front and raised his hands to quiet the officers. "As most of you know by now, we've been asked to help out the UC Campus Police with an anti-war demonstration in Sproul Plaza tomorrow."

There were a number of hoots. One patrolman called out "Red Square," and actually got a couple guffaws from rookies who hadn't yet heard that joke.

"What the hell are we doing here?" Richard whispered to me.

"What did Fanelli say about the Cantwell investigation yesterday?"

"Nothing. I didn't even see him."

I stood up to get the Captain's attention. "Excuse me, sir, we're homicide inspectors."

"Thank you for enlightening us, Inspector Wolfe." That got more than a few laughs. "And the deputy chief appreciates Lieutenant Fanelli volunteering your experience to work as the liaisons between Field Ops and the U.C. Campus Police."

I was the first one out the door after the meeting and I caught Fanelli at an inspector's desk. The lieutenant was on his way out of the office, wearing a sportcoat and holding his briefcase.

"Since when do you assign homicide inspectors to babysit a bunch of college kids?" I asked.

Fanelli pulled me out of earshot of the others on the floor. "They needed experienced officers to supervise the operation. I said you two weren't tied up on anything important."

"How about the Cantwell case?"

"Forget it," Fanelli said. "I talked to the D.A. There's nothing there."

"I was down at the morgue this morning. Cantwell was there, too, chatting with Wilson."

"So?"

"They're recording it as food poisoning."

Fanelli thought about this a moment. "I'd probably do the same if it was my son."

"Even if you suspected he'd been murdered?"

"I don't," he said.

"What do you think?"

"The kid was with a hooker and he accidentally took an overdose of heroin. When she saw he was dead, she got the hell out of there."

"So that's what you want me to put in the report?"

Fanelli didn't appreciate my tone. "Just put whatever the hell's on the coroner's report and seal the damn thing."

All juvenile records were sealed.

"Have you ever heard of a hooker carrying pure morphine?" I asked.

"There's no morphine on the street."

"My point exactly," I said.

"Who told you that?"

"Not Wilson, that's for sure. And what kind of pro shoots up her john, anyway? Numbed up like that, even a seventeen-year-old would take half the night getting off. These girls like to turn their tricks fast, especially in a fleabag joint like that."

Fanelli nodded for me to continue.

"How about the makeup in the sink?" I said. "Why would she be washing up with a dead kid in the other room? Like you said, she'd want to get the hell out of there as fast as she could."

"That's all?"

"He didn't die of food poisoning."

"Tell you what," Fanelli said. "I'll talk to the D.A. about it again. I'm heading over to his office now."

"Thanks," I said.

"I'll need a full report on your discussions with the campus liaison and Field Ops by the time I get back."

Figuring Richard and I could take care of that in an hour or two, I headed down to Records. I found Willie B. reading the sports page, perched on a cheap wooden stool that looked as if it was about to collapse under his 275 pounds. Ten years past his prime as an amateur heavyweight, he couldn't stay on his feet longer than a half-hour without having to "take a load off."

"You don't happen to know if there's any sealed files on a kid named Chris Cantwell—Congressman Cantwell's son?" I asked.

I thought it might be the kind of thing he'd remember. Records officers gossip and they'd be sure to talk about a high-profile case involving a politician's son. Besides, Willie B. had one hell of a memory. He could name every fighter Archie Moore had ever knocked out, all 141 of them. Give a round by round of any important fight in the last fifteen years, including scoring. And talk about Ali's first-round punch that took out Liston as if it lasted fifteen minutes—what position each fighter was in, where the kayo punch landed, how the bigger man fell, taking you step-by-step through Ali's victory shuffle. His memory was the reason Willie B. had been assigned to Records after popping his knee chasing a dealer down Powell Street.

"You bring me the Brotski files?" he asked, not bothering to look up from the newspaper.

"When's it due?" I asked, trying to remember if it was mixed in with a stack of overdue paperwork on my desk.

"You know damn well it goes to trial next week." He kept his face buried in the paper. "You've never turned in anything on time the two years I've been down here. You have any idea how much extra work that causes me? Half my time's spent on the phone with the D.A.'s office."

"I'll have Richard bring it down this afternoon."

"That's the only time I ever see any paperwork out of you—when your partner brings it down."

Now that I thought about it, I probably should've brought Richard. He claimed to be tight with Willie B. Among the few black officers on the force, they called themselves brothers. But I'd left Richard behind on the phone with Field Ops, knowing he wouldn't have approved of this visit in the first place.

"This is really important," I said.

"Everything's important with you," he said, finally looking up from his newspaper.

"Can you just tell me if you remember seeing anything on Chris Cantwell?"

"They're long gone." Willie B. smiled, knowing he was whetting my appetite.

"They? How many were there?"

He shook his head.

"Where'd they go? The juvenile courts? The D.A.'s office?"

"Maybe," he said, glancing down at the newspaper again.

"No cases pending?"

Willie B. shook his head again without looking up.

"You don't remember anything about them?"

Willie B. smiled even more broadly this time. "Those motherfuckers are all sealed, man. I could lose my job just for opening them."

"Especially with a U.S. congressman standing over us, making sure we all stay down on the mat," I said.

Willie B. kept reading as if I was no longer there. But just before I hit the door he said, "There was five."

***

I finished my report by lunchtime. The most difficult part was getting hold of the Campus Police liaison. Once I reached him on the phone, though, he only had a few minutes for me. He was busy coordinating with the Oakland and Berkeley Police, which were sending much larger Forces than the token SFPD offering. I asked Richard if he wanted to grab a bite.

"Do you have any idea how many damn forms have to be completed just to send a few men over the bridge for an afternoon?" he asked.

"Anything I can do?"

"Yeah, you can leave me alone so I can take care of it."

"You sure?" I asked.

"Just go. Eat your lunch."

I hiked over to Top Dog and picked up two hotdogs fully loaded with onions, pickle relish and thick ribbons of mustard. Chips and a couple of Cokes too. Then carried it all a few blocks up to Norm's Pharmacy on Harrison.

I'd met Norm Kovaly in the mid-50s at a pickup soccer game in Golden Gate Park. He was from Kosice in Slovakia and spoke very little English at the time. My Czech was grammar school level, but good enough to strike up the acquaintance of immigrants—minus the nostalgia. Neither of us wanted to reminisce much about our lives before we got to the U.S.

After soccer games we'd get foot-longs off a pushcart and make small talk about adjusting to our new life in America. I was focused on becoming a cop. Norm, a small wiry guy, was overwhelmed with visions of towering American honeys who loomed very large in his overactive imagination.

Norm had already earned his medical degree when he was shipped off to Treblinka with his parents, who were selected for the gas chambers right off the platform. He escaped during the uprising of '43, one of only seventy Jews to survive that revolt. He said that was enough excitement for one lifetime. When he got to the U.S. he decided it would be quicker and easier to earn a good living as a pharmacist rather than going through the rigmarole of becoming a doctor. Now he simply wanted to make as much money as possible and spoil his wife and kids. A big fan of American capitalism, Norm couldn't understand why I didn't hate the communists as much as other Czechs.

"It wasn't the communists who sent us to the camps," I told him.

"No, but it's the same fascist mentality running the Communist Party today," he said.

"That mentality is everywhere," I said. "On the surface everybody looks normal and friendly, but under the right circumstances even Americans could be calling some other people an enemy race and goose stepping all over their lives."

***

I found Norm in the backroom of the pharmacy, filling orders. He usually skipped lunch, but said he'd make an exception today for old time's sake. I spread the hotdogs, chips and Cokes over his desk and got right to the point: "So what do you know about morphine?"

"You depressed or something? You could pick up some heroin a lot easier off the street. I hear upper Fillmore's a good spot. But in the long run you'd be better off with a good wife." He didn't look at me as he bit off the puckered end of his hotdog. Norm was a painstaking eater who liked to create patterns with his food.

"Thanks, I'll keep that in mind," I said. "I'm investigating a kid who died of a hot shot."

"It's not a bad way to go," he said. "Compared to something like arsenic... You ever hear about those SS officers in the German DP camp after the war?"

I nodded. But I didn't tell him I was part of the group who'd snuck into the Nuremberg bakery that supplied those German soldiers with bread, and painted the tops of loaves with arsenic. If we hadn't gotten interrupted by security guards in the middle of the night we could have killed them all. We never did find out the exact number who got sick and died. Everybody—Germans, Americans, British and Israelis—wanted it hushed up. But a fairly reliable source told us we'd gotten about a thousand.

"Accident or on purpose?" Norm asked. "Because if it was suicide, that's the way I'd do it. Just about as painless as you can get, with pharmaceuticals anyway."

"How would somebody get their hands on morphine?" I asked.

"Just takes a prescription. But the docs don't hand them out like Valium."

I watched for a few seconds while Norm worked on a potato chip, taking small nibbles around its edges.

"Same with pills?" I asked.

"How's a kid gonna shoot up pills?"

"Like they do heroin?" I asked. "Crush it up and cook it in a spoon."

"Back in the 30s they used to have little pills that dissolved in water," he said with a chuckle. "But now it would take more trouble than it's worth. You'd need a mortar and pestle. Besides, you can order vials from a pharmacy."

"Where else can you get vials?"

"Hospitals."

If the fatal morphine came from a hospital, it probably would have been picked up in a burglary. But I hadn't heard about any drug heists lately.

"Are you cautious about filling morphine prescriptions?"

"If it was one of my regulars, I'd handle it like any other scrip."

"You keep records of narcotics prescriptions here at the pharmacy?"

"Everything from this year's in those files." He pointed to some metal cabinets. "Then I box 'em and store 'em up there." Dusty cardboard boxes were piled on a wooden shelf above the filing cabinets. "I keep the narcotics prescriptions separate."

"Is that law?"

"It's been so long I'd have to look it up, but I think all pharmacies do it that way."

"So if a cop like me wanted to have a look, you think you'd make me get a court order or something?"

Norm shook his head. He'd just finished off the last protruding hotdog end, getting ready for a major offensive on the bun. "I'm not saying you're not a very special hepcat, Simon." Norm saluted me with his hotdog. "But I'd probably show 'em to any cop who didn't come in here acting like some Gestapo asshole and promised to keep his mouth shut about where he'd seen 'em."

***

It was two o'clock before I finished looking through the last six months of Norm's narcotic prescriptions. The signing physicians' and patients' names were illegible on a quarter of them. Norm was able to identify all the doctors' names, but couldn't figure out a few patients. He showed me how to narrow my search by looking for prescriptions with the notations *vl* for vial and *ml* for milliliter. I found fourteen morphine prescriptions for tablets and two for vials. Norm knew both patients who were injecting the drug. The first patient's wife had come down to the pharmacy to pick up the opiate for him, and a nurse had picked it up for the second one.

Before I left, I used Norm's phone to call headquarters and talk to Lieutenant Hallman, who was in charge of investigating burglaries. He said the last hospital break-in was over a year ago. I ruled that out. I didn't think the kind of people who stole morphine would let it sit around aging like wine. I considered checking in with Richard, but decided it would be better for both of us if he didn't know what I was up to.

I walked back to the Hall of Justice parking lot and got into my Citroen. Then dropped by five neighborhood pharmacies as I drove west across town. Four allowed me into their files. The owner wasn't on the premises in the fifth. They said I'd have to come back when he was there. In all, I found seven patients with prescriptions for morphine vials. The pharmacists were familiar with five, none of whom sounded suspicious. I jotted down one of the two names the pharmacists couldn't identify. I'd locate that person later, if necessary. I couldn't make out the other patient's name. I arrived at the beach below the Cliff House at a quarter to four.

CHAPTER NINE

Not wanting to park my car in a conspicuous place like the Cliff House Restaurant, I left it on the Great Highway's dirt center divider next to a brand new '69 powder-blue Cadillac Convertible DeVille, one of the first of the model year. It had to be Cantwell's. The top was down and the white leather seats exposed to the elements. They'd probably dry out and split apart in a few years, but he'd have already sold the car and that would be somebody else's problem. The Caddy was parked next to a white Camaro with a license plate from Hertz Rent-A-Car. Those were the only vehicles in sight.

I crossed the southbound lanes on foot, entering a fog rolling in from the ocean. The air was heavy with sea life and sea death all mixed up together. I headed north along the shoreline, which paralleled a sloping sandstone embankment that elevated the highway above the beach. The soup got thicker as I made my way along the hard-packed wet sand. I could hardly discern the spidery outlines of cement columns a hundred feet ahead, supporting a span of road where there was a break in the embankment. Just beyond, on top of the bluff, I made out the white blur of the Cliff House.

Cantwell emerged from the mist with a man in his late 30s who wore a leather bomber jacket, khaki pants and steel-toed combat boots. The man walked with an easy gait over the soft sand—too easy for somebody who didn't look anything like a beachcomber.

Cantwell extended his arm to me. "Thank you for making yourself available, Inspector."

"I think you're the one who deserves credit for that, Congressman," I said, cautiously taking his hand.

"Inspector Simon Wolfe, I'd like you to meet Milan." Cantwell put his hand on the man's shoulder.

Milan gave a nod and measured smile.

"Just Milan?" I asked.

"Like Twiggy," he said with an accent I immediately recognized.

"What did they call you when you were a young roustabout in Old Town Square?" I asked in *Praguer Deutsch*, the German dialect shared by both upper-class Jews and Gentiles who'd lived in Prague before the war.

If Milan was impressed, it didn't show in his smile. In fact, his pleasant Nordic features gave away very little.

"I'd appreciate it if you two spoke English," Cantwell said.

I took out my pack of Camels.

Milan reached into his inside coat pocket and pulled out a box of English Navy Cut Players. "If I'm not mistaken, you preferred these when you lived abroad." He tilted the pack toward me.

"Sorry, have we met before?" I asked, taking one.

"Many people feel that way around Milan," Cantwell said with the hint of a smile.

"Is that right?" I asked, glancing into Milan's placid eyes as he lit my cigarette.

He held out the pack to Cantwell, who waved them away, saying, "Never touch the things."

I didn't think Cantwell caught Milan's wink as the congressman turned to go back to his car. It was meant for me, anyway, and I got the drift: war-ravaged Europeans thought that coddled Americans' fear of death was ironic, to say the least.

The three of us walked silently, with the barking of seals off in the distance.

"I don't take this kind of personal interest in just anyone, Inspector," Cantwell finally said. "Only those I want to make into friends."

"And just how did you two become friends?" I asked.

"I came to Washington to advise the congress on the Czech situation," Milan said.

"And since he was already in the States," Cantwell said, "I thought he could make a little side trip to do me a personal favor."

"So you're more or less political bedfellows," I said.

"Everything and everybody is political," Cantwell admonished.

"Just a bit of harmless *baksheesh*," I said, keeping my focus on Milan.

He appeared to be smiling at both Cantwell and me, the corners of his mouth and laugh lines around his eyes slightly upturned. But when I glanced directly into his pupils they reminded me of cameras unemotionally taking in everything: our bodies' relative positions, how many seconds before the next wave broke, the configuration of seagulls floating overhead, the direction of the wind.

"*Baksheesh*," Milan repeated, his facial features twinkling around fixed lenses that narrowed their focus on me. "Didn't you get paid under the table in your cousin's handkerchief business, at least until he was able to get you legal papers?"

And now I understood exactly who this Milan was and what he was up to.

"Am I supposed to be impressed?" I asked Cantwell. "That kind of information can be easily gotten from half-a-dozen sources."

Milan squinted into the bright mist, which had become incandescent in the late-afternoon sun. "Yes, but how many people know you were in the U.S. for six months before ever contacting your cousin?"

"There is no official record of how you supported yourself during that period," Cantwell said. "That was conveniently left off all of your paperwork, including your police employment records."

My stomach knotted. Where had Milan gotten that information? Certainly not from any documents. The date of my arrival in the U.S. was never accurately recorded. I'd sneaked in under an alias with forged papers provided by the Mossad. I got real ones later when my cousin sponsored me as a Jewish refugee.

Cantwell looked smug. Since I'd put a false immigration date on my SFPD employment application, he could get me fired. Milan, on the other hand, seemed almost blasé about the whole business, as if gathering information for blackmail was one of his less taxing assignments. Yet I had to admit he was damn good at it. And I wondered where he'd so quickly found sources with information on me.

"What part of Prague are you from?" I asked.

Milan picked up a piece of driftwood. "My father had a factory in Karlin. Small world—your father bought steel springs from him." He drew a curlicue in the sand. "Funny thing about springs—they all look alike until they're tested under pressure. It's only then that you know which ones will remain true." He gave me perfunctory smile. "Anyway, we had nothing personally against the Jews. It wasn't our choice to stop doing business with you. My father was conscripted into making artillery parts for the Germans."

"Against his patriotic objections, I'm sure, like all the other Henleins," I said.

"My father was hung for his beliefs in Wenceslas Square by the Soviets." Milan poked the sand with his stick. "The Henleins were the only ones who truly understood the dangers of communism. Still, he brought me up to respect the Jews' intelligence and racial loyalty."

"Which made our world conspiracy all the more dangerous," I said.

Milan halted in front of a jellyfish lying on its back. "Jews weren't the only ones who suffered. Do you know how many millions were killed in Siberia, alone?"

He stabbed the driftwood into the center of the jellyfish and hoisted the animal above his head like a trophy.

"Jesus," Cantwell said, turning on Milan. Their eyes locked. Milan's were numb and fearless. Cantwell backed off, muttering, "Put the damn thing down."

Milan hurled the driftwood, impaling the jellyfish on the sand. He then put his boot on it, twisting the sole back and forth, rupturing the creature, which oozed over the sand.

Cantwell led us away from the water and across the street to our vehicles, where we stopped in front of his DeVille. He turned to me expectantly.

"It looks like we've reached the parting of ways," I said.

"We're not necessarily saying the D.A. would bring charges against you for attempted murder sixteen years ago," Cantwell said.

So they knew that too! Feiertag must have been one of Milan's informants. Yet I was fairly confident the war criminal would never risk testifying in court. He wouldn't expose his own past to help out Cantwell or anyone else. And even if Milan used his powers of persuasion to force Feiertag to come forward, I doubted the D.A. would have dared press charges against me. It would turn into a political nightmare.

"Based on what?" I asked.

Cantwell raised a suggestive eyebrow and opened the Cadillac's heavy door. He got inside and slammed the door, lowering the car's electric window to have one last word with me. "Just remember, Inspector, I have a well-deserved reputation as a hard-nosed politician who will do whatever it takes to win."

I leaned down close and pointed with my thumb back to Milan, "Do you have any idea who you've gotten yourself involved with?"

"A professional," Cantwell said with a patronizing smile and drove off.

I turned to find Milan looking at me over the top of his Camaro.

"Americans," he said. "Can't live with them and can't live without them. Even your Israelis feel the same."

"They're not my Israelis," I said.

"My point is that we may have been on different sides once, but that was a long time ago. Now the Russians are everybody's enemy, and we're all obligated to do everything we can to defeat them."

"Even if it means working with Nazis?" I asked.

He gave a long sigh to let me know I was being impossibly stubborn.

"Or cooperating with the SS by joining Theresienstadt's ghetto guard?" he said, giving me another wink.

CHAPTER TEN

I'd been posted in the *Schleuse*, a dank cement hall in Theresienstadt's Jaeger barracks. They called it the *Schleuse* because it was like a sluice through which the newly incarcerated were funneled. The first step in these newcomers' indoctrination was for the SS to *Schleusen* their luggage of everything of value. We Ghetto Guard made sure none of the prisoners hid any of their valuables. These greeners were lucky to be left with a half-can of toothpowder and a torn pair of socks. And if they didn't watch out, those meager possessions might later become *geschleust* by marauding SS women called *berusky*, or even liberated by one of their fellow inmates.

The real purpose of the *Schleuse* was to beat into the Jews' heads that their value had plummeted to zero and they should be thankful for any little thing they had. Any rag on their body, any crumb of food that entered their mouths. Even a little keepsake like the top of a tin can crudely crafted to resemble a heart had to be carefully guarded.

I was leaning against a brick wall in a dark corner, smoking and eavesdropping on a couple of Czech guards who were also smoking. Like everybody else, I smoked even though the SS forbade it for prisoners. I'd picked up the habit when I was part of the *Aufbaukommando*, a group of young Jewish men who rebuilt the Terezin Garrison into Theresienstadt, Hitler's "model ghetto." Among the laborers, cigarettes were considered more valuable than money and I wanted to see what all the fuss was about.

The SS could have condemned me to the next transport east if they'd found out I was smoking, but I wasn't worried about the Czech guards ratting on me. Since the Ghetto Guard had relatively free run of the grounds, we did all kinds of black market business that profited the Czechs. Also, one of the guards had once been a friend when his younger brother and I were classmates. I'd visited their house, sharing meals and playing soccer with both brothers.

I had my eye on a wealthy couple in the *Schleuse* who'd taken up residence around one of the support columns. The wife was dressed elegantly, as if she had been taken captive on her way to the opera. Her husband stood off to the side in a dress hat and black tie with folded arms, waiting for somebody to figure out they'd made a mistake by including him. Others had tried to explain the facts of life to this stubborn man, but he was far too proud.

So why should I feel sorry for some fop whose head is too thick to get the message, I thought. He was just bringing trouble on himself. I felt differently about his wife, though. With fresh spirits still fluttering high from yesterday's freedom, her dark eyes shimmered in our gloom. I knew I should have looked away. It would have been better not to remember her glittering like a treasure today when tomorrow she'd look as gray and violated as the rest of us.

By her side was a young boy who began to cry. She tried to quiet him, but the child was hungry and wouldn't stop. The guard I knew barked at the mother to make the child shut up. She glanced over to her husband who went up to him and protested that he had no right to speak to them like that. That's when the guard winked at me. I didn't think much of it at first. As a younger man, he'd been a jovial and basically decent sort. So I figured he was only going to have a little fun with this dandy.

But without warning he slammed the butt of his rifle into the man's face. After giving a naked stare at the man's beautiful wife, the guard went back to chatting as if nothing had happened. The wealthy man had been thrown to the floor by the force of the blow. His nose was broken. Blood was flowing down his chin. He crawled back to his wife and began to sob, still on his hands and knees. I looked away, pretending nothing had happened. And by Theresienstadt standards I guess it was nothing. I'd seen men beaten to death or hung for less.

When I went to sleep that night I'd put the incident out of my mind. The next morning on the way to my shift, I strolled past the camp's bakery. I wanted to enjoy the day's first cigarette while taking in the scent of baking dough. I stopped in front of two stone demigoddesses on the bakery's front lawn. The statues were erected when the garrison was built in the late 18th century as a tribute to the Empress Maria Theresa herself. And there they'd sat for a hundred-and-fifty years in togas with their ankles exposed, during

Terezin's evolution from garrison to Czech village and finally a way station for the destruction of my people.

A lopsided three-quarter moon hung between the shoulders of these indifferent goddesses, as if tossed up into the sky by some careless child's hand. A heavy fog had rolled in from the direction of the Labe River to the east. To the west, shreds of mist slid across the face of the moon that flickered as though it too were winking at me. When I got to the States I'd hoped to put that compromising wink behind me. Now it had returned with Milan.

CHAPTER ELEVEN

I arrived at Richard and Miriam's nearly an hour late for Rosh Hoshana dinner. Richard told me straight off that if it was up to him they would have eaten and let me fend for myself, but Miriam wouldn't hear of it. He pulled me aside and asked where the hell I'd been all day and why I hadn't even had the courtesy to call and let him know what I was doing. I didn't want to tell him Cantwell was trying to blackmail me. Neither he nor Miriam knew what I'd done before arriving on her father's doorstep in the fall of 1952. As I tried to come up with a half truth to placate Richard, Miriam saved me by reminding us of her rule—no shoptalk at family get-togethers.

Yet things got even worse when Miriam asked me to put on a yarmulke. We'd been through this discussion before. The first time, she'd told me she didn't care what I believed or didn't believe—I should wear it to honor our traditions. Later, she'd said I should do it for Jason, who was beginning to pay more attention to the adults around him. Tonight she tried another approach: "After all you've been through, Simon, don't you care enough about being part of Judaism to at least make the gesture?"

"I don't have to," I said. "The world has made it clear that I'm a Jew, like it or not. Besides, false gestures are worse than no gesture at all."

As a convert, Richard took Jewish tradition even more seriously than Miriam. He'd learned the prayers in Hebrew and was frequently called up to the *bima* in synagogue. He also owned several fancy yarmulkes. On this particular evening he was wearing one Miriam had crocheted for him in orange and black, with connecting triangles she'd copied from an African pattern. In the past Richard had left the yarmulke discussion to Miriam and me. But he wasn't about to remain silent this evening.

"Then do it for her," he said, opening a drawer in the china cabinet. Inside were several synthetic yarmulkes given away at weddings and funerals, or when people arrive at temple without one. Richard held out a black one and white one.

I didn't reach out for one.

"Take it or—"

"Richard!" Miriam said before I could hear if he was actually going to kick me out. She grabbed the yarmulkes.

"He's got the nerve to come to my house—"

"It's our home," Miriam said, "and Simon's family, no matter what."

Miriam put a lace handkerchief over her thick brown hair, bowed her head and began the Hebrew prayer over the candles. Jason became entranced with his mother, as if speaking in this husky tongue had transformed her into a different woman. I remembered when I'd stared with the same fascination at Miriam's mother Hannah, watching candlelight brush the underside of her rounded cheekbones. Neither woman was a classic beauty, but they had a maternal aura I found far more alluring than hollow models in magazines.

Things eased up a bit after dinner when Jason and I sat down to play chess. For the last four years, since about the time he'd turned six, he wouldn't let me get away without playing at least one game. Each time we set up the board he said this was the game he was finally going to win. I started playing chess with my father before I was five and was considered a strong player when I was ten years old like Jason. But the way he was improving, he was getting dangerously close to being just as good.

I didn't know if I was distracted by the day's events, but Jason had me on the run pretty quickly. Part of my problem was that I'd tried attacking too early, not realizing how much stronger the boy had become in the three months since we'd last played. He fended off the attack and scattered my pieces. Then he planted his rooks in the center files, ready to ram them down my throat. With his queen bearing down on my king, I had no idea how I'd get out of it. Taking one last desperate measure, I threw my queen into the middle of the board *en prise*.

I frowned at Richard who was squirming around behind his son. It was all he could do to hold his tongue. But Jason did not want his father kibitzing any more than I did. The boy lifted his knight and dangled it above my queen, mulling over the ramifications. He'd never seen me do anything so flat-out stupid before. Yet how to refuse the most valuable gift one chess player could give another, short of stumbling into checkmate? His eyes widened as they scanned the pieces, confirming his suspicions that if he took my queen I could not retaliate by taking his.

I lit a cigarette and waited for Jason to make his move. Miriam was sitting on the arm of my chair, her hand outstretched near my shoulder. She reached over to an end table, picked up an ashtray and set it on her thigh for me to use. She'd brought in a tray of coffee and rugalach for dessert, and sat close to let me know I was forgiven for what had happened earlier.

I glanced up at Richard. He looked down at the chess board. I could tell by the twinkle in Jason's eyes that he was about to snatch up my queen. He set her down proudly with the other pieces he'd captured, then came over and sat on my knee. "Resign, Uncle Simon?"

Richard turned his back on us, muttering, "Shit."

I rubbed Jason's loose cinnamon-colored curls with one hand, while with the other I captured his king's knight pawn with my bishop. His knight that captured my queen had been protecting that pawn. He'd fallen prey to a fatal gambit. His king was trapped in the corner. Checkmate. Jason stared at the board for a long time, at first to see if there was any way out, then to digest exactly what had happened to him. He silently got off my knee and left the room.

"You bastard!" Richard said. "He's just a kid."

I stood up. "I think it's time for me to leave."

"What is going on with you two?" Miriam asked.

"Don't try taking his side again," Richard said.

"His side of what?" she asked.

I got my coat and kissed Miriam goodnight. When I tried to nod goodbye to Richard, he lowered his heavy eyelids.

As I was going out the front door I heard Miriam tell Richard to go after me.

"Just who do you think you are?" he said, slamming the door behind him.

"I don't know what you're talking about," I said.

"You don't respect anybody, do you? When I think of how hard Miriam's tried to include you, but have you ever called her once, just to say thank you for dinner?"

I understood why Richard thought I was taking advantage of his wife. He hadn't been privy to a conversation she and I had a number of years before. I'd told her I didn't want to go to her house for the holidays anymore. I felt like an intruder. She asked me to do it for her; after her parents had died, she felt bereft of family during the holidays. She said she could accept that I divorced myself from the religion, although she hoped someday I'd develop more positive feelings toward our heritage.

Richard resented the fact that Miriam seemed to appreciate my presence all the more when I showed up grudgingly. In his mind, all the effort he'd put into being part of Judaism didn't seem to count as much as the mere accident of my being born a reluctant Jew. He didn't want to hear it when I told him it had nothing to do with Judaism and everything to do with the fact that I was all that was left of Miriam's family. Richard said that he and Jason were her family now.

"Is it really how I treat Miriam that's bothering you?" I asked.

"It's how you treat everybody, man. Where the hell were you today?"

"Meeting with Cantwell," I said, still undecided about how much to tell him.

"You don't even have the decency to allow a father to grieve in peace."

"You think I ought to back off, just like everybody else, don't you?"

"To tell you the truth, I don't give a shit what you do," he said. "But if you want my opinion, I think you're pressing it just to piss everybody off and show 'em you're above us all."

I shook my head and went down the stairs.

"No?" Richard called out after me. "Then you tell me what you're looking for."

"Nothing in particular," I said. "I simply refuse to look the other way on a wink and a nod, that's all."

***

It was about nine o'clock when I'd finished my walk from Richard and Miriam's to my apartment. David and Wiki—the young neighbors I'd seen outside the night before—were sitting under the front porch lights making picket signs. David wore an old long sleeve shirt he'd probably kept from high school. Wiki had on one of David's white T-shirts and a pair of tattered jeans so spotted with paint they had to be from art class. She didn't have to worry about style, though; whatever she threw onto her shapely body was automatically "in."

She was perched on the top step above him with her chin on his shoulder and blond hair fanned out across his chest. With an arm draped over him and her hand on his, she helped him outline the letter *W* on a poster board.

David was not much of an artist. He was more the political type, with a bumper sticker on his motorcycle that said *Question Authority.*

When he looked up and saw the cop across the hall coming his way, his hand must have slipped. Wiki laughed, playfully calling him "klutzmo," and dark, brooding David actually giggled. A likeminded shiksa who could crack wise through his existential angst, Wiki was David's reward for having been born in the U.S.A. and coming of age in the 60s.

We lived in such different worlds I usually walked past without acknowledging my young neighbors. I figured they'd be more comfortable that way too. Besides, I knew they smoked pot. I'd smelled it while walking past their apartment door. Kids were smoking weed all over, even in public, and cops mostly looked the other way. Still, if somebody had decided to arrest them, it would be pretty tough to remain free spirits in jail. And I hadn't wanted to get involved trying to explain any of that—assuming they'd listen in the first place. Maybe it was because I hadn't heard the word *klutzmo* before and it made me smile; but whatever the reason, this evening I did stop.

"Is that for the demonstration on campus tomorrow?" I asked.

David glanced up furtively and then looked away, probably wishing I'd stuck to our previous arrangement pretending they didn't exist.

Wiki smiled as if she'd been waiting for me to make the first move. "How do you know about that?"

I glanced down at the unfinished poster. It said *Make Love Not W.* "I'm gonna be there too, with a bunch of other cops."

"Great. That's all we need, another Chicago," David said. "What do you guys think we're going to be up to, anyway?"

"I don't know," I said. "It's not like we all think alike."

"Once you put on your uniforms you do," David said. "And then, bang, we're not your neighbors anymore, we're the enemy."

Wiki put her arms around his neck and said, "Mellow out." She leaned over him and pointed to the words *Make Love.* "I know you know how."

As I climbed the stairs, I heard her slap David's shoulder and say, "He was just trying to be friendly, asshole."

CHAPTER TWELVE

Richard and I were in uniform with a contingent of twenty SFPD patrolmen stationed fifty yards north of the campus demonstration. We hadn't spoken more than a few words to each other all morning, and those were about police matters. So I thought it might be a good idea to try smoothing over our differences from the day before.

"Why don't you brief our unit this morning?" I asked him.

"You're the senior officer present," he responded with his shoulders thrown back as if he were talking to some officer in charge he'd never met before.

"You're better than me at public speaking," I said. "What with my accent and all."

"That's never stopped you before."

"Do it anyway," I said.

Richard got up in front of our unit and explained where to take up positions, how to schedule breaks and follow contingency plans in case violence broke out. Yet by lunchtime, even though the demonstrators' numbers had swelled to about 1,500, trouble seemed a remote possibility. Many of the male students had taken off their shirts to enjoy the autumn sun. In the adjacent plaza below, a group of black youths beat African drums and kids with dogs played Frisbee. To them, we pistol-packing police, sweating in our long-sleeve uniforms, were the only sign of aggression.

There was some tension with a small group of anti-communists who stood on the sidelines jeering the demonstrators. But most of these counter-demonstrators wore ties and did not appear to be looking for a physical confrontation. One of them held up the front page of a newspaper with the headline: "Communist Tanks Invade Prague." An anti-war demonstrator stood up and called him a fascist.

Richard said, "*Fascist*—that's their response to everything. Fucking commies."

"I thought about joining a young communist group once," I said.

"You would, too—just to be different," Richard said, not really that angry with me any longer.

"In the 30s most people didn't think Bolshevism was such a terrible thing," I said. "Besides, the communists were the only ones standing up to the anti-Semites. Back then, communism, Zionism, even fascism were all just different kinds of answers. That was before Hitler had slaughtered six million Jews and we'd found out Stalin had murdered anybody who'd ever had a creative thought."

"So how do you feel about what we're doing here?" he asked.

"Sometimes I remember when all men in uniform were bad news."

"I guess I can relate to that," Richard said. "A black kid growing up in the Oakland flats, cops weren't our best friends either. I wasn't like my sister, though—she hated cops. Sometimes I'd even pretend I was one, marching around like I knew what was right and wrong—like in comic books. You probably never heard of Flash Gordon, but—"

"We got all that stuff when I was a kid," I said.

"No shit." Richard gave me a boyish grin. "Remember Ming the Merciless with that pointy-collared cape?"

I nodded. In Prague I used to rush to the movies to see the latest Flash Gordon episodes. Being an only child, I'd drag along my mother or father or sometimes even my nanny.

"Flash would always be trying to protect some lily-white blonde from Ming," Richard said, "when all the while we knew it was Ming's raven-haired daughter Princess Aura that really turned Flash on. Sometimes I'd be on Flash's side, but I gotta admit other times I'd picture myself in a cape with all the other dark-skinned cats." Richard laughed at himself and pointed to a young couple sitting cross-legged on the blacktop with their heads touching. "Young and under the sun, man. Remember how free you felt at their age?"

"At twenty?" I said. "I felt anything but free."

"Okay, that was right after the war," Richard said. "But how about before all that shit happened? You know, when you were a young teenager? You must have had some good times growing up."

"By fifteen we were surrounded by guns night and day, and I was just as stupid and oblivious as these kids," I said, gesturing toward David and Wiki who had their arms around each other, swaying to Joan Baez singing *Amazing Grace* on Sproul steps.

"Well, yeah, at that age all you can think about are chicks anyway. You must have had a girlfriend, right?"

"I guess," I said.

"Did you meet her in school?"

"No. We met at a public swimming pool."

"What was her name?"

"Sarah," I said.

***

I came up with the idea of going in the water when she did. Since Sarah was at one end of the pool and I was at the other, I thought it wouldn't look so obvious. Anyway I'd seen her smile in my direction when she caught me glancing at her. I began swimming toward her, but when I lifted my head to take a breath, she was no longer there. Mysteriously my rhythm broke and my smooth stroke faltered into a dog paddle. She slipped up from under me, her water-slick body gliding along mine. With a loud splash accompanied by her laughter, she flew above and came down with her hands on my head, pushing me under. Although she held me for a long time, I sensed she knew exactly how much I could take. I came up gasping for air.

"Had enough?" she said, still laughing.

"Why did you do that?" I asked.

"If you wanted to talk to me, why didn't you just come over and say so?"

Sarah got out of the pool and went back to her towel. I got my towel and other stuff and laid them beside her. From then on we were inseparable, even though I didn't think of her as a girlfriend right away. Somehow I knew Sarah would decide about that when and if she was ready. She wasn't someone to be rushed or slowed down. And I was happy just to keep up with her.

At first we only met at the pool. Although neither of us wanted to talk much about our lives away from each other, we never ran out of things to say. We brought books and shared stories from them. Mostly we'd talk in Czech, but sometimes we'd switch to German so nearby Czech speakers wouldn't understand what we were talking about. Every now and then we'd even practice English. Sometimes we didn't talk at all. We'd merely lie next to each other and read. Secretly, I'd peek over, startled at how she looked like a woman when she was reading, her brow furrowed with lines of concentration. When she caught me staring, she'd turn right back into a silly girl, gently slapping my face or putting her hand over my eyes like a blindfold.

We both wanted to be like any other boy and girl living in a normal place. After a while we believed so much in each other, we pretended there were no Nazis. We began to take chances we shouldn't have: staying out late and walking the streets after curfew; stripping off the yellow fabric stars we were supposed to wear sewn over our hearts, and hiding them in her purse. We went to movie theaters and other places Jews were not allowed.

Once, we got stopped on the street by two Czech policemen who asked for our papers. I froze. Sarah distracted them with a flirtatious look and said that she had them somewhere in her purse. As she began to take out one item at a time, I was terrified she would make a mistake and accidentally pull out one of our yellow stars. Or that they would guess from her unruly dark hair that she was Jewish. When her hands were full she asked the policemen to help, as she laid comb, lipstick and hairclip in their hands. She came to a photo of Clark Gable and held it up to show them, clasping it to her heart.

"Isn't he wonderful!"

One of the policemen said, "Yes, yes," and dismissed us without waiting to see our papers. "You should be more careful. We could have been Gestapo."

Sarah didn't just love Clark Gable, she loved everything about films, introducing me to a passion that became even stronger than reading. Although Hollywood movies had been officially banned by the Germans, we found an out-of-the-way theatre that still showed them. When the lights were turned off we felt hidden and safe. Sometimes we even held hands, but mostly we just wanted to get lost in the stories unraveling before our eyes. Films with epic tales like *Gone with the Wind* took us on journeys with heroic people who were able to overcome any challenge.

Our absolute favorite film was *The Wizard of Oz*. I can't remember how many times we saw it. But I do remember the last time in late August—just before Heydrich the Hangman's crackdown—getting frightened like small children, yet delighted that we were old enough to laugh at our own foolishness. Sarah jumped out of her seat and screeched as the Wicked Witch of the West sent out her army of flying monkeys. Then she fell back down and buried her head in my shoulder to muffle her laughter. Her slight body sent a charge through me that felt like lightning arcing between heaven and earth.

After the movie, there was a wonderful and terrible quiet filling the dark street. It was like the hush after a violent storm. So almost holy, I didn't want to do or say anything to spoil it. I was waiting for Sarah, who for some reason seemed as solemn as the night. She finally laughed at nothing and slid her arm through mine, pulling me after her as if there were no danger anywhere.

That's when she decided it was time. Yanking me off the road behind a Roman column under a cavernous portico in front of a department store, she swung me around so my face was very close to hers. Then pressed her determined lips tightly together. When I took the dare she parted them, and I couldn't believe how soft they were and how warm it was inside her mouth. I twisted in a tornado of emotions—impossible things that shouldn't exist together, soaring and plummeting at the same time, her wild hair prickling my neck as if all secrets were coiled in those electric tangles.

***

"She gave me this." I showed Richard the tin token I kept in my pocket. "It was hidden in the yellow star she was supposed to wear. I didn't realize at the time she'd given me her star instead of mine."

"Weren't they all the same?" Richard asked.

"It was a present," I said, distracted by Milan coming down the steps of Wheeler Hall. "Cover for me. I'll be back in fifteen minutes."

I followed Milan around the side of Dwinelle Hall and caught up to him in an isolated spot between the building and some shrubs.

"Where were you just now?" I asked.

"Doing my job, same as you," he said with a genial smile.

"Your job's not anything like mine," I said.

"I think you've forgotten what the world's like out there where wolves run free," he said, laughing me off. "Wouldn't you like to see our birthplace the way it was before the communists took over?"

"You mean when Hitler was in control?"

"Forget Hitler. I'm talking about before that, when we were boys playing on the banks of the Vltava."

I shrugged.

"What does it matter what happens to an American congressman or his spoiled son?" he said. "I couldn't care less about them. I want to make our homeland like it was. And that's why I'm counting on your help."

He put his arm around my shoulder.

I shook him off as I pulled out my cigarettes. He went into his pocket for his pack of Players, but I shook my head: not this time.

"What are you expecting to accomplish?" he asked.

"Justice," I said.

"How very American of you," he said with a collegial smile, "but justice is simply the self-justification of those in power."

I nodded as I lit my cigarette. I inhaled and blew out a thick plume of smoke, trying to figure this man out. With a boyish mixture of innocence and mischief, he actually looked as though he believed he could persuade me to come over to his side. I wondered what he was capable of when he became disappointed.

"Were you visiting Dr. Meyers?" I asked.

His whole face shut down at my tone—the cop's superior air of entitlement. His eyes focused on Wheeler Hall.

I turned to see what he was looking at.

"She needs to learn her place," he said.

When I turned back he had already slipped behind some bushes.

CHAPTER THIRTEEN

Dr. Meyers' office door was ajar to catch a cross draft from the open windows behind her. She sat at her desk, wearing a stylish black scoop-neck jersey top and dime-store reading glasses that had nothing at all to do with style. Her eyes peered over the half-frames at a page in a typewriter. Not aware that I was standing in the doorway, she silently mouthed what she'd written on the page. Then her lips fell still. At rest her mouth had the graceful downward arc of a gull's wing in flight.

"Jesus!" she said, glancing up. Her hand leapt to her throat.

"Did you think I was Milan returning for one last word?" I asked.

"What!" Her fear turned to anger as she got to her feet.

I took a few steps forward. "Why didn't you tell me Chris Cantwell had been arrested?"

"You left so fast I couldn't tell you anything. What were you so upset about?"

"I can't blame you for trying to shift things back on me," I said. "I can only guess what you'd risk by talking. Is that why Cantwell's stooge dropped by? To remind you of the stakes?"

I couldn't tell if she was shaking her head *no* or warning me off. She sat down at the table adjacent to her desk and I sat opposite, trying to get a read on her.

"This is a very frustrating case," I said. "I don't think what happened to Chris Cantwell was an accident, even though everybody else is going to want to see it that way. At least until Cantwell's election is over."

"He may never want the truth to come out," she said softly

"Why? What's he trying to hide? What's in his son's arrest records?"

"You know I can't talk about that," she said. "You're not even supposed to know they exist."

Without a court order there was no way to make her talk. And Cantwell would make sure no judge would grant one.

I pulled out my cigarettes, tapping the pack against my fist until one staggered halfway out, and tilted it toward her.

"I told you I'm quitting."

"Mind if I do?" I said, laying the protruding cigarette against my lips.

She didn't say yes or no. Just got up and went into her desk drawer to pull out a cheap metal ashtray. The kind you see in Paris cafés. I thought maybe some day I'd get to ask her how she came by it.

"You didn't even like the boy, so I can understand why you wouldn't want to risk your reputation and career to help find out what happened to him," I said, taking a foolish stab at reverse psychology.

She slid the ashtray across the table. "Can we drop the bullshit for a minute?" She sat and faced me. "I'd like to ask you something."

I felt my shoulders stiffen.

"Relax, it's not about your war experiences," she said. "I know you don't want to talk about those."

"I don't remember saying that."

"What you said is you'd rather take care of present day injustices you can do something about." She reached across the table and helped herself to one of the cigarettes from my pack. I lit it for her. She took a drag before speaking again. "If nobody else gives a damn about Chris Cantwell's death, you're not going to be able to *do* much about it, are you? So what's the point? Why do you care?"

"I could ask you the same thing," I said. "You drag information out of people who don't want to talk about it for a world that doesn't want to listen. Why? Do you really think you can speak for the dead?"

"I speak for the living," she said. "Perhaps it's you who's trying to speak for the dead."

"A woman who looks like you can probably get away with putting words in other men's mouths."

"I don't put words in anybody's mouth. Both men and women speak freely here because they treasure their freedom to finally speak the truth."

"Okay, you want to hear a story from my past?" I asked. "Have you ever heard of *musellmen*?"

I knew she must have come across that word from people she'd interviewed, but I wanted to hear how she defined it.

"Those were people in the camps who didn't care if they died."

"A lot of people stop caring about their own death," I said. "Soldiers in battle. Mothers who give their lives for their children. People who are angry enough to risk themselves in order to take the lives of others. You can still care about things and not care about your own death. But for a deeply religious man—an Orthodox—to stop caring about God, that is quite another story."

"Are you religious, Simon?"

I wasn't sure if there was a smile playing at the corners of her mouth. Or perhaps it was in my mind as I watched her pronounce my given name for the first time.

"No, thank God," I said.

Now she was smiling—small, suggestive, just the right amount.

Suddenly I wanted to confess everything, but crushed out my cigarette and looked away, trying to get a grip on myself.

"I had a friend named Kurt," I said, automatically pulling out another cigarette.

She did not try to fill my silences, which made me more aware of her.

"We played music together in Theresienstadt," I continued. "He played violin and I played piano. He was so religious that even music was a dilemma for him. He was afraid it wouldn't leave room for God. In the end he justified it by saying it was an expression of the divine spirit. I met him again during my first days in Birkenau. But we weren't playing music there."

I glanced up to see if she understood. She tipped her head once to let me know she was well aware of the difference between the ghetto Theresienstadt and the death camp Auschwitz-Birkenau.

"At first I didn't recognize Kurt. It wasn't only because he'd lost so much weight. He wasn't the same person. When I went up to him and told him who I was, I couldn't tell if he remembered me or not. He was already detached from everything important to the rest of us, including memories.

"The night before he died, I saw him on his knees on the floor in front of the bunks, rocking back and forth as if *davening*. It was after we were all supposed to be in bed and I knew the night guard would beat him if he saw him there. I crawled over the outside man on my bunk to get Kurt and put him to bed. He pulled away with a strength I would not have guessed possible from a man in his condition."

"'What are you doing?' I asked.

"'I'm saying goodbye to God.'"

"He said His name?" she asked, knowing that it was taboo for Orthodox Jews to pronounce God's name.

"Yes. The next morning at roll call Kurt stepped out of line, knowing he'd be shot. I'd seen prisoners purposely run into the electrified fence to commit suicide, but I'd never seen anybody with the nerve to face the SS."

I stopped talking.

"Why do you think he did it?" she asked, knowing I needed to hear another voice.

"The SS man in charge killed Jews with the same lack of concern that we kill ants in our kitchen," I said. "Still, Kurt went right up to him. Neither of them moved—they didn't want to give up what they shared at that moment: like light and dark, each completed the other. I can't tell you how long they stood like that, but I can tell you there was a flock of maybe a dozen black birds flying overhead and that one of the few green things around—a milkweed growing by the side of a barracks—was blowing north by northeast. I thought I heard the laugh of a child from the women's camp—but I'd never heard one before or after. The last sound before the shots from the Luger was a hiccup from a prisoner near me. The SS officer turned and shot him first, then Kurt.

"I wanted to laugh. That was God's answer to the whole thing—a hiccup! From that moment on, I didn't even question if he existed. I knew he was irrelevant. I would decide what was just, since there was no one left to judge me."

Dr. Meyers' green eyes momentarily met mine. She looked at my cigarette in the ashtray, almost burned to the filter. And crushed it slowly and deliberately as if it were her own.

"I think it's a story the world deserves to hear," she said, finally looking up.

"It was for you, not the world."

"Perhaps someday," she said.

"Yet the story's not really about me, is it?"

"I wouldn't say that," she said with a shrug, "but it doesn't explain why you care about Chris Cantwell's death."

"No, it only explains why I don't have to justify it to you or anyone else."

She reached across the table. I thought she was going to lay her hand on mine. She put her fingers on my shirt's cuff button. "May I?"

I pulled away and unbuttoned the cuff myself, rolling up my sleeve. She stared at my unmarked forearm for several seconds before looking up for an explanation.

"It was toward the end of the war," I said, sliding my sleeve back down. "The Germans were in such a hurry to get all the Jews exterminated, they'd quit tattooing us." I fumbled trying to redo the button.

"They didn't even leave you that," she said, reaching out again and pulling my hand to her. "Let me."

"I'd thought about getting a number tattooed after I escaped," I said. "But it wasn't for the reason you're thinking—so I'd never forget. Other refugees who hadn't been in the camps were getting them. Some of them weren't even Jews."

"I hadn't heard that before," she said.

"Those numbers could be a free pass with the Russian troops—to get by the roadblocks, or a seat on the overcrowded trains, or simply not to be executed 'cause they couldn't figure out where you fit in. But somehow I managed to get by without it. Just lucky, I guess, huh?"

She realized she'd been holding my hand and released it without buttoning the cuff.

"Everybody I talk to says they were lucky," she said. "One woman told me she survived because she carried a horseshoe the whole time. But I think for all of you it was more than just luck."

"What do you think it was?" I asked, fastening the button.

She thought for a while, but in the end simply said, "That you cared more."

"How could I have cared more than a man who had dedicated his life to God?"

"I think your friend ultimately felt alone."

"And I didn't?"

"I believe you survived because you had a deeper sense of connection to something."

"To what?" I asked.

"You tell me," she said.

I shook my head and rose from my chair. "Perhaps someday... " My voice trailed off.

"Someday, Simon?" She gave me a smile faint beyond reading. "Well, if someday ever comes, you seem like the kind of man I might be able to share some things with too."

I didn't even realize I hadn't gotten any information about Milan, until I was out the door and down the stairs of Wheeler Hall.

CHAPTER FOURTEEN

I took a shortcut from Dr. Meyers' office back to Sproul Plaza, cutting through the trees that grew along Strawberry Creek. The creek bed was only a few feet wide. I jumped the water easily, landing on the dark moist earth on the other side. Pushing through underbrush, I came out into sunlight shining onto Faculty Glade, and stepped over a sign that said *Keep off the Grass*. A group of barefoot students were holding hands, folk dancing in a circle on the lawn, looking radiant, the way we're supposed to when we're young and full of blind hope.

The music ended and a couple of students glanced my way. I felt like a fascist in my heavy uniform and ducked under some tree branches, coming into Sproul Plaza the back way, along the side of Sproul Hall. Positioned behind the loudspeaker, the voice coming from the top of the steps sounded muffled, like somebody talking into their hat. After skirting the demonstration to get back to our unit I saw Fanelli with Richard.

"That must have been one hell of a dump you took," Fanelli said to me.

Richard shot a look behind Fanelli's back to let me know he'd been covering for me.

"Must be a quiet day back in the City," I said, wondering what a lieutenant from San Francisco's homicide detail was doing on this side of the Bay.

"I *wish*..." Fanelli's eyes scanned the crowd of students. "I wish I could be that age again for just a week."

"Married or single?" Richard asked.

"Are you kidding? Man, if I knew then what I know now, I'd score with a different girl every night."

"Don't even think about it," Richard said, giving me a furtive glance. "Some of those girls look young enough to be high school kids."

I'd known Fanelli when he was younger, and he was no different than he was now. Overly cautious both as a man and a cop, he'd gotten married while still in the academy. Each month he took a set percentage of his salary and invested in blue-chips. He knew he'd retire in eight years at fifty-five with a good pension and solid nest egg. He was going to buy a motor home so he and his wife could drive across the country and see the national monuments. It was all planned. No surprises.

"You'd probably make the same mistakes all over again," I said.

"Oh, no," Fanelli insisted. "I'd make some very different fucking mistakes. Ones I'd love to take to the grave with me." With that, he turned his back on the crowd. "I just came from a meeting you need to know about, Simon."

"What meeting?"

"Campus police want us to help them out again. We've put you in charge."

I glanced over at Richard, who averted his eyes just enough for me to know something was up.

"Why isn't somebody from Field Ops handling it?" I asked.

"Deputy Chief told me to assign it to you," Fanelli said. "There's word on the street things might get out of hand, and it'll be good to have somebody with your experience around."

"This is crazy," I said. "You don't assign homicide inspectors this kind of work. Why can't they find somebody else with experience downtown?"

"I don't know." Fanelli shrugged. "Maybe they're all busy planning the Policeman's Ball."

Richard smiled.

"There hasn't been a Policeman's Ball since 1960," I said, too pissed to think anything was funny. "What about the Cantwell case? What did the D.A. say?"

"I forgot to talk to him about it." Fanelli glanced at his watch. "They're getting back together at three-thirty at the campus station." He turned away before I could say anything else to his face.

"Will you phone him about it?" I called after him, but he didn't seem to hear.

"You know as well as me he talked to the D.A. about it," I said to Richard. "I just wonder who else was in there with them."

Richard half turned away. "The chief."

"When were you planning on telling me?"

"After I closed out the case tomorrow. Anyway, Fanelli said he'd rather talk to you himself."

"And you agreed to that?"

"Gimme a break, Simon. What was I supposed to do?"

"The kid's got five arrests," I said.

"He probably got drunk and stole a couple packs of cigarettes."

"The records are sealed. But if you really wanted to know, I think we could get Willie B. to—"

"I'm not helping you, Simon. No way, no how."

"And you talk about me not respecting anything," I said. "How about that oath you took, so help you God? Or does your God have a different set of bylaws for bigwigs?"

Richard folded his arms and turned his back on me, facing the demonstration. The crowd was thinning out. I glanced at my watch. It was just a little past three. It would only take five minutes to walk to the campus police station, but I was afraid if I hung around any longer I might say something I'd regret.

In the Campus Police meeting room, about thirty officers had broken into small groups, waiting for things to get started. They were mostly younger, recently promoted off the street. Not a single grizzled, familiar face. I grabbed a Styrofoam cup and poured what the coroner's assistant Dale Smoot referred to as *civic brew*: "lukewarm tap water spiked with phenolic acids."

Weaving between officers sharing jokes and street lore, I overheard somebody say that the next campus demonstration wasn't planned until the following Monday. It was Wednesday. That would give me a few days to do some more digging into the Cantwell case. I was hoping it might be enough time to either find something to persuade the brass it was necessary to do a full-blown murder investigation, or at least convince myself to drop it.

It wasn't until they began handing out assignments that I understood why I didn't know anybody in the meeting room— I'd been the lone officer tagged with the responsibility for all the San Francisco districts. Both the Berkeley and Oakland forces had assigned a number of men. I did a slow burn as I thought about the corner I'd been backed into. A homicide inspector assigned to a staff job that should have been handled by four or five desk jockeys!

At the end of the meeting I reviewed my duties. They included planning and coordinating logistics and transportation for all nine district stations, as well as filling out the various required forms and reports. When I counted how many pieces of paper had to be completed, I wondered if Fanelli and the deputy chief hadn't added a few just for my benefit. Now that my hands were tied with bureaucratic crap, they could get Richard to write up a report on Chris Cantwell's death saying exactly what they wanted.

CHAPTER FIFTEEN

After the Campus Police meeting broke up around five-thirty, I didn't bother returning to my post at the demonstration. I flung all the meeting notes and sample forms into the back of my Citroen. Half of them slid down onto the floor under the seats. I really wanted to throw them all in Fanelli's face.

I ripped off my uniform as soon as I got inside my apartment. After changing clothes, I grabbed a Bireley's from the refrigerator and made a peanut butter sandwich before heading over the Bay Bridge to the City. Instead of getting off on Bryant Street and going to headquarters to do paperwork for next week's demonstrations, I took Highway 80 to 101 and got off at Van Ness. Then I cut over to the Castro District.

I parked on Noe Street across from the corner grocery where Mara and I had shopped when we'd stayed at the jump-site sixteen years before. It was the same old shabby wood-shingled storefront. Other than a new coat of bright yellow paint, the wood exterior of the Edwardian across the street was also unchanged. After climbing the house's five wooden stairs to the front porch I scanned the rusted mailbox's nametags. I hadn't bothered to check up on Feiertag's whereabouts for several years, and the paper name strip was too faded to read. It was also too weathered to have belonged to a new tenant.

The interior stairs leading to the upper units had been carpeted in the intervening years. That made climbing up much quieter, although it didn't matter this time. I pounded on the door. No answer. I pounded again and was about to take out my pocketknife, thinking I'd get in the same way I had before, but a deadbolt had been installed above the entry lock. A high-priced

Schlage I guessed Feiertag had installed at his own expense. I wasn't about to open it without lock-picking tools.

A gray-haired woman in her 60s was waiting for me downstairs on the front porch. I didn't recognize her at first in her faded terry bathrobe. Last time I'd seen the apartment owner she was a good-looking blonde just a bit older than I now was. I remembered thinking she was pretty with a plump milk-and-honey appeal.

"He takes a catnap at this hour and can't hear anything without his hearing aid," she said in High German, testing my pedigree.

"He told me he'd be waiting up for me," I responded in the same upper-class dialect. "I came all the way from Fresno to see him."

She peered over her nose at me. She couldn't have remembered who I was. I'd seen her during surveillance, but never let her get a good look at me.

"Not a *hinter Berliner*?" she said with a coy smile. I'd passed: I didn't speak like some backwoods Bavarian.

I shook my head and smiled.

She told me to wait, went back in her apartment and returned with a large ring of keys. I followed her up the stairs.

"You know him from Litomerice?" she asked over her shoulder.

I named the small Czech Sudeten town where Feiertag had been mayor, about sixty kilometers outside Litomerice.

The way she sized me up, I thought she might be assessing my age. I'd been just a kid back then.

"I was a friend of Berthe," I said. Feiertag's daughter was only a few years older than me and it was entirely plausible.

The woman kissed her fingertips to let me know Berthe was one classy Aryan.

"Betty," I said with a smile, remembering that's what Berthe's American friends called her.

She unlocked Feiertag's door. When we got inside, she pointed to a sagging chair with stuffing poking out of its arms. "You can wait here."

After I sat down in what must have been Feiertag's favorite chair, she went into the bedroom and closed the door—not all the way—just enough so I couldn't see inside. I heard her rouse Feiertag. She came out and told me it would take him a few minutes to get dressed; then stood there, hovering over me.

"I won't steal anything," I said with a reassuring smile. "Promise."

She gave me a lingering look before leaving. As soon as she'd closed the door, I got up to check out the living room. Feiertag had replaced the heavy drapes with white lace curtains that let in light. But the same Biedemier cherry-wood vitrine with leaded-glass doors took up an entire wall, dwarfing everything around. My parents had one like it when we'd lived in our large flat in Vinohrady, an affluent suburb of Prague. Unlike Feiertag's, ours did not look out of place in my parents' vaulted-ceiling living room. Perhaps Feiertag's vitrine had also come from his family home in Czechoslovakia. I hadn't bothered to research his home furnishings when I was devising the plan to kill him.

The TV was new. He'd splurged on a large color console, which had more room on top for framed photos than his old black-and-white. Now he had so many pictures that some were hidden behind others. I picked up a photo of a beautiful young woman, whom at first I mistook for his daughter. Then I saw another recent photo of Betty with her family. With all the weight she'd gained, I hardly recognized the statuesque woman I'd last seen running up the stairs yelling for her son Martin. Standing next to her was the teenage girl from the first photo. It had to be Betty's middle child, who bore a striking resemblance to her mother in her lovelier days. Next to the girl was a boy I guessed to be a few years younger. Standing taller than his father was the oldest boy, Martin, in an army captain's uniform. He'd barely come above my waist when he'd seen me suspending a toaster above his grandfather in the bathtub.

I turned my attention to a floor-to-ceiling bookcase and picked up a wood carving of Christ on the cross, sitting in a small easel. Behind it were Feiertag's old German edition of the *New Testament* and a recent German-English translation called *Good News for Modern Man/Die Gute Nachricht*. Feiertag had always been interested in religion. In addition to being mayor of his Sudeten village he'd been one of the leaders of the local Lutheran Church.

I pulled out a volume called *Ethics* by the religious philosopher Dietrich Bonhoeffer, who was hanged by Hitler for opposing the Third Reich. I opened it to a book-marked page and read an underlined passage: *History rewards and punishes only men's deeds, but the eternal righteousness of God tries and judges their hearts.*

Feiertag came out of the bedroom, dressed in a suit and tie with his thick gray hair freshly combed. His aftershave was supposed to mask the stuffy smells of an old man who kept his windows shut; instead its lime exhumed long-imprisoned odors impregnating the walls. Aside from the hearing aid, at first glance he looked much the same as the man who'd knelt at my feet awaiting a bullet to the head. He had not forgotten me either. He stopped in the middle of the room, close enough to let me know he wasn't cowering, yet far enough to keep his distance.

"Why can't you people leave me alone?" he said.

"Who else has been bothering you and what did he want?" I asked.

"You're both looking for a man who no longer exists."

I used the book *Ethics* to push Feiertag into his favorite chair. "You're exactly the same man I could have killed sixteen years ago."

"Why didn't you?" he asked.

"The only thing you need to know is that you owe me for your life and I'm here to collect." I jabbed the air in front of his nose with the book. "Now, tell me about this man who came asking questions about me."

"Why would I know anything about him?" Feiertag asked.

The old man no longer had much power to his hoarse voice. He *had* aged. I could see that now. His face folded in upon itself with fear, deep furrows from cheeks to chin reminding me of the twisting *f*-holes on a violin. Even though he strained to sit erect, he looked more sad than hard.

"He's a Henlein like you," I said. "Awfully coincidental, don't you think?"

"There are tens of thousands of ex-Nazis from all over the world in America. All legal, upstanding citizens, invited over by the U.S. government."

"Tens of thousands?" I said.

I'd only heard about a few hundred scientists who were snuck in under the cover of Projects *Overcast* and *Paperclip*. When I was with the *Nokim* any of us assassins would have loved to have gotten our hands on a rocket scientist like Wernher von Braun, who had supervised the use of Jews as slave laborers under the Nazis. Yet neither the Haganah nor the Mossad would dare touch him or any other prominent scientist adopted by the U.S., which had become Israel's most important ally.

"Germans?" I asked.

"Not just Germans," he said. "Also anti-communists recruited from Soviet Bloc nations like Czechoslovakia."

I furrowed my brow and shook my head.

"They came under cover of something called *Bloodstone*," he said wearily.

There were so many covers worldwide under which Nazi war criminals escaped justice I shouldn't have been surprised I hadn't heard about this particular one.

"And what about Milan? What's his cover?"

Feiertag looked frightened. He was more comfortable talking in generalities than getting specific about an operative who might turn on him.

"Why can't you just leave an old man alone?"

"Forgive and forget," I said, leaning in close.

"I don't care about your forgiveness," he said.

"Of course you don't." I handed him the open book. "You'd rather leave that to the eternal righteousness of God."

Feiertag looked down at the marked passage. "It's something you might want to think about."

I reached into my pants pocket for the tarnished tin top. Feiertag's eyes alighted on the oxidized metal. Out of my jacket's breast pocket I took a stained yellow fabric star that had not been laundered since it was given to me twenty-seven years before.

"Here's something you might want to think about," I said, slipping the metal top into four pockets sewn onto opposing points on the backside of the fabric star. "A friend gave it to me so I could keep her heart close to mine." I held the star against my breast pocket, where Nazis forced Czech Jews to stitch them to their clothing. "You were one of the last people to see her alive. Perhaps you remember? She was just about this age." I took the picture of Feiertag's granddaughter off the television top. "Just a naive young girl who wouldn't have understood your lofty concepts of forgiveness."

Feiertag got out of the chair and took the photograph from me. "I only wish I could explain to her now," he said, putting back the photo.

"Explain to me, then," I said. "Who is this man Milan? What's he doing here gathering information on me?"

"You'd just better hope he confines his activities to gathering information." Feiertag gave me a bug-eyed stare, as if to say, "Now do you understand?"

I shook my head.

"Have you ever heard of the Gehlen Organization?" he asked, sinking back into his chair. "I suppose not. When you belonged to the Mossad, Gehlen was still in its infancy."

I took out my cigarettes, giving myself time to digest what he'd just said.

"How do you know I belonged to the Mossad?" I asked, touching butane flame to tobacco's tip.

"Who else would have sent you after me?" he asked.

"But you never told anyone?"

He shook his head. "Our community of Czech ex-patriots is small enough that we can keep track of everybody, even those like you who have nothing to do with us. However, the last thing we'd want is to have anyone start digging up the past. It's a house of cards."

"And the Gehlen Organization—is that a Czech group?"

"There are a few Czechs in it, Henleins such as Milan. But mostly it's made up of Germans. Ex-Nazis and SS officers like the founder General Gehlen, who was one of Hitler's top intelligence men. They're the CIA's primary source of information about the Soviet Bloc."

"Nazis working for the CIA?"

"Thousands of them," he said. "Officially, they don't work directly for the CIA anymore. They're more of a contract organization now. And if it weren't for politicians like Cantwell they'd have probably lost their funding years ago."

"You think Milan got information about me from the CIA?"

"How would the CIA know about you? Israelis wouldn't have admitted to them that they'd sent an assassin over to the U.S." He paused for a moment, shrinking into himself before imparting the next piece of information. "It's more likely Milan got it informally from intelligence agents in the Mossad."

"You're trying to tell me Israelis work with these ex-Nazis!" I said, leaning in nose to nose.

He turned his head to escape my cigarette smoke. "They have a common enemy now, the Soviets."

"You think Jews would expose me to a Nazi!" I said, grabbing hold of his lapels.

"You have to admit it would be a good way to even the score for your defection."

I didn't ask how he knew about my rift with the Mossad. Maybe I'd get to that later. Now I had more urgent business.

"So what is this Milan—an intelligence agent?" I asked, letting him loose.

"He's a ghost!" Feiertag whispered. "A ghost who can do whatever he pleases." He lowered his eyes fearfully. "And once he's back behind the Iron Curtain, it will be as if he never existed."

"What's he doing while he's here? Blackmailing people to keep them silent about Cantwell?"

"He's something of a legend among émigrés who have recently come over. His father was killed by the Russians who then turned his mother into a whore. Do you know what that can do to a man?" Feiertag asked.

"Tell me," I said.

"They send him back to Czechoslovakia to take care of certain men—maybe a high-level Russian or just a Czech sympathizer."

I leaned in close again. "Are you more afraid of him or me?"

"He wouldn't have let my grandson stop him," he said with an apologetic smile.

I'd become tired of Feiertag's voice and turned to leave.

"If you cross him," he said, "you'd best draw a circle around those close to you and do whatever it takes to survive."

"I don't have anyone close to me," I said as I went out the door.

CHAPTER SIXTEEN

It was about ten o'clock when I opened my apartment's front door. I was about to reach for the light switch, but instinctively drew my gun. Easing my left hand under my right, I steadied my aim at a shape that did not belong, outlined by dim light coming through the open window.

"You don't lock your door," a woman's voice floated through the darkness. "Interesting, for a cop."

Without lowering my weapon, I reached up and turned on the overhead light. A tall blonde wearing a red Afghani sheepskin coat was standing in front of my couch. Although her voice was familiar, I couldn't place her.

"If somebody wanted to get in, a lock's not going to stop them," I said.

She walked over, pushed aside the muzzle of my gun and handed me my card. "Your address is also listed in the phone book."

As I holstered my weapon I glanced up. She was several inches taller than me.

"When I'm sitting, people don't realize I'm such a long drink of water." Lari suggested the shape of a woman in the air with both hands. "Short waisted, lotsa' leg."

"The three-inch spikes don't help," I said.

"Hazards of the occupation."

"You weren't wearing the wig last time I saw you either."

"Like it?" She combed her fingers through the shoulder-length hair.

I shrugged and said, "Make yourself at home."

"Not too big on compliments, are we?"

I went into the bedroom where I took off my coat and tie and rolled up my sleeves. After using the john I hid my gun and holster in a middle drawer, then returned to the living room. Lari had made herself at home in a corner of the couch, with legs curled under and head resting on a throw pillow Miriam had given me five years before as a housewarming gift.

"Want a drink?" I asked.

"Whatever you're pouring," she said in a contented purr.

She must've been good at her work. I was sure she'd said the same words in exactly the same way a thousand times before, yet it still sounded spontaneous. I went into the kitchen cupboard and got down a bottle of 15-year-old Macallan scotch I kept for special occasions. I poured one neat and one on the rocks. I liked Macallan's smoky taste any old way. Returning to the living room I held out both glasses. She took the one with ice. Very ladylike.

I sat down on the chair facing her and pulled out my Camels. When I offered her one she shook her head.

"You got something to tell me?" I said.

She remained silent as she watched me light my cigarette.

"Like that you were up in the room with the Cantwell kid the night he died."

She held up her glass as if to say *Salut*. "Wrong night."

"But you've been with the kid before?"

Hesitating a moment before standing, she pulled off the wig and tossed it on the couch. Her dark hair was tied back in a knot. She stripped off the Afghani coat and threw it on top of the wig. She was wearing yellow-and-blue-striped hip-huggers and a spaghetti-strap top with little lace loops not quite concealing her navel. A knife hung on her right hip, its leather sheath strapped onto a wide silver-studded belt.

"You know that's illegal," I said, pointing to the carved-bone handle.

"And wouldn't it be just like a cop to bust me for carrying something to defend myself instead of going after the assholes I have to defend myself against."

I reached out my hand. She slipped out the knife with her left hand and laid the blade on her right, offering me the bone handle. It was a 6 ½ inch double-edged fighting knife. A nice one. Light to the touch with good balance. I gave it back to her the way she'd given it to me, handle first. She slid it into the sheath without looking down.

"You seem to know how to handle that thing," I said.

"One of my customers works for the government, above your pay grade," she said with a wink. "We made a deal: he taught me how to defend myself and—"

"I get the picture," I said.

"It's because of that kid I bought the damn thing," she said.

"Chris?"

"He had one pretty much like this, maybe even a little bigger," she said. "He worked me over pretty good while he held it to my throat."

I gestured for her to sit down again and took a few drags off my cigarette. "You know what you've told me is motive enough for killing him."

"It sure is." She picked up her drink and took a sip. Her hand was shaking. "But I'm not the only one who's got motive. I got off lucky. You should see what that sadistic little fuck did to my friend's face."

"What friend?"

"She called herself Karma. You can forget tracking her down, though. He sliced both her cheeks and just for good measure cut her bottom lip in half—fucked her up so bad she split town. Now she's just plain old Jane in Ohio or someplace. A waitress—no one's gonna pay to kiss that mouth anymore. Congratulations." She saluted me with her glass again. "Another one off the streets."

"Did either of you file a police report?" I asked.

"What a fucking joke that was. The way they were grilling me, you'd think I'd beat myself up. They said there's no way a green kid could've gotten the best of a whore like me."

"Where'd you go? Northern?"

"No. Downtown. Went in to report an assault with a deadly weapon and ended up being handed over to Vice."

"Vice? Are you sure it wasn't Violent Crimes?"

"Puh-lease," she said, fluttering a half-closed eyelid, taking another sip of her drink.

"Who questioned you?"

"Some fascist named Ellingsworth. What a fucking prig!"

"What did you tell him?"

"The truth. But he'd already worked out his own version. Why confuse himself with facts?"

"How *did* it happen?"

She set down her drink and looked at me as if she hoped she wasn't wasting her time with yet another cop shining her on.

"I didn't know he was Cantwell's son. If I had, I would've told him to get lost."

"You know Congressman Cantwell?"

"Jesus," she said. "I think so."

Remembering the way Cantwell had looked at his young aide, it struck me that he must have slept with whoever struck his fancy, legal or illegal. "Was he as brutal as his son?" There might have been more important questions I could have asked, but nothing I was more curious about.

Lari laughed while downing her drink.

She was the second woman I'd run across that day invoking client privilege, except I didn't think she had any legal basis.

She pulled out her Benson and Hedges. "How about a gentleman's cigarette?"

I crushed out my own and took two. Lit them and handed one back to the lady. "You want me to guess?"

Lari laughed and wagged her cigarette like a naughty finger.

"He liked to be tied up," I said.

"You've earned your stripes, in-spect-her."

"What did you use? His belt?"

"Sometimes," she said, pleased with our game.

"Then you called him a heel."

Lari cracked up laughing. A full-out, tooth-and-gum laugh that probably wasn't sexy enough for her johns. "*Heel's* like out of some thirty-year-old flicker."

"I like the flicks," I said.

"I bet you do. Not the shoot-em-ups, either."

She lowered her sharp chin and looked up at me out of eyes like half moons eclipsed by sultry eyelids.

"Are we talking full-blown S&M?" I asked.

"I'm not into labels. A man's got everybody looking up to him, so it gets him off to have a chick be a little sassy once and a while. Then when I'd let him loose, it would be his turn and I'd get down on my knees. That's the only way he could get off," she said with a clinical air.

"But his son didn't work that way?"

"Shit!" she said, downing her drink. "That cat was real scary. You just looked at him crosswise and... That's what happened to Karma. She told him off for what he did to me and he spent the entire night raping the shit out of her. After Karma tried reporting it to the cops, he cut up her face. Told her he could kill her and nobody would do a damn thing about it." Lari fell silent.

I offered her another drink. As I went into the kitchen to refill our glasses, I became aware that the one scotch had gone to my head. I couldn't remember that happening since right after I'd been liberated. All this talk of torturing women must have triggered something in me. Still I needed to concentrate. She'd thrown out a lot of information—with twists and turns I hadn't expected. Chris Cantwell could have just as easily been the perp as the victim.

When I brought the drinks back into the living room, I said, "Sounds like an awful big coincidence the kid would end up with a prostitute his father'd been seeing."

"It wasn't a coincidence." She grabbed the drink and took a swig. "The little creep had been tailing his dad. He told me I should do him for free because he was younger and better looking."

"Why'd you go with him in the first place?"

"He didn't tell me who he was until he got me up in the room. He just looked like some hot young boy with a smile that could charm apples off a tree. But talk about a Jekyll and Hyde. Man, he turned so fast I never saw it coming. When I told him I didn't do freebees, he hit me square in the jaw. Didn't even change the expression on his face. I came to naked. He'd tied my hands and feet with my own clothes. I started to yell, so he gagged me with a pillowcase, not that anybody in the Fool's Gold would give a damn about a woman screaming her lungs out." She shook her head, trying to look angry.

I pulled out my handkerchief and handed it to her.

She wiped away tears. "The creepiest thing was, when he was done he got all sweet and innocent again and said how much he liked me and how beautiful I was. All with that fucking smile! It was like everywhere, all over his face. Except his eyes," she said looking away. "They were somewhere else."

"Did the police go back to the scene to see if the physical evidence matched your story?"

"Thanks to Big Al, they didn't even drive me home," she said, handing back the handkerchief. She downed her second drink. "That kid could've gotten away with killing the president the way his father protected him. He's got the whole fucking system wired."

"If you really believe that, why are you here telling me all this?"

"I don't know. Something about you seems different. Besides, what do I have to lose now that he's dead?"

"It sounds like you should be happy the kid got what's coming to him," I said. "Why not leave well enough alone?"

Lari laughed. "I get it. You're not about to take on dad, either, right?"

She snatched up the wig from under her coat and shook it out on her way to the bathroom. And came out looking more natural as a blonde than a brunette. Slipping on her coat and going to the front door, she said, "Just once, I'd like to see that asshole get down on his knees for the finish."

CHAPTER SEVENTEEN

On the way into the office the next morning I stopped by the lab to drop off a few hairs from Lari's wig I'd found on my couch. I told the lab techs to check if they matched the ones I'd picked up at the Fool's Gold Hotel. Then I dropped by Records and asked Willie B. to meet Richard and me for coffee later that morning. When I got upstairs I found Richard at his desk filling out a report on a typewriter. I slid over a chair and sat down, handing him a cup of coffee the way he liked it, three sugars and a drop of milk. He didn't thank me, but at least took a few sips.

"I was wondering if you could help with some of this demonstration paperwork," I asked.

"Is that why you're buttering me up?" He set down the coffee and went back to hitting the typewriter keys with both index fingers. "I don't have time now," he said, hitting the wrong key. "Shit." He rolled the triplicate form up several lines to make the correction.

I glanced down and saw a copy of Chris Cantwell's death certificate by Richard's elbow.

"Don't even say it, Simon," he said without looking at me.

I lifted my eyes to Chris Cantwell's Case Report in Richard's typewriter. In the space marked *arrests* Richard had written *none*.

"I think I know what's on his sealed sheet," I said.

Richard scratched his mistake off a carbon copy with a razorblade. "What? Whizzing in public?"

"Try Jack the Ripper in training."

He stopped to look at me. "What are you talking about?"

"He tortured prostitutes."

"No way," he said. "Who told you that?"

"Remember that call girl I talked to at Northern? He tied her up and beat the shit out of her. Then he sliced up her girlfriend's face."

Richard gave me an incredulous look.

"It's true. When she came downtown to report it she got stonewalled. Cantwell stuck his nose in to protect the kid. And, oh yeah, the good congressman also happened to be one of her regulars."

"You gotta be shittin' me!"

"She came to visit me last night, wearing a blond wig, no less. I dropped a few hairs off at the lab."

"She's a suspect?"

"I've got a few suspects now. And just as many reasons for Cantwell to put a lid on this investigation. You think he wants it in the papers that he and his son were having sex with the same prostitute—the one who might just be guilty of killing the boy?"

"Just before the election?" Richard said. "It would make one hell of a headline." He caught himself gloating and gave a sober look at the report in his typewriter.

"It's like a parking ticket," I said, getting up from my chair. "Once you start, you've got to finish. Besides, the chief's probably drumming his fingers as we speak. But that doesn't mean you can't have coffee with me and Willie B."

***

I told Richard I'd meet him at the coffee shop in Union Square that Willie B. and I had agreed on. I left early to stop by a few more pharmacies. First, a couple mom-and-pops in the Mission District that only took a few minutes. I found one prescription for morphine vials. Nothing suspicious. The pharmacist knew the patient, a woman terminally ill with cancer.

Then I stopped at a Payless downtown that took longer. Unlike the smaller drug stores, it had several pharmacists behind the counter, all so busy I probably could have walked back without anybody asking what I was doing. The problem was, though, all these pharmacists kept records differently. Some separated narcotic prescriptions while others mixed them in with normal prescriptions. One had a several-month backlog he hadn't even gotten around to filing. And just like every other pharmacy I'd visited, a lot of the information on the prescriptions was illegible, so it was difficult to tell exactly what I was looking at. When I'd ask one pharmacist for help, he'd say someone else had filled the prescription.

I kept glancing at my watch and cursing under my breath as I tried to make headway. There were twenty or thirty prescriptions for morphine tablets over the last several months. Only three for vials. One was a large order for a missionary traveling to Africa. The pharmacist vouched for the missionary's integrity, but I jotted down his name anyway.

I ran twenty-five minutes late for coffee. On the way over, something important dawned on me, though: if I'd wanted to get my hands on morphine for illegal purposes, I'd go straight to one of those larger pharmacies where the left hand didn't know what the right hand was doing. The confusion would be a perfect smokescreen for anybody who wanted to hide their tracks. And since San Francisco was long on pharmacies and I was short on time, I decided to focus my attention on chain pharmacies like Payless, Owl and Longs. It might take longer to look through their files, but I had a hunch that's where I was going to find what I was looking for... if it existed.

***

Hot Buns was Willie B.'s favorite coffee shop. The coffee was nothing special, but they had enormous homemade cinnamon rolls. When I arrived three were piled on his plate. He and Richard were sitting on bar stools at the end of a narrow counter in front of the window where they wouldn't be overheard. I apologized for being late, but neither seemed to care. They were having a grand old time without me, talking about whether Ali could beat Frazier, if Ali were allowed back in the ring. Richard thought Ali could win with speed and intelligence, while Willie B. said Frazier's brute strength and determination would wear down the ex-champ.

I didn't have much to add. The last boxing match I'd been interested in was thirty years before when Joe Louis knocked out Max Schmeling in the first round. So I kept my mouth shut, waiting for the conversation to flow naturally in my direction.

Out of nowhere, Willie B. turned to me and said, "So you really think somebody might've killed the Cantwell kid?"

I glanced over at Richard, surprised that he and Willie B. had been talking about Chris Cantwell before I got there.

"Richard's already told me about pressure from the top to close out the case," Willie B. said. "We know all about that kind of clambake down in

Records. Still, certain shit's interesting enough for the water cooler, no matter what, and Cantwell's been one of 'em for years. Like I told Richard, though, we don't normally share outside. It comes back down the pike, somebody's gonna get canned."

I nodded: it wouldn't get back on my account.

"Okay," Willie B. said. "So you tell me what you know first."

I went over what Lari had told me the night before. Willie B. kept nodding as if Chris Cantwell's brutality was no big deal. Richard shook his head as if it was indeed a very big deal.

"That takes care of two prostitutes," I said. "But you said there were five reports."

Willie B. stared out the window at a young mother pushing her infant down the sidewalk in a stroller. "Before the prostitutes there were two girls from his school. Same kind of MO."

No wonder Patricia Walker had been so pissed off. She hadn't just had sex with Chris Cantwell. She'd been raped by him.

"Jesus," Richard said. "And his father helped him squirm out of those too?"

"Yup," Willie B. said, taking a sip of coffee to wash down a bite of bun.

"You know their names?" I asked. "Of the girls at school he raped."

"They black all that stuff out with minors," Willie B. said. "One happened maybe a year or so after the other. He spiked the first girl's drink with LSD. I remember that 'cause I thought it was some pretty cold shit."

I glanced over at Richard who looked as though he was about to put his fist through the window in disgust.

"How about the fifth one?" I asked.

"The file just kinda up and disappeared. I'm pretty sure it wasn't one of the girls at his school or a prostitute, though."

"You remember the judge on any of them?" I asked.

"Yeah. Same one on all of them. Wattley."

"I know him," I said to Richard. "Frank Wattley. One of Cantwell's buddies."

CHAPTER EIGHTEEN

I told Willie B. I wanted to drive Richard back so we could talk. Richard wasn't very chatty, though. He sat in sullen silence all the way to the Hall. Even after I'd parked, he looked stonily out the windshield. Finally he turned to me and said, "Fathers are supposed to look out for their kids, not get mixed up in the same crazy shit they do. As far as I'm concerned that bastard Cantwell's just as guilty of his son's death as anybody."

"Maybe, but no court's ever going to try him."

"No, he'll never go to jail for it," Richard agreed. "But there's other kinds of justice."

"The only thing he cares about right now is that election," I said. "Any scandal that comes to light afterwards, he'll have six years in the Senate to outlive it."

"How about if the prostitute took her story to the paper?"

"They'd never print it, even if Cantwell and the editor weren't friends. But if we could find the killer and she started talking, nobody could put a lid on the press then."

"She?" Richard said.

"So far, everything points to a female."

Richard nodded. "You want me to do that demonstration bullshit for you?"

We had to slide the front seats of the Citroen forward to dig out paperwork from under them. I told Richard to leave it for me to type up that evening. The main thing was to phone internal contacts during the day when they were likely to be at their desks.

"Don't worry," he said, "I'll take care of it."

"If you've got extra time after that," I said, "sort out the reports and requisitions by priority."

"Got it," he said.

"Top priority are the ones that will have to go up the chain of command and eventually land on the desk of the deputy chief, and—"

"Like this one?" Richard held up a form that was torn and greasy from being yanked out of a seat runner.

***

When we got inside the Hall, Richard went up to the fourth floor while I looked for Judge Wattley's chambers downstairs. I found his assistant sitting at a reception desk, stamping legal forms with the court's seal. He didn't skip a beat, pounding the stamp and blowing on the seal, as I introduced myself. "He won't be back until twelve-thirty."

"Twelve-thirty exactly?" I asked.

The clerk nodded and stamped the next form.

"How do you know? Does he have anybody else scheduled for that time?"

"That's when he always takes his lunch."

"Always at twelve-thirty?"

"Sharp," said the clerk, who then stamped three forms in rapid succession. "Attorneys plan their arguments by the clock in that man's courtroom."

Now that I thought back, I remembered Wattley had been a stickler when I'd testified in front of him. He also came to snap decisions about people. Once he'd made up his mind about a defendant, he was quick to dismiss evidence he thought irrelevant. In short, he was exactly the kind of judge who could easily justify helping a friend's son stay out of jail, simply by seeing things one way instead of another—youthful indiscretions as opposed to torture and rape.

"Where does he usually go?"

The clerk looked up blankly.

"To lunch," I added with an irritated smile.

"Nowhere."

"Does he eat?"

My impatience didn't seem to register on the clerk, who continued his work. "Yogurt and fruit. Mondays and Thursdays it's peaches and apricots, respectively, when they're in season. Prunes when they're not. Tuesdays and Fridays, apples."

"What about Wednesdays?"

"That's the fascinating thing about Judge Wattley." He slammed the seal down on another form. "You never know."

I glanced at my watch. It was about eleven-thirty.

"Tell him I'll be back," I said.

I got in my car and skirted the downtown traffic by taking Sutter to Van Ness, then headed north to a Payless on Jackson in Pacific Heights. It would have seemed almost too convenient if the morphine that killed Chris Cantwell had come from a pharmacy near his house, but I thought it was worth a try. This Payless's files weren't quite as easy to get access to as the ones downtown, though. I told the manager I was in a hurry, but he said he'd have to call their main office to get permission.

"I don't have time to wait around," I said. "Do me a favor and call Congressman Cantwell's house. I'm investigating the death of his son. I forget his number. You must have it on file somewhere. Just leave a message and tell him or his wife or whoever answers that Inspector Wolfe won't be able to drop by this afternoon with the information he wanted. When you get hold of your main office, you might as well get permission to make copies of all prescriptions on file for the last five years." I handed him my card. "Have them boxed up and sent to me here, will you?"

I was pretty sure I'd need a court order to force him to send copies of old prescriptions. I think he suspected that too. Yet if he called the main office he'd be taking the chance they'd tell him to do it anyway, and he'd be stuck with a mountain of paperwork.

"I didn't realize you were in *that* kind of hurry," he said, pocketing my card. He took me to a chair in the back and showed me the file cabinets.

This Payless was organized a lot better than the one downtown. The pharmacists kept their prescriptions filed together, all in the same place and in the same way—narcotic prescriptions kept separately, everything in chronological order by day with tabs separating out weeks and months. I didn't have to go back much more than a month to find prescriptions for the Cantwells: Seconal for Mrs. Cantwell and Dexedrine for Mr. Cantwell. Nothing at all for Chris Cantwell and no morphine prescriptions of any kind for the family. When I went back five months, though, I also found penicillin prescriptions for both Mr. and Mrs. Cantwell.

Pacific Heights Medical was the heading on all the Cantwell family prescriptions. That was it—no address or phone number. I laid the prescriptions on the desk in front of me. After comparing them, I came to the conclusion that the signing physician's name was either Evan or Edgar—Williams. A wealthy doctor of wealthy patients probably wouldn't give me the time of day. I put him on my list of people to contact when I ran out of better things to do.

***

I got back to the Hall at 12:45. Judge Wattley's clerk wasn't in. He must've been in the habit of taking his lunch just as promptly as his boss. I knocked on the judge's door and got no answer. I opened it anyway. The judge was in the visitor's chair in front of his desk, watching a soap opera on one of these new solid state portable TVs sitting on a table to the right of his high leather chair. A jar of fruit and yogurt were next to a legal pad on which he was scribbling notes. His robe hung on a coat rack in the corner. He was hunched over his work wearing a white T-shirt. His arms were paler and thinner than I would have guessed. Although he was in his early fifties, about Congressman Cantwell's age, he'd always had an upright, athletic bearing—a man with a respectable golf handicap and a reputation as a mean tennis player. Like the congressman, the judge had also married a beautiful woman whose smile had often lit up the society pages.

"Excuse me, Your Honor."

He did not look at me as his eyes bobbed up from the notepad to the TV. "You'll have to wait a minute," he said, lifting a restraining finger.

"It's important, sir. Otherwise I wouldn't bother you like this."

He didn't say anything else. Just kept watching TV and taking notes. When a commercial finally came on, he turned to me.

"Inspector Wolfe," he said, lifting a spoonful of yogurt, which he then shoveled into his mouth. "What can I do for you?"

"I'm investigating the death of Chris Cantwell, Congressman Cantwell's son, and I wanted to ask you about a couple of Chris's cases assigned to you."

The judge got up and turned off the TV, waving me into the chair behind his desk. That seemed strange to me. The Judge Wattley I'd known never would have so readily given up any seat of power. I took his chair while he scribbled a few more notes.

"My wife had a stroke eight months ago. She can't follow TV programs anymore. They go too fast for her. But she's been watching *As The World Turns* for almost ten years. Did you know that they recently aired their 3,200th episode?"

"No, sir, I've never watched it. Would you like me to wait a few minutes until the program's over?"

"That's all right," he said, pushing aside the notepad. "I'll make up the ending. I have to do that sometimes and darned if I'm not almost always right. I used to make fun of her for watching drivel. Now I feel as if I'm missing something if I don't know what happened. I thought it was a very satisfying turn of events when Claire stabbed Michael. The cheating bastard had it coming."

He took another bite—a large chunk of apple mixed with yogurt. I sat waiting for him to finish.

"Life throws us all curveballs sometimes, doesn't it, Inspector?"

"Yes, Your Honor, it does."

"And then we just have to take our best swing—hit or miss."

I nodded and he nodded and I could tell it was my turn to talk.

"I think there's a possibility one of Chris Cantwell's victims may have killed him."

"That went through my mind too," he said.

"I'm interested in knowing more about them."

"I got a call from Allen Cantwell warning me you might be coming. He said he didn't want me talking to you."

"But here you are."

Judge Wattley put down his spoon and took a few seconds before speaking. "Strange thing. Gloria and I have actually become closer since her illness. We talk a lot more. About everything. Don't keep secrets like we used to. I know about her relationship with Cantwell. Different things matter to me now, though, and Allen Cantwell isn't one of them."

"Did you tell him you were going to talk to me?" I asked.

"He reminded me of my legal responsibility not to divulge confidential information to you or anyone else."

"What did you say?

"I told him I would comply with my legal obligations as I have always done. And I will, too, Inspector." He gave me an uncomfortably long stare whose drift I didn't get; then picked up the spoon and put it in the empty jar.

I thought that meant our conversation was over, until he leaned forward on bare elbows. "You know your problem, Inspector Wolfe?"

"Which one?" I asked.

The judge stood up and smiled down on me as if he were gazing from the height of the bench. He went over to the coat rack for his judge's robe. "You're not a political animal."

"I could probably use some help in that regard," I said, coming out from behind his desk.

He slid the robe over his shoulders. "You need to take more of an interest in things."

"What kind of things?"

"Little things. Big things. Political things. For example, do you have any idea who's recently been appointed to local federal positions?"

"You mean judges?" I asked.

"You cops might not have any regard for a colleague's privacy, but we judges respect one another," he said sternly. He took my hand and shook it perfunctorily. "Don't be a stranger now, Inspector Wolfe."

This time I did get his drift: he never wanted to see me again.

CHAPTER NINETEEN

I had a pretty good idea what judicial appointee Wattley was referring to: Judge Roger Smith. Cantwell and Smith had been partners in the same law firm, and Cantwell had helped him get a seat on the federal bench earlier that year. At the time there was a big stink about Smith's appointment, with opinion pieces accusing Cantwell of cronyism. One editorial said that President Johnson would have selected any judicial nominee submitted by Cantwell, in order to get the wholehearted support of a conservative California Democratic congressman.

But why would Wattley have steered me in Judge Smith's direction? The thought passed through my mind that Wattley might still be a friend of Cantwell's and was sending me on a wild goose chase. I decided against it, though. If Wattley wanted to trick me, he wouldn't have used a lie that compromised his wife's reputation. No. Cantwell was a backstabber who'd stabbed one too many backs. And this was payback.

So what connection could a federal judge have with Chris Cantwell? Had the boy committed a crime that broke federal laws? I didn't think so. He sounded more like a sadistic rich kid who acted on impulse. Why bother to transport some girl across the state line when he could get away with whatever he wanted in his own backyard? Besides, it was a fairly lengthy process to get a federal judge appointed. Even if Chris had broken federal laws, it was unlikely that his father's buddy would have been confirmed quickly enough to be assigned the kid's case.

Yet the idea that Cantwell had helped appoint a friend in return for some sort of favor did make sense. Perhaps Roger Smith had represented Chris Cantwell, and the congressman needed Smith to keep quiet about criminal behavior that had not come out during the hearings. But that didn't hold water, either. If Smith had been Chris Cantwell's attorney, he'd have had to keep silent about whatever he knew. Confidentiality was even a more serious matter for attorneys than for shrinks and call girls.

Whatever deals Smith and Cantwell had made, I didn't think the judge was going to tell me about them. So rather than going over to the Federal building to look for him, I used a pay phone in the Hall of Justice's lobby to call upstairs to Richard.

He said Fanelli had been radioing me for the last hour. The lieutenant wanted to know why Richard was working on the demonstration preparations instead of me.

"What did you tell him?" I asked.

"That you had to go to a meeting with the Campus Cops and I was helping out. Also, that your fucking radio was broken." He grunted. "I don't like lying."

"But you're getting so good at it," I said.

Richard's silence let me know he didn't think I was funny.

I gave him a recap of my talk with Judge Wattley. When I got to the part about Cantwell having an affair with Wattley's wife, Richard said, "He's even a bigger snake than I thought."

I asked Richard to look up Roger Smith's home address. The judge lived on the other side of the Bay, in the Piedmont hills. Richard offered to call first to make sure that Smith's wife was home, but I told him I wanted to catch her by surprise.

***

Undisturbed by static from my police radio I listened to the news while driving over the Bay Bridge. Before leaving the Hall, I'd reached under the dash and pulled out a wire. The broadcast reported that Czechoslovakia's First Secretary Dubcek and other Czech leaders had been kidnapped by the Russians. There were rumors they'd been assassinated. Cantwell was flying back to Washington that evening for an emergency meeting. Although I knew that the congressman's going out of town might buy me some breathing room, I could not be happy about his reason for leaving—the world might have heard the death knell of freedom from my birthplace.

The Smiths lived in an old brick Colonial on top of a hill in upper Piedmont. After knocking several times and ringing the doorbell, I heard the flush of a toilet upstairs. The bathroom must have been over the front door, perhaps adjacent to a master bedroom that had a view of the street. I heard footsteps coming down the stairs inside the house. Marlene Smith spoke out of a speaker mounted next to the door while viewing me through a peephole.

When I told her who I was, she asked to see ID. I flipped open my wallet and held up my badge and picture in front of the little glass eye. She opened the door with a heavy chain attached and asked me to hand it through. Normally I wouldn't let my ID out of my possession, but I didn't want a federal judge's wife alerting headquarters to my whereabouts while trying to verify who I was. She looked at the picture on the ID several times and then back at my face. She had large blue eyes and perfectly coifed short hair like Doris Day in *Pillow Talk*—both the movie and hair style were now almost ten years out of date.

"What can I do for you, Inspector?"

"I'm investigating a homicide. Do you mind if I come in for a minute?"

Mrs. Smith handed back the ID and glanced at her watch. "I'm sorry, I don't have time now. I volunteer to assist with art classes at my son's school."

I stared at her through the narrow door opening, without making any movement to leave.

"If that's all, Inspector," she said, without even offering the obligatory smile of a Piedmont housewife.

"If it's not too much trouble, Mrs. Smith, I was wondering if I might use your telephone. My police radio's broken and I have to call into headquarters."

She sighed heavily, making her irritation even more apparent by rattling the door chain as she fumbled to unfasten it. When the door was open and she came into full view, I was struck that everything about her looked like a 50s' version of Doris Day. Including her starched white blouse and red gingham swing skirt flared with petticoats. Everything, I should have said, except her vacant eyes, with dark circles that pancake makeup was unable to conceal.

The living room's décor was early American froufrou spruced up with way too many knickknacks, most of them handcrafted by the artsy-craftsy homemaker. Kitschy needlepoint aphorisms and shadow boxes with multi-colored beans hung on the walls. She led me to a telephone on a side table near the fireplace. Homemade Christmas ornaments were already platooned on the mantel awaiting their holiday parade. Interspersed with these baubles were family photographs in frames painted with psychedelic colors. Gaudy as they were, I was relieved to see some reminder that we were living in the current era.

When I got through to Richard, he said, "Jesus, Simon, I was about to put out an APB out on you. You're supposed to be meeting with Fanelli and the deputy chief."

"What about?"

"I don't know, but Fanelli's really pissed that he had to go in without you. You'd better eighty-six whatever you're doing and get in here."

I'd quit paying attention to what he was saying, though. Among the lineup of family photos I noticed one with a pretty girl holding pompoms, standing in a cheerleader's pose. *Claremont Prep* was written on her sweater.

"When should I tell him you'll be here?" Richard pressed.

"I have to make one more stop," I said.

"One more stop where?"

"I can't talk now. I'll tell you when I come in." I hung up the phone.

Mrs. Smith led the way to the door and glanced back at me to follow.

"You didn't ask me whose homicide I was investigating," I said.

"If you must," she said, throwing up her hands.

"He was one of the students at Claremont Prep. From the photo on the mantel I see your daughter also goes there."

"Not anymore," she said. "She transferred to Judson."

"She probably knew him at Claremont," I said. "It's a small school. His name was Chris Cantwell, the congressman's son."

"My daughter never talked about him," she said, escorting me out.

As she was closing the door on me, I asked, "Where is Judson?"

"In Phoenix," she said.

***

Driving from Oakland to Berkeley I pondered why an attentive mother like Mrs. Smith would send her daughter off to Arizona. Wouldn't she want to watch the girl go out the front door on prom night, with an orchid on a formal dress that mom had hemmed? I suspected the girl's absence was the key to answering why Judge Wattley had pointed me in the Smiths' direction. And I could think of only one person who might confirm my suspicions.

Dr. Meyers lived in a single-level three bedroom house on Euclid Avenue in the hills north of campus, where a lot of other professionals and professors resided. Nobody answered the door when I knocked. I went back to my car, which was parked across the street a few houses up. It was 3:30. Fanelli had to be fuming at my absence and Richard probably wasn't too happy with me either.

As I sat in my car waiting for Dr. Meyers to return home, I lit a cigarette and thought more about Mrs. Smith. She reminded me of my own mother when she was in Theresienstadt, keeping up outward feminine appearances, distracting others' attention from eyes so defeated they were no longer even capable of guile.

I'd planned on waiting about thirty minutes before heading back to the Hall. But when I tossed a spent cigarette out the window, I realized I'd lost track of time: three others were on the blacktop below.

It seemed my life could be summed up in spent butts. And why not account for an existence in cigarettes? After all, they'd been our chief currency in Theresienstadt. I couldn't remember how many I'd traded to make sure my mother lived in relative comfort compared to most other prisoners. I'd even been able to organize her own *kumbal*, a private little corner with a chair, table, mattress, and a bedspread hanging over a rope to give her the privacy she said she so desperately needed.

In return, she gave me looks. At first, I thought she blamed me for my father's death. Later, when she'd shed all pretense, her eyes seemed even less alive; no longer taking in others, they'd simply become instruments of selfish expression. A few times when I'd caught her behind the bedspread with a man, they were accusatory. What right did I have to judge her? If I could trade favors, why couldn't she? At least that's what I inferred at the time. But I never asked. Perhaps if I had another chance I might. Except the last look she ever gave me. I knew exactly what it meant and would never want to hear those words spoken.

As a part of the Ghetto Guard I'd been able to keep both our names off the transport list. My mother's had gotten included a few times, but I'd pulled strings to get it removed. I tried not to think about the fact that somebody else would take her place. The Germans handed the Council of Jewish Elders a quota and the trains had to be filled with exactly that number of Jewish bodies. No more, no less. The German accountants were as coldly accurate as their soldiers. If not her, it would have to be somebody else.

Each time the transports required their few thousand Jews, there was a hubbub of activity in the ghetto. People traded whatever they had left, and in the case of still desirable women, that was sometimes themselves. The types of people who ended up on the trains changed over time. For the first few years, prominent citizens, the wealthy and famous, as well as WWI veterans were left behind. Also the elderly, because the Germans wanted to maintain the ruse that people were being transported to work camps, and older people were obviously incapable of work. But as time went on and there were fewer of us to choose among, it was more difficult to protect loved ones. Finally the day came when neither my mother nor I had anything valuable enough to trade for somebody else's name to be put in her place. The Nazi quotas had to be filled.

As I'd done before when my mother's name fell on the transport list, I went to Jakob, my contact on the Council of Elders. He had been a close friend of my father's. Jakob had also been one of the leaders of the *Aufbaukommando*, the group of mostly young Jewish men who reconstructed Theresienstadt into a ghetto. He vouched for me when I lied about my age and got me a job with the *Aufbaukommando*. Later he helped me get assigned to a post with the ghetto's Jewish Police and watched out for me in other ways after the Nazis murdered my father.

"There's simply nobody we can put in her place," he said.

Everybody else was protected by people of higher rank than me.

"Put me in her place," I said. "I'm younger and stronger and I'll have a much better chance of surviving the work camps."

We all had a foreboding about these camps in the East from which nobody returned, but like the Germans we continued to call them work camps because it made us feel better. Sometimes people would even volunteer for them, trying to keep their families together, pretending things would get better when they left the disease-ridden overcrowding of the Theresienstadt Ghetto.

"It can't be done," Jakob said. "We don't send members of the Ghetto Guard unless they've been caught breaking rules. Even the SS would question it."

I had no idea if he was telling the truth. I didn't think the Germans gave a damn who went on the transports. Perhaps he'd made some sort of promise to my father to protect me at all costs. Or maybe he'd heard about my mother's immoral activities and judged her in my father's stead. In any event, I had nobody else to turn to.

When I told my mother there was nothing I could do about getting her name off the list, her accusing eyes said it all: she was taking my place. I had traded her off.

Jakob tried to console me by reminding me of the elegant lady my mother had once been. But I didn't need any reminders. She was a beautiful, pampered woman who'd grown up surrounded by wealth and culture. The last thing she'd been prepared for was dealing in lives. As far as I was concerned, Jakob had no right to judge her. Nobody did. Except perhaps a mother who'd put her own future on the line to save her child. And I believed any woman who'd been through that would be well beyond judging another.

CHAPTER TWENTY

I'd gotten about halfway through my fifth cigarette when Dr. Meyers' Saab pulled into the driveway. A gangly teenager wearing a Berkeley High letterman's jacket got out on the passenger's side—all arms and legs, tangled hair and faded jeans. The girl reached into the backseat for a picket sign that said *KISS A FASCIST PIG TODAY*.

Dr. Meyers would have a daughter like that, I thought, flicking the cigarette into the middle of the street as I got out of the Citroen. The doctor didn't pay attention to my door slamming. She was too busy opening her car's trunk to get some bags of groceries. While her daughter reached into the Saab's back seat to scoop up her schoolbooks, her mother turned over the picket sign lying on the grass.

"What's this?" Dr. Meyers asked.

"I told you. It's for the demonstration," the girl said.

"Yeah, but you conveniently laid it face down so I couldn't read it." Her mother put an admonishing hand on an outthrust hip.

The girl cocked her elbow akimbo with equally dramatic flair. "You got something against free speech?"

As Dr. Meyers was about to answer, she glanced in my direction. "Nikki, go into the house." She held out the keys.

Nikki grabbed them. "Who's he?"

I flashed my badge at the girl and said, "Don't forget your picket sign." Giving a Charlie Chaplin smile, I pointed a finger to my cheek and leaned toward her.

Nikki curled her lip in disgust and took off toward the house, leaving the sign on the grass.

"There's nothing sadder than a rejected fascist pig," I said to her mother.

"What are you doing here?" she asked.

"Just dropped by to help you take in the groceries." I lifted out two bags.

She picked up the last grocery bag and closed the trunk. Scooping up her daughter's picket sign, she said, "I don't have time for this bullshit."

When we got inside, she told Nikki to go to her bedroom and do her homework. I followed Dr. Meyers into the kitchen, where I set the bags on a counter. As I stood around watching her put away food, I noticed how orderly she kept the cabinets. When she'd run out of room on the tin-can shelf, she cleared cereals off the shelf below, relocating them to make available two adjacent shelves with military rows of cans.

Nikki came into the kitchen and glanced at her mother straightening dry goods. "You've gone over the deep end."

"I don't notice you helping," Dr. Meyers said.

"You told me to do my homework."

"And?"

"I'm hungry," the girl said, opening the refrigerator and pulling out an apple. Her final statement before leaving was a loud crunching bite out of the forbidden fruit.

"If you'd categorized the tin of oatmeal as a can rather than a cereal, you wouldn't have had to go to all that trouble," I said to Dr. Meyers with a cheerful smile.

"Wait out there." She lifted an arm and pointed to the door.

Like the kitchen, everything in Dr. Meyers' living room was as it was supposed to be: matching couch and overstuffed chairs, color coordinated with a round oriental rug whose pattern was clearly visible through the glass-top coffee table. If the room had belonged to anybody else, I'd have bet it was put together by a decorator. In Dr. Meyers' case, I had the feeling she wouldn't have wanted to give up that much control.

I'd have also given odds she'd chosen the art herself. Rough-hewn pottery and lopsided glass objects were scattered just so on table tops. This modern art lent a Bohemian spontaneity to the doctor's Prussian order, making me think of the arty coteries my mother used to assemble in her fashionable Vinohrady drawing room.

I stopped in front of a print by Camille Pissarro with its title at the bottom, *Avenue de l'Opéra, Place du Théatre Français: Misty Weather*. Of course Dr. Meyers would have chosen the only Jewish Impressionist. The picture showed a bustling Parisian street scene vanishing into a fog at the center of everything. People were depicted in broad brush strokes of pink, amber and blue, merging indistinguishably into their white world. Yet the painting's hazy forms captured a breath of life that was missing in the corpse-like portraits hanging in the Cantwell's house.

I wandered over to a wall unit. A stereo took up the upper shelf. Some family photographs were below. In one photo, Nikki was lighting candles at her Bat Mitzvah celebration, surrounded by other thirteen-year-old girls. She looked so prim in her party dress it was difficult to connect her to the rebellious girl I'd just seen in faded Levis.

I noticed a drawer opened a few inches. I helped it along with my finger. On top of what looked like a bunch of old papers and letters was a silver-framed photograph turned upside down. I flipped it over, leaving it in the drawer. It was a wedding picture. Dr. Meyers had long wavy hair piled loosely on her head, interwoven with small white flowers. She was as thin then as her daughter was now, the full-length white satin wedding dress hugging the slopes of her hips. Her groom was dark and brooding and handsome, but looked almost ten years older, perhaps thirty. I tried to calculate how old I must have been when the portrait was taken. Somewhere in my mid-twenties.

"What are you doing?" a voice came from behind me.

I closed the drawer and turned around. Nikki stood in the middle of the living room with folded arms. We eyeballed one another. Actually, she glared and I tried not to smile at her gutsiness, convinced she would have taken it the wrong way.

Dr. Meyers came in. "I thought you were in your bedroom doing homework."

"He was snooping around," Nikki said.

Dr. Meyers gave me a reproving glance before saying to her daughter, "Go on now."

Nikki stood her ground, looking from me to her mother and back again, trying to figure out what was going on.

Dr. Meyers went up to her and ran her fingers through the girl's hair. "Please, Honey, it won't be long. I'll call you for dinner."

"Are you sure everything's okay?" Nikki asked, giving me the eye.

"Yeah. It's fine. Go on."

When the girl had gone into her room and shut the door, Dr. Meyers turned to me and said, "What the hell's eating you, anyway?"

"How about Patricia Walker and the Smith girl?" I said.

Her face dropped. "Oh, God."

"I know what's in those sealed files."

She bit her lower lip.

I smelled coffee brewing in the kitchen.

"If you're pouring, I take a lot of milk."

She shook her head as if she was making a big mistake. "Leave my stuff alone, okay?"

I held up two fingers. "Scout's honor."

By the time Dr. Meyers had returned with a tray of coffee, I'd thought through my approach. I didn't expect her to tell me everything outright, but like Judge Wattley maybe she'd find ways of saying things without saying them directly. I even left my notebook in my pocket so our conversation would seem off the record.

She set the tray on the glass coffee table and sat on the chair opposite me. "Help yourself."

"You were called in to counsel Chris Cantwell after he raped the Smith girl," I said while pouring milk into my coffee.

"How do you know that?" she asked.

"Timing. You quit seeing him about a year ago and you said you saw him for a year. That would be some months after Patricia Smith's rape and—"

"I'm afraid to ask where you got this information, Inspector," Dr. Meyers said, setting down her coffee. "It couldn't be anyplace legal."

So she wasn't denying that either Patricia Walker or Judge Smith's daughter had been raped by Chris Cantwell.

"Was he your patient when he assaulted those two prostitutes?" I asked.

She lowered her eyes.

"I'll take that as a yes," I said.

She lifted the cup to her lips—an excuse, I thought, not to look at me.

"How about I lay my cards on the table and you do the same?" I asked. "It will stay here between you and me."

Dr. Meyers set her jaw and looked directly at me. "I don't trust cops who say that."

"I can't even begin to tell you what kinds of chances I've taken by coming here. I don't see you risking a goddamn thing."

"I have more to lose," she said, glancing back at her daughter's room.

"So Cantwell wins again. Is that what you want?"

She lowered her head and pressed her lips together: I'd hit a nerve.

"I'll start," I said. "I already know Cantwell was having sex with the same prostitute as his son. You think he has something more to hide than that?"

I'd sized up hundreds of people the way she was sizing me up now. It all came down to the slope of my shoulders, the angle of my hands resting on the table, the tension in my brow, the tautness of my upper lip, the small fluctuations in the electrical charge around my body. Could I really be trusted?

"I never told you any of this," she said in a low voice.

I nodded. "Do you remember him mentioning any enemies?"

"Other than the girls he'd destroyed and their family and friends?" she said with an acerbic laugh.

And she was right—that could make for a fairly long list of suspects. I reached into my pocket for my pack of cigarettes. I laid them on the table and looked up at her.

"Go ahead," she said. "Nikki's always sneaking them. She's probably in there with the window opened now. Use this." She passed over a hand-thrown bowl.

"Did the court order him to see you?"

She rolled her eyes and ran her fingers through her short thick hair, which rippled directly back into place. "The court never ordered him to do a damn thing. Everybody verbally agreed to drop the charges if Chris would seek counseling."

"Why did they choose you?" I asked, flicking an ash into the bowl.

She took the cigarette from my fingers without asking. After inhaling one deep drag she quickly handed it back, as if it never happened. "I'd met the Cantwells socially at a Halloween party," she said choosing her words carefully. "They liked me."

"Could he have been doing things you didn't know about? Things that never got reported to the police."

She shook her head.

"How can you be so sure?"

"Because he was proud of himself. He wanted me to know." She took my cigarette again.

I lit another one.

"You know what he said about Patricia and Joyce?" she asked. "He didn't know what they were whining about. They should have thanked him for choosing them."

"Like his father," I said.

"At least his father asks first," she said with a knowing look.

"Did he ask you? I mean his father."

"I know what you meant." She took a drag off the cigarette. "I was just wondering why you asked the question." She exhaled smoke while scrutinizing me out of the corners of her eyes. "He came on to me at the Halloween party, pretty much in front of his wife."

I crushed out my just-lit cigarette. "Did anything happen between you and Cantwell?"

"Did you come here to find out about Chris Cantwell or my love life?"

"I just have trouble picturing you with somebody like Cantwell," I said.

"And why would you be trying to do that?" she asked, breaking into a wonderfully irrepressible laugh, which reminded me of the bold brush strokes in Pissarro's street scene, alive with both darkness and light.

CHAPTER TWENTY-ONE

It was about eleven o' clock at night and the office coffee pot had just finished perking. I'd gotten lucky when I'd arrived at the Hall from Dr. Meyers' house—Fanelli had left for home about a half hour earlier. I was able to get down to work without any distractions. Richard and I had been sitting back to back, pounding nonstop at our typewriters for the last three hours straight. Richard said if we worked all night, by morning we might be able to look reasonably well prepared for next week's demonstrations, and maybe—just maybe—I might have a chance of bluffing my way through with Fanelli.

I'd told Richard about my conversations with Mrs. Smith and Dr. Meyers, but he seemed most interested in talking about "vibes" between Dr. Meyers and me.

"What vibes?" I asked.

"She asked you if you were there to talk about her love life—you should have said something cool, like—'"

"Something unprofessional, you mean."

"Man!" Richard said, shaking his head. "You don't mind stepping over the line at other times."

"Not when I'm interviewing a—"

"That's exactly what I'm saying—how can you be so smart interrogating suspects and—"

"Speaking of suspects," I said, ignoring Richard's grin at my changing the subject. "Mrs. Smith had a motive."

"Taking revenge for what the kid did to her daughter?" he asked.

"The way I'm calculating, though, Patricia Walker was raped before the summer of '66 and Joyce Smith later that fall. Two years is a long time to wait for revenge."

"Same thing with Judge Smith," Richard said. "If Cantwell was buying his silence, you think he'd wait a year to get paid off?"

"Federal judgeships don't open up every day," I said. "He might have had to."

We'd taken our coffee back to our desks to continue typing up paperwork.

"Maybe Cantwell had something to do with the death of his son," Richard said, rolling three forms and two pieces of carbon paper into the typewriter. "He had motive. The kid was out of control—a danger to his career. Who knows, maybe the little creep even threatened to expose the old man."

I wandered over and looked out the fourth-story window, trying to imagine all the unimaginable possibilities tangled up in the glittering web of the city's lights: desires on the brink of fulfillment; dreams about to be thwarted; and nightmares so twisted at conception they were doomed to be abortive. My eyes floated up to the black sky above Nob Hill and a thought emerged from its emptiness.

"How would Cantwell have done it?" I asked, turning to Richard. "Hid in some dark corner of the hotel waiting for the prostitute to come out? He had no way of knowing she'd leave first, before the kid even had sex with her. Then what would he have done? Snuck into the hotel room, somehow knowing that a lethal dose of morphine was inside, and talk his kid into shooting up?"

Richard continued typing as he listened to my argument. I turned back to the window, thoughts racing through my mind like the blur of late-night traffic on 101 below.

"Cantwell could have put her up to it," Richard said. "You said he and that call girl knew each other."

"Do you think he'd take the chance of working with an amateur like Lari?" I wasn't ready to tell him about Milan. Too many personal secrets I'd have to disclose.

"He'd be afraid she'd leave too many loose ends?" Richard said, hitting the carriage return several times, advancing down to the next box on the form. "Still, she did have a personal score to settle with the kid."

"Why would she have come to see me, then?"

"Wanting to get something off her chest? Or maybe she planned the murder with Cantwell and decided to double-cross him. Like you said, she wanted to see the congressman down on his knees."

"She's too smart to try to make someone that powerful into a fall guy," I said.

"Sometimes people do stupid things if they're pissed off enough," Richard said. The phone rang and he picked it up. "Evans."

And people can get pretty pissed off when they believe the world is purposely remaining blind to injustices committed against them or those close to them, I thought.

After hanging up, Richard said, "Get your coat. We're going to the Haight."

***

Lari Zohn lived a few blocks above Haight on Broderick Street, in an airy upstairs flat with floor-to-ceiling bay windows. The front room was filled with furnishings you'd expect to find in the apartment of any young woman who wanted to impress friends and lovers: an unframed rock poster (*Jefferson Airplane Takes Off*) flanked by chrome-framed Dali prints; madras sitting pillows on the floor; batik-draped end tables; candles of every shape and color; and a vase of dried flowers in the center of her dining-room table. A small bookcase included *Soul on Ice* and *Pride and Prejudice*. The blond hardwood floors were waxed and polished.

Lari lay naked on her back in a queen-sized bed. Throat slit. One clean cut. Her left arm bent back above her head and long legs parallel to one another, reminding me of a model posing for an old master. Her death-clenched right hand stretched over the edge of the mattress. Congealed semen clustered in her pubic hairs. A fist-sized stain of blood on the sheet below her armpit. Her double-edged fighting knife on the floor next to the bed, blood still tacky on the blade.

An anonymous call had been taken by the duty sergeant in the Mission Street Station, who dispatched two patrolmen. The officers on the scene told us they guessed the caller had been a john; either he'd killed Lari or he'd found her that way. Maybe she was killed by his predecessor. Whichever, they'd said, the caller refused to give his name.

"Why would a customer slit a prostitute's throat?" I asked. "She was obviously open for business and he'd gotten what he came for."

"What was she doing naked in bed if she wasn't with a john?" Richard asked. "Unless... did she mention a boyfriend?"

"No," I said, picking up the phone.

My call got Dale Smoot out of bed. "Don't make house calls," he grumbled. "Have the photographer develop the snaps and bring 'em down to the morgue in the morning."

"I may not be on this case come morning."

"Huh?" Dale replied sleepily.

"Remember the kid who died of food poisoning? You may find yourself writing up another certificate on a call girl who bled to death because she cut herself shaving."

"Don't want to hear anymore," Dale said, finally waking up.

"Does that mean you're not coming over?"

"Nope. It just means the less you tell me, the better."

"You worried about your objectivity?" I asked.

"Subjectivity" Dale said. "And it's not mine I'm worried about, but Wilson's."

No doubt Dale's boss would eventually take the party line that Lari was an unfortunate victim of the inevitable hazards of her evil profession. But like Chris Cantwell's death scene, Lari's seemed too tidy. Her clothes were folded on a chair in the bedroom. On top lay a wide leather belt looped through the knife's sheath. Her purse, watch, rings and earrings were on the dresser.

"Where do you put your holster and gun when you get home?" I asked Richard.

"I lock them in a desk drawer," he said.

"How about before Jason was born?"

"I don't know. I guess on top of the dresser."

"With your wallet and personal effects."

Richard nodded and stepped over to the chair, staring at the belt and attached sheath on Lari's midnight-blue satin blouse.

"For one, it's a knife not a gun," he said. "For two, she could use that belt with or without the knife attached, so in a way it's just another article of clothing. And for three, maybe women are different about the way they treat their weapons."

Maybe they were, I agreed.

After a cursory check of the front room and kitchen we came to the conclusion there was no evidence of a struggle. Nothing appeared jostled or out of place. No sign of a break-in, either. So I told Richard we should go on the assumption that Lari had let the killer in through the front door.

"With most women that would probably mean she knew him, but... " Richard let the sentence dangle suggestively.

"Used to letting strange men in," I said unnecessarily, wishing the tough bravado Lari had displayed at my house had done her more good when it really counted.

We went into the bathroom where I examined the contents of the medicine cabinet. I was looking for morphine. I didn't find any, but something else caught my eye. "So she takes off her clothes, gets into bed and they have sex, but for some reason he doesn't come inside her." I held up a circular dispenser of birth control pills.

"She didn't miss any days," Richard said, studying the dispenser.

We returned to the foot of Lari's bed to speculate on what might have happened.

"He probably didn't have the knife in his hand while they were having sex," I said.

"Maybe he told her he had to go to the bathroom or something." Richard walked from the bed toward the bathroom, stopping at the chair. "She's not paying attention to what he's doing. He pulls the knife out of the sheath." He pretended to do that. "Turns around and takes her by surprise." Richard pressed his knees against the side of the bed opposite Lari's corpse, holding out his right fist at stomach level, as if he were grasping a knife.

"Too awkward," Dale said, appearing in the doorway dressed in a brown plaid shirt, bolo tie with turquoise slide and yellow suspenders. If I hadn't known him better I'd have thought he'd haphazardly thrown the outfit together on his way out the door. "Where's all the blood?"

"I figured he cut her windpipe and she died instantly," I said. "Once her heart stopped beating the blood stopped flowing."

Dale walked around the bed to the body. He took a penknife out of his pocket and pried open the wound the way he would a gill on a fish. "Knew what he was doing. Cut clean through trachea and artery in one go. Could've sucked down her own blood and drowned. Death wouldn't have happened in a snap, though. The bed should be soaked in blood."

Dale looked down at Lari's bloody knife on the floor and knelt beside it, being careful not to push it out of position before it was photographed. Putting his ear against the naked girl's chest, he studied the incision.

"Blade tilted slightly upward," Dale said. "He'd have to be on his knees to get that kind of angle. The knife went through her left carotid and then the trachea. He could have done it with a backhanded slash." Dale used the penknife in his right hand to simulate the way the blade would have moved.

"How about if he was left-handed?" I asked, remembering that Milan had impaled the jellyfish using his left hand.

"He might have held it like this." Dale shifted the penknife to his left hand, palm inward with his thumb pointed up and the blade down. "Like Zatoichi, the blind samurai." He chuckled while moving his fist toward Lari's throat in a slow punching motion, the blade angled back like a shark's dorsal fin. "Get a nice deep bite that way." Dale got to his feet. He brushed himself off and, concurring with himself, said, "Yup."

"I don't see her as the kind of girl who'd have lain there passively," I said. "Even with an experienced killer, if he'd walked all the way around the bed and gotten on his knees, she would have had a chance to lift an arm."

"No defensive wounds I can see," Dale said.

I stepped over to Lari's folded clothes, hung the belt and sheath over the back of the chair and picked up her blouse. It looked newly pressed. No wrinkles from being worn. No perfume or body odor. Just the smell of cleaning fluid. Same with the other clothing. All of it looked freshly cleaned and pressed.

"Maybe she wasn't killed in bed," I said. "She could have been moved there after she was dead. The killer stripped her and disposed of her bloody clothes to make it look like she was killed by a customer. Would you expect to see bruising if he dragged her over to the bed?" I asked Dale.

"Possible," he said, inspecting Lari's ankles. "I'll be able to take a better look when I get her downtown."

By now a couple of lab techs, a photographer and the original two patrolmen with us were in the apartment. I told the patrolmen to check the trash for bloody clothes, rags, paper towels or anything else that might have been used to wipe up blood. I then assigned sections of the apartment and we began searching for blood traces. It took less than five minutes for Richard to spot a section of the hardwood floor in the front room that was shinier than the floor around it, newly scrubbed.

I pulled out my penknife and scored a joint between floorboards. Fresh blood emerged on the tip. We found other evidence of blood in the same area: a stain that hadn't been fully washed out of the couch's valance and two small splatters under the couch missed by the obviously rushed killer. They were elongated, probably ejected as the body was falling.

Now that we knew where she was killed, I wanted to establish how. I sent the lab techs into the bedroom to collect evidence and the photographer to take photos of the body and murder weapon. The patrolmen had not been able to find any bloody remnants in the trash, so I told them to check trashcans downstairs and question anybody who might've seen anything. Richard, Dale and I remained in the front room where we got to work trying to recreate the murder.

"She probably had the knife strapped to her waist when she opened the front door and let him in," I said. "He must've said or done something to upset her before they got to the bedroom."

"How did he get the knife away without a struggle?" Richard asked.

"Let's say she pulled the knife to back him off during an argument," I said.

Dale handed me a wooden spoon he'd gotten out of the kitchen, about the same length as Lari's knife, encouraging me to proceed with a demonstration.

"In heels, she'd be taller than the average man," I said, handing the spoon to Richard, who was six-one, perhaps an inch taller than Lari in high heels. I positioned him facing the door and stood opposite. I guessed Milan to be about five-eight, an inch shorter than me. Comparatively the height difference between Richard and me would be the same as between Lari and Milan, about three inches.

Richard held the wooden spoon in his right hand, the spatulate end protruding back toward his body, pointing the handle at me as if it were a knife blade. I looked to Dale for confirmation. He nodded. Without warning I stepped into Richard, brushing my left hand over his right. Grabbing the back end of the spoon as if it were a knife handle, I snatched it away and shoved it into his gut.

"He could have hit her much harder," I said, "and knocked the wind out of her."

Richard and I were so close, his arms were outside of my body, unable to hit me effectively or block a knife blade. Lifting the spoon to shoulder level, I threw a left, just missing his chin. The wooden spoon followed, sweeping across his throat.

"That's the ticket," Dale said. "Your shoulder's a few inches lower than his neck. The blade would've cut up through the left carotid first and then the trachea."

"She looked pretty strong," I said to Richard. "Maybe you let go of the spoon too easy."

"It's a double-edged knife, man," he said. "No way she would've been able to keep hold of the blade."

We looked from one to the other, simultaneously coming up with the same deduction, then made a beeline to Lari's corpse. Dale opened her rigor-clamped right hand one finger at a time. A knife cut ran down the center of her palm.

Richard gave a look of disgust. "He had sex with her after she was dead?"

And that's when Fanelli came through the bedroom door.

CHAPTER TWENTY-TWO

"All we need right now is some perverted wacko on our hands," Fanelli said.

"I don't think that's what we've got," I said.

Fanelli stuck his nose in my direction. "Yeah?"

I'd spoken before thinking. If I'd continued—saying it was more likely that a professional killer had deposited semen to make it look like a john had killed her after having sex—Fanelli would ask how I'd come up with that. Even if I'd wanted to tell him, I didn't think he'd be open to hearing that the killer worked for Cantwell.

"But it's too early to tell," I said.

"Look, if this is some sort of sex-crazed... I need to know and fast. The press will be all over us like... " Fanelli outstretched his arms, turning his head from one of us to the other, as if addressing an audience. He fixed his attention on me. "What do you need to solve this case?"

"Time," Richard said. "With all you got us doing—"

"I think what Richard's trying to say..." I glanced at Richard to let him know I was purposely cutting him off. "... is that you probably want to call in another team. We can't possibly give this the attention it deserves."

Richard gave me a puzzled look, but was smart enough not to say anything else—for now.

"You've been using every possible excuse to get out of working on the demonstration," Fanelli said. "Why the change of heart?"

"I know I've put you in a bad light with the brass," I said.

"Yes, and we need to talk about that." Fanelli gazed around the apartment, which was buzzing with police activity that required somebody's leadership. "I'll get this squared away first and meet you in the office later this morning. You'll be there, right?"

"Of course, we're going to work the rest of the weekend to make sure the SFPD is properly represented on Monday," I said with a salute in my voice.

Richard waited until we were in the privacy of his car before he let me have it. "If you'd told Fanelli to have somebody else take over the demonstration bullshit, he would have done it."

"Then changed his mind by sun-up and pulled us off this case," I said.

Richard stared at me for a good long time, sizing me up. "There's a whole bunch of shit you're not telling me."

"I know who killed her and by now Cantwell does too."

"Cantwell?" Richard said.

"If he thinks you and I aren't on the case, maybe he'll lie low, hoping the department will believe she was killed by some sex-crazed slasher."

I heard sirens in the distance. They were heading our way. A Ford Fairlane pulled up and double-parked across the street. A reporter jumped out, Graphlex in hand.

"Let's get out of here," I said.

***

For several blocks Richard concentrated silently on driving, keeping an eye out for police vehicles and press cars speeding toward Lari's apartment. He turned off Haight Street and took a less busy, circuitous route to Market Street, which he used to angle across town.

"So who do you think killed her?" he finally asked.

"A pro."

"And you think he was hired by Cantwell?"

I nodded.

"The same killer who knocked off his son?"

"I don't know," I said. "It's a different MO, and I'd pegged the kid's killer for a woman. This is a man."

"How do you know?"

"Because I met him."

Richard's head snapped in my direction. "Shit!"

The car's front tire got caught in a streetcar track. He returned his attention to the road, carefully guiding the wheel back onto pavement.

"When?" he asked.

"That night I was late to your house on Rosh Hashanah."

Richard pulled the car over to the curb and gave me the piercing look he used in the interrogation room. "Why are you just getting around to telling me now?"

"I wasn't sure I was going to tell you at all. Cantwell's using this guy to blackmail me."

Richard's face dropped. "Don't tell me he's got something on you."

"Yes."

Disappointment swept over him as he looked away and shook his head. "Did you do this while we were partners?"

"It's got nothing to do with police work," I said. "It happened before I was on the Force, just after the war."

Richard turned to me again, relieved. "Does Miriam know?"

"I've never told anybody."

He nodded just once and pulled the car out onto Market again. The normally bustling street was eerily quiet. I sat silently, allowing him to mull over what I'd said.

"With all the shit you went through back then, whatever you did to work it out is your business," he said. "I'm not even going to ask. If you ever feel like talking, though, you can trust me."

"Thanks," I said.

"How did this guy get information on you?"

"I don't know. He's Czech. An ex-Nazi. He must have his sources. He works with the CIA."

"The CIA!" Richard nearly swerved into another streetcar track. "You've gotta be shitting me."

"I think what he's doing is off the books, though. A personal favor for Cantwell."

"Still and all, man, that's some heavy shit," Richard said.

"That's why it's better you stay out of it."

For the rest of the way he kept his eyes focused on the road and I couldn't tell what he was thinking. After parking at the Hall of Justice, he left the engine running.

"So what are you saying?" he asked. "Cantwell had her bumped off to—"

"I'm not so sure Cantwell wanted her killed. I think he just wanted this guy to intimidate her into silence. But she pulled a knife on him and—"

"But if this guy's a pro... "

"She was a big girl, trained to use the weapon," I said. "And I don't think the guy's all there. Having a woman stand up to him may have pushed him over the edge."

"I don't put anything past Cantwell," Richard said. "I could see him ordering her to be bumped off."

"It makes no sense that Cantwell would send somebody out to kill Lari," I said. "If he started knocking off everybody with scandalous secrets about him—"

"The list would be pretty damn long," Richard admitted. "But this one might have been different. With her Cantwell might have had to tie up a lot of—"

"Loose ends," I said.

"Loose ends!" Richard slapped the steering wheel, turned off the engine and grabbed the keys. "Didn't you turn her wig hairs into the lab to see if they matched the ones you found the night the kid died?"

"The lab reports," I said, opening the car door and hopping out. "Maybe Lari's hairs came back as a positive match, and Cantwell's department snitches slipped him the news that she'd been with his son the night he died."

"That would be motive," Richard said, using his longer legs to rush ahead of me as we got closer to the glass entry doors.

But when we got inside, the lab was locked.

I pounded on the door.

"They've gone home," Richard said. "We're going to have to wait." He put his arm around my shoulder, guiding me toward the elevators. "You look tired. Why don't we go home and grab a few hours shuteye then meet back here around nine?"

***

I didn't get a lot of sleep. Maybe that's because I got up too early and the few hours I did get were fitful. I couldn't stop wondering why Milan had killed Lari. If some other woman challenged Milan, would he kill her too? With one death on his hands, he had nothing to lose. Hell, if Feiertag was right and the man was a ghost, he'd never had anything to lose. What would happen if he came up against another uncooperative girl? That thought bolted me out of bed at a quarter to seven.

I was at Claremont Prep by 7:30. The school's administration office told me that Patricia had called in sick both yesterday and today. They tried phoning so I could have a word with her, but nobody answered. Yet they refused to give me her phone number and address. When I demanded to talk to the principal, he said Patricia's father's approval would be required to divulge the girl's personal information. But the way his eyes slid off to the side, I had a feeling somebody had gotten to him and told him not to cooperate with me.

My car was parked at a Safeway across the street from the school. I found a phone booth in the corner of its parking lot and looked up *Walkers* in the phone book. There were too many to call and Richard wouldn't be at work yet, so I couldn't get him to use the department's resources. I was afraid if I called anyone else at the department it would get back to Fanelli. Anyway, Richard was expecting me to come into the office and pitch in with paperwork for the demonstration. I'd have to go down to the Hall myself to find the girl's address and explain to Richard why I had to go warn her.

As I was about to get in my car I noticed a Payless Drug across the street on College Avenue. It wasn't even 8:00 and since it would only take forty minutes to get to work, I jaywalked to have a look. The Payless didn't open until 8:30, but I saw a light on in the back and knocked on the door. Nobody answered. I made a loud clatter for several minutes, rattling the door and banging on the window, before a pharmacist in a white lab coat showed up and pointed to the store hours stenciled on the glass front door. I pressed my badge up against the window. He unlocked the door.

Before the pharmacist could ask any questions, I pushed my way in and told him I was in a hurry and didn't have time get into a whole rigmarole. I said I'd been to all the Payless Drugs in San Francisco looking for information regarding a murder. They'd already checked with the main office and been given permission to let me look through the filled prescriptions. I'd appreciate it if he'd show me where they were kept, tell me how they were organized and leave me alone.

I probably didn't need to lie about getting permission from the Payless head office. The pharmacist was too busy to care, trying to get late orders filled. He led me to a desk where I could look through old prescriptions and said they were supposed to be sorted by month and week. It was company policy to separate narcotics from the rest of the prescriptions, but he didn't think anybody had really bothered. He left me and went about his own business, counting, weighing and bottling medications.

I began my search six months back in April's file and didn't find anything of interest until I got to September. A day before Chris Cantwell's death, a prescription for a five-milliliter vial of morphine was filled under the name of Mrs. Sylvia Cantwell. The scrip heading read *Doctor's Association*. The doctor's signature was illegible—a few curlicues.

"You know why this patient had a prescription for morphine?" I asked the pharmacist.

He looked over the scrip. "My partner took it."

"How much morphine are we talking about?"

"This is pretty concentrated stuff—made to be diluted." He went over to a red reference book called a PDR. Running his finger down a page he said, "200 milligrams. That's a lot of morphine."

"What do you mean by a lot?"

"The average dose is somewhere between five and 15 milligrams."

"What happens if you take the whole vial at one time?"

"You're a homicide inspector, right?"

I nodded.

"Then I have a feeling you already know."

CHAPTER TWENTY-THREE

Mrs. Cantwell sat at a breakfast table, her gaze fixed out French windows overlooking the Bay dotted with whitecaps and sails, which were nearly indistinguishable in the crystalline distance. Her dress was partially unzipped and her hair sleep-tousled. She didn't seem to notice me standing in the doorway, nor the housekeeper lingering behind, reluctant to approach her distracted boss with the news that a police inspector had arrived.

When the housekeeper had answered the door she'd said Mrs. Cantwell was not expecting visitors and could not be disturbed.

I flashed my badge and said that I was sure the lady of the house would prefer talking to me here rather than downtown.

"You wouldn't want to talk to her now," the housekeeper pleaded. "She's in one of her moods."

"I won't be long," I said, pushing past her.

The housekeeper scurried around me to lead the way to the kitchen.

I had purposely not phoned ahead, hoping to catch Mrs. Cantwell off guard, before she'd had a chance to put herself together. But I hadn't expected that she would have absolutely failed at her daily attempt at perfection. Something had gotten under her skin. If the death of her son hadn't thrown her, I wondered what could.

I gestured with my head for the housekeeper to leave us. Mrs. Cantwell did not look my way, even though the kitchen's old pine floor groaned under my feet. As I approached her, I saw a full cup of tea to the left of her folded hands. To the right the *San Francisco Chronicle* was opened to a back page.

"That kept me up all night too," I said, pointing to the headline *Slasher Murders Woman in Her Apartment.*

"I must look a mess," she said, brushing back her hair.

I made a zipping motion and pointed to her half-undone dress. She reached around and fumbled with the zipper. "Would you mind?"

I laid a finger lightly on her back and she readily complied, leaning forward. As I slid up the zipper, Mrs. Cantwell said, "The newspaper didn't mention if you had any suspects."

I patted her on the shoulder. "There—lovely as ever."

"Liar," she said and got up from the table with her teacup. She set it down on the sink and turned on the stove to reheat the kettle. Returning to sit at the table, she asked, "Why are you here, Inspector?"

I picked up the newspaper and dropped it in front of her. Circling the table to look at her square on, I said, "I think you know this woman."

Her eyes darted nervously to a rubber band that had been used to bind the paper. She pulled her hair back in a ponytail and tied it with the faded pink elastic.

"Do you have a suspect?" she asked.

"Your husband's in Washington, right?"

Mrs. Cantwell looked up at me, smiling at my inference. "He'll be back Sunday night. He has to prepare a speech for the demonstration on Monday."

"Nobody told me he was going to be at the demonstration," I said.

"See, you don't know everything," she said, rolling open her palms.

The teapot whistled.

"Hildy!" Mrs. Cantwell called out.

"I'll do it," I said.

I opened the cupboard to the left of the stove, looking for teacups and saucers. I found the tea instead.

"Sugar?" I asked.

"Right here," she said, gracefully arching a finger on a white oval bowl in the center of the table.

I found the dishes in a cabinet to the right of the stove. Mrs. Cantwell didn't give any directions, as if she enjoyed my investigation of her cupboards. I poured the boiling water into two cups, using one teabag for both.

"We didn't get a chance to talk about your son last time I was here," I said, setting the teacups on the table and sitting opposite her. "It was probably too soon for you, the morning after he died."

Mrs. Cantwell put some sugar in her cup and stirred the tea.

"It's difficult to sort out all your feelings so quickly," I continued. "To separate grief from—"

"Relief," she said under her breath. Then shaking her head: "That's not right, is it?"

"If you'd been expecting the worst to happen," I said.

"My relief had nothing to do with him, but... "

"With the women he might have hurt?"

She set the teaspoon on the edge of the white china saucer and leveled her gaze at me. For a second I thought she was angry. Maybe at herself.

"Why don't you just get to the point, Inspector? What did you really come here to ask me?"

"I found a morphine prescription in your name at the pharmacy across the street from his school," I said. "You don't know anything about it?"

She shook her head, her ponytail swaying in counterpoint.

"Perhaps your son found a way of getting morphine in your name. He was a very resourceful boy."

"I don't know anything about any drugs," she said, giving me a doe-eyed stare, dilated pupils floating on the lilac blue of her irises. Quite lovely, really, even if it was Seconal induced.

"What are you high on now, Mrs. Cantwell?"

"High?" She said. "I simply took some pills my husband picked up to calm my nerves."

"Prescription?"

"I guess. Why?"

"And you didn't think to ask him what he'd given you?"

"I trust my husband."

"Even though you know he was having affairs."

She remained unfazed.

"Did you know before he brought home the clap?" I pressed. "Or was it syphilis that the penicillin was for?"

"What has any of this to do with my son's death?" she asked in a monotone.

I held up the newspaper article again. "Both your son and husband were having relations with the same prostitute—the one who got her throat slit." I slapped the newspaper down on the table and she flinched. "You must have been aware that she'd been with your son because she filed a police report."

She regained her composure.

"But I doubt your husband would have told you the names of all the women he'd been with, especially prostitutes."

"I think I've heard quite enough," she said.

"You have to admit it's one hell of a coincidence that this same call girl gets murdered when your husband's trying to keep a scandal from ruining his campaign. Think about it, Mrs. Cantwell—a prostitute was with your son the night he died. Perhaps even the same one who shot him up with the overdose that killed him."

"My husband didn't have anything to do with it. As you said yourself, he was out of town."

"But his goon wasn't."

"I have no idea who you're talking about," she said.

"A man with an accent like mine. He calls himself Milan."

I could tell by her hesitation that she knew exactly who I was referring to.

"Good day, Inspector."

"You probably told yourself there was nothing you could have done when your son attacked those girls."

"I want you to leave," she said, looking down at the table.

"He damaged them for life," I said, getting up out of my chair.

"Please," she said.

I walked over to the kitchen door and stopped to face her. "You have a chance to help this time."

"How could I possibly do that?" she asked, still staring down at the table.

"I need to understand why Milan murdered that prostitute."

She shook her head.

"If you could find out, you might be saving the lives of other women."

She gazed up at me.

"Please, Mrs. Cantwell, will you help?"

She looked out the window into the pale blue sky, which was almost the color of her eyes.

CHAPTER TWENTY-FOUR

When I arrived at the office at half-past ten Richard was on the phone trying to commandeer extra buses for the demonstration. After hanging up, he explained that the Berkeley Campus Police were now requesting that other departments bring their own, in case it became necessary to make mass arrests. Also, our patrolmen would have to be bussed over. Making matters worse, it was now Friday and all the bureaucrats who could expedite the transfer of vehicles from other governmental agencies would be sneaking out early to get a head start on the weekend.

I let Richard vent for a while about "ridiculous departmental bullshit," before I asked about Fanelli. He grabbed my arm and led me into the bathroom where we'd have some privacy.

"You were supposed to meet with him this morning," Richard said, turning his frustration with the bureaucracy to my unexplained absence. "I told him I was helping out with the paperwork because you were down at the motor pool checking up on buses under repair. The chief's been asking for a status report and said he wanted you and Fanelli in his office as soon as you got in."

Richard forgot about bureaucrats and buses when I filled him in on Patricia Walker's absence from school and Mrs. Cantwell's morphine prescriptions. That's when he remembered to tell me the lab reports had come back on Lari Zohn's hairs. Negative.

"Which means she probably wasn't with the little prick the night he died," he said.

"She could have been wearing a different wig."

"I've been thinking maybe it wasn't even a prostitute at all," Richard said. "All the desk clerk really saw was a miniskirt, long gloves, fishnet stockings and blond hair. At the Fool's Gold, hell, even Miriam could have passed dressed like that." I wasn't sure I liked Richard's comparison of my younger cousin to a prostitute, even if she was his wife, but before I could object, he added, "It could have been any one of the kid's victims in disguise."

"That's one less motive for Cantwell to have had Lari murdered," I said.

"Maybe he ordered the hit before we got back the lab results—jumped to the conclusion that she gave the kid a hotshot, and he took revenge, pure and simple."

"Revenge is much too pure and simple for Cantwell," I said.

Yet Richard was beginning to convince me that maybe I should take the congressman more seriously as a suspect.

"More likely he didn't want his son's killer apprehended," I added. "Too many dirty secrets could get exposed."

"What's going to happen when Cantwell finds out Lari's hair came back negative?" he asked.

"He's not dumb," I said. "He might come to the same conclusion you did—that one of his son's other victims could have been in the room with the kid the night he died. Willie B. told us there were five sheets—five victims. One we don't know. The second is Lari and she's dead. If she told the truth, the third is another prostitute that left town. Joyce Smith is number four and she's out of the picture, at a private school in Phoenix."

"So who does that leave?" Richard asked.

"A seventeen-year-old girl named Patricia Walker. She's been missing from school for the last few days."

"We've got to find her," he said.

Richard agreed that it made no sense for me to stay in the office while he went out looking for Patricia. It would have taken us too long to play catch-up if we exchanged work loads, and we were racing the clock. Come Monday, we had to have all the demonstration preparations completed. Also come Monday I'd be effectively derailed from the investigation into Chris Cantwell's death. Sidelined with my hands in my pockets, listening to a bunch of cocksure kids and one arrogant congressman taking black-and-white positions about a very gray Vietnam war.

***

I reconnected the wires to my police radio so Richard could send me information as I drove across the Bay Bridge. He told me that Patricia

Walker lived in Berkeley with her father who was a geology professor at Cal. Her mother was deceased. Their house was in the hills north of campus, about a mile or so above Dr. Meyers'.

Built on a hill slope, only the garage of Patricia's house was visible from the street. A red Firebird in the center of the driveway left no room to pull up on either side. The street in front of the house was so narrow that parking was only allowed on one side and it was crowded with bumper-to-bumper cars. As I drove up the hill looking for an open space, I saw Milan's white Camaro five cars up. Throwing the Citroen into reverse I screeched back into the driveway, almost sideswiping the Firebird's bumper as I swung in behind it.

The wooden stairs leading down to the house from the driveway were badly in need of repair. Taking two steps at a time I nearly tripped on a loose wooden tread. I grabbed the two-by-four banister to steady myself, but it wobbled so badly that for a second I thought both it and I would go tumbling off the side onto the cement patio below. The front door was locked. I was about to pound on it, but decided sneaking up might be more effective.

I noticed a gate to the left of the house. It too was locked, but made a surprisingly soft thud as I gave it one swift kick. The gate flew open with the latch dangling by a screw. I crept down the hill on a brick walkway that bordered the house. The path led to a small deck at the back of the house, which acted as an entry porch to a sliding glass door.

I heard a muffled male voice as I yanked at the door. It was latched, but I could see through a gap in the drapes. Holding my hand over my eyes to block out the sun's glare, I put my face to the glass. Inside I saw a large playroom that was being used as a storage facility, with wood crates and cardboard boxes covering the floor. Nobody was in the room. The voice must have been coming from the other side.

A grassy slope fell off sharply from the house's twenty-foot-high rear wall, offering no path along its back. I lost footing several times as I scrambled toward the other side. Halfway across, I slipped onto my hands and knees, sliding five feet down the slope. I climbed up the slick grass on all fours, angling toward the corner of the house. When I got there I was close enough to recognize Milan's voice coming from inside.

As I climbed the hill along the side of the house, I kept my hands plastered against the stucco wall as if I were scaling the face of a cliff. The first window I reached was too high to look through. Now that I was closer I heard Patricia crying. I could also hear Milan's voice clearly enough to understand what he was saying:

"I'll show you what we do to spoiled little girls who fraternize with the wrong people."

"I've already promised I won't say anything," Patricia managed to get out between sobs.

"It's a bit too late for that," Milan said.

I was far enough up the slope that I was just able to get my eyes over the second window ledge. Milan had his back to me, blocking most of Patricia. With her bare legs spread out on both sides of him—bent at the knee, feet on the floor—I guessed she was sitting on a chair.

"Now we have to make sure you don't make the same mistake again," he said.

I slid my .38 out of its shoulder holster, but the window was too high for me to get off an accurate shot. With the pistol held above my shoulders and nothing to rest my hand against, it was far too risky. I'm not sure I would have taken a shot even under the best of circumstances: a bullet might have taken an odd ricochet or even passed through Milan and hit Patricia. I grasped the barrel and broke the window with its butt.

Milan turned, scowled at me and looked back at Patricia. I couldn't see his hands, but the way his elbows were cocked, they seemed to be on her head. Glass shards studded the base of the window frame, preventing me from using it to steady my aim. I smashed out several larger glass spears and grabbed onto the sill to climb inside, cutting my palms on smaller pieces lodged in the frame. Milan stayed where he was, as if he had eyes in the back of his head and knew I couldn't get off a shot, or that if I tried to climb through the window I'd slice open my belly on the broken glass.

Adrenaline made me more sure-footed as I ran along the house and leapt onto the small deck leading to the back entrance. I put two bullets into the sliding-door handle, breaking its latch. When I pulled open the door, I couldn't see a clear path between the boxes and crates scattered everywhere. Stepping into boxes, I crushed file folders marked with the geological names of dirt and rock samples. Hopping into an apparent opening between containers I tripped on a hidden boulder, landing with one hand in a crate of rust-colored soil.

I scrambled to my feet with dirt stinging the cut on my palm. The door leading out of the room was locked by a key. I kicked it open and it banged loudly against a wall in the passage. At the end of the hall, the door to

Patricia's bedroom was ajar. I pushed it open with my foot, holding my weapon in a three-quarter hip position, elbow slightly flexed, anticipating that Milan could appear from any direction. When I didn't see him I continued to nudge the door open. Patricia was sitting naked on a chair with her back to me, head lowered, buried in her hands. Milan was not in the room.

Down a hall to my right a flight of stairs led up to the house's main level. I took five silent steps to the base of the stairwell and bent onto one knee on the bottom stair, my left hand cupped under the .38 that I held pointed up thirty degrees. The staircase was empty. Halfway up the first flight I leaned over the banister and swept the gun barrel up and down the second flight. It was also empty. I saw light streaming in from above and guessed it was coming from the open front door.

I charged up the second flight of stairs and onto the front patio. Before I'd hit the top of the neglected wooden steps I heard the Camaro's engine as it raced past the house. By the time I got to the street the Camaro was rounding a bend. I couldn't even get off a shot at its rear window.

When I returned to the bedroom Patricia was sitting in the same position. She had not bothered to dress. I went to her bed and pulled off the flowered bedspread, trying to keep my eyes averted from her naked body. But I couldn't help glancing down at her feet, where her thick auburn hair lay on the floor.

"Did he—"

"No," she said, glancing in the mirror at her sheared head.

I lay the bedspread over her shoulders and gazed away, looking anywhere but at her. On the desk a photo showed a laughing Patricia at fourteen or so with her arms around two other women—by the resemblance I guessed them to be her mother and older sister—Patricia's left leg high-stepping like a Rockette. The happy-go-lucky girl in that photo was nothing like the haughty one I'd met a few days before or the one now bent before me. My eyes drifted down to the bloody nicks and small tufts of remaining hair on her skull.

I thought about women in the camps who'd also had their heads shaved. Unlike those prisoners who got numbers tattooed on them, Patricia had razor scars on her wrists, which looked to be at least a year old.

I dropped to one knee and pulled the bedspread tight around her.

"It grows back," I said.

"But not the same," she whispered.

"Sometimes stronger," I said, without telling her that might also mean it would be coarser. "Get dressed, please."

I went upstairs to give Patricia some privacy, washing and bandaging my hands in an upstairs bathroom. Then I called Richard. Before I could tell him what had happened, he said, "Dr. Meyers called you about an hour ago to report a theft."

"Me, personally?"

"She asked for you by name."

"Why didn't you transfer her to Burglary?"

"Chris Cantwell's files are missing. She asked if you'd stop by on your way back in."

"I've got this girl to take care of first," I said, and told Richard about Patricia. "I can't bring her into headquarters for questioning. We don't know who we can trust anymore."

"I'll track down her father," Richard said.

After hanging up, I called Dr. Meyers to say it would be at least an hour before I dropped by to investigate the burglary of Chris Cantwell's files.

"I'm with this girl who got into a little trouble and I have to wait for her father to take custody of her," I said.

"What girl?" Dr. Meyers asked.

"You know who she is—one of Chris's victims—Patricia Walker."

"Patty!"

"Have you met her?"

"She's a friend of Nikki's. What happened to her?"

I paused, thinking about how much I wanted to tell her. Normally I would have been evasive. But at this point, except for Richard, I trusted Dr. Meyers about as much as anybody. Certainly more than anyone on the Force, especially my superiors who wanted to keep me boxed in by protocols and procedures.

"Cantwell's hired somebody to keep a lid on things. I'm pretty sure he's the one who had your files stolen."

"I don't care about files now. What about Patty?"

"She... uh... got roughed up a little."

"What do you mean? What exactly happened?"

If Milan had simply raped her, I think I would have had an easier time explaining it. Police dealt with that on a routine basis.

"Bring her down here, please," Dr. Meyers said without waiting for me to answer.

"Her father should be here soon—"

"Her father! Have you met him? Bring her to me."

Patricia wandered in wearing a pink-and-orange granny dress and a lime-green floppy hat. Perhaps clashing colors were in fashion now. And then again, at that moment she might not have cared.

"I'm on the phone with Dr. Meyers," I said. "She wants you to wait for your father at her house."

The girl gave me a far-off look.

I raised an eyebrow to prompt her.

"Will Nikki be there?" she asked.

"Where's your daughter?" I said into the phone.

"At school."

I shook my head.

She nodded. "Okay, then. But I want to be gone before she gets home."

Patricia opened the front door and waited until I hung up the phone. I went out first and she locked the door with a steady hand. Nodding impassively to let me know she was ready, she reminded me of how we *Nokim* would steel ourselves from unwanted emotions, locking them tightly away before we'd go off to do a job.

As I opened the car door for Patricia, she smoothed down the back of her dress so it wouldn't slide up when she sat down, and righted her hat after it brushed the car's headliner. She nodded again and I closed the door. No tears. In fact, she looked as though she might never cry again.

After putting the keys in the ignition I glanced over to make sure she was prepared to leave.

It took several seconds before she returned my gaze, laying her eyes numbly on mine as if she were blind. "Have you ever killed anybody?"

I nodded.

"I bet you didn't feel a thing your first time, like a hunter shooting a deer."

CHAPTER TWENTY-FIVE

Even if I'd wanted to, I could not have explained to Patricia or anyone else how it felt the first time I took a man's life. One thing I could have said, though, was that I wasn't haunted by his face. He had none, departing without eyes, ears and nose. When I'd finished with him he could have been anyone. Or nobody, his blistered corpse looked so inhuman. Yet I would never allow myself to forget his deceptive smile.

Emil was part of a workgroup that was trucked each morning out of Auschwitz-Birkenau to bombed-out factories where we gathered scrap metal—corrugated tin, old machine parts and steel girders. Some of the cleaner scrap we loaded directly onto trucks. But if the metal was painted or badly corroded, it got dumped into an acid wash. We'd tie whatever we could find over our noses and mouths to block out the vat's burning stench, which was more painful than the cold invading through blown-out windows and entryways whose doors had been looted. At times I used rags off my feet that had taken the place of shoes. Toes could freeze beyond pain, but nothing could anesthetize lungs from the searing sting of hydrochloric fumes.

Although Emil was officially attached to our workgroup, he managed to avoid the acid vat. Unofficially, he was the best damn scavenger the SS had ever run across and they'd instructed our Polish guards to give him free run of a series of damaged factories. He spoke Polish and German and could talk his way past anybody, homing in on the best hiding places, always coming back with a little extra to make the Poles happy and managing to squirrel away something for himself.

Of course the SS got the lion's share of Emil's booty, even though they rarely bothered to come inside to ensure their take. Brushing up against the machinery might have soiled their uniforms. Besides, it was often colder inside the metal and concrete walls than outside under the pale winter sun. They were sure that even without their direct oversight, neither the Jews nor the Poles would have dared cheat them too badly.

The SS preferred to stay outside on the lawn beyond the factory gates where they could flirt with local women coming and going from work. The Nuremberg laws concerning *Rassenschande* forbade the SS from contaminating themselves with Jewish women, yet Polish women were acceptable for sexual purposes even though Slavs were also considered sub-humans.

Yet there was one SS officer named *Untersturmfuhrer* Stuckart who sometimes did wander among us slave laborers. I once overheard him tell a fellow officer that the twisted interior of the factory ruins at least had some architectural interest, which was more than he could say for the thick-ankled Polish secretaries.

Untersturmfuhrer Stuckart was different in a number of ways from his SS counterparts, who took their role more seriously, truly believing that their duty in "the battle of destiny for the German people" was to rid mankind of the disease of inferior races. I had a feeling he probably agreed that the Aryan race was superior. But I don't think he was ever able to shake his strict Lutheran upbringing, which taught that all of us were defiled by Original Sin and in the end only God could decide who would be saved. Simply killing off everyone except the Aryans would not have solved the Lutheran problem of mankind's future. So what was the use? At least that's what I eventually came to read into the cynical smile that seemed to play on the edges of his finely chiseled lips.

The first time *Untersturmfuhrer* Stuckart approached me he was carrying a slim volume of Goethe's poetry. He'd heard me speaking German to another prisoner and asked with a sardonic smile if I was familiar with the author. I mumbled that I'd read *Faust* and the *Sorrows of Young Werther*. From then on he would have a word or two whenever he passed, and after a while it seemed to amuse him to pose philosophical puzzles from one of his many books.

Normally I kept working without reacting to his remarks, fearing that any answer I gave would get me in trouble. Yet *Untersturmfuhrer* Stuckart never really seemed to expect an answer. He'd walk away before I had a chance to lift my head in acknowledgment. Not that I would have looked directly at him. Looking into the eyes of an SS officer could mean a bullet in the head.

Once I did look up. He'd asked whether Faust's pact with the devil to regain his youth was a mortal sin or a forgivable human weakness. For some reason the question struck a chord in me and I must have glanced into his face, looking for some inkling of his opinion. I didn't see one. Nor was there any indication I was going to get punished. Just the hint of ennui in his expression before he walked away.

Three other German speakers were in our workgroup: Herman, who was in his early forties; Alfred, about thirty; and Emil, only a year or two older than I. Although Herman, Alfred and I came from different backgrounds, we spent a lot of time together. We tried to get assigned to the same workgroup and sat with one another during meals whenever possible.

Herman had a stocky frame. Even though he'd lost a considerable amount of weight in the camp, there was still something solid about him. An ex-banker with an accounting degree, Herman questioned everything from a dry, logical perspective. Whereas others might use a gambler's instinct to guess who'd be condemned in the next selection, Herman thought it through in terms of debits and credits. Who was healthy and who was sick? Who had important friends and who had isolated himself? Who was assigned to a useless job and who was doing work required for the Reich's war effort?

"Why do you think Stuckart talks to you?" Herman asked me, using a crust of bread to wipe the last drops of potato-peel soup off the sides of his dented tin bowl. "In my opinion, the only possible reason he might ask such difficult questions of an eighteen-year-old would be to add an extra twist of cruelty to his already sadistic humor."

Alfred had already finished his bread and watery white soup. I can't remember him ever eating. I don't know if that's because he did it so stealthily or I could not imagine his ascetic physique requiring nourishment. A Sephardic, he had the long angular features of a Spanish nobleman from an El Greco painting. I don't know how his family got to Germany. Perhaps wheeling and dealing their way around the world. They'd been in the jewelry trade for generations. Unlike his father, though, Alfred had not bought and sold raw gems. He'd chosen to become an artisan who designed rings, earrings and pendants that had once gone for top prices among the German aristocracy.

"I think the SS officer truly likes our young Simon. As much as a Nazi can like a Jew, in any case," said Alfred, who almost always took a contrary position to Herman.

"You think he likes boys?" Herman asked.

"Nothing so simple. Besides, our young Simon's got the eyes of an old man. You were probably born that way," Alfred said to me.

Most often we talked about Emil, who was the topic of many Jews' conversations. Emil was developing a reputation for ruthlessness. He stalked new prisoners and stole their bowls and spoons before they learned to guard them while washing up in the morning. Later, he would trade these utensils for food or cigarettes. When bowls and spoons were in short supply, they could be worth a ration of bread or more. Prisoners who had them stolen were forced to trade for replacements or they would not be able to receive soup. Going without soup meant even more extreme hunger and weakness, which could easily spiral into death in our Darwinian jungle.

Both Herman and Alfred had been personally touched by Emil's cruelty. Alfred's sister was one of the Jewish women Emil pimped to the Poles. When Alfred found out, he confronted Emil in front of our barracks, saying he should be ashamed of himself. A Jew taking advantage of other Jews! Emil responded that he thought Alfred ought to be grateful to him for keeping his sister alive. Being a prostitute was the only reason she had not been selected.

Emil was responsible for the death of more Jews than anyone could count. Herman's brother had been one of his victims. Emil wanted his brother's bunk, which he considered prime real estate because it was on the outside close to the bathrooms. From there it would be easier for Emil to sneak in and out to do after-hours' business. When his brother refused to give over his bunk, Emil greased the right palms to have him selected for the gas chambers.

"He's a scourge on all of us," said Herman. "He lacks *Ahabath Israel.*"

"What have I ever done to show a love of the Jewish people?" I asked.

"Just because you don't show it, doesn't mean you don't have it," Alfred said.

"It doesn't matter what Simon feels or doesn't feel," Herman said. "Something has got to be done about Emil."

"What are you proposing?" I asked.

"Exactly what he did to my brother. No more, no less."

"An eye for an eye," Alfred said. "It suits you perfectly."

"Even if we all agreed to it," I said, "Emil has SS connections. He trades with them and always has something to offer. What do we have?"

"Your SS friend, I suppose," Alfred said, looking over to Herman to see if he'd guessed correctly.

"He's always stopping to talk some nonsense or other to you," Herman said.

"Maybe you could bring up the question hypothetically at first," Alfred suggested. "Couch it in metaphysical terms. Who knows, having one Jew selected at the request of another might fit perfectly into his perverse view of things."

Although I had no personal grudge against Emil, I agreed to try talking to *Untersturmfuhrer* Stuckart. I did not want to jeopardize the camaraderie I had developed with Herman and Alfred. On some level, I felt it was all that was keeping me alive. Anyway, I never thought *Untersturmfuhrer* Stuckart would agree. Why would an aloof SS officer be bothered by the fate of any particular Jew?

The next afternoon after spending the day loading back-breaking steel beams onto a truck I spoke to *Untersturmfuhrer* Stuckart. He was leaning against a tree, reading Rilke. Keeping my head bowed as I passed, I muttered that if it still pleased him I'd like to attempt to answer his question about *Faust*.

"Continue," *Untersturmfuhrer* Stuckart said, without looking up from the pages.

"Was it a mortal sin for Faust to make a pact with the devil?"

"I remember the problem," he said.

"It depends on how you look at it."

Untersturmfuhrer Stuckart lowered his book. "You think the story of Faust is like a crystal ball that will give a different answer to each reader?"

"In a manner of speaking," I said. "Guilt and innocence are often subjective. Say, for example, the death of one man will result in the greater good. Is the person who takes that man's life truly guilty?"

"That's an interesting question coming from a Jew facing extermination for the greater good of the Reich. But I suppose you believe God is the final judge."

"Perhaps God simply *is* the greater good."

"That sounds more like this new philosophy called existentialism, rather than Judaism," *Untersturmfuhrer* Stuckart said. "I'd like to know where all this is leading."

"Assume a bad man was selected in place of a much better man, wouldn't the world be a better place because of it?"

"Are you talking about anyone in particular?" *Untersturmfuhrer* Stuckart asked.

My eyes drifted over to Emil who was dividing some booty among several SS officers.

"Ah, now I see," *Untersturmfuhrer* Stuckart said. "Are you actually admitting that even one of God's chosen people can be a treacherous psychopath?"

I'd never really thought of us Jews as God's chosen. In my mind that was as prejudiced as saying Jews were inferior or smarter or greedier. But I wasn't about to say that to *Untersturmfuhrer* Stuckart.

When I didn't respond, he raised the book, covering his eyes. "I won't actively take a hand in his death, but I might look the other way if you did it yourself. I can assure you, nobody else will get too bothered about the accidental death of a Jew."

Untersturmfuhrer Stuckart lowered his book again and looked down on me with the dispassionate interest of a scientist studying a specimen under a microscope. It seemed to me that he was thinking it would be a fascinating experiment to see if this little worm could actually kill another human being—one of his own race, no less.

When I reported back to Herman and Alfred, they both agreed that *Untersturmfuhrer* Stuckart had given me and only me permission to kill Emil.

"I can't do that," I said. "I refuse to raise my hand against another Jew."

"I don't think he really is a Jew," Herman said.

"Why would anybody in his right mind pretend to be a Jew, here of all places?" asked Alfred.

"To have the opportunity to be among us," Herman said. Prisoners were segregated by race; you had to be a Jew to live among Jews. "He thinks Jews are easier to take advantage of. Besides, even if he was born a Jew, he's proven himself unworthy of our people. At heart he is just another Nazi."

"I don't know what he is at heart," I said. "I've never even spoken to him. In my opinion we have to at least give Emil a chance. I think the three of us should ask him to reform his ways and see what he says."

Since I had the SS connection, my opinion counted most. We approached Emil, who seemed eager and accommodating, offering us cigarettes so the four of us could "enjoy an intimate chat." At that time cigarettes were in such short supply that one was worth several rations of bread.

"I have been meaning to speak to you too," Emil said, looking from Herman to Alfred. "I have done things I've regretted and I've found it increasingly difficult to live with myself. Of course we all have had to do terrible things to survive. Each time a prisoner goes up in smoke he's taking our place. I'm sure that weighs as heavily on you as it does on me."

As Emil smoked and talked, smiling easily as if we were all close friends, I noticed how healthy he looked compared to the rest of us. Strangely, even though I knew he'd robbed and cheated, his robust physique caused me to trust him more. How could his prospering not be right and our withering on the bone not be wrong?

"Others might try to excuse their misdeeds with the words of Maimonides, who said it is our duty to the future of our people to find any way to survive," Emil said.

"The Rambam forgave Jews who posed as Catholics to save themselves," Herman said, "but he never excused the sacrifice of fellow Jews."

"Of course he didn't," Emil said genially. "That's why I say I can't agree with those who have misquoted him. Anyway, whatever we've done, I think, like the Rambam says, we need to forgive ourselves and move on to live better lives, don't you?" He left us with that thought and one more cigarette each.

I was not sure I agreed with Emil. But the thought of being responsible for killing him, if I did not agree, must have colored my opinion.

"Who can judge our actions here in this purgatory?" I argued to Herman and Alfred. "Everybody's doing whatever they can to simply survive from day to day. Forgiveness of one another is all we have left."

Alfred said there should be limits to what anyone, especially Jews, should be forgiven for, but he was willing to forget about Emil and concentrate on his own survival. Without our help there was nothing Herman could do about Emil, but he still maintained that the man was a snake who would do or say anything to get what he wanted.

Several days later Herman was selected, even though by his own debit-and-credit logic it should not yet have been his turn: our work party was considered necessary for the German war effort and Herman was still capable of doing a good day's labor. This happened only weeks before the gas chambers were shut down for good due to the advancing Russian troops.

Alfred said Herman's selection had to be Emil's doing. I was not convinced until the next day. We were working in the factory and an I-beam fell on Alfred's head, killing him instantly. Emil appeared less than a minute later and told me how very sorry he was and how much he'd liked Alfred, despite their disagreement over his sister.

"I sympathize with how a well-meaning person like Alfred might have had confused feelings in the chaos here. It's difficult for all of us to keep level heads," Emil said, handing me a cigarette and lighting it.

"How did you learn about Alfred's death so quickly?" I asked. Emil was the first person not working with us to arrive on the scene.

"I saw from up there," Emil said, pointing to a walkway in front of the upstairs offices, where several tall girders leaned against the banister. With a little added muscle from somebody who owed him, it would have been easy for Emil to have arranged for Alfred's "accident."

Untersturmfuhrer Stuckart strolled by with his usual half smile, except this time I read a warning in its irony: act now or you will be responsible for your own selection. He headed away in the direction of the acid vat. From a distance it seemed smooth and complacent, its hunger hidden beneath the surface. I knew I would also have to appear calm if I wanted to lure Emil into my corrosive trap.

"Come on," I said to him. "*Untersturmfuhrer* Stuckart wants us to go with him."

We followed *Untersturmfuhrer* Stuckart as he circled the vat. The other workers had taken away Alfred's body and nobody else was around. I stagger-stepped, flicking my cigarette into the vat. Its non-flammable acid gave out a small hiss. Emil continued a few feet ahead of me. I lifted my arms toward his back, about to lurch, when *Untersturmfuhrer* Stuckart turned to face me. I waited for him to smile. I wanted him to. I knew exactly how I would read his smile this time: *who can blame you for entering a pact with the devil when your God has forced you into making such horrendous choices?*

As Emil broke the impassive surface of the piss-colored pool, the SS officer cocked his ear toward the sound of his sizzling flesh. Yet *Untersturmfuhrer* Stuckart did not seem like somebody who'd witnessed an agonizing death; he appeared more like a deer in a meadow startled by a rustling branch, perhaps catching sight of an upright figure as it disappeared into the brush. The figure had nothing to do with Emil's melting body, though. It was me, or at least what I once called my soul, banished into dark silence.

CHAPTER TWENTY-SIX

I was pacing back and forth in front of Dr. Meyers' front picture window, keeping one eye on the street. She sat on the couch across the room from Patricia who was brooding in an overstuffed chair. It seemed like a good ten minutes since any of us had spoken. I kept glancing at Patricia to see if she seemed ready to talk. Time was running out before the girl's father would arrive to pick her up.

I hadn't bothered interrogating the sullen girl on the short trip from her house. I was hoping that Dr. Meyers might be able to help me get through to her. When Patricia saw her friend's mother waiting for us on the front porch, she jumped out of the car before I'd turned off the engine and ran up to Dr. Meyers. The girl shivered as she released herself into the security of the woman's outstretched arms. I walked up the porch steps and heard Dr. Meyers whisper, "You'll be fine, sweetheart." She kept hold of Patricia's trembling hand as she opened the door.

I motioned to Dr. Meyers that I wanted to talk to her. She shook her head *not now*. I nodded my insistence. She let loose of Patricia and told the girl to make herself at home, we wouldn't be long. After Patricia went inside, Dr. Meyers turned to me and said, "What!"

"I'm going to have to ask her some questions about Chris Cantwell."

"Are you blind? Can't you see how traumatized she is?"

"I'll give her a little time to calm down, but I have to talk to her before she leaves," I said, following Dr. Meyers inside.

Patricia stood in the middle of the living room with her floppy hat in hand, looking around as if she had no idea where she was or how she'd gotten there. Since I had not told Dr. Meyers exactly what had happened to the girl, she was stopped short, breathless, by the girl's shaved head. When Patricia saw the cloud that momentarily darkened Dr. Meyers' brow, it seemed as if the bond between them had been severed. Perhaps the girl had awakened to the reality that this was somebody else's house and somebody else's mother. Hers was dead.

After that, all of the doctor's attempts to comfort Patricia only seemed to make her more distant. When Dr. Meyers pushed aside pillows for the girl to sit next to her on the couch, Patricia instead curled up on an overstuffed chair. She shook her head at Dr. Meyers' offer of tea, food and a hot bath. The girl hadn't spoken since she'd asked me about killing a man for the first time. Her curiosity on the subject made the question regarding her whereabouts on the night of Chris Cantwell's death all the more pressing.

I glanced out the window, past the treetops across the street to the Bay. San Francisco was hidden by a haze that hung over the entire peninsula. Soon I'd return to headquarters, also disappearing into that haze. I told Dr. Meyers I'd like some coffee and offered to help her make it.

"I can't wait any longer," I said when we got in the kitchen. "I'm going to have to question her."

She turned away, taking down a can of Yuban from the cupboard. "I still think it's too soon," she said softly, without her usual authority.

"It would be better if you waited here in the kitchen," I said.

She nestled the coffee can against her stomach, arms wrapped around as if it were an infant, and turned to me. Tears welled in her eyes.

"I'm sorry," she said. "Hearing about things from clients I interview and seeing them first hand—I couldn't catch myself in time. It wasn't fair to her."

If it had been anybody else I'd have left her to the silence of her own regrets and gotten down to business with the girl. But I couldn't leave Dr. Meyers alone like that—not about to cry.

"After the liberation," I said, "the others who hadn't been in the camps... their eyes were like mirrors, and in them we saw how deathly we looked. They couldn't see past our sallow flesh, inside us, the way we did with one another. We were in our own separate world and had no way to communicate with them. You know this and yet you still to try to step through the looking glass—the reason has got to be because of your indomitable heart."

She set down the coffee and reached out to me. For a moment I didn't know where her hand was going to land. It ended up on my forearm. "Can you at least tell me what you want to ask her?"

"I have to find out where she was the night Chris Cantwell died."

Dr. Meyers slowly withdrew her hand and gave me a look somewhere between curiosity and disbelief.

"She talked to me earlier about how it must feel to kill a man," I said.

She nodded. "I'm sure she meant she *felt* like killing somebody."

"You don't know that," I said.

"I know character types and she's not a murderer."

"I don't think this boy was killed by somebody who's homicidal by nature. It could have been almost anybody."

Dr. Meyers shook her head, unable to hold back tears. "Not her." She wiped her face with the back of her hand. "And even if it were, she wouldn't be a threat to anybody else now. Can't you wait a few days before accusing her?"

"Look what that man did simply to silence her. If he finds out she was involved in the boy's death, her life might be at risk."

She shook her head more slowly this time, not seeming to register what I'd said.

"Do you remember the call girl Chris beat up?" I continued. "The one his father also frequented? She was one of my suspects and she got her throat slashed last night."

"Jesus!" Dr. Meyers stopped crying. "But you don't know for sure that her death was connected to... It's unbelievable that Allen Cantwell would... " She ran out of words.

"We both know unbelievable things happen," I said.

"Yes." She glanced toward the living room, where Patricia was waiting for us. "I think she'll feel more comfortable if I'm there when you question her."

When we got back into the living room, Patricia was lying on the couch with one arm draped to the floor. She had that old haughty look on her face. She took off her hat again and tossed it onto the overstuffed chair, daring us to stare at her skull. I didn't need to be a psychologist to know she'd retreated into herself—to hell with the world that had betrayed her.

Dr. Meyers broke the silence: "The inspector has a few routine questions he needs to ask you, Patty."

As the girl folded her legs up to her chest, her dress rode up and exposed her calves.

"Did you agree to play good cop?" she asked Dr. Meyers.

"Where were you last Sunday night when Chris Cantwell died?" I asked.

"You think I murdered him!" Patricia declared almost gleefully. "Say I did kill the animal, would I even be guilty of a crime? I mean, Chris killed a dog and the law never touched him."

"Nobody's accusing you of anything," Dr. Meyers said.

"Did you dress up as a prostitute and meet Chris Cantwell in a hotel room?" I asked.

"I bet you've had a lot of fun picturing that one," Patricia said. "Think I'd make a tasty little morsel, huh, Mr. Inspector?" She raised a seductive eyebrow, which seemed sad and awkward above her tight mouth and rigid jaw.

Dr. Meyers fell to her knees in front of Patricia. "Don't, Patty, please."

"I thought shrinks were supposed to be interested in the dirty truth," Patricia said, her voice cracking.

"What Chris thought is not your truth," Dr. Meyers said.

"You're mistaken if you think I'm like your precious little Nikki," Patricia said, sitting upright. "She can act as slutty as she wants because she has a mother who knows she's not one."

"Neither are you," Dr. Meyers said.

"You want the dirty truth, don't you, Mr. Inspector?" Patricia asked, turning to me.

"It depends on what it is," I said.

"That was bullshit I told you—not about Chris being a shallow asshole, but about not being interested in him. I wanted him, just like all the other stupid girls. I asked for it."

"You didn't ask him to spike your drink with LSD," I said.

"It just brought out what was already inside of me. Besides, I wasn't stoned when I went up into the hills with him."

"You were frightened," Dr. Meyers said.

"Sure, and it turned me on. The truth is, I was so fucked-up I would have done whatever he wanted even if he hadn't pulled the knife."

"Then why did he pull it?" I asked.

"To show me who I was." She folded her legs under herself, this time making sure the dress covered her ankles. "While he was doing me he held the knife to my throat, saying I was wet like a whore—that's how he could tell I liked it." Patricia dropped her head so we couldn't see her face.

"Did you go to the police right away?" I asked.

"While I still had the evidence inside me?" she said, smiling fiercely. "It wouldn't have done any good. You pigs still would have said it was my fault."

There was a knock at the door. We all glanced at one another. Something had passed between us that could not be shared with whoever was outside. Dr. Meyers rose slowly, gathering herself as she must have done hundreds of times before when an intense moment had to be broken. She ducked out of sight, turning into the entryway to open the door. Patricia glanced up in fear. I was no longer the enemy: now she wanted my protection.

Still out of sight, Dr. Meyers said with a veneer of friendliness, "Hello, John."

Patricia winced at the thud of her father's heavy boots, even before he came striding into the living room. He was a tall, gangly man with an Adam's apple that looked like a sharp rock lodged in his throat. He wore a khaki jacket and jungle hat and looked down at his daughter with hawkish eyes, as if she were far below—dirt. "Now, what the hell have you gotten yourself into?"

"Please, John," Dr. Meyers said, putting her hand on his arm.

I stepped between them, nudging her out of the way.

"Come with me a minute," I said, taking hold of his upper arm and pulling him outside onto the front porch. As soon as I'd closed the front door, he grabbed my wrist. His hands were rough and strong from digging soil and lifting rocks.

"I don't care who the hell you are," he said. "Keep your goddamn hands off me."

He was open to a knee in the groin and I was sorely tempted. I probably would have, too, if it'd done his daughter any good. But right now he was all she had, and the last person she needed caring for her was an enraged father.

"Do you have any idea what's happened to your daughter?"

He blinked away my question. "Why don't these things happen to the other girls?" Looking down at his muddy boots, he said, "Everything sinks to its natural level. Soft dirt gets stripped away by—"

"And there's nothing like a hard father to make a daughter soft," I said.

There were many ways he could have taken that, and he hesitated long enough to think through a number of them. "What the hell are you insinuating?"

I grabbed him by the throat and pushed him up against the wall, while sliding out my .38 and putting it to his head. "I'm not insinuating anything. I'm telling you straight to your face, there's a man out there who wants to do this to your daughter and he might just pull the trigger."

He glared at me but did not fight back.

I let him loose and lowered my gun. "Where was Patricia last Sunday night?"

He straightened his collar as his gaze lowered to my weapon. "Staying with her older sister in Piedmont."

"All night?"

"Kelly drove Patricia to school Monday morning."

"Take her away for a while," I said, handing him my card. "Check in with me every day and I'll tell you when it's safe to bring her back."

He shook his head. "I've got commitments. I'll talk to Kelly."

"Her sister's is the first place he'll come looking for her. Cancel whatever you have to do."

He smiled like his daughter, exposing teeth as if threatening to bite.

"I'm giving you fair warning," I said. "I can make your life very difficult."

He sized me up.

"Child neglect and assaulting an officer of the law, for starters," I said, sliding my gun back into its holster. "Even if those charges don't stick, you have to wonder what the Board of Regents—"

"Okay," he said. "I know a place up—"

"Don't tell me where it is! Don't tell anybody. Just take her there." As he turned the doorknob to go back inside the house, I said, "If anything happens to her, it will be on your head."

CHAPTER TWENTY-SEVEN

Dr. Meyers and I watched through the front window as Patricia and her father got into his WWII-vintage Jeep and drove away.

"I hate that man," she muttered. "He's as dumb as his rocks. He doesn't have a clue."

"How well do you know him?" I asked.

"We went out a few times." She turned to face me. "He's the kind of man who thinks everything has its place, including women."

"He asked you to marry him and you turned him down."

"I'm not even going to ask how you figured that one out, Inspector. He wanted a mother for Patty and I regretted not being able to be that. She tried to kill herself, you know, after Chris raped her."

I nodded but didn't tell her I'd seen the scars.

"There were five police reports about women who were attacked by Chris," I said. "Patricia Walker was the first, Joyce Smith the second, a call girl named Lari Zohn the third, another prostitute named Karma something the fourth—I need to know who the fifth victim was."

"I can't tell you," she said.

"Why? Was it your daughter?"

"Jesus!" she said, taking a step back. "Look, if Chris Cantwell had raped my daughter I wouldn't have let Allen Cantwell or anyone else stop me from doing something about it."

"I don't doubt that," I said. "But you didn't answer my question."

"The answer is no—Nikki was not one of Chris Cantwell's victims." She glared at me until I looked away.

"And you still won't tell me who it was."

She shook her head as if I was a man like John Walker who didn't have a clue. "I thought you came here to investigate some files that were stolen."

***

Dr. Meyers kept old patient files locked in a metal cabinet in the small middle bedroom she used as an office. She'd discovered the burglary after returning from taking her daughter to school. The lock on the filing cabinet was easy enough to pick without leaving evidence that it had been tampered with, but the thief had not bothered to relock the drawers. Nor had he closed them. If he had, she might not have noticed for months or even years.

"Did he take anything else?" I asked.

"No."

"How can you be so sure?"

"I looked thoroughly while I was waiting for you," she said in a sharp tone that let me know she didn't appreciate my questioning her answers.

I began checking around the rest of the office for anything else unusual. It was a fairly cramped space. Dr. Meyers had positioned a large antique desk several feet into the room so she could sit facing out with her back to the wall. I understood—I didn't like facing a wall either—but in a ten-by-twelve bedroom, it made things rather tight.

The filing cabinet was tucked in a back corner beside a large double-hung window. I pulled back the curtains. The window's latch was secured. The thief had not come in that way. Aside from the opened filing cabinet, I found no evidence of a break-in. The intruder had worked carefully, which made it all the more likely the drawer was left open on purpose.

"Nothing else has been touched," she said impatiently. "All he wanted were the files."

I went behind her desk to look at several mementos hanging on the wall. A framed photograph showed Dr. Meyers in her early twenties, wearing a graduate's cap and gown, receiving a diploma. When I looked more closely, I noticed that the man shaking her hand was the groom I'd seen in her wedding photo.

Next to that picture, positioned behind Dr. Meyers' chair, was an old photo of a young couple, which looked to be taken in the 20s. The man in the picture had a pleasant round face and gentle eyes. The woman's gaze seemed to escape the photo's two dimensions, leaping the barrier between past and present. Now I knew where Dr. Meyers got her penetrating gaze.

Mounted to the left of the photo, in the same frame, was a handwritten letter in an older German script called *Sütterlin*, which was taught in German schools before World War II. I learned to read and write it when I'd been trained by the *Nokim*.

The letter began, *Meine liebe madchen.*

And loosely translated, continued:

> Events are transpiring so quickly, it is difficult to keep you abreast. Your father and I will soon be moving to a resettlement camp. Because of his status as a WWI veteran, we are among the last. Please thank Fred and Irma for their generous offer. We love you very much and would have desired nothing more than to be near you. However, your father insists that we find a way that does not break German law, so we can keep our good name when all this blows over. With God's will, we will see you soon.
>
> Your loving mother and devoted father.

"What are you looking for?" Dr. Meyers asked.

"I'm not sure," I said, pulling my hands out of my pockets, letting loose of the tin heart, which fell back among my loose change.

The final memento hanging on the wall was an old tapestry evening bag strung on a hook by its pewter chain. My mother had owned one very similar in the early 30s. The chain was attached to the purse by a filigreed brass frame. I noticed that its clasp was open. Knowing Dr. Meyers was not a woman to leave anything dangling, I stepped aside to show her, putting my finger between the two brass balls that interlocked to close the purse. She gave a puzzled look. I slid my fingers inside and pulled out a folded piece of yellowed paper.

"That wasn't there," she said.

When I unfolded the paper I found a crudely drawn caricature of a hook-nosed Jew. Beneath the drawing it said *Deutschland Judenfrei.*

I handed the Nazi flier to Dr. Meyers. "Are you sure it didn't come with the purse?"

She crumpled the paper into a ball and threw it at my feet.

"It wasn't there!" she said, dashing out of the room.

I picked up the flier and smoothed it out. A message was handwritten on the back in ballpoint pen, which immediately struck me as odd; ballpoint pens were seldom in use in the 30s when the flier was printed. The ink looked fresh. I rubbed it with my finger and it smudged. It was probably written immediately before the intruder put the flier in the handbag.

Dr. Meyers returned with an antique amethyst pendant and matching earrings. "Look. This is all I brought over with me—in that bag—all my mother was able to leave me. I've been saving them for Nikki." She went over and clasped shut the purse, then wrapped her arms around herself as if she'd felt a sudden chill. "I have to get out of this room."

She went into the hall and stopped in front of the office doorway. I had to brush her to get past.

She shot me a back-off look.

"Stay out there," she said, pointing to the living room and went into her bedroom at the end of the hallway.

I waited a few seconds before trailing her, and peered into the room from the doorway, where I saw Dr. Meyers gazing into an open closet.

"Was that closet door opened when you got home?" I asked.

"This is my bedroom," she said putting her hands on her hips, continuing to stare at the closet. "It's private, if you please."

I noticed an empty space on the top shelf, between boxes that were as neatly lined up as books on a shelf. "What was there?"

"God! The box these were in," she said, holding up the jewelry. "Can't I have a moment's privacy?"

I went down the hall to the living room. Before I sat down to wait for her, I folded up the anti-Semitic flier and put it in my pocket. I decided not to show her the handwriting on its back. Not simply because I thought the message would upset her all the more. I had a strange feeling the quote from *Oedipus* was meant for me: *What misery to be wise when wisdom profits nothing.*

***

Dr. Meyers sat on the sofa with her head in her hands. "Why take the files?" she said. "I'd remember most everything in them if I was ever called upon to testify."

"They were leaving you a message," I said.

"What kind of message?"

"That you're not even safe in your own home and you'd better keep your mouth shut."

"But there are a million ways they could have left that same message. Why steal files?"

"There might have also been something in them they wanted to know," I said.

"Like what?"

"If Chris had any victims you knew about that they didn't."

"When you say *they*, you mean Cantwell. How can you be so sure he's involved?"

"Why would anybody else steal Chris's files?"

"But why would Allen leave that disgusting flier?" she rushed on, not really listening to me.

"Cantwell didn't do it himself. He's using a Czech contractor to do his dirty work. That's where the flier came from."

"A contractor?"

"An ex-Henlein. Maybe the guy owes Cantwell a favor. Maybe he's buying a favor. Maybe he and Cantwell just see the world the same way."

Dr. Meyers noticed me glance down at her hands. They were shaking.

"I haven't eaten anything since last night," she said. "I can hardly think."

"Then let's get you some lunch," I said.

"I have appointments," she said, obviously putting me off.

"Right now?"

"Back to back, from two to five."

I looked at my watch. It was twelve-fifteen.

"Come on. We'll eat on campus."

***

The outdoor patio of the Terrace Restaurant was crowded with students, studying, drinking coffee, eating lunch and soaking up the autumn sun. Empty tables were hard to find at lunchtime, so I told Dr. Meyers to grab one while I went inside to pick up our lunch. She tried to give me a few dollars to cover a tuna sandwich.

"It's on me," I said.

She shook her head and pushed the bills into my hand.

After I returned with the food, I carefully counted out her fifty-seven cents change. She didn't think it was funny. We ate silently for several minutes. The sun and exuberant chatter of students were a welcome diversion.

"I always feel out of place here," Dr. Meyers said.

"You don't look much older than they do," I said, sliding a French fry in one side of my mouth while blowing smoke out the other. I'd never totally gotten out of the habit of consuming everything I possibly could while it was still in my possession.

"Right," she said sarcastically, "it's been over ten years since I was even a teaching assistant."

"Anyway, that doesn't matter now," I said. "It's the age of Aquarius."

She shook her head and laughed. "What *are* you talking about?"

"You're an Aquarian, aren't you?"

"And you are one very puzzling man, Inspector Wolfe."

"Simon," I snuck in between bites. "Weren't those amethysts?"

"Okay, Simon," she said, setting down her ice tea. "Elaine." She reached across the table and we shook. "Now that we're on a first-name basis—what the hell are you talking about?"

"The stones in the pendant and earrings—your birthstones, right?"

She held up an *ah-hah* finger. "You don't strike me as the astrological type."

"My mother was. She said analytical Aquarians and emotional Cancers complement one another."

She tore a small piece of lettuce off the end of her sandwich and pointed it at me. "And I suppose you're a Cancer."

I shrugged.

"Anyway, you're the analytical one," she said. "Don't you figure everything out using hard, cold logic?"

"The crab has a hard shell to protect its soft inner body," I said.

She smiled and leaned back, closing her eyes to take in the sun. The skin on her face was the same rich olive tone as her arms and shoulders.

"Did she make it through the war—your mother?" she asked hesitantly.

"Same as your parents."

"Not exactly." Her playfulness disappeared. "Your parents probably didn't have any choice in the matter."

"My father was murdered by a Czech policeman and my mother was sent to Theresienstadt before we knew what was happening," I said.

"Mine did know," she said. "That's why they sent me here to live with my aunt and uncle, who later raised the money and arranged to smuggle my parents to Denmark. But they refused."

I remembered the letter on Elaine's wall that said her father did not want to break the law.

"Germany was their home," I said.

"You know what they say about the Germans, Simon?"

"Germans or German Jews?"

"Jews were the best damned Germans ever made," she said. "They say the reason Germans never had a revolution was because they had to keep off the grass."

I tried to picture her as a young girl who felt abandoned by her parents, even though they'd sent her away to save her life.

"But what right do I have to complain?" she said, pushing away her half-eaten sandwich. "How can I possibly understand what you survivors had to go through?"

"It's not like you missed some sort of rite of passage," I said.

I heard a female voice call out, "Simon, Simon."

I turned and saw Wiki at a table with a few girlfriends. She nodded approval in Elaine's direction and gave me the peace sign.

"My next-door neighbor," I said.

"She's beautiful," Elaine said. "She seems awfully friendly."

"Not really. I don't even know how she learned my first name. My mailbox, I guess."

There was an awkward silence.

"Elaine," I finally said.

She looked at me casually, as if we were now truly on a first name basis.

"I need to know who his fifth victim was."

She leaned back in her chair and crossed her arms.

"I think it's pretty clear," I said, "that Cantwell's silencing people who can damage his reputation."

She nodded and hesitated for several seconds before speaking: "Allen called me last Monday to tell me Chris was found dead. He said I would be breaching both my ethics and the law if I divulged any information about either him or his son. If I did, he said he would personally make sure I never practiced again"

"What did you tell him?"

"That I understood my professional obligation," she said staring off into space. After several seconds she turned to me again. "But threatening someone legally is one thing. Murder is quite another, and I don't believe Allen is capable of that."

"Patricia was not just threatened legally, neither was that prostitute who got her throat slashed. I don't think you're going to want it on your conscience if something happens to that fifth victim."

"And you really think you'll be able to help—working all by yourself?"

"If I go to the department and ask for support, will you tell me who the fifth victim was? I promise I'll leave your name out of it."

Our eyes met for a second. She looked away. From past experience, she had no reason to trust the police in matters where Cantwell was concerned.

"Are you coming onto the grass or not, Elaine?"

CHAPTER TWENTY-EIGHT

After I reviewed most everything I knew about the Cantwells with Fanelli, the lieutenant quickly got hold of Chris Cantwell's sealed files, using the power of the chief's office to jump legal and bureaucratic hurdles. He wasn't nearly so fast about reviewing the files, though, mulling over each word like a Talmudic scholar. He would have described himself as meticulous and careful. But I knew he was lost. I'd seen it written all over his face when I'd said we needed to protect Chris Cantwell's killer.

Fanelli had no idea how to analyze a situation without being spoon-fed priorities by his superiors, and none of them had ever said it was okay to spend precious resources protecting a suspected murderer. To make the situation even more difficult for the lieutenant, I'd told him I thought Cantwell had been exerting undue influence on the department. Each time Fanelli turned a page and then went back to a previous one, presumably crosschecking information, I knew his quandary was not about moving forward carefully, but about moving forward at all.

Richard stood at parade rest in a corner of our boss's office ("Once a Marine, always a Marine," he used to say), keeping his gaze as far from me as possible. He had not been very happy when I'd told him my plans to enlist the chief's support, especially since I'd been the one who'd talked him into sneaking around and lying about it. After all, he had a lot more at stake than I did. He had a family to feed.

"So what are you saying?" Fanelli asked. "The congressman is out on the streets silencing people?"

"I think he's got somebody doing it for him," I said, glancing at Richard to let him know I didn't want him saying anything else on the subject.

"Prove that one," Fanelli said. "We've got no way to tie Cantwell to any of these cases. As far as your theory that one of Chris Cantwell's victims was involved in his murder, what have you got? One dead prostitute who's not talking and another you heard was out of town the night the boy died. Unless you think it was one of the schoolgirls?"

"No," I said. "Joyce Smith's going to school in Arizona and Patricia Walker has an alibi. Still, one of Chris Cantwell's victims has already been murdered and I think the others could also be in danger."

"Let's say you're right," Fanelli said. "I still don't see the urgency. Let's say you've got four victims who are possible targets. One's already dead and the other three are safely out of town."

"There's one more victim," I said.

"I've only got four files here." Fanelli tossed me the pile.

"Then the other one must have gone conveniently missing," I said, glancing down at Joyce Smith's file, which fell open. A photograph showed her with a black eye and badly bruised arms. It took a few seconds to get over reconciling this image with the one I'd seen of the pretty cheerleader. "I know for a fact a fifth rape was reported and I know who it is."

"Who?" Richard said, looking at me as if I'd been holding out on him again.

"The mother of one of Chris Cantwell's previous victims and the wife of a federal judge."

"Holy shit," Richard said. "You gotta be kidding."

"What the hell are you two talking about?" Fanelli asked.

"Marlene Smith," I said. "Judge Smith's wife."

"And you know for a fact she filed a complaint?" Fanelli asked me.

"I don't know how much got written down, but part of the deal was that if she went away so would any record of the occurrence."

"Why would she agree to a deal like that?" Richard asked.

"Cantwell turned the tables on her. He told her the rape of her daughter would be inadmissible in court if she tried pressing charges against his son. And if she didn't back off, she'd be the one charged with a crime—contributing to the delinquency of a minor. Chris Cantwell would say that she invited him into her house and seduced him. With that, and a few other inducements—"

"What kind of inducements?" Fanelli asked.

"Who do you think recommended her husband for the federal judiciary?"

"Where the hell did you hear this?" Fanelli asked.

The truth was I hadn't heard it. When I'd asked Elaine if Marlene Smith might have dropped her complaint in exchange for a recommendation from Cantwell for her husband, Elaine said she didn't know. So it was a wild guess. One I would have bet on, though. In fact, I might have been betting my career on it.

"How long ago was Mrs. Smith supposed to have been raped?" Fanelli asked me.

"About a year."

"You think she killed the boy?" Richard asked.

I shrugged.

"Why would she wait until now to get back at him?" Fanelli asked.

I shook my head. I hadn't figured that one out yet.

"A judge's wife dressing up like a prostitute?" Richard said. "You'd think she could have come up with a better way to—"

"I don't think there was a better way for her," I said. "She doesn't have the psychology of a killer. Putting on a costume would not only help her hide her identity from the police—it also helped her conceal herself from herself."

"Still, you'd think a judge's wife would be smart enough to know she couldn't get away with it," Fanelli said.

"Maybe she didn't think it would be thoroughly investigated," I said. "She knew Cantwell wouldn't have wanted a scandal hitting the press before an election. But the congressman can also figure out that if we interrogated her she'd be the kind of woman who'd want to relieve her conscience and confess everything."

"Exactly the kind he'd need to silence," Richard said.

"So what were you planning on doing?" Fanelli asked me. "Going out to her house and accusing her without any evidence?"

"I've already questioned her once, but she wasn't a suspect then. I'd like to take one more crack at her. If I'm right, confessing will be her only guarantee of safety."

"And if you're wrong?" Fanelli asked.

"We're talking about a federal judge's wife," I said. "If anything happened to her because we ignored the trail of evidence... "

Fanelli reached across the desk and took back the file folders. "You never told me where you got this information about Mrs. Smith."

"Can you give me a guarantee that my source will be protected?"

"I don't have time for this bullshit—the chief is waiting," Fanelli said, glancing at his watch and getting up from his desk. "Any other last-minute bombshells either of you want to drop on me before we go up to see him?"

"Yeah," Richard said, looking over at me. "Mrs. Cantwell called and said she wants to meet you at a club on Broadway later tonight."

CHAPTER TWENTY-NINE

On the way up the elevator to the chief's, Fanelli grilled Richard about Mrs. Cantwell's phone call. Richard said he'd tried to get more information out of her, but she said she'd only speak to me. Fanelli asked what I thought she might want to talk about. I decided not to mention the morphine prescription. At least until I saw how the chief reacted to all the other information we were going to throw at him. If it looked like he was in collusion with Cantwell, there would be no sense in tipping my hand any more than I'd already done.

When we got to the chief's outer office his secretary told us he was running a few minutes late. That wasn't bad for the chief; I'd waited all morning to see him before. Richard and I sat on two chairs on one side of the secretary's desk and Fanelli sat alone on the other. Richard fidgeted with his car keys, beads of sweat collecting on his forehead.

I leaned over and whispered, "Don't worry. You've just been in the office doing what you were supposed to."

He didn't look reassured.

After that, we waited silently for ten minutes before Lieutenant Ellingsworth of Vice and two senior inspectors came out the office door. The chief was right behind them and said, "You'll supervise this yourself, Leo, right?"

Ellingsworth said, "Of course, sir."

"We can't have any screw-ups."

Ellingsworth's smile put the chief at ease. He had a way of making the right people feel assured. I was sure part of it was his good looks. He had large, sympathetic-looking brown eyes, a square jaw, thick wavy hair, and a well-trimmed moustache, which some of the younger cops were adopting to show that in their own small fashion they too were part of the 60s revolution. And somehow, even with San Francisco's gloomy weather, Ellingsworth managed to keep a year-round tan.

I wasn't the only cop who thought Ellingsworth was a phony. But as long as he was on the fast track he didn't care what we thought. Besides, he didn't like me any more than I liked him. That might have been because I'd turned down his prized position of lieutenant of Vice before it had been offered to him. Cleaning prostitutes off the streets and waging war on homosexuals every time the mayor was up for election—that was not my idea of police work.

"Inspector Wolfe," Ellingsworth said with a slight flourish. As always, he was in uniform, custom tailored and freshly pressed.

"Planning your latest raids on the YMCA and Club Baths?" I asked.

Ellingsworth raised a questioning eyebrow.

"It is election season," I said.

"And I always back the winner. You should try it sometime." He touched his cap. "See you later, Inspector."

Richard and I got up off our chairs and followed Fanelli to greet the chief, who remained standing at his office door.

"I'd like to talk to Lieutenant Fanelli first, if you don't mind," the chief said. "Why don't the two of you go downstairs to the coffee shop and come back in a half hour or so."

***

I ordered two cups of coffee while Richard went to the pay phone to call Miriam and let her know he was going to be late again. I felt frustrated about being caught up in a political web, unable to help Mrs. Smith. To take my mind off her, I turned my attention to a portable TV mounted on a plywood shelf in the corner, broadcasting the late-afternoon news. One of these new-style TV anchormen who had more looks than brains said that Czech President Ludvik Svoboda had flown from Prague to Moscow in an endeavor to secure the freedom of First Secretary Dubcek and the other Czech leaders being held hostage by the Russians.

"Everything okay at home?" I asked Richard as he sat down next to me.

"Yeah. Miriam's taking Jason to the Merritt for dinner." He poured more milk than usual in his coffee. He did that when he had a nervous stomach. "She didn't like the idea that I was going to let you take all the heat."

"What did you tell her?"

"What I'm telling you—I'm not risking our mortgage by going against the chief if he tells us to pack it in."

I nodded, then turned my attention back to the TV. A political commentator—the old type of reporter hired for his erudition—joined the anchorman and said he was relieved to hear that Dubcek and the other kidnapped leaders hadn't met with the kind of unfortunate accidents that had been known to befall dissidents in Moscow. The Russians had probably refrained from disposing of these Czech leaders because they were afraid that the student demonstrations in the streets of Prague could turn into a bloody revolt like the one the Soviets had been forced to quell in Hungary twelve years before. The Russians didn't want a repeat of the bad world press they'd received from their handling of the Hungarian uprising.

The commentator said he'd heard rumors that First Secretary Dubcek had been isolated and sedated while the Russians tried to put the screws to the other captured Czech reformers, but so far these brave leaders were holding out. The Russians wanted them to sign a statement calling for *normalization*, which basically meant the Czech people would have their hearts laid down on the Soviet chopping block. The commentator quoted a headline from an article printed in a Czech underground newspaper satirizing this new round of Soviet doublespeak: *Normalization? Kafka Lives!*

The anchorman looked lost with the political commentator's reference to the great Czech writer, Kafka, and glanced down at his notes to fill in with a humorous anecdote his hacks had prepared for him. "Now we'll see if the Czech president can live up to his name. You know, Al, Svoboda means *freedom* in Czech."

"I can't keep track of all these Czech leaders," Richard said.

"Svoboda was a Czech general who teamed up with the Russians to kick the Nazis' asses during World War II," I said. "But he's an old man now and I'm not so sure he'll be as tough with his former allies."

Only half listening, Richard took a sip of coffee.

"Face it, man," he said, "Cantwell may not be the devil exactly, but ain't no way you're gonna avoid jumping into the fire to go after him."

***

Chief Murray opened a box of Muriel Cigars he always kept on the far-left corner of his desk. Richard and I declined his offer, but Fanelli took one to be polite. Richard and I waited while the chief lit Fanelli's and his cigars. Whenever the chief stuck one of those fat Muriels in his mouth I always thought about the sexy blonde on TV, singing, *Hey big spender, spend a little dime with me.*

After we'd settled around his meeting table the chief said to Richard and me, "I want to tell you boys right off the bat that I'm on board with you one-hundred-and-ten percent."

I glanced over at Fanelli. He wouldn't look me in the eye.

"Nobody wants to see a judge's wife in harm's way," the chief continued. "It's a disgrace. Captain Murdock has already been in touch with the chief of the Piedmont Police and I've asked Murdock to personally update me on Mrs. Smith's welfare."

The Piedmont Police Department was so small they didn't even handle their own homicides. The Alameda Sheriff's Department did that for them. But then, of course, no homicide had occurred in Piedmont—Mrs. Smith was still alive. As a matter of fact, there hadn't been a homicide in Piedmont since I'd joined the SFPD. And I could picture what would happen when the Piedmont police were sent out to question Mrs. Smith—she'd deny that any threats had ever been made against her. The patrolmen would leave satisfied that the "City of Millionaires" was as safe and secure as ever.

"I'd still like to question her in regard to my investigation," I said.

"What investigation?" the chief asked. "Lieutenant Fanelli has already got another inspector on the murder of that prostitute. But if you think it's necessary, go ahead and contact the Berkeley police about the assault on that schoolgirl and the theft of Chris Cantwell's files. That should tie it up as far as you're concerned."

"Without Chris Cantwell's homicide investigation at its center, none of those incidents make any sense," I said. "They're just odds and ends that are going to get overlooked."

"Captain Murdock's looking at all the evidence," Fanelli said, gazing forward at no one in particular. "He'll get back if he wants us to follow up."

"What about Congressman Cantwell?" I asked Fanelli. "Did you tell the chief about him?"

Fanelli glanced at me before dropping his eyes. That's when I knew he'd folded.

"Don't force our hand, Simon," the chief said. "There's nothing to be gained and everything to be lost." Unlike Fanelli, the chief was not afraid to look me in the eye.

"You've thought about it and it's best for all concerned," I said.

The chief's smile might have seemed ambiguous to somebody who didn't know him. To me it said a window had opened for me to slip away and be free. Free from the department's judgment, at any rate. He couldn't help with the way I judged myself.

"But I'm afraid I can't see it the same way," I said.

"Afraid of what?" the chief asked in the intimate tone he'd used as my mentor.

I got up and walked to the window that overlooked the Hall of Justice parking lot. Just beyond it the freeway on-ramp was crowded with cars leaving work. Their headlights were only slightly dimmed by the last rays of sunlight.

"Of losing your way home, boyo?" I heard the chief say. When I turned around his smile was now large and welcoming. "If this isn't your home, what is?"

"I don't know," I said, taking out a cigarette.

"You go out into the grimy streets, you're bound to get some dirt on you at the end of the day," said the chief, holding up his lighter. I walked over and he lit my cigarette. "What's the answer?" he continued. "Go back to your apartment, take a shower and get the hell out there again the next morning."

I went back to the window. I couldn't believe how quickly darkness was falling.

"Go home and sleep on it. You'll see the light come morning," the chief said.

I turned around, walked over to the table and sat down. "No, I won't."

"All right, have it your way." The chief turned to Fanelli. "Lieutenant, I've received a complaint regarding Inspector Wolfe's attempts to blackmail Congressman Cantwell into remaining silent about some very disturbing information he knows about the inspector's past. That's the reason Inspector Wolfe's been pursuing this pointless investigation into the death of the congressman's son."

Oddly, for a moment I felt a sense of relief. Now I knew where everybody stood.

"Where did he get this information?" Fanelli asked, giving me the kind of sidelong glance he'd give a suspect.

"From an extremely credible source—a respected member of the intelligence community," the chief said.

"You mean the assassin who murdered one woman, attacked an underage girl and stole medical files?" I said to the chief.

"Assassin?" the chief said. "If I were you, I wouldn't plan on trying to defend myself with counter-accusations."

Richard glanced at me in disbelief.

"Defend myself?" I said.

"Yes," said the chief. "Congressman Cantwell wants us to meet with him and the mayor on Monday night to get everything out in the open. By the way, he sounded as though he might be willing to be reasonable and civil about all of this, if you are."

"Reasonable and civil," I repeated, wondering why the chief hadn't simply shown me the door and put me on suspension pending a disciplinary hearing. Something was stopping him. I could only guess that he'd gotten orders to keep me within the fold. If they cut me loose I might decide to talk to the press. They didn't want me doing that, at least not before the election. After that it was anybody's guess what they'd do with me.

"It would help your case immeasurably if you were willing to show good will by committing here and now to stand down and stop pressuring the congressman," the chief said.

"While possibly allowing another woman to be murdered," I said.

The chief set down his cigar and shook his finger as if admonishing a schoolboy. "If you must persist," he said, again turning to Fanelli. "Lieutenant, I'd like you to attend this meeting also, since it involves two inspectors who work for you."

"Two inspectors?" Richard said.

"Yes, you're implicated as an accomplice in Inspector Wolfe's misuse of power. And I'm afraid your wife's activities may also come into question. It's been suggested that her family illegally harbored Inspector Wolfe when he first came to this country. She could lose her job as a teacher and perhaps even her citizenship."

So Richard had been right, there was no chance of going after Cantwell without jumping into the fire. And I'd been willing to do that. But I couldn't take Richard, Miriam and Jason with me. I remembered what Feiertag had said about drawing a circle around myself and those close to me. And how I'd arrogantly said that I didn't have anyone.

"And if I don't pursue the investigation?" I asked.

"The congressman indicated he might be willing to let sleeping dogs lie," the chief said.

I glanced over at Fanelli. He was able to look me in the eye again now that we were about to become co-conspirators. I turned to Richard, but he seemed oblivious to everything around him, as if he'd slipped into a terrible darkness. That's the irony of stepping into the fire. There's no light at its heart. Or maybe we just become blinded as we pass through its outer glare.

"In other words," I said, "everything is fine, so long as I stay away from anyone involved with the death of Congressman Cantwell's son and—"

"With one exception," the chief cut me off. "We want you to meet with Mrs. Cantwell tonight and report back tomorrow morning on what she said."

CHAPTER THIRTY

The bare-shouldered Marlene Dietrich impersonator straddled a café chair on a runway extending halfway into the intimate drag club with perhaps twenty tables crowding the stage. The performer wore lace-gartered black stockings and a Fred Astaire top hat, with a thick Gaulois cigarette erect between slender fingers. The perfect mimic: left hand bent vainly back, spine arched wearily and throaty androgynous voice. If it had been thirty years before, I'd have been fooled into thinking it was the Blonde Venus in her prime.

Mrs. Cantwell leaned in close over the small table and said just loudly enough to be heard over the music, "Don't you think it might be better for all concerned if he simply disappeared."

I'd been distracted by a woman slipping between my table and the one a few feet away, wearing a Day-glo dress that hid only the bare essentials. It had taken a few seconds to realize—since the essentials were hidden—that it might not have been a woman at all I was glancing at. So I thought maybe I'd heard wrong. But when I looked directly at Mrs. Cantwell and saw she was deadly serious, I understood why she'd been confiding in me.

We were sitting to the left of the shallow stage in a dark corner of Finocchio's. She was dressed straight out of *La Dolce Vita*, a woman stepping off the Via Veneto: black evening gloves, diamond-studded shades, and wide-brimmed black hat concealing her eyes when she so much as dipped her head. A strange disguise, since anywhere else it would have made her conspicuous. But everyone in this North Beach club was on display, each patron's style more outlandish than the next.

"It's one of the few spots in town I wouldn't ever be noticed, at least not as myself," she'd said when we'd first sat down. "Can you imagine my husband being seen here?" She adjusted the rake of her hat to conceal one eye.

"I would have preferred some out-of-the-way coffee shop," I said, staring at a table of loud women I thought might be men in drag, though the room was too dark and smoky to tell for sure.

"Don't be grumpy, Inspector." The rim of her hat eclipsed the playful pout on her fluorescent-pink lips. "Really, it's the ideal place for a little chat." She leaned back dramatically, holding out an empty cigarette holder. "After all, people come here to express their inner selves."

"I'm not interested in getting all that deep," I said. "What's this about anyway?"

"You wanted me to talk to my husband, and now that I have, you're the only one I can confide in. Everyone else is in his back pocket."

I hoped that in her haze of booze and pills she hadn't noticed me glance down to hide my guilt. If she found out I'd become one of those people in the congressman's back pocket, our little chat would be over.

"At least appreciate the irony," Mrs. Cantwell said, staring at two young men in motorcycle leather at the next table.

They held hands and gazed into one another's eyes, singing along with the moaning performer: *Falling in love again, never wanted to, what am I to do, can't help it.*

"What irony?" I asked.

She turned to me and said in a low Dietrich voice, "A clandestine meeting in a club the Nazis would have outlawed."

"Nazis?"

"Isn't that what you wanted to talk about—my husband and his Nazi friend?" She waved to the passing waiter. "Alberto."

He stopped on a dime, bowed and kissed her hand. "*Bellisima Madonna!* Where have you been? I've missed you."

She batted her false eyelashes and ordered another martini, her third. I got a second Scotch.

"My husband is such a child sometimes," she said when the waiter was out of earshot. "His adolescent affairs are one thing, but all this cloak and dagger business... he's really out of his depth." Mrs. Cantwell pulled a pack of Virginia Slims out of her alligator purse. "Would you mind?" She slid the cigarette into the holder and I lit it for her. "You're still interested in making that deal, aren't you?"

"What deal?"

"Listen," she said, waving her cigarette holder around like a conductor's baton, "What's really to be gained by digging up skeletons?"

"It's my job, for one thing," I said, glancing nervously at the four men in drag who were beginning to pass around a suspicious-looking cigarette.

"I've heard you're capable of going your own way," she said.

"So what exactly are you asking of me? To help protect your husband?"

"If it's mutually beneficial."

"Aren't you the least bit curious to know how your son died? Don't you care about him at all?"

"Don't talk to me about my son," she said, poking her cigarette dangerously close to my eyes. "I grieved enough for him while he was alive, despite the fact that he almost destroyed my life. I'm not going to let him ruin things now that he's dead."

She took a sip of her drink and gave me an apologetic twist of a smile. "Even as a child we knew he was missing something—he couldn't experience emotions more complex than immediate pain or pleasure. Can you imagine how bleak his inner world must have been?" Mrs. Cantwell took off her shades so I could see her eyes. They were bloodshot, but otherwise seemed surprisingly sober. "I probably should have warned Elaine when Chris chose her as his counselor."

"I thought the courts assigned her," I said.

"Chris had a genius for making people think things were their idea."

"Why did he want to see Dr. Meyers?"

"Because he guessed Allen was interested in her. We'd met her at a party—"

"A Halloween party," I said, remembering that Elaine had mentioned it.

"Her costume got all the men's attention, but only Allen had the nerve to approach her. He's never lacked for nerve, my dear, sweet husband."

"How did Chris find out?"

"Allen had arranged a meeting at school with the Smiths to talk about what had happened between Chris and their daughter."

"Joyce Smith," I interjected, smelling marijuana from the direction of the four men in drag.

"Yes. It was Joyce that time," she said. "We were sitting in the car in front of the school while Allen gave Chris last-minute tips on how to behave during the meeting. He told our son to say that he and Joyce had been drinking and he wasn't thinking straight—of course, implying all the while that neither was she."

"Wasn't the girl bruised up pretty badly?" I asked, remembering the photo from her file.

"Oh, but accidents *will* happen when kids get drunk," Mrs. Cantwell said, raising the brim of her hat with an arched thumb so I could see her lift a disapproving eyebrow. "My point is, I know they hadn't discussed in advance the idea of Chris's volunteering to see a therapist. If they had, it would have come up in the car while Allen was briefing him."

"Chris brought it up out of the blue in the middle of the meeting?"

"It wasn't out of the blue exactly. While they were sitting in the car discussing strategy, Elaine drove up to drop off her daughter. Allen started asking questions, as if he were interested in Nikki. If he was an open book to me, he must have been totally transparent to our scheming son."

"I thought Nikki went to Berkeley High," I said.

"She didn't then," Mrs. Cantwell said.

"Did Chris say directly that he wanted to see Dr. Meyers?"

"He rarely said anything directly. At one point during the meeting he blurted out tearfully that he wanted to see somebody about his problems. At first I thought it might have been a ploy to persuade the Smiths to refrain from pressing charges. But when he said that he'd be embarrassed to see a therapist who was a total stranger, I knew exactly what he had in mind. As if it were his own idea, Allen suggested Dr. Meyers." She smiled at the pained expression on my face. "Don't worry, Inspector. Allen wasn't her type."

"Why say that?"

"I've heard you've taken quite a shine to her."

"How would you know anything about me and her?" I asked. "Has your husband been spying on me? Did he send you here to talk me out of investigating your son's death?"

Mrs. Cantwell laid her forearms on the table and squared her shoulders. "If Allen continues to handle things the way he has so far, he's going to get us deeper and deeper into trouble."

"He's already an accessory to a murder," I said. "I hope you weren't involved."

"That Czech idiot was simply supposed to intimidate people into keeping silent, not kill anyone."

"Operatives do what they're told," I said.

"Apparently not this one."

"Can't your husband call him off?"

"Now that it's gone this far, I don't think Allen knows what to do." And that's when she said, "Don't you think it might be better for all concerned if he simply disappeared." She slipped her shades back on so I couldn't read her eyes. "Nobody will miss him."

"Are you kidding? There will be a federal investigation. Even a congressman couldn't put a stop to that."

"Milan doesn't even exist," she said. "So they'll be forced to cover up his disappearance. And believe me, they know how to rewrite history just as well as the Germans."

"Do you realize who you're asking to do what?" I said.

Mrs. Cantwell smiled and shook her head. "Come, come, Inspector, it wouldn't be your first time."

The room fell into a breathless hush. Along with the silence, it seemed a wave of paralysis had also swept over the club, freezing everyone in place, from the front door to the stage, where the performer who'd stopped singing cried out, "Pigs!"

As I turned toward a commotion at the front door, my attention was drawn to the men in drag, who'd pulled out police-issue Smith & Wesson .38 Specials. Beyond them, several patrons who'd rushed to get out the front door began backpedaling. As one fell to the ground, the others looked on, terrified. I saw a baton land on the skull of the fallen man and then a uniformed cop wielding the club stepped into view.

The four undercover cops fanned out, pistol-whipping men back into their chairs, yelling, "Get down, you fucking faggots."

I didn't know what came over me, but I rushed forward and grabbed the arm of a plainclothesman as he was about to bring his pistol down on the head of a man in motorcycle leather. I swung him around and decked him with a solid right. I was about to go after his partner, when I felt myself restrained from behind. I turned to take care of whoever it was, but stopped short before laying into Mrs. Cantwell, who'd grabbed hold of my arm.

"You set me up," I said.

"Allen set us both up," she said.

A bullhorn broke through the pandemonium. "Everybody stay exactly where you are. This is a police raid." It was Ellingsworth. "You are in violation of local criminal ordinances regarding moral decency and state drug laws."

More uniformed cops streamed through the front door, throwing patrons into chairs and on the floor, grabbing others with choke holds. Ellingsworth set aside his bullhorn and pushed two men down by their heads, palms flat on the table, kicking out their legs into spread-eagle positions. As he patted one down, he grabbed hold of his balls until the man cried out in pain.

I couldn't hear what Ellingsworth was yelling at his victims, but the lieutenant's head was rotating back and forth, looking around the club. I was sure he was searching for me. I had to be Ellingsworth's prime target; he was going to cuff me and take me in. By the time the department was finished, I'd be so damaged Cantwell would never have to worry about me again. Nobody would ever believe a word I said.

"Come on," Mrs. Cantwell said, tugging at me.

I pulled away from her. I wanted to take care of another undercover cop in drag, who'd shoved his pistol down a man's throat and was pumping the barrel in and out. I hesitated when I saw Ellingsworth make his way toward the back of the club. He hadn't yet spotted me through the dark haze.

"There's a back door," Mrs. Cantwell said.

Just then the club's overhead lights went on and Ellingsworth saw me.

Mrs. Cantwell stepped in front of me and pointed out the way to escape. "If I set you up, why am I helping you out?"

It was all happening too fast to figure out who was setting up whom. I had no choice. Ellingsworth was closing in. I jumped onto the stage and looked back at Mrs. Cantwell who purposely bumped into the lieutenant, knocking him onto the lap of one of the guys in motorcycle leather. She fell on top of him with her arms around his neck and her hat covering his face.

I flew through the back door, where two uniformed patrolmen were posted on the landing, blocking the way down a flight of metal steps.

"The Lieutenant said nobody gets past, sir," one of the officers said.

I pushed him aside. "You think he meant me, you idiot?"

I clanged down the stairs and came to a dark alley that led out to Broadway. Halfway down the alley I heard Ellingsworth call from the landing, "Wolfe! Come back here!"

I knew too many shortcuts in the neighborhood. He'd never be able to catch me.

CHAPTER THIRTY-ONE

A fog hung over the dark water, blacking out the warning lights on the Bay Bridge's suspension towers. The fog hovered far enough above the bridge span that the road lights were visible as far as the eye could see. But I had no idea where I was going.

I cranked down my car window. The smack of wind was biting—cold and salty. It didn't matter. I kept cranking. I couldn't get enough air. It was about midnight, but I didn't see another car on the road. I was alone in the dark, dangling on the bridge's strung-and-saddled cables, unable to see heaven or earth, detached from everything and everybody.

I stopped and gave a quarter to the woman in the tollbooth. She receded into my side-view mirror. The tiered lights of San Francisco's high-rises were cropped in my rearview. Ahead of me the house lights of Oakland's hillsides were suspended like stars. Somewhere among them was my apartment. I couldn't go there. That was the first place they'd come looking for me.

I remembered how Elaine had said that every survivor she'd talked to seemed to have some deeper sense of connection to something. And it was true that during the worst of times I'd felt inwardly drawn by some mysterious future. Even when I'd made my escape on the Auschwitz death march, I did not feel as though I was running away so much as willing myself forward through that hostile landscape toward something hopeful.

I sat outside Richard and Miriam's house in my car, listening to a country station playing Patsy Cline's *So Wrong*. From the street I could see a yellow glow through the living room's parted drapes. Miriam walked past in flannel pajamas, probably going to the kitchen for Jason, who often woke up around this time to ask for a glass of juice. Miriam would do anything for those she loved, probably even forgive me for jeopardizing her happy home.

I thought about the time I'd felt most homeless, after my escape from the death march into war-ravaged Poland, where murder was so random that everybody, Jew and Gentile alike, was on the run. When I found a group of partisans hiding in the forest I had no choice but to trust them, even though a few wanted to shoot me on the spot. Since I spoke German they said I must have been a German deserter. I did not tell them I was a Jew who'd escaped the Nazis. Poles were killing Jews, and that included Polish partisans who were also fighting Nazis. I claimed I'd been attached to a division of Svoboda's independent Czech battalion and we'd scattered after getting ambushed by retreating SS marauders.

A pretty girl lightly freckled with reddish hair was assigned to question me to see if I was really Czech. Her name was Anna and she'd studied at Prague University. At the end of her interrogation she announced to the group, "His German's impeccable but his Czech's only passable." Rifles began to rise in my direction. Meanwhile Anna went up on her toes and did a ballet turn with one hand arched above her head and said, "He's definitely a Praguer—upper class like me." This caused uproarious laughter as the guns fell back down to the partisans' sides. I was not sure if it was the confidence of her pronouncement, her humor or simply her grace that saved me. Whichever, I was happy to be taken in.

I'd never felt so immediately close to any group of people. We were young, isolated from the rest of society and united by a common purpose—surviving the world's madness. We felt guiltlessly free to do anything in the name of that resolve.

Within days the leaders gave me one of the few precious rifles and sent me out with their fighters to kill our enemies and gather up more weapons and other supplies. I had never shot anything before. Not even a squirrel with a slingshot. The only man I'd ever killed had been with my bare hands. But after watching thousands of prisoners die by the guns of Germans, I did not mind shooting back. And I was rewarded with the uniform and boots off the first German soldier I killed. Not that I needed any rewards. Being a part of the group was enough. I was content to do whatever duty I was assigned and sleep wherever they told me.

I could tell where each person fit in the hierarchy by where he or she bunked. At first I was on the outskirts, which was one of the more dangerous spots due to the chance of ambush. Anna had claimed a place in the center of the group. She'd made a lean-to from a slain soldier's blanket, which she'd strung over a tree branch to give herself protection from the elements and privacy when she slept and read. Up until three weeks before I'd joined the partisans, she'd shared this dwelling with her boyfriend, who was one of their leaders. After he was killed in a skirmish she slept there alone.

Anna and I became friendly while going out on raids. She'd insisted on carrying a gun instead of doing domestic chores with the other girls. She became a different person when she strapped on a rifle. So did I, for that matter. Killing came surprisingly easy to me. I was neither attracted nor repelled by it, and was able to do exactly what was necessary—no more, no less. That's why Anna eventually asked to be partnered with me.

Together we were assigned some of the most difficult tasks. Once I slit a man's throat from behind so quickly he was not able to utter a sound. Anna's smile distracted his attention so he would not look back when he heard my first footstep. On my second step he began to turn. By the third he was dead.

Despite Anna's good looks I never saw anyone in the group make a pass at her. Although I was beginning to have thoughts about her, I would not have dared to pursue her. Not that I really knew how. My previous romantic experiences in Theresienstadt had been settled like business transactions. I'd traded something in return for a night's company. Sneaking around the ghetto barracks to these dark trysts was how I learned that I had a photographic memory of the physical layout of places, even ones only briefly seen.

After I'd been with the group a few months, we'd acquired a number of new members and lost others to death and desertion. The leaders called a meeting one night to discuss work assignments, guard duty, gun and ammunition distribution, and other logistics. When they got to our sleeping arrangements, Anna announced that I would join her under the lean-to. There was not one sidelong glance or snicker; it was taken as matter-of-factly as she'd said it.

I momentarily considered backing out. If I had, though, not only would I have insulted Anna, but the other men—all of whom would have surely traded places with me—might have wondered why. I thought it would be safer to entrust my secret to her alone. Besides, for a boy of eighteen, an offer from a girl as lovely as Anna was almost impossible to refuse.

As I slipped into her lean-to that evening I had to ask, "Why me?"

A smoky kerosene lamp cast an amber glow, throwing the recesses of her face into relief. "Since you don't allow passion to cloud your judgment while you're killing, you certainly won't let yourself get carried away by me." She took off her shirt as coolly as if she were in front of the family doctor and smiled at what she supposed was my modesty: I'd slipped into her sleeping bag without taking off my pants.

"Is this your first time?" she asked.

"No," I said.

"Ah." She slid off her pants. "Did you have a real and proper girl in Prague before the war?"

I nodded.

She lay next to me in the sleeping bag and placed her hand on my shoulder. "You can think of her now, if you wish."

As she closed her eyes, I imagined she was thinking of her boyfriend who'd died only months before in these woods. Yet I could not think of anyone. My mind was like an empty boat, unmoored, bobbing, belonging to no one.

"Did you picture her?" she asked afterward.

A bright moon shone through the opening in the tepeed blanket, casting a blue wash over her ruddy face. I propped myself up onto one elbow, trying to stare so hard that I'd never forget her classic Aryan beauty.

"Sarah?" I asked.

Anna blinked several times, batting away the darker girl's Biblical name.

"It would have seemed like a betrayal," I said.

"To her or to me?" she asked.

"To myself, I think."

She sat up and folded her legs Indian style, bending slightly forward so that her breasts fell into smooth cones.

"Graven images," she said with a strange smile.

I lay back and fell asleep so quickly that her words seemed from a dream. When I opened my eyes Anna was no longer by my side and the lean-to's blanket had been removed, exposing me to a circle of partisans. As I sat up and slipped on my pants Anna came forward with a rifle strapped across her shoulder. She was not the same woman who'd given herself to me the night before.

"Why did you lie to us?" she asked, addressing herself to the group as much as me.

I stared at her speechlessly.

"Do we have to make you pull down your pants so everybody can see?" one of the men in the circle said.

"I was afraid you'd kill me if I told the truth," I managed to say.

An argument ensued, with half the group wanting to take me deeper into the forest to shoot me in the head. Some said that since I'd lied I could no longer be trusted. Others wanted to kill me just because I was a Jew.

In order to resolve the dispute one of the leaders looked to Anna: "You decide."

"He may have been brought into this world a Jew, but he's also a born killer and we can still use him," she said, turning her back on me, disappearing into the forest.

I slipped away the first chance I got, before the Jew killers could get their hands on me. This time I had no illusions—I was on the run. My blind hope had fallen along with the bodies littering the roads and fields of that charred landscape. I had no idea why Anna had betrayed me. Perhaps if asked, she would have said I was the one who'd betrayed her and the rest of the group. Or simply, that betrayal itself was beside the point in this desecrated land; and to survive in a world torn asunder meant to betray and be betrayed.

***

The light inside Richard and Miriam's house went out, but the porch light remained on, tempting me to come forward and knock on their door. Yet whatever words I rehearsed in my mind sounded like excuses. I might have told Miriam that I'd lied to her father about why I'd come to the U.S., to avoid implicating him. But I no longer believed that myself.

I'd lied to others as well as myself because I was ashamed, not so much of what I'd done, but why I'd done it. I once believed I was taking lives in the name of humanity. When it got down to it, though, I'd killed in an attempt to make myself feel whole, hoping that would help me become part of the world again. Perhaps in some way it had—as a cop I sought justice in the names of others. Yet that did not make up for the fact that I'd murdered men in my own name. And even if I had not betrayed anyone else, I had betrayed myself.

That truth was all I had to offer Richard and Miriam, I thought, as I reached for the knob to turn off the radio. But I was stopped by an announcement on a news broadcast. A woman had been murdered in her house in Piedmont. The newscaster did not give the victim's name, but I knew who she was.

CHAPTER THIRTY-TWO

The air reeked of sulfur from flares patrolmen had dropped at both corners of the block to keep out unauthorized cars. Curious neighbors huddled outside a police-tape barrier strung around a telephone pole, several trees and a cast-iron streetlamp whose acorn globe threw an incandescent light that blanched onlookers' faces. I found a parking place among the jumble of official vehicles crowding the normally sleepy residential street—cars from the Alameda County Sheriff's Department, Piedmont Police Department, county coroner and medical examiner. Also government-issue Ford Fairlanes used by lab employees on twenty-four-hour call. Then, of course, there were the media vans. And even a couple of Oakland cops out of their jurisdiction leaned against their patrol car, as curious as the other spectators. It seemed little Piedmont had a big-time homicide on its hands and nobody wanted to be left out. The question was who was in charge?

I asked the Piedmont patrolman checking IDs at the front door how the killer had gotten into the house. He said as far as he knew there were no signs of forced entry. He never asked how I'd found out there'd been a homicide or what my business was. I probably could have walked straight upstairs to where the murder had been committed, but decided to get permission first. I located the chief of the Piedmont Police stationed in the middle of the living room, who was technically heading up the investigation.

"This is too much," he said when I introduced myself. He collared a sergeant and told him he wanted everyone out except Piedmont Police and the Alameda County homicide unit. "That includes you too," he said to me. "What's the SFPD doing here, anyway?"

"I'm working on a case that might be connected. I know my way around a crime scene and won't disturb a thing. Promise." When he hesitated, I added, "If these cases are related it could help your investigation."

"Okay," he growled. "Go ahead upstairs. But stay out of the way. When you're done, report back." The chief dismissed me by waving his hand to the left toward the staircase.

"Thank you," I said.

But when he was summoned outside, I wandered off to the right to look at two open drawers in a china cabinet next to the kitchen door. One contained a felt-lined silverware box that had been emptied. The other drawer also appeared to have been cleaned out. I bent down to look inside and saw a silver ladle hidden in the back. It might have been overlooked by a burglar. And then again, it could have been left there on purpose to let the police know that valuables were inside.

I glanced over my shoulder. Those in a position to see me were involved in other matters. I was more or less on my own for the moment. Using my handkerchief I slid open a drawer in the cabinet. It contained street maps and a Boy Scout compass. Another held dinner candles. A third, letters and papers of some sort. Whoever had opened the drawers must have known where the valuables were. A burglar unfamiliar with the house would have opened every drawer to see what was inside, and either closed them all to cover his tracks or not bothered to close any. So why were only two left open?

I heard voices through the open kitchen door and peeked inside. An Alameda County Sheriff's detective sat at a kitchen table interviewing a dark slender man with a heavy five o'clock shadow, dressed in a suit and tie. It had to be Judge Smith.

"I always do the same thing when I get home," he said in an almost inaudible drone. His eyes were immobile as if riveted on a nightmare. "First, I walk upstairs and go to the bathroom—"

The detective interrupted: "You're sure you didn't do anything else before you found your wife's body?"

"Yes, I'm sure. I always do the same thing," the judge repeated. "First go to the bathroom, then empty my pockets and take off my coat and tie, watch and ring. As you can see, I didn't get the chance." He stretched out his arm to show his wristwatch. Then he pulled a wallet out of his inside jacket pocket and reached into his pants pockets to show his keys and change.

"You didn't notice the looted drawers downstairs?" the detective asked.

The judge shoved things back in his pockets. "I guess not."

"So you went upstairs to go to the bathroom and... "

"I found her," the judge said, lowering his eyes as though he were finding her all over again.

"And that's when you called the police?"

The judge shook his head. "I took my son to a neighbor's. Somehow he hadn't heard a thing. He still doesn't know."

As the detective turned his head to write in a notebook he must have caught sight of me. He looked up. The judge also glanced over; his eyes were as hollow as those of the *musellmen* in the death camps. The detective frowned. I got the message and left.

I climbed the stairs past a lab tech dusting the handrail. A patrolman was blocking access to the bedroom. I showed him my ID and told him the chief said I could have a look around. After he let me through, the first thing I noticed were clothes from an open chest of drawers strewn around the floor. A lanky Sheriff's Department detective with a shock of tousled brown hair was down on his hands and knees sifting through the litter.

"Anything interesting?" I asked, flashing ID, which he didn't bother to look at.

"Never could get used to the durn things, myself," he said in a Southern accent, holding up a pair of blue polka-dot boxers. "Like wearing a lady's blouse down there."

I smiled to stay on friendly terms in case I wanted to ask him more questions.

In the bathroom a portly medical examiner squatted next to Mrs. Smith's body, which lay on the floor in front of the toilet. She was dressed in a white tennis skirt, red sleeveless jersey top and tennis shoes with white peds. No blood was visible on her clothing, but a splatter or two on the red top might not have been distinguishable from where I stood.

The toilet seat was up. A small pool of blood had puddled near Mrs. Smith's head, which appeared to have hit the side of the toilet as she fell. She didn't look as though she'd been struck, though; no bruises were on her face or arms. I was trying to figure out how she'd died when I noticed her head twisted to one side like the chickens dangling by their feet in the windows of poultry shops in Chinatown.

I inspected the bathroom door. The jamb was damaged around the strike plate, which dangled from its bottom screw. A scuffmark next to the knob was the only footprint on the door.

The detective in the bedroom peered beneath the bed. "Lookee here," he said, reaching underneath with a pencil. He fished out a ring and slid it down the pencil's orange shaft for me to see. "Must've rolled under. Guess that's why he missed it."

"Who?"

"The killer when he was digging through the drawers." He studied the ring. "Not bad. Eighteen karat." He spun the ring around on the pencil to get a different view, and read aloud the inscription inside: *Marli and Dodge forever.* "Roger dodger," he said with a chuckle.

"You sure it's a man's?" I asked.

He shouldn't have slid the ring onto his finger to check its size. But maybe he figured it didn't matter since the killer had probably never touched it. Anyway, the ring fit and he nodded. "Why? Something wrong?"

I shook my head and went back to the bathroom to have one last look. "Was that toilet seat up when she fell?" I asked the medical examiner.

He nodded and pointed to a smear of blood on the porcelain rim of the bowl.

I nodded back: I knew everything I needed to know for now.

I rushed down the stairs, through the front door and past the Piedmont Chief of Police, who was on the lawn talking to a captain from the Alameda Sheriff's Department and the newly arrived assistant D.A. Nearby, a TV news crew was folding up its equipment.

"Hey you," the chief called, snapping his fingers at me as I rushed by.

"I don't think there's any connection," I called back, now running full speed to my car.

CHAPTER THIRTY-THREE

"You open the door in the middle of the night without even asking who's there," I said to Nikki, who'd answered my knock with eyes half shut and bed-hair corkscrewing out from her head. So she'd know I meant business, I repressed even a hint of a smile at the willful young woman who now resembled a little girl in Winnie-the-Pooh flannel pajamas. Except for her mouth:

"Gimme a fuckin' break." She ran off, leaving the door wide open.

She returned dragging her mother by the hand. Elaine wore a faded *BEARS* sweatshirt that looked large enough to have belonged to her ex-husband, covering about as much as those minis young girls now wore. She had a pillow crease on the right side of her face and her short hair was wedged up to the left.

"May I come in?" I asked.

"At this hour?" Elaine said.

"I need to speak to you alone."

"No way!" Nikki stomped her foot. "I want to know what's going on too."

Elaine stepped aside and motioned for me to enter.

In the living room the three of us stood in silence until I turned to Nikki and said, "Please."

"Okay, but you have to tell me everything," she said to her mother before skulking off to her bedroom and slamming the door.

Elaine raised an eyebrow. "So?"

"Mrs. Smith's been murdered," I said.

"Oh, God, Marlene," she said, dropping onto the couch.

"I think you're in danger."

"Shit! Shit! Shit!" She banged her fist down, punctuating each curse, then looked up at me and said, "You promised if I confided in you—"

"I'm sorry," I said.

She got up, pulling the sweatshirt down over her thighs. "Wait here for me." She went down the hall into her bedroom.

I sat on the couch for a minute not knowing what to do with myself. I'd killed people and investigated the death of those who'd been killed, but it had never before been my duty to protect anyone. It wasn't now, either, at least not my professional duty. In fact, I'd be betraying my oath if I didn't return to headquarters and report everything I'd seen and heard. But with Judge Smith's haunted eyes fresh in my mind, I was reminded that the most severe penalty came from betraying oneself.

I paced around the living room, thinking Milan could get into the house no matter what precautions I took. Normally I prided myself on doing only what was needed, but unable to sit still I began checking points of entry.

The living room's bay window was fixed. The front door was solid with a good three-quarter-inch dead bolt. The two double-hung windows on the wall facing the driveway were locked and painted shut. They hadn't been used in years. Nikki's bedroom door was the first I came to in the hallway. I knocked. She opened it straightaway. Her light was on; she hadn't gone back to sleep.

"I'll just be a second," I said, stepping inside.

"What are you doing?" she asked, backing into the corner of the cluttered room. She turned around the sign that said *KISS A FASCIST PIG TODAY* so the words faced the wall.

I sidestepped a portable stereo and walked over a jumble of clothes, books, papers and what looked like plastic rollers for straightening her hair, although I couldn't believe she ever really used them.

"Is the front gate locked?" I asked, testing latches on two windows that faced a side-yard walkway.

She nodded and whispered, "Is this about what happened to Patty?"

I turned to her. "What do you know about that?"

"Did she get raped?" She swallowed hard to get out the question.

I shook my head.

"My mother interviews people who were... you know, like slaves. She says a piece of their souls got stolen, but you can learn to live that way, like people who've lost a limb. I'd rather live without an arm or a leg, though."

I put my hand on her shoulder, not knowing what to say. I was half surprised she didn't pull away.

"Do you want to check under the bed?" she asked.

"Maybe later," I said, patting her before withdrawing my hand.

I closed Nikki's door behind me and went into Elaine's office. The paint had worn off the side channels of the well-used double-hung windows. I made sure they were locked. Back in the hall I found the bathroom door shut. I thought Elaine might be inside and didn't bother to knock. I'd already worked out in my mind that the bathroom was backed by the kitchen and wouldn't have an exterior entrance.

I edged through the partially open door at the end of the hall that led to the master bedroom. Elaine had slipped on a pair of slacks and was sitting at a vanity. "A woman I knew has just been killed and like an idiot I'm futzing with mascara."

It was a good way to buy time, since she must have been wondering how much she could trust me. Last time we'd talked she'd told me about Mrs. Smith and then Mrs. Smith got killed.

"My mother would never see anyone unless she was totally put together," I said. "Old-world habits. I wear a tie when I go to the local hotdog stand."

I slipped between her chair and bed to inspect the closet.

"What do you think you're doing?" she asked.

The closet was arranged with dresses on the far left, followed by pants— evening separated from casual—skirts in the middle and long-sleeve then short-sleeve blouses on the right.

"Jackets and coats in the hall closet?" I asked.

"Underwear and bras in the top dresser drawer," she snapped. "You didn't answer me. What are you doing?"

I pushed aside the shoes on the closet floor. "Looking for an access door to the crawlspace under the house."

She gave me a reproving look and turned away. But when I glanced at her face reflected in the mirror she looked frightened.

Unable to find an access door on the closet floor, I put back the shoes. The shelf above the hanging clothes was piled almost to the ceiling with boxes for hats, shoes and other accessories. I pushed them aside into the empty space on the left to make room in the center to reach up to the ceiling.

"What happened to those missing boxes up here?" I asked.

"I thought you were looking for a door," she said.

I glanced at her reflection in the mirror and our eyes met, before hers slipped away.

"I found one," I said, using a wooden hanger to reach up and test a piece of painted plywood that covered the attic entry. It lifted without any trouble. I'd have to check the outside vent to see if Milan could climb into the attic. My guess was that breaking in that way would be unnecessarily difficult, though.

I went over to a sliding wood window above the king bed, which was covered with decorative pillows hiding the ones used for sleeping.

"You didn't have to make the bed for me," I said.

Elaine responded with a few angry strokes as she brushed her hair.

The window was unlocked. I leaned over the bed and rotated the latch into the catch, but it wouldn't hold fast. That was probably how Milan had gotten in when he'd stolen Chris Cantwell's files.

"Did you know this window won't lock?" I asked.

She got up and leaned over the other side of the bed to have a look, then shrugged. "Is all this fussing really necessary?"

"No more than you fussing with yourself," I said.

She narrowed her eyes to let me know I'd stepped over the line.

I went down the hall to the bathroom. Elaine must have closed the bathroom door to hide the mess from Nikki's and her toiletries, which competed for space in the house's only bathroom. It looked to me as though Elaine was supposed to have the left side of the cultured marble sink top, where things were lined up in some semblance of order. On the right, Nikki's tubes, jars and brushes spilled not only into her mother's territory, but on top of the toilet tank and even onto the floor where a hair dryer was lying in the corner. The only things that seemed to coexist harmoniously were yellow and pink toothbrushes cozily reclining inside a glass.

I found a toilet plunger behind the toilet. Pulling the wooden handle out of the rubber head I returned to the bedroom and laid it on the bottom channel of the window. If Milan tried to slide open the window, the handle would act as a stop. I turned my attention to a glass-paned door that opened onto a redwood deck. He could break in almost silently with a glass cutter. There wasn't much I could do about that.

"I've got a few more things to check," I said.

Elaine kept applying lipstick as if I hadn't spoken.

I found an access door to the crawlspace built into the hall closet's floor. Its brass handle lifted and turned to release a brass bolt. The lock wasn't much and could easily be broken. But I didn't think Milan would bother entering from under the house. It was too dark and confined.

Elaine came out of the bedroom, wearing a bright lime-green top that made her eyes sparkle.

"You're staring, Simon."

"You changed clothes."

"If you were a good detective you'd know it's not for you. Anyway, let's get this inspection—or whatever you want to call it—over with."

"I still have to look outside."

"Let's go," she said, sweeping her arms through the air and leading the way through the kitchen to the back door.

"Where's the attic vent?" I asked as we headed up the driveway.

"I don't even know where the fuse box is," she said, dismissing me with a laugh I didn't much like.

On the back lawn I pointed up under the roof's gable and said in a lecturing tone, "That's called an attic vent. If you'll notice, it's a little over a foot square. Too small for a man to crawl through."

She turned on me. "Look, this bullshit—"

"Isn't getting us anywhere."

"And where exactly do you think we're going, Simon?"

I was taken aback.

"You think I'm some gullible woman who believes putting a stupid toilet plunger in my bedroom window is going to stop Cantwell's hit man?"

I shook my head and took out my pack of cigarettes. She didn't take one when offered. I lit two anyway and handed her one.

"I don't know what you're doing here," she said, "but I do know that nobody else gives a shit what happens to me or my daughter." She took a deep drag. As she exhaled I could see faint edges of the smoke in the moonlight. "How much danger am I in?"

"Two women have been killed and you saw what happened to Patricia. If I hadn't been there—"

"I'm taking Nikki into hiding," she said.

"He'll find you."

"What do you suggest, then?"

"Get Nikki as far away from you as possible."

"No fucking way," Elaine said. "I'm not letting her out of my sight."

"You want her in the line of fire when he comes after you? She's impulsive enough—"

"To try to save me," Elaine said. "Shit!" She stomped out her cigarette. "Why are you helping us?"

"That's my job," I said.

"If you were really doing your job, you'd be trying to convince me to be a witness against Cantwell."

"Why do you think I'm trying to help you, then?"

"I don't know. I think for some reason you've crawled out on a limb, and I'm not sure I want to be the only one keeping you company."

I stared out into the night sky. The stars were so thick I felt their weight upon us.

"You need somebody to protect you," I said.

"The way you protected Marlene Smith?"

CHAPTER THIRTY-FOUR

Elaine reluctantly agreed to take Nikki to a friend's house tomorrow morning. But that's all she agreed to. When I asked if I could sleep on her couch to keep watch, she said I'd be just as likely to attract trouble as repel it. So I spent the night in my car parked across the street. It was a sleepless night, but I must have nodded off for a few minutes after dawn. I was awakened by the smell of coffee through the car window, which I'd left open to hear the sound of slamming doors, screams or other indications of trouble. Nikki had crossed the street barefoot in jeans and a tie-dyed T-shirt and now stood outside the car door with a steaming mug.

"Lots of milk." She handed it to me. "The way my mom's other friends with foreign accents take it."

I slipped my hand off the .38 Special lying on my lap and took the coffee. It was rich and warm with just the right touch of bitterness. "Did she ask you to bring it?"

Nikki shook her head. "She just got up and doesn't even know you're here."

"She won't like it when she finds out," I said.

"Once she knows I'm okay, she'll be okay." She pointed to my pistol. "Do you always sleep with that thing?"

"How come you're not in school?" I slid the .38 into my shoulder holster.

"On Saturday?"

"Berkeley High, right?" I got out of the car and set the coffee mug on the roof. "Did you like Claremont Prep better?"

"How would you like being separated from your friends?"

"How come you left?"

"Like cops never make deals?" She gave a self-satisfied smile, probably proud of keeping up with a cop in this game of answering one question with another. "You want to go on the back porch where it's sunny?"

We walked out of the long shadow of an elm, across the street into the low morning sun. The air had a hint of sea salt and balm from eucalyptuses farther up the hill. I welcomed the first pangs of hunger. Even though I'd spent the night in my car and needed a shower, I couldn't remember ever having felt quite so ready for the world.

"What kind of deal did you make?" I asked when we got onto the porch.

Nikki rested her spine against the waist-high wood railing and arched her neck, stretching with the nonchalance of youth. Black tangles of hair tumbled free, soaking up rays of the rising sun.

"Are cops like always cops?" she asked.

I took out my cigarettes and she playfully filched one out of the pack, as she might from one of her school chums.

I lit the cigarette for her. "What kind of deal did you make?"

She took a long drag and held up the cigarette to say thanks.

"Mom didn't like some of the kids I was hanging around with at Claremont and sent me down to live with my dad. I hated it with him. So the deal was I could come back and stay here if I transferred schools."

"Where does your dad live?"

"L.A. I ran away and hitched back to Berkeley," she said, blowing one smoke ring into another.

The sun, cigarette and coffee were too comforting for me to get worked up about any threat that wasn't immediate. So I simply said, "Hitchhiking's dangerous, especially for a young girl."

"You're as paranoid as my mom. It's like the 60s, man."

"Peace, love and world harmony," I said.

"You don't believe in that?"

"If the world hasn't changed in six thousand years, why should it start now?"

"Anyway, nothing bad happened, but it sure freaked Mom out."

She blew three more quick smoke rings.

"I guess that was the idea, huh?"

"I told her I'm not leaving Berkeley. The rest of the world's too fucking materialistic." She shook out her hair as if to rid it of excess wisdom.

"So you didn't like living with your father?"

"Are you kidding? I swear, everybody down there has sold out. He's a shrink, too, you know, but even more successful than my mom. She's into all this do-good jazz. He's just into money. And he'd better be, the way my stepmom spends it on herself and their two brats."

Nikki's eyes darted to the door as she dropped the cigarette behind the porch onto the driveway. But not fast enough. Busted by Mom. Elaine hadn't changed the clothes she'd worn last night and had dark circles under her eyes.

"I felt sorry for him out in his car, so I brought him coffee," Nikki said.

Elaine pursed her lips while evaluating the situation. "Go get ready to leave, Nikki." The girl went into the house and closed the back door. "You won her over, anyway," Elaine said, glancing down at smoke from Nikki's discarded cigarette rising up over the side of the porch.

"You want me to drive you?" I asked.

"I'm not going to get rid of you, am I?"

I shook my head and thought I detected a smile from her.

***

Elaine and Nikki jockeyed for the bathroom for over an hour. Neither looked as if she'd done a whole hell of a lot to herself after they'd finished. Not that either could look bad. The idea was to be attractive without appearing to have tried. A reversal from what I'd known growing up, when women wanted others to notice how much effort they'd put into preparing themselves for the world.

Yet I could see the evidence of how much work they'd done to themselves when I went into the bathroom to wash up before leaving. Things were thrown every which way, making the small space appear somewhat more cluttered, even though Nikki had taken many of her toiletries and cosmetics.

I drove a circuitous route to Nikki's friend in Orinda, circling the campus on deserted side streets to make sure we weren't being followed. When we finally pulled up in front of the house, Nikki said, "So are you two having a weekend thing? Is that why you're trying to get rid of me?"

"I think you know better," Elaine said, giving her wiseass daughter a fond chuck on the cheek.

As Elaine watched Nikki carry her overnight bag toward the house, she said, "I hope to hell you're right, because if anything happens to her... "

I would have blamed myself, too, I thought as I drove away.

"How about I take you to wherever it was you wanted to hide out," I said.

"And then what?" she asked.

"I'm going to try to contact Cantwell and see if I can make a deal."

"What kind of deal?"

"I'll tell him you've agreed to keep your mouth shut. You'll even lie in front of a judge if you have to."

"And what makes you think that'll satisfy him?" she asked.

"I spoke to the call girl who got killed—"

"A dead prostitute—great source."

"She came to my apartment and told me what happened with Chris and his father."

"Pillow talk from a dead prostitute—even better."

"Look, if you want to know about my sex life—"

She turned away and looked out the passenger window.

"She reminded me of you," I said.

"I'd like to hear you explain that one."

"She couldn't stop herself from mouthing off, either."

Elaine slowly broke into a smile and put two fingers up to her lips, motioning for a smoke.

"I figure that's what got her killed," I said, handing her the pack.

She lit a cigarette for each of us with the car lighter and handed me one.

"What happened to Marlene Smith?" she asked.

I gave her an overview of the circumstances surrounding Mrs. Smith's death.

"How can you be sure it was Milan?" she asked.

I explained that an average burglar, more used to quietly entering through windows than kicking in doors, would not have known how to kick down a bathroom door with one well-placed boot. Nor would he have known how to break a person's neck. That was an assassin's trick: it was sudden, silent and did not require a weapon.

She gave me a questioning glance when I mentioned assassins.

"Since there was no forced entry," I added, "somebody must have let the killer in."

"Why would Mrs. Smith have invited him in?"

"I think the judge did," I said.

"But Judge Smith said his wife was dead when he got home."

"He lied about a lot of things," I said. "He emptied out those silverware drawers to make it look like the motive was burglary. He also used the toilet when he got home."

"How do you know that?" she asked.

"His wife used that same toilet during the day so the seat should have been down."

"He wouldn't have stepped over her body to pee," Elaine mused haltingly, probably stopped by the picture conjured in her mind. "Still I can't believe that Roger Smith would let Milan into his house to kill his wife."

"Milan didn't come to kill her," I said. "If he had, he would have waited for her to be alone. And he would have done his business downstairs, fast."

"So he came to pressure them into silence," Elaine said.

"But why would Cantwell worry about her talking now, a year after the rape?"

Elaine lowered her eyes.

"What?" I said.

"I told you Marlene came to see me after Chris raped her."

"That's how you knew so much about her," I said.

"What I didn't tell you, though, was that she called me a week ago to tell me Chris had come back and done it again. She was still alive then and I'd promised her—"

I waved off the apology—we'd both kept secrets from one another for our own good reasons. "Since his father and her husband had made a deal, Chris knew he could get away with it again."

"She swore she wasn't going to let him this time," Elaine said. "She said she was ready to talk to anybody who'd listen, including the press."

"Do you know if she did?"

Elaine shook her head. "Her husband talked her out of it. He told her to wait a week or two so—"

"He and Cantwell could figure out another way to shut her up," I said. "Maybe she decided the only way to care of things was by killing the kid."

Elaine gazed out the car window at the green Orinda hills. "You think Cantwell had her killed for revenge?"

I shook my head. "He's attacking women who are uncooperative, whether he thinks they've murdered his son or not."

"You think they know I told you that Chris raped Mrs. Smith?" she asked, eyes downcast with fear.

"They seemed to have found out about everything else," I said. "But what worries me most was that Milan said you needed to learn your place."

She looked at me indignantly, but that visceral reaction was quickly overcome with the reality of her situation.

"I guess I haven't been all that cooperative."

We entered the darkness of the Caldecott Tunnel, heading back to Berkeley. We'd left Elaine's house without eating breakfast. I was famished, and Elaine said she might be able to eat something too. As we took the Berkeley exit off Highway 24, she suggested we stop at the Claremont Hotel for breakfast. I'd never been to the Claremont. It was a bit pricey for me.

"Let's go to the Merritt," I said.

"I'll pay," she said.

I was the one who usually read other peoples' minds.

"I don't let women pay for me," I said.

"Really?" she said, lowering her eyebrows in disbelief.

"It's custom, that's all," I said.

"Maybe it's time for you to leave some of that old-world baggage behind," she said.

We may not have been in the Old World, but the Claremont did everything to make it seem as though we were, including little round tables with white table cloths and cloth napkins. Waiters who bowed from the hip too. Yet when all was said and done, their pancakes, bacon, eggs, hash browns and toast were no better than at the Merritt Coffee Shop. Elaine had ordered a fruit cup and poached egg, but had yet to eat more than a few bites of unbuttered toast.

"So where do you want me to take you when we leave here?" I asked.

"Home," she said.

I shook my head emphatically.

She picked up a grape and threw it back into the fruit cup. "If he can't find me he'll go after Nikki for bait."

"He won't get anybody if I'm waiting at your house for him," I said.

"You'd just sleep out in your car if I didn't say yes," she said with a wan smile.

"You should eat something," I said.

She popped the discarded grape into her mouth. "Satisfied?"

"Do you think Mrs. Smith murdered Chris?" I asked.

"I don't know. You've dealt with more killers than I have."

"Do you think a normal woman could be driven to kill so coldly and deliberately?" I rephrased the question.

"A normal woman under abnormal circumstances," she said.

"For a person with a conscience, taking another person's life on her own—without being a soldier or a cop or part of some other group she believed in—that act would separate her from everybody. She'd end up feeling absolutely alone."

"She was already alone," Elaine said.

"Not that way," I said. "Even when the world turns its back on us, we still want to be a part of it. Very few people are willing to take the chance of never being included again."

"Who are you talking about?" Elaine asked.

"For example," I said, "there were members of the *Nokim* who were incapable of actually handling the murder weapon."

"The *Nokim*?" she said, looking at me quizzically.

"They were the Haganah's avengers."

"I know who they were." She pushed aside her poached egg cup. "Let's get out of here. I suddenly can't stand the smell of food."

CHAPTER THIRTY-FIVE

We cut across the Berkeley-Oakland hills toward my apartment to pick up clean clothes and toiletries. Mostly we were silent. I waited for Elaine to ask about the *Nokim*. I thought I might have been willing to talk about the terrible freedom that came from being abandoned by the world. When I remembered the millions of lives "legally" taken under the orders of one country or another, acting on my own against a few genocidal murderers didn't seem like a crime. Yet I wondered if a woman with clean hands could ever get past where mine had been.

David and Wiki were out front with two sleeping bags opened on the lawn. He was on his knees pinning one down while she swept it with a kitchen broom. When Wiki saw Elaine, she said, "Hey, you're the chick from the Terrace, right?"

"That very chick," Elaine said, with a playfulness that hadn't been present in the car. "Going camping?"

"If you call sleeping out in Sproul Plaza camping," Wiki said.

"Quiet, Wiki," David said, getting to his feet.

Wiki glanced in Elaine's direction and raised an eyebrow.

"What's going on?" I asked.

"Like you don't know that an army of cops is going to blockade the campus Monday morning," David said.

"I never heard anything about a blockade."

But I didn't tell him that I'd been out of touch with police demonstration plans for several days now. I hadn't even spoken to Richard in nearly twenty-four hours.

"It's not going to work, man," David said. "We'll have our own army sleeping over Sunday night."

"I bet the blockade's a rumor," I said, "and spending the night's a waste of time."

"Never know," Wiki said, winking at Elaine. "Could be romantic,"

"You'll get to cuddle up and share ghost stories under the stars," Elaine said.

"Hey, you two can join us," Wiki said. "We'll loan you one of our bags. It'll be like an old-fashioned sleepover."

"Sounds cozy," Elaine said, heading toward the front porch, "but we're over thirty."

"Hey, I never bought into that shit," Wiki called after her. "I've always trusted my parents."

As we entered my living room Elaine folded her arms across her chest. At first I thought it was because the apartment was chilly—I always left the windows open—but then I noticed how she was taking in the barrenness of the place. No colorful paintings on the wall or abstract sculptures or lopsided pottery, not even curtains to hide the yellowed window shades. I'd rented the apartment furnished in brown Herculon and Formica. My only additions had been a fake wood-grained TV and a few inexpensive ceramic ashtrays, also brown.

"If you don't mind, I'm going to shower and shave," I said, removing my jacket.

She sat down on the couch and said, "Make yourself at home."

I left the bedroom door ajar so I could hear out into the living room, got out of my clothes and tossed them on the bed. I grabbed a clean pair of underwear and T-shirt from a drawer. From the closet I pulled down a pair of brown wool slacks and a white dress shirt. I was about to add a brown-and-gold striped tie, but decided to eighty-six the neckwear. I'd roll up the shirt's sleeves and open the top button.

I was fully prepared to shed some of that old-world baggage Elaine had talked about, until I came out of the bathroom after my shower and found her packing a small valise that I'd kept hidden in a corner of my closet.

"What are you doing?" I asked.

She balled up a pair of socks she'd taken from one of my bureau drawers and said, "You went in my closet."

"I'm talking about that," I said, pointing to the valise.

She threw in the socks. "It's a suitcase, isn't it?"

I stepped up to the bed and pushed her aside.

"Hey!" she said.

She'd folded two piles on my pillow: the first was clothes I'd haphazardly thrown on the bed before showering; the second, stuff I'd kept packed in the suitcase.

"Why did you take those clothes out?" I asked. "They're clean—haven't been worn."

"In how long?" she asked.

"Sixteen years."

"Where were you planning on taking them if things got bad, Simon?"

Once I'd dreamed of Israel or even Prague, but where was home now?

She put her hand on my forearm. "We all dream of getting the hell out sometime," she said, smiling and crinkling up her nose, "but—"

I jerked my arm away.

"You think you're cute?" I said, patting the inner pocket along the back of the suitcase. "Okay, what did you do with it?" I ran my hand under the elastic strap, inside the pocket.

"Do with what?" she said.

"Don't play games, Elaine, it's loaded."

She watched coldly with hands on hips as I dumped the contents of her purse onto the bed: lipstick, compact, comb, wallet, Kleenex, parking stub— no pistol.

She raised her eyebrows, asking if I was satisfied.

That's when it dawned on me that Milan must have broken into my apartment and stolen the Beretta.

"You don't trust me," she said.

"Do you trust me?" I asked.

She thought about it. "Would you have been so eager to come to my rescue if I'd been twenty years older?"

When I didn't answer she glanced down at the valise I'd kept since my days with the *Nokim*.

"Why would any woman in her right mind trust a man who's just marking time?" she asked.

"How about you?" I said. "What do you think all your folding and refolding and putting everything in its place is about?"

She flashed those piercing eyes to tell me to back off.

"You're waiting for your parents to come back and tell you you've been a devoted daughter."

She balled up a T-shirt and threw it into the suitcase.

"But they're dead, just like mine," I said, heading out of the bedroom.

Halfway into the living room I heard her call out, "Hey, asshole."

I turned around.

She stood in the bedroom doorway with my T-shirt in her hand and tears streaming down her face. "Fold your own fucking clothes," she said, flinging the shirt across the room. It landed on my Formica dining room table.

She wiped her eyes and nose with the back of her hand and stormed back into the bedroom, returning with the suitcase full of my clothes.

She dumped out everything and kicked pajamas, shirts and underwear across the floor. She caught a pair of blue boxers on her toe and they flew up in the air, landing on top of my floor lamp, covering the yellowed shade.

I didn't know why, but everything suddenly struck me as funny.

"I guess the place could use some color at that," I said, smiling and flicking the corner of my boxer shorts.

"You're not getting off that easy," she said, kicking the last garment at her feet, a pair of trousers I'd worn before I took a shower. I dodged the pants as they slid past me and were stopped by a leg of my plaid Herculon-covered chair.

"I'm sorry I said those things about your parents," I said.

Her eyes met mine for a slight moment before looking down at my feet.

"What's that?" she asked.

"What's what?"

She walked straight toward me, veering away at the last second and bending from the waist, purposely bumping me aside with her hip as she reached under the chair.

"This," she said, straightening up, holding my tin heart in her palm.

"It was in my pocket," I said.

Something about the way the object had stopped under the chair triggered an unconscious connection that wouldn't surface, like a word stuck on the tip of my tongue. One thing I was conscious of, though, was that Elaine could sense I was controlling the urge to snatch the tin heart out of her hand. But taking away my keepsake would have brought up the issue of trust. So I waited until she laid the heart in my palm.

"But what is it?" she asked.

"Somebody made if for me. It was like my horseshoe." I slipped it into my pocket. "Something that got me through."

"Or perhaps it was the thought of the person who made it that gave you hope," she said, picking up my pants from the floor, folding them and laying them over the back of the chair.

"At most a thought," I said.

"Sometimes that's all we have to go on." She smiled with a kind of sated exhaustion as she sat on the arm of the chair. "I guess neither of us is perfect."

I sat in the chair with her close above me, straining my neck to look up at her.

She shook her head dolefully.

"What?" I asked.

"I can't get that whole thing with Marlene out of my mind. You think her husband followed them upstairs?"

I nodded.

Her eyes grew wide, bright and blank, like a movie screen when the film has broken.

"He watched that animal kill her," she said. "Can you imagine what it must be like to stand helplessly by while—"

"Yes," I said from somewhere deep in my throat.

Elaine waited for me to say more. When I remained silent, she got off the chair's arm and crouched in front of me, putting her hands on my knees.

"Talk to me, Simon, for God's sake."

"We were in the middle of packing our bags," I said. "All set to go. My father's cousin who lived in Oakland had agreed to sponsor us. My parents had been saving my mother's most valuable jewelry. They'd lived in poverty, holding it in reserve for that moment. I don't know how the police found out. Anyway, they came for us that morning."

"The SS?"

"No. Czech police. Henleins. No other Czechs would have treated us as if... They might have turned us over, but they wouldn't have... In cold blood, without any provocation."

"Both of your parents?"

"They spared my mother, if you can call it that. And left my father alive long enough to hear her pleas and moans from the bedroom. Then they dragged her out naked to watch. One of the cops who said he wouldn't dirty himself with a Jewish cow was still dressed in uniform when he put the gun in my father's mouth. I was huddled in a corner. I wanted to yell, but couldn't find my voice. I soiled myself when my father's blood splattered my mother's arms. Still I recovered faster than her. I had to hold her hand until we got to Theresienstadt and they separated the men from the women."

"Was she ever able to take care of herself again?"

"She was able to care for her body—everything else became a lie to her."

Elaine put her hand on my face. "But not to you." She lowered her hand, which fell into a fist by her thigh. "I don't think I could remain sane and watch someone I loved being... "

I let my gaze settle into hers. Everything was clear, like still waters, which I wanted to remain undisturbed.

It was she who stirred the waters first: "Simon, I need to tell you something."

I took hold of her hands, wanting to tell her that I trusted her beyond question.

"You don't need to tell me anything," I said.

CHAPTER THIRTY-SIX

We stopped for dinner at Kaspers where we sat with other Lake Merritt locals at the counter around the hot-dog steamer. I'd wanted to take her someplace nicer, but she'd insisted on one of my regular haunts. She even said I could pay this time.

"You'll let me treat you to a taste of my cheap, solitary existence," I said.

She'd laughed as she took a bite of her dog dressed like mine with French's mustard, tomatoes and even onions. She'd been laughing ever since we'd gotten out of my bed, even at the fact that I didn't laugh much.

"It's just that I'd rather go someplace we can be ourselves this evening," she'd said.

We didn't get back to her house until after dark, where we sat together on the sofa and made small talk until about ten. She went into the bathroom to get ready for bed. She'd been in there a while when I heard running water and figured she was brushing her teeth. I got up off the couch and considered going out onto the back porch for a cigarette. Instead, I took a few more turns around the living room. Truth was, I didn't know what to do with myself. Too many things were pulling at me.

Why hadn't Milan come after Elaine? She knew at least as much about Cantwell as Lari Zohn and Mrs. Smith, if not more. What made her different? Or maybe he was waiting in the shadows, trying to rattle my patience?

Then there was this new turn of events between Elaine and me. It wasn't just that we'd made love. I'd told her what happened to my mother and father. And after my mother's death, I thought I'd never again have to face the shame of that moment reflected in someone else's eyes.

I couldn't deny the sex had also been different, as we stripped ourselves of past, present and future. No shame, guilt or regret in those wordless moments. Just animal sounds carried by our breaths along one another's skin. No thoughts. Simply the restless journey to discover how our limbs best fit one another's body. It was afterwards, when the words and thoughts returned, I'd found myself stranded with the image of Sarah's heart in Elaine's hand.

Lying in my bed with her head on my shoulder, Elaine again had asked about the lucky charm. I wanted to tell her everything about Sarah and my childhood life in Prague before Theresienstadt. But the more I talked, the less substance it all seemed to have, as if words only served to rob my life of its gravity: "Just a girl I kissed once."

Elaine propped herself up on one elbow, her face hovering above mine like an impossibly close moon. "Growing up is difficult enough without having to hide from Nazis. You shared the last moments of your innocence with Sarah. You locked part of yourself away for protection, the part with her in it."

"I can do without the shrink talk," I said, turning away.

Elaine rolled me on my back and got up on her hands and knees, straddling me. She stuck a big, fat, fake smile in my face. "Better?"

"Worse."

"Grump," she said, climbing off.

"So now you know who you jumped into bed with," I said.

She pressed her body to mine, breasts flattened against my back. "Yes. And I only wish I had as much courage." She kissed me on the neck.

Now, standing in front of Elaine's kitchen waiting for her to get out of the bathroom, I was reminded of all I hadn't told her. All the parts of myself I'd withheld. Those last seconds of life I'd shared with the men I'd slain as they'd unveiled layers of themselves: first animal fierceness, then primitive fear, and finally—as they lay their heads against the floor or wall or even a few times on my legs—a kind of bloody trust that goes beyond words. Mine was the last face they'd ever see, and we could not help but share an otherworldly kind of bond.

Elaine came out of the bathroom in the CAL sweatshirt she'd worn the night before. It was hard to believe that only twenty-four hours had passed since then.

"I'm going to bed," she said. "Are you coming?"

"In a few minutes."

She looked at me questioningly but did not ask why. "I'll be reading, waiting for you, okay?"

As I heard the bedroom door close, I was again plagued by the image of her picking up Sarah's heart. Why had it bothered me so much? Was I so lost in my past that I would never be able to allow myself a future?

I went over to the cabinet and opened the drawer where I'd seen Elaine's wedding photo. I leafed through handbills from performances at the Berkeley Repertory Theatre, American Conservatory Theater and the San Francisco Opera. I picked up a letter without a stamp or return address, with *Doc Lady* handwritten on the envelope. Inside was a sheet of blue-lined notebook paper. It was printed in a childlike hand.

> I hear Nikki's back in town from her dad's. Guess she couldn't stay away from me. I can be oh so charming when the mood's right. She says I'm a "cutie pie." I haven't shown her much different yet. It's too much fun watching cool cucumbers like you waiting for the other shoe and we both know it's going to drop. I'll be helping her out though. It's no good for little girls to be stuck up. I look forward to passing you on the street and watching your eyes scamper away like frightened little mice. It won't be because you don't want to see my cutie pie face either. It'll be all about that other cold mug you know real good now. I'm going to make sure you see me every day for the rest of your life, remembering what it was like to watch your damaged goods come home from school with her head down like a good little cow. Watch your back, mom... Moo!

I put away the letter, knowing who it was from, and went into the bathroom to wash up. As I pushed aside sundries in the medicine cabinet, looking for toothpaste, a jar of pancake makeup caught my attention. I'd only noticed lipstick, mascara and perhaps a little blush on Elaine and Nikki. Pancake makeup wasn't part of their look. Of course, it could have been left over, something Elaine had once used. Yet some disturbing connection between Chris's threatening letter and Elaine holding Sarah's misshapen heart caused me to open the jar. Its rose fragrance took me back to the hotel room where I'd last smelled it.

I pictured myself lifting Chris's wallet out from under the chair the way Elaine had picked up Sarah's gift. How had it gotten there? If his wallet had simply fallen out of his pants when they were being folded, it would have landed in front of the chair, not under it. Chris must have thrown his pants the way Elaine had thrown mine, and that's when his wallet slipped out of the pocket and slid under the hotel chair. If he had discarded his clothes in a reckless moment of passion, why would a prostitute have picked them up? Why not get down to business? And after Chris had OD'd, who would bother wasting valuable get-away time making sure everything was folded?

Then there was Chris's menacing note. I recalled how Nikki had told me her mother had sent her to Los Angeles to live with her father to get her away from bad kids she was associating with at Claremont Prep. She must have been talking about Chris. But after Nikki hitchhiked back home, Elaine knew that transferring the girl to Berkeley High would not be enough to protect her from an obsessed psychopath. Since the police weren't going to help, she had nowhere to turn.

I went into the hall and saw light coming from under the bedroom door. The thought briefly passed through my mind of going to Elaine. But I turned into her office and closed the door behind me. Taking three steps through the dark to the corner of the desk, I lifted my hand chest high to where I remembered I'd find the switch to the desk lamp.

I sat behind the desk. The three drawers on the right did not have locks. The bottom one contained pamphlets and brochures on various academic programs and conferences. Letters from professionals were in the center drawer. In the top, stationery, envelopes and business cards were laid neatly between angled wooden slats. I picked up one of Elaine's cards. When she'd first given it to me at her campus office, saying I should call her if I wanted somebody to talk to, I'd shoved it in my pocket without reading it carefully. I studied her title: *Dr. Elaine Meyers, M.D.* It struck me that she was not merely a psychotherapist, but a medical doctor too.

Now I wanted to get into the locked drawers on the left. I was prepared to break into them. But first I opened the wide center drawer, pulling it out as far as it would go before it stopped on catches. Crouching under the desk I located the metal levers that released the drawer. When I pulled it out I found the spare key that comes taped to the back of these drawers when desks are sold. Most people don't even know they're there.

The key unlocked the drawers on the left. The two bottom drawers contained private correspondence with other doctors, various Holocaust groups, government agencies and writers working on manuscripts about the Holocaust. It was in the top drawer that I finally found her prescription pad. Across its top was written *Doctor's Association*.

"Simon?" Elaine said, opening the door and surveying the mess on top of her desk.

I got up and handed her the prescription pad. "I found your morphine prescription at Payless Drugs with Mrs. Cantwell's name forged on it."

She crossed to her desk, laid down the pad, gathered herself and turned to me. "I wanted to tell you the first time you came to my office. I couldn't bring myself to. I was about to say something at your apartment, but we kissed and—"

I shook my fist in the air. "God, can't you leave anyone alone?"

"What?" she said, backing away.

I lowered my hand. "I wasn't talking to you."

"You don't believe in God."

"He couldn't have planned it better," I said, pushing past her.

***

I walked down the hall, cut through the kitchen and out the back door, thinking of the quote Milan had left on the Nazis flier: *What misery to be wise when wisdom profits nothing.* On the porch I lit my last cigarette, crumpled the pack and threw it on the ground, then stomped out the smoke after a few drags. I headed toward the street past Elaine's Volvo, which was parked in the driveway, blocking my car. I'd purposely hidden the Citroen in the garage, hoping to take Milan by surprise if he attacked.

When I got to the end of the driveway, across the street I saw the disembodied ember of a cigarette floating under a smudge of black sky where elm leaves blocked out the stars. As my eyes adjusted to the light from a partially clouded moon, I made out the silhouette of a figure leaning against a white Camaro.

I bounded across the street and swiped the cigarette from his mouth. Grabbing hold of his coat, I pulled him to his feet and slammed him up against the Camaro's rear fender. I felt the .38 resting against my ribs. Mrs. Cantwell's words, "Nobody will miss him," crossed my mind as I reached under my jacket. Milan smiled like a boy playing a game of cops and robbers.

I pulled out my weapon and put it against his temple. "Do you also find this amusing?"

"Ironic, perhaps," he said. "What are you going to do with her?"

My eyes had adjusted to the darkness, and our faces were close enough to see he didn't show the slightest trace of fear.

"If you think I'm going to let you and Cantwell—"

"He's the reason she's still alive," Milan said. "Politicians can afford to be sentimental, I guess."

"Not too sentimental to put the clamps on her when she's under police custody," I said.

"He doesn't want her arrested. That's why he wants your help to—"

"I'll help him" I said, pulling back the hammer with my thumb.

"You want to leave me by the roadside the way you did the SS—fine, you'll have cops crawling all over this street, right up to her doorstep. That's the last thing a woman concealing a murder needs."

He was right.

Milan slowly raised his left hand, pushing aside the gun barrel with an index finger. I eased down the trigger, forgetting the advantage he had by being left-handed. He made his move, grabbing the barrel with a powerful forehand. He must have backhanded the butt across my temple. I blacked out. When I came to, I was lying on the street, tasting a salt-sweet trickle of blood. I sat up and thought I saw the blurred image of my .38 Special tucked into his belt. But I had trouble focusing. With my head spinning, I rose to my feet.

It seemed in slow motion that Milan whipped around his foot, the heel of his boot catching me in the solar plexus. I doubled over, putting my hands on my knees as I fought for breath. I tried to straighten up but felt as though my gut was being twisted from the inside. He took one long step forward. I saw his fist coming, but didn't feel it connect. The uppercut lifted me off my feet.

He must have been standing over me, waiting for me to open my eyes. When I did, the sole of his combat boot slammed into my face. Next the steel toe caught me just below the heart. I wasn't sure if I heard the crack or just felt the vibration travel up my torso and through my head. I pulled my knees up to my chest, curling into the fetal position. The fluttering of my heart seemed to come from just outside my body.

Milan pulled out his pack of Players. He took a moment to light a cigarette, taking a long self-satisfied drag. "Ready to talk now?"

"About what?" I asked, trying to sit up, but with the pain in my gut I could only prop myself on my elbows.

"Making sure she remains silent."

"Unlike you, I've never been very good at silencing women," I said.

The sole of Milan's boot connected with my temple. He wanted to hurt me bad, but not bad enough to use the steel toe. Next thing I remembered, he was lifting my head by the hair. I felt the sting of the cigarette on the crown of my skull, then came the stench of burning hair and flesh. He pounded my head against the blacktop and lifted it by the hair. The only way I knew my head had hit the pavement again was by the sound of my teeth clattering against each other. Warm blood spread through my hair and dripped down my neck.

When I opened my eyes, Milan had Sarah's heart in his hand. He tossed it onto my sleeve, saying "But men like us can't afford to be too sentimental."

He walked over to the Camaro and opened the door. "Cantwell wants to meet you at Fort Point at ten o'clock tomorrow night. Come alone."

He opened the door to the Camaro with my .38 still in his belt.

"I don't care what Cantwell says—we know what's best for him," he said. "Anyone who doesn't agree to keep silent is dead and that includes your girlfriend."

He got into the Camaro and started it up. I lay on the street and heard the engine recede into the night. The sound faded away into the darkness descending over my mind.

CHAPTER THIRTY-SEVEN

I was not aware that Elaine had come to get me until I was already on my feet with my arm around her shoulder, taking step by faltering step toward her house. Nor did I remember her examining me on the bed, and only vaguely recalled that she took off my clothes and bathed me. She wrapped my broken rib with an Ace bandage, dressed me in pajamas that had been packed in my suitcase, laid me down and covered me. Later, she said she'd given me something to make me sleep. I didn't remember that either.

I awoke to the sunlight coming through the weave of persimmon curtains. I tried to get up but my body was not so cooperative. It was impossible to sit up directly from a lying down position. When I flexed my stomach muscles, the pain was unbearable. Only by swiveling my legs over the edge of the bed was I able to rock myself into sitting. Getting onto my feet was not as easy, though: I nearly passed out. But once I was standing, it wasn't so bad. I could more or less walk normally if I kept my back straight.

Elaine sat at the dining room table, already dressed, drinking coffee. "You should have called out for me," she said, jumping up and putting her arm around my shoulder for support. She held my hand as I eased into a dining-room chair. A new carton of Camels was on the table. She'd opened it and taken out a pack. Several extinguished butts were already in the bowl. She sat down and leaned forward, elbows on the table. "Can I get you anything?"

I picked up Elaine's lit cigarette propped against the side of the bowl, put it in my mouth and took that first drag of the day. It wasn't what I'd hoped for.

"Here," she said, getting me a fresh one out of the pack.

I shook my head and half extended my arm to give her the cigarette. She reached across the table and took it. "Coffee?"

"Just a sip." I stretched to reach her cup, but was stopped short by a pain in my side. "I haven't felt that one before," I tried to joke.

But my pain was reflected in her face as she pushed over the coffee. My lower lip throbbed to the touch of the warm cup. I could only imagine what I looked like. The coffee was black with a little artificial sweetener, but I didn't mind as I drank through the only corner of my mouth that wasn't painful to the touch. My slurps echoed through the silence of everything not being said.

"Hungry?" she asked, handing back the cigarette. "I went to the grocery and picked up—"

"Maybe in a little while."

"You need to eat before we leave."

I set down the cup. "Where do you think we're going?"

"To the police station," she said.

"Why?"

"Don't you remember? I'm turning myself in."

I crushed out the cigarette, pressing down so hard it burnt my fingertips. "I must have been delirious. That's the last thing—"

"When I saw you on the street last night, I thought you were dead and... " She put her hand on top of mine. "Once I confess, Nikki will be safe. Everything will be out in the open and nobody will have any reason to go after anybody else. But I want to go to San Francisco, not Berkeley. I want you to be in charge of my case."

"I won't be in charge of anything," I said. "Cantwell will, and he doesn't want you to confess. He'll bury the whole business somehow, perhaps over your dead body."

"How could he get to me if I'm in custody?"

"He'll have somebody do it for him. Listen, he may not have wanted anybody dead when this thing started, but a third murder will seem a lot less serious now that he needs to cover up the other two. And you're the last person he wants talking."

"What does he want me to do?"

"I'm supposed to meet him at ten o'clock tonight."

"You can't even drive in your condition," she said.

"I'll manage."

She got up, walked to the front window and looked into the bright morning. For the first time I noticed that a small triangle of the green-blue bay was visible between the elm tree and two houses across the street.

"If you promise to keep quiet about him," I said, "he might get the D.A. to agree to a lesser charge."

She returned to sit at the table and reached over for the coffee. After taking a few sips she passed it back to me.

"I'm sorry about what happened between us," she said.

"I'm not," I said, trying to reach across the table for her hand, but she lowered it onto her lap. Her lips settled between a smile and what it was covering up.

"I thought about giving up my practice and moving," she said, "but Nikki would have run away again and come back to Berkeley. I couldn't have stopped her."

"And Chris would have gotten to her," I said. "How long did you take to plan it?"

"It was pretty impulsive. If I'd thought too much—"

"Some things seemed well thought out—disguising yourself as a hooker so you wouldn't be identified."

"It all began with an innocent remark by one of the survivors I interviewed who said I was young and pretty and should let my hair down once in a while. So for a lark I wore something slutty to a Halloween party. If I hadn't worn that costume, Allen wouldn't have noticed me. Nor would he have asked his son about me. Chris never would have been aware of my existence and wouldn't have befriended Nikki as a way to get to me."

"Where is the costume now?" I asked.

"I don't have it."

"Did you dispose of it?"

"No. I thought it might look incriminating if somebody found it right after Chris's death. It used to be up in my closet in some hat boxes."

"In that empty space on the shelf," I said.

She nodded. "He took it when he stole the files."

"That means Cantwell has the one piece of physical evidence that can link you to the scene of the crime."

She pressed her lips together and gave me a stoic smile.

"What about the prescription in Mrs. Cantwell's name?" I asked.

"I took the chance that the pharmacy wouldn't call Mrs. Cantwell for confirmation."

"You got a lethal dose, Elaine. The prosecution can construe that as premeditated murder."

"You think?" she said, then dropped her head onto her arms.

"You need to tell me about it," I said.

"I need to tell the world," she said. "That's why I want you to take me downtown."

"You need to tell me first."

Neither of us spoke for a time. She finally took out a cigarette, lit it, and looked at me, hoping I'd let her off the hook. I knew how to remain impassive while waiting for a confession. She looked down at the table and shook her head over and over, slow as a grandfather clock's pendulum. Then she began to tell me what had happened the previous Sunday night...

CHAPTER THIRTY-EIGHT

When I'd called Chris about a note he'd written threatening Nikki, he told me there was only one way I could save my daughter. I remembered a hotel he'd mentioned where he took prostitutes and told him to meet me there. I arrived a little late and he was waiting on a chair with his hands folded over a hunting knife on his lap.

He rose with a superior air as he slid the knife into a sheath on his belt. Keeping his hand on the knife's handle, he took his time evaluating how I looked. He began with my stiletto heels, worked his way up fish-net stockings, bare stomach and halter top. He passed over my face as if it didn't matter and his eyes finally rested upon my wig.

I'd put on the same costume I'd worn to the Halloween party where I'd met his father. In one of Chris's sessions he mentioned that his father talked about how hot it made him to see an uppity bitch like me dressed as a whore. I'd hoped to throw Chris off balance by bringing his father's fantasies into the room.

"You made it pretty clear on the phone what price I'd have to pay to keep you away from Nikki," I said.

"Price?" he said with a boyish pout. "You act as if I'm ugly or something."

In his letterman's jacket, with thick hair brushed over to the side and big blue eyes, he looked anything but ugly.

"You know that's not your problem," I said.

"I hope you're not here to talk about problems, Doc," he said, approaching me.

I stood my ground, waiting to see how close he'd come. "That wouldn't do much good, would it?"

"Not in a million years." He stopped about three feet away.

"Exactly," I said, giving him a resigned smile.

"So not even a little part of you's interested in doing this?" he asked.

"You want me to be willing?" I said in a casual tone.

I knew that for him the question of *willing* only had to do with breaking my will. I reached in my purse and took out the vial of morphine.

"Maybe with this... " I said, raising an encouraging eyebrow.

"What is it?" he asked.

"There's a long medical term for it but—"

"I know everything there is to know about drugs," he said. I'd never yet found a topic Chris didn't claim to know everything about. "Some neuro-aphrodisiac like Spanish fly."

I didn't tell him that the medical profession did not believe in aphrodisiacs, neuro or otherwise.

I veered around him and sat on the bed, setting the vial on the nightstand. "You'll have a lot more enthusiastic partner."

He snatched up the vial and held it to the light.

"Don't you want me to enjoy it as much as I did with your father?" I asked.

"Liar," he said, tossing the vial into the air and catching it. "He would've told me if he'd scored with you."

"Would he?" I asked.

Chris gave me a boyish smile. "He couldn't pass up the chance to lord it over me if he'd nailed my therapist."

I leaned back casually on my elbows. "Even if I made him promise that silence was the only way I'd give myself to him?"

"Give yourself!" he said, laughing. "Poor Dad never did realize things aren't worth shit when they're given."

"Why's that?" I asked.

"When you take something you know somebody's gonna miss it."

"So there's got to be winners and losers," I said, tilting my head as if seeing him in a new light.

"Don't look at me like that," he said.

"How do you want me to look—ashamed?" I snatched the vial out of his hand. "You've won, Chris. I give up. I might as well enjoy it."

He grabbed the morphine back. "What did you say it was, again?"

"My own secret recipe," I said with a smile. "A special cocktail I put together, you know, to enjoy sex with strangers... or... other unusual circumstances."

"Say we split it?" he said.

I got up off the bed and circled him, stopping in front of an overstuffed chair. "I didn't bring enough for two. I didn't think you'd need it."

He set the vial back on the nightstand. "Forget it, then," he said, taking off his jacket and throwing it at me. I let it slide down the front of my legs.

"Your turn," he said.

I picked up his jacket and folded it over the back of the chair.

"For what, Chris?"

He licked his lips, trying to look salacious. Truth was, he looked too much like a boy. It was almost humorous. But mostly sad.

"You have to tell me what you want," I said.

"Show me your titties."

I noticed his fingers tremble and again looked into his face as I lifted my hands to remove my top.

"Keep your eyes down like one of those Jap gashes," he said.

"Geishas."

"What-the-fuck ever. Just do it."

I lowered my eyes and reached back to untie the knot on my halter top. I peeled back the cloth slowly, exposing my flesh inch by inch. I took off the top and held it up in front to hide my breasts while folding it. I didn't lower it until I turned around and unfurled the spangled cloth on top of his jacket. When I finally showed him what he'd asked for, I turned my head in shame.

His eyes lit up, as if I'd given him exactly the right amount of everything. He took off his shirt and threw it on the chair.

"Take off your shoes next," he said.

I bent from the waist to un-strap my heels, wondering if he derived any pleasure from the shape of a woman, or if it was only about power. He dropped one of his shoes as I laid mine under the chair. He unsnapped the sheath and slid the long blade in and out of its leather slit. "I bet my dad beats off thinking about you."

I picked up his shirt off the chair and folded it, keeping my eyes lowered.

"Take off your skirt now," he said.

I heard his other shoe drop as I undid the chain-mail belt on my miniskirt and laid it over the arm of the chair, careful not to crease my top. I unzipped my skirt and folded it next to the blouse. I was in black panties, black garter straps, black stockings and a blond wig: a two-dimensional magazine foldout. Like Chris, I'd put on a mask molded to the requirements of the moment. But he couldn't take his off—there was nothing underneath.

I looked up at him imploringly as if I could no longer stand the humiliation. "Let me get high, Chris, please."

He threw the knife at the table top and watched it wobble around the embedded point. He tossed his pants across the floor. As I bent down to pick them up, he lifted a shoe above his shoulder as if to throw it at me. I kept one eye on him while folding the pants. That's why I didn't notice that his wallet had slipped from his pocket under the chair. I laid the pants on top of his other clothes. He dropped the shoe haphazardly. It landed on top of the other one. Now naked, he lay back on the bed.

"Go ahead and get it ready," he said, pointing to the vial.

"Thank you," I said, stopping to straighten Chris's shoes with my feet. I sat on the edge of the bed, took the syringe out of my purse and placed it on the nightstand. I could see him out of the corner of my eye, stroking his penis and staring at me.

"Watch me beat off," he said.

"I need to do this first."

I picked the vial and peeled off its foil cover. After filling the syringe I went over to the chair to look for something to use as a tourniquet. I pulled the leather belt off his pants.

"Use yours," he said.

I draped his belt over the back of the chair and picked up mine. Bringing it over to the bed, I sat next to him. Laying down the syringe, I began wrapping the belt around my bicep.

"You really thought I was going to let you have all the fun?" he said, yanking away the chainmail links so hard they almost cut my arm. Tilting his head to one side he winked and said, "Tie me off."

I removed his hand from a full-blown erection and wrapped the belt around his arm.

"Bite me hard, Doc. I'm into your kind of pain."

I yanked hard and slapped his vein with the back of my fingertips. When I picked up the syringe to shoot him up, he grabbed it away from me.

"Jack me off while I do it," he said.

I felt like vomiting as I wrapped my hand around his cock, but I wasn't sure if that was because of what I was doing or what I was about to do.

He inserted the needle and began injecting the morphine.

"I get to have all the fun," he said like a taunting child.

"Yes," I whispered, trying to imagine I was stroking a sick child anywhere but where my hand actually was.

After he finished injecting all the morphine he handed me the syringe. The drug hit him immediately and his eyelids began to droop.

As I looked down on him, the entire story must have been written all over my face.

"That was no fucking aphrodisiac you gave me," he said, muscles tensing along his arms, legs and neck. "But I already knew that." He gave me a prankster's smile.

"I don't think so," I said.

"Doesn't matter." His voice was beginning to slur. "I've had you coming and going from the get-go."

He was right. He did have me coming and going. Either I sacrificed my daughter or killed him. One way or the other he'd prove I was as soulless as he was.

"Now I'm all full up, Doc, and you'll be running on empty 'till kingdom fucking come."

Slowly his muscles went slack. He began to wheeze. His chest heaved. Then his breathing became inaudible. I laid my hand on his and put my ear to his chest. When his breathing stopped, my fingers were still touching his.

CHAPTER THIRTY-NINE

The midmorning sun was already high over the roof. Its rays reflected off the front lawn, inclining through the bay window and illuminating Elaine's down-turned face. In the wash of that reflected light her features seemed classically balanced: rounded nose softening a slightly square chin; pixie bangs exposing a high forehead that offered an ample stage for the play of her eyes; the downward arc of her mouth perfectly resolved in silence. Decaying shadows that fleshed out the contours of her cheeks made her look like a girl, at least as young as Nikki, perhaps even Sarah.

She closed her eyes for several seconds; when she opened them I saw no connection between us. She'd shut me out. Did she think I was staring at what she'd called her mask when I should have been looking deeper, down into her heart? Perhaps I should have tried to convince her that I'd glimpsed the innocence of her soul, but she knew I didn't believe in souls. Whatever transpired, things were no longer the same.

"It was an icy moment," she said, just to say something.

"Is that why you laid the bedspread over him before leaving?" I asked.

"Little things kept calling me back." She swirled a cigarette around the side of a bowl, shepherding stray butts down to the cluttered bottom.

"You left makeup in the sink when you washed up."

"I still feel like I haven't gotten it all off." She lifted her face into the light, rubbing fingertips over her cheeks.

"What about Nikki?" I asked.

"She'll have to go live with her father," she said in a matter-of-fact tone.

"Why not at least wait until I talk to Cantwell before you make that decision?" I asked.

She smiled, all teeth and no humor. "So the two men can cut a deal over the little woman."

"Me and Cantwell?" I said. "What about you and me?"

"It was a mistake," she said.

"I don't believe you."

"Of course you don't." She lifted the cigarette to her lips but lowered it without taking a drag. "After all, we touched souls, right? And then we had so much in common—I interviewed Holocaust survivors. Or was it that our parents shared the same dismal fate?"

"I was drawn to you before I knew all that."

"Love at first sight," she said, stabbing out the cigarette.

"It wasn't just your looks," I said. "Even if you'd been less attractive, something about you made me feel like... like before I'd ever been—"

"Compromised," she said, looking more sympathetic. For a second I imagined she knew exactly what I was unable to say and was about to tell me she felt the same. "By killing men?" She leaned back in her chair, crossing her arms. "I can put two and two together. You were an assassin. A member of the *Nokim*. I know what you did. But that's a very different situation from mine."

"It doesn't matter," I said.

"It doesn't?"

Her smile cut right through me, and just like that it faded like a wisp of cloud into an empty sky.

***

Mara once asked me to say I loved her.

"I read words like tea leaves," she said. "Even if you don't think you mean it, I'll know by the shapes of sounds and silences in between."

We'd spent the week in a posh resort built against a sea cliff on the Amalfi Coast. The water seemed to have melted away our cares, and for a few sun-drenched days we were consumed by playful laughter, feeling almost as young as we were. If she'd asked me to say something before our target had arrived I may have even reacted differently.

He was a wealthy German industrialist. A respected citizen the Fatherland wanted to protect. As an ex-Waffen SS *Obersturmführer*, he'd been low ranking enough that with his country's help he was able to evade war crimes investigators. Although his official position with the Waffen SS did not involve him in any criminal activities per se, we had eyewitnesses who'd seen him participate in ad hoc executions during Germany's invasion of Russia.

For the next several days on the beach Mara and I laid down our towels close to him. Mara said he was one of the best looking men she'd ever seen—as handsome as John Garfield—enjoying the irony of comparing him to a Jew. She paraded around topless, trying to catch his eye and lure him off alone. Her body got the attention of most men on the beach, but our target was too busy doting on his plump wife and making sand castles with his two children.

We probably could have killed him in front of his kids and gotten away with it. One day they went out on a paddle boat and were a good half hour from shore. But after watching my father get slaughtered, I couldn't subject other children to the same haunted future. Mara agreed that we needed to get him alone. But not for the same reason. She was a perfectionist who liked to keep things clean. That meant no witnesses, not even young children who probably wouldn't be of much help to the police.

On the fourth day, at about one o'clock in the afternoon, he went alone to his hotel room to make a business call. For the last three days the children had stayed on the beach late with their mother, once until past five. That would give us at least a few hours head start. In any case, the Italian police weren't known for their efficiency. Our plane out of Rome would probably get off the ground before their investigation.

The hotel rooms had old locks with key slots large enough to be picked by an Allen wrench. Mara's hands worked quickly and silently. We were upon him in less than a minute. He took the ambush coolly and didn't deny a thing. He described his involvement in the slaughter with the same regret as a loyal family man who'd slept with a prostitute on a business trip. There was no trace of the killer in his eyes. I imagine there was in mine, though, as I held the Beretta to his head.

On the drive to Rome I said, "It was as if we murdered the wrong man."

"Nobody's the same as they were six years ago, six months ago, or even six minutes ago," Mara said. "If we worried about that, there'd be no such thing as justice."

I didn't tell her I always felt like the same man, carrying the weight of everything I'd ever seen and done.

We checked into a small hotel near the top of the Spanish Steps and ordered a late dinner in the room, having decided we wouldn't go outside until the taxi came the next morning to take us to the airport. It was hot. Mara opened the sagging French windows, heavy with centuries of white paint. She stripped and laid her lithe body on the creaky bed. Guilt infused my lust like the hot wind sweeping out of the night into our room. All my emotions were ignited, most of all the primitive aggression I'd always kept under wraps. It was the first time I'd taken her without question.

Afterward, when she asked me to say I loved her, my body went numb. I could no longer feel the crumpled sheets beneath me. It was not the same kind of numb as when I was about to kill a man. That deadened nerves and flesh. This went deeper.

"You think that love has gone the way of the soul," she said. "Like God, it's become irrelevant."

"What has the soul got to do with it?" I asked.

"The soul is the part of us that can love and be loved," Mara said.

"I don't have one," I said.

Her body gathered effortlessly into a sitting position, one leg crossed over the other—head, neck and back forming a classical arch. Straight blond hair hanging down concealed her mouth. I could only imagine her cutting smile.

"If that were true, you'd simply lie to me," she said.

CHAPTER FORTY

I drove blindly through a fog, relying on memory to race through the turns along Marine Drive, which skirted the shoreline and dead-ended at Fort Point. When I'd dropped Elaine off at Richard and Miriam's, Richard had handed me a note saying that Feiertag had called me at the office. I'd planned on stopping by to see him first, but a fatal accident on the Bay Bridge had held me up for hours. And now I was late and worried that Cantwell had not waited for me.

When I parked and got out of the car, the night was so impenetrable I couldn't even see silhouettes of the Golden Gate's steel struts a quarter mile away. I followed the sound of lapping water to the concrete parapet's edge, reaching out for the iron boundary chain. Fingering the rust-pitted links I edged around the point to the west side of the fort, thinking Cantwell would want to meet close to the base of the bridge where it was more secluded. I didn't stray from the water's edge until I heard a shoe scrape the ground.

I made my footfalls louder.

"Over here, Inspector."

And slowly approached.

In his black wool overcoat Cantwell first appeared like a smudge against the mist, as featureless as a brush stroke in the Impressionist street scene on Elaine's wall.

"Thank you for being prompt," he said. "It's been one hell of a day, and I still haven't prepared my speech for the students tomorrow. Did you see me on TV?"

I shook my head.

"I hate letting those Russian bastards get away with it again."

I took out a Camel. As I turned up my butane lighter's flame to light my cigarette, he said, "Jesus, what in the blazes happened to your face?"

"Why don't you ask your Nazi friend?" I said, increasing the size of the flame and moving it between us to see his reaction.

Cantwell squinted at the light and pushed back my hand. "I apologize for that. Hopefully we can get past his stupidity and move on to a beneficial resolution."

I extinguished the flame. Traces of light came from somewhere else. An obscured moon? Warning lights refracted by the fog off the invisible bridge towers and high walls of the fort? Whatever their source, standing within a few feet of him I could just make out his overanxious expression.

"Beneficial for whom?" I asked.

"You mind letting me have one of those things?"

"I thought you didn't smoke."

Before I could hand him one, he grabbed the pack from me. He slapped the foil top against his fist and a cigarette fell to the ground. He paused a moment to see if I'd pick it up for him, and bent down as if that's what he'd intended in the first place. He took his first drag without inhaling and coughed out the second one.

"Let's get to the point, Inspector," he said, holding the cigarette between his thumb and index finger. "We both know who you're worried about—I don't want to see her go to jail either."

"Are you worried about her or yourself?" I asked.

"I want to do the right thing, for Christ's sake," he said, taking a quick puff off his smoke. "It's not as if it was her fault."

"Whose fault was it?"

"Hell—" Cantwell was cut off by a container ship's horn blast. He scuffed his foot on the ground, waiting for it to stop. "I'll take responsibility if that makes you feel any better." He glowered in the direction of a second blast from the horn. "Maybe if I'd set some limits for the boy—" He took a deep breath to calm himself during the third blast. "Look, I think we both agree that although technically she might be guilty, she's not a murderer."

"We might agree," I said, "but I'd like to hear your reasoning, just the same."

"I already told you I take responsibility." He turned toward the ocean, where the fog formed like condensing breath from the waters' impatient murmuring. "She had no choice. She was forced into it. Okay? Now, can we find some way to put this business behind us?"

I stopped and listened to the random squawks of seabirds, which seemed almost melodic over the rhythmic slap of the restless water.

"She wants to confess," I said.

He stomped out the cigarette. "Talk her out of it."

"How far did *you* get with her?" I asked.

"She doesn't think too highly of me." Cantwell laughed nervously. "I guess I can't blame her. But you're more her type. I'm sure you can reason with her."

"And say what?"

Cantwell relaxed a bit. Thinking out strategies of persuasion was familiar territory for him.

"Okay, tell her this," he said. "She sacrificed herself for her daughter's happiness. What kind of life does she think Nikki will have with a mother in prison, always being forced to communicate through a wall of steel and glass?"

"She might think that's better than communicating through a wall of dishonesty."

Cantwell paced out a circle. On his return, he said, "Maybe we can find a way for her to have the best of both worlds. Let's say she waits until after the election to confess. Then I'll help her. I'm sure we can convince a jury she's sorry for what she's done."

I didn't think the word *sorry* would hold any relevance for Elaine. But Cantwell wouldn't have understood that.

"And, of course, in return for your help, you will remain clean of any scandal," I said.

"With a soft judge, she might not spend a day in jail." He looked away again, summoning up a picture-perfect future out of the fog.

"What about Milan?" I asked.

"He's not a problem anymore." Cantwell waved his hand through the air to dismiss the assassin. "He's been called back to gather intelligence on the Russians."

"So now there's nothing to tie you to the death of those two women."

"That's how a cop might look at it," he said. "A man who cares for a woman might see it another way."

"Either way, Elaine's the only one left who might talk."

"That wouldn't be good for anyone," Cantwell said.

"What about my cousin and her husband?"

"They were implicated by your past, which vanished with Milan. We might even be able to work something out about that little incident with you and that woman at Finocchio's the other night."

"You mean your wife?"

I thought he raised a reprimanding eyebrow. I couldn't tell for sure, though; the night seemed to have suddenly gotten darker.

"Do we have a deal?" he asked.

"I'll see what I can do."

"I need to know for sure," Cantwell said.

"I can't speak for her," I said, straining to see his reaction. But the night had become so murky I could no longer read his face.

***

I arrived at Feiertag's after eleven. When nobody answered I tried the doorknob. It was unlocked. I stepped into the lightless room and smelled sulfur. My first thought was that the odor hadn't necessarily come from a gun; it could have simply been from matches. But then came the faint metallic odor of blood.

After sixteen years I still remembered where the light switch was. I reached out in the dark and turned it on. Across the room Feiertag was stretched out on the floor with his torso curved above his legs, his corpse forming the shape of a question mark. A perfect final expression of a repentant child killer. Would his God forgive him after all?

I closed Feiertag's eyes and mouth. He was still warm. I didn't think he'd been dead much more than an hour. My .22 Beretta lay in a pool of blood by his head. I wiped it off with my handkerchief. I wondered if he'd wanted to tell me not to trust Cantwell. Anyway, that didn't matter now. Maybe the congressman had lied outright or maybe he was no longer in control of the situation. The only thing that mattered was that Milan *was* a problem. And I was certain he'd be going after Elaine next to keep her from confessing.

CHAPTER FORTY-ONE

I spent the night in my car across the street from Richard and Miriam's house with the .22 Beretta on my lap. Milan had emptied the magazine and left one bullet in the chamber. A taunt, I was sure: that was all I'd once needed, right?

At five o'clock a boy on a bicycle threw the *Tribune* on Richard's driveway. It was still dark but I glimpsed the reflection off the newspaper's plastic wrapping under the yellow-orange glow of a streetlight. I went across the street and brought the paper back to my car.

Using the car's overhead light I studied a front-page photo of a poster boy Russian "liberator" being given a cigarette by a pretty Czech coed. In the background a mother could be seen grimacing and clutching her child. Further back, almost totally obscured in coarse black-and-white photo dots, I spotted a group of students sitting on the street in front of a tank whose gun was pointed at them.

The Russians were too arrogant to care about a few disaffected men like me who could see past images posed in the foreground. They were again about to prove that power trumped truth. The once great lion of a man, General Svoboda, who had single-handedly taken on the Nazis after the rest of the Czech army had capitulated, was now a docile lamb in Soviet hands.

The old Czech general had stepped into their trap by going to Moscow to gain the freedom of the kidnapped Czech leaders. Soviet Premier Brezhnev wore the mask of a kindly grandfather as he hugged Svoboda and kissed him on the cheek. Nobody knew exactly how many men Brezhnev had destroyed after similar embraces, but it had come to be known as his kiss of death. In this case, it would be the death of Czechoslovakia's soul.

I must have slipped off for a few minutes. It couldn't have been too long, though, before Richard woke me by rapping at the car window. It was drizzling and he wore a regulation yellow slicker over his uniform.

"What happened with Cantwell?" he asked.

"I'll explain later. I need to talk to Elaine."

"She left with Miriam about an hour ago," he said, reaching into his pocket and handing me a note hastily scribbled on a lunch bag.

> Hon,
> Gone to help Elaine look for Nikki who snuck out of her
> friend's house last night.
> Love you,
> M

"I found it when I got out of the shower," Richard said.

"Do you have any idea where they went?"

"First to drop Jason off at school and then Elaine's house, I guess."

"You'll be at the demonstration?" I asked.

Richard nodded. "Everything okay?"

"Keep an eye on Cantwell, will you?" I said.

"If anything goes wrong at the demonstration," Richard said, "the chief says he's our number one priority."

"Stick close to him," I said, turning over the engine.

"By the way," Richard said, "if you run into anyone from the SFPD, we have orders to arrest you for the assault of fellow officers."

"Thanks," I said, pulling away from the curb.

***

Elaine's car was in the driveway. I knocked on the front door. No answer. I went around back and tried lifting myself up through the bedroom window where Milan had broken the lock. Pain spread from my ribs throughout my entire body. But it wasn't the pain that made me drop back onto my feet. If I did something stupid like puncturing a lung I wouldn't have been able to go on. I went to the door off the patio that opened into Elaine's bedroom. Instinctively I reached for the .38. Then remembered Milan had taken it. Pulling the small .22 out of my pants pocket I broke the glass with its butt.

Elaine's bedroom looked exactly as it had before. The bed made, perfumes and lotions arranged on the vanity, closet shut. I opened the door leading to the hall and went into the living room. It also looked undisturbed. I checked the kitchen. Before we'd gone to Richard and Miriam's, Elaine had washed and put away everything including the candy dish we'd used as an ashtray. Nothing had changed. I entered Nikki's open bedroom door. Clothes were strewn on the floor, and books and records scattered around her unmade bed. With all the clutter I couldn't tell if she'd been there or not. But when I surveyed the bathroom, her toothbrush was still gone.

I was about to head down to Berkeley High to see if Miriam had driven Elaine there to look for Nikki. But I remembered that before we'd left, Elaine had shut Nikki's bedroom door to hide the clutter. She kept it that way even when nobody was home. So why was the door now open? She must have checked in there for clues to her daughter's whereabouts, and then something sent her off in such a big hurry she neglected to close the door again. I returned to the teenage disorder to figure out what Elaine had seen. It took a minute before I realized that the picket sign that had been lying in the corner was missing. Then I knew where Nikki must have gone and that Elaine was sure to have followed.

CHAPTER FORTY-TWO

Edging up a narrow campus lane to the main north-south road, I honked at kids in jeans and T-shirts, traipsing through a fine drizzle. Most were slow as cattle getting out of my way onto the bordering dirt and grass. My plan was to connect to that main road and drive directly to the demonstration, tucking my car away behind foliage or an official vehicle. But access was blocked by a chain barricade at the bottom of a knoll.

I got out of my car and left it in front of a *No Parking* sign hanging on the chain. The sky was nasty with black-and-white clouds tussling in the high winds. A biting wind swept under my jacket and cut across my ribs, causing a dull throb. Looking for an easy way over the knoll I tailed two boys carrying picket signs saying *Hell No We Won't Go*.

I climbed up a dirt footpath that wound through a eucalyptus grove and trampled azalea bushes to get onto a lawn that was enclosed on three sides by the back wings of Dwinelle Hall. Wriggling through a boxwood hedge, I angled to the far side of the sprawling structure. After climbing halfway up the sloping front courtyard, I passed a loosely assembled line of Berkeley police blocking the doors of the building. Across the main road, five more uniformed officers were stationed on the steps of Wheeler Hall. I guessed they wouldn't have allowed Elaine entrance to her office. Good. One less place to have to look for her.

The boys I'd followed went one way and I veered off the other, toward the sound of a muffled voice coming from a loudspeaker. Climbing to the main road I caught sight of the tail end of the demonstration. Twenty or so patrolmen stood outside a sea of students; the backs of their heads blocked my view. I couldn't even see the speaker's podium on top of Sproul steps. I wasn't about to push my way into the crowd and become trapped, unable to maneuver.

Although I couldn't see who was addressing the demonstration, her voice was now clear as she quoted a speech by the student activist Mario Savio: "There is a time when the operation of the machine becomes so odious, makes you so sick at heart, you can't take part. And you've got to put your body upon the gears and upon the wheels, upon the levers, upon all the apparatus, and make it stop."

Great! But from where I stood the apparatus was impossible to locate. I had to secure a higher vantage. Skirting the demonstration, I found myself pressed against a waist-high concrete wall abutting Sather Gate's wrought-iron arch. Onlookers were packed shoulder-to-shoulder, standing on top of the wall. Normally I would have flashed ID, hopped up and pushed somebody out of the way. But given the shape I was in, I wasn't going to be able to do that.

I caught the eye of a boy with rain-frizzed hair directly above me, and before I could think twice he'd reached down and grabbed my hand. It felt as though hundreds of stilettos were jabbing the insides of my rib muscles as he pulled me up. That pain subsided into waves of cramps once I'd squeezed in among the line of students. The kid kept his arm around my shoulder until I straightened up. He said he respected somebody my age coming out to support the cause. Just the kind of encouragement I needed at that moment.

Below us, many thousands of standing spectators surrounded a few thousand sitting in the center of the plaza. The participants overflowed the huge plaza onto bordering sidewalks and stairs. They were pressed up against railings of the Student Union balcony, which gave a bird's-eye view of the proceedings. A few had sneaked into Sproul Hall and were hanging out of windows. Kids had even climbed trees to see over the heads of others. Hundreds of uniformed police stood guard around the protestors. Elaine and Miriam could have been anywhere and I wouldn't have been able to pick them out. Same with Milan. I'd have to think like him to have half a chance of catching him.

If it was me, I'd try somehow to get Elaine alone, but from where I stood, students and police were everywhere. Yet there were places I couldn't see from my position on the wall: lonely spaces behind columns at the back side of the Student Union; secluded areas in the lower plaza; dark corners beneath overhangs. Maybe even some deserted hallway or backroom inside Sproul Hall.

Police were blocking access to Sproul. They were also spread out over the steps, guarding the speakers who were protected from the weather under cover of the Greek-columned portico. Cantwell sat up there with his wife who wore a floppy black straw hat and sunglasses. The chief was next to them with two plainclothes cops acting as bodyguards. Milan would stay as far from them as he could. He'd need bait to lure Elaine away—like Nikki.

I might not have been able to pick people's faces out of the crowd, but I could read a lot of their picket signs. Many said the same old thing: *Make Love Not War*; *Get Out of Vietnam Now*. Nikki, however, being the unique young woman she was, had the only placard reading *Kiss a Fascist Pig Today*. Having broken into Elaine's house, Milan might have also known about Nikki's sign. And he too could have located her sitting about twenty rows from the Student Union steps, right in front of the speaker's mike. Like David and Wiki, she must have slept over to have gotten a good seat.

The quickest way to Nikki would be to skirt the demonstration to avoid stepping over people sitting on the ground. I'd have to weave through a cordon of Oakland police standing in front of the Terrace Restaurant, but they wouldn't know who I was. Scanning the route further up, though, I noticed the SFPD contingent strung out along the top of the steps to the lower plaza. If I kept to the outskirts of the demonstration, I'd have no choice but to pass in front of them.

Richard stood next to Fanelli, who was staring up at Sproul steps. When I glanced over to see what he was looking at, I saw Cantwell gazing back at me. As soon as our eyes met, he turned away and whispered something to the chief, who took several steps to the side and gestured in my direction with his head. Lieutenant Fanelli put his arm around Richard and said something, then turned his back on me. Richard looked directly at me and shook his head, signaling something was wrong.

I didn't feel much pain as I jumped to the ground, adrenaline pushing me through the sitting demonstrators toward Nikki. Although its electric jolt could have given me the strength to shove anybody out of my way, I didn't need to. The seas miraculously parted as demonstrators swung their knees aside and pointed out places for me to find footing. When I stepped over David and Wiki, she yanked my pant leg to get my attention and said, "Welcome to our side, neighbor." Her smile seemed as bright as eternal youth.

The four uniformed SFPD patrolmen who'd been sent after me did not get such a welcoming reception. Protestors purposely blocked their path.

When the cops tried to muscle their way in, more kids stood up to keep them back, forming a wall ten deep that obstructed the uniforms' access into the crowd.

Cantwell didn't notice this peripheral ruckus as he stepped up to the microphone with one of the plainclothes bodyguards who held an umbrella over the congressman's head.

"The Soviets have begun firing on students in Prague," he said.

The crowd became hushed, and for a moment I stopped wending my way through knees and ankles to listen to him.

"Casualty reports are sketchy, but I speak for all Americans when I say that we condemn in the strongest terms this brutal and illegal action taken against law-abiding citizens."

I continued forward as the crowd broke into applause. I had to hand it to him—Cantwell was one hell of a politician—a well-known hawk getting a group of anti-war demonstrators to clap for him. Hell, even God seemed moved as the skies thundered.

If everybody else was fooled by Cantwell, smart little Nikki was not. "Sneaky fascist," she muttered as I came up from behind and tapped her on the shoulder. She looked aghast at the sight of me. I wasn't sure if she was shocked by my bruised face or simply my presence.

"Have you seen your mother?"

A few umbrellas flipped open around us. Other students held notebooks and newspapers over their heads as the drizzle turned to a fine rain.

"What would she be doing here?" Nikki asked, staring forward as if she didn't want to be associated with an adult or cop, or maybe both.

"Looking for you," I said, grabbing the sign out of her hand.

I held the sign high above the crowd. I wasn't sure who I hoped to attract—Elaine or Milan. Either way I'd be a step ahead. If it was Milan, I had one bullet and one advantage—I didn't care if I was apprehended. Let the shit fly where it may.

The rain wasn't heavy enough to disperse the crowd or deter Cantwell. Now that the congressman had the demonstrators' sympathies, he wasn't about to let up.

"As we are witnessing today," he said, "free societies allow their citizens to express all points of view without resorting to repressive measures."

I was still holding up the sign when I heard Elaine call out Nikki's name. I waved my free hand in the direction of her voice. But I still couldn't locate her as she yelled my name this time.

First scanning nearby faces and then working my way back, I spotted Elaine next to Miriam, standing in the crowd on top of the Student Union steps. I waved my hand and called out her name.

She cupped her hands around her mouth: "Where's Nikki?"

I was about to point down at the girl when I saw Milan draped over the railing of the balcony above Elaine. He'd probably seen Nikki's sign long before I had and waited for Mom to join her daughter.

Although he couldn't yet sight Elaine—she was hidden from his view under the balcony—he now knew where she was. I'd given away her position by yelling her name and waving. Milan could also figure out that she'd soon come into his line of fire, rushing to join Nikki. He slipped behind a column and appeared on the other side, holding my .38 Special. He rested the weapon on the railing. The gun was hidden from the view of those around him by his body and the column.

"That's the difference between these free and democratic United States of America and totalitarian Soviet Russia, and why we have to fight the spread of communism in Vietnam." The congressman had finally made the point he'd come for.

Nikki stood up to boo Cantwell, making it possible for her mother to see her. Elaine pushed forward into the crowd, calling out, "Nikki! Nikki!"

She would have made a good target soon after landing at the bottom of the crowded steps. I placed my body in front of Nikki and held up my hand like a traffic cop. Elaine halted at my signal and looked around. Seeing no danger, she continued. Within seconds Milan would have a bead on her. Then he'd slip into the crowd and be gone before the police knew that the shot had come from above.

Milan gave a flicker of a smile as I pulled out the .22 he'd used to kill Feiertag. I'd be lucky to hit the person next to him with that short-range assassin's weapon. He now focused his attention on the place where any second Elaine would step into his sights. I fired my one shot into the air. The Beretta might have been small, but surrounded by stone walls and glass windows, it made one hell of a reverberating bang. And got immediate results. Elaine, who'd just stepped among the sitting demonstrators, was stopped as panicked people jumped to their feet.

"What are you doing!" Nikki said as she watched me slip the pistol back into my pocket.

"Your mother's in danger, Nikki, please," I said, pointing up to Milan.

Nikki spotted the assassin holding a gun. Things were happening too fast. She'd have to trust me. She grabbed my hand and followed my lead toward her mother.

As if the chaos on the ground wasn't bad enough, thunder ripped open the sky to a grievous downpour. The mob surged away from the demonstration's center to get out of the open plaza. This mass hysteria was Elaine's only salvation. She was pushed back by the tide of out-rushing humanity, giving me time to get to her before she came into Milan's line of fire.

I glanced up and Milan gave me a cold nod as he slowly shifted the angle of the pistol, which he now pointed at David and Wiki. He'd given me a choice: them or Elaine. I threw down the picket sign and kept dragging Nikki toward her mother, yelling over my shoulder, "David, Wiki, down!" I motioned with my free hand for them to get to the ground.

The young couple was among a handful of people standing in place. David looked vexed at his fellow protestors running past like frenzied animals. Wiki tilted her head to one side and gave me a resigned smile. The .38 Special's explosion boomed. I couldn't see her face as she was spun by the impact of the bullet and fell to the glistening blacktop.

David yelled, "The fucking pigs are shooting!" Then fell protectively on top of his downed girlfriend.

I swung Nikki into her mother's arms and pushed both of them up to where Miriam stood on top of the stairs, under the balcony, out of Milan's sight. A rock flew over our heads and crashed through a plate-glass window. I pushed the women behind a column, sheltered from the stampede of students rushing through the broken window into the safety of the Student Union.

"That man up on the balcony shot a girl," Nikki said.

Elaine crept to the edge of the steps to look down into the plaza. Her gaze drifted toward David. Several patrolmen were manhandling the frantic boy. One hit him across the back with his baton.

"Leave him alone, you bastard!" she screamed.

It wasn't until the cops finally managed to pull David to his feet that Elaine realized what he was fighting over—Wiki's dead body.

Sensing she was about to rush into the plaza, I grabbed hold of her.

"That's where he wants you," I said.

I scanned the campus for exit routes. The four SFPD patrolmen who'd come after me had pulled out their batons and were battling a dozen or so students who fought back with picket signs and fists. Toward Telegraph Avenue, a trash can under a kiosk had been set ablaze. An Oakland cop dragged a girl by the hair around the corner onto Bancroft Way where the buses for arresting students must have been parked. Out on the street, protestors rocked a police car in an attempt to overturn it. Across the plaza on Sproul steps, a group of SFPD patrolmen had formed a circle around Cantwell and his wife. Richard was with them, as was Fanelli and the chief. Richard glanced my way and pointed toward the center of campus.

"They plan to use the Campanile as a command post," Miriam said.

They could get a view of the whole campus from the clock tower.

"Let's go with them," Miriam said. "We'll be safe up there."

"Elaine's not going to be safe anywhere around Cantwell," I said.

"The streets are well guarded," Miriam said. "You'll get caught if you try to get off campus."

"I have a key to Wheeler," Elaine said. "We can wait it out in my office."

CHAPTER FORTY-THREE

We decided that Nikki would be safer away from Elaine. We sent her off with Miriam to find Richard and tell him about Milan.

"Let's head for those trees on the other side of Sproul," I said to Elaine.

As we passed Wiki's body Elaine stopped. The girl had been shot in the heart. A flash of lightning brought into relief the rain-diluted blood spreading over her breast. The pink splotch formed a shape similar to the dead girl's lips, which lay easily, one against the other, as if she'd said her peace.

"We're not safe here," I said, yanking Elaine's arm.

She glanced up at flames spitting out of a second-story window of Sproul Hall and made eye contact with me, nodding assent.

We zigzagged across the plaza to avoid skirmishes between patrolmen and enraged protestors who believed the police had killed a demonstrator. The sound of their fighting was drowned out by thunder and the downpour drumming against concrete, brick and stone.

Elaine and I paused to get our bearings under an old oak by Strawberry Creek, sheltered from the rain by its umbrella of leaves. Scattered students ran past. They picked up their pace as we heard a rumbling that at first sounded like another round of thunder. A searchlight swept the grass in front of us, as a helicopter lowered into view. We slipped around to the creek side of the tree to hide, Elaine crouching behind its thick trunk. I tried to do the same but the pain in my side had returned, and I ended up sitting on a protruding root. The wind from the hovering copter whipped up rain at hurricane speeds.

Elaine yelled over the engine's roar, "Do you think they're looking for us?"

I no longer had any idea what the department's priorities were—beating up students and coming after people like us who were a threat to Cantwell? I felt drained by a lack of sleep and overexertion. My pain was worse than ever.

The tree root trembled under us. The rotors had increased speed as the copter lifted above the trees and lowered over the road in front of Wheeler Hall. We had to get to our feet, cross the creek and make a run for it over that road, possibly exposing ourselves to Cantwell looking down from the clock tower, or even a bullet from Milan.

I clambered down the weedy incline. Elaine passed me and leapt over the creek. I couldn't jump and had to wade through. With muddy feet I slipped while climbing up the other side. She took hold of my hand and pulled me up the slope. Emerging from the trees we saw across the road that the steps of Wheeler Hall were now empty. No more patrolmen. The helicopter circled toward Sproul Plaza.

"I'll run ahead," she said. "It's going to take a few seconds to unlock the door."

I hoped adrenaline would kick back in as I lumbered across the road. Yet I didn't feel the slightest surge. Not even when I glanced up at the granite clock tower's Plexiglas barrier and thought I saw the dark shadow of a face looking down at me. Elaine was holding open the door when I got to the top of the stairs.

The power was out in Wheeler Hall. I'd noticed it had been out in other buildings too, maybe from the storm. Little light filtered through Wheeler's glass front doors, barely revealing an outline of stairs. We grasped the banister to guide us up through the darkness of the stairwell. Although Elaine was more familiar with the building, without the benefit of light she relied on my memory to locate the double doors on the third floor landing. I depressed the release bar, unlatching the lock. We felt our way along the wall, counting doors to the fifth, Elaine's office. She fumbled, finding the right key by touch, and handed it to me. I slid it into the lock, opened the door and edged in first. With its wall of exterior windows, the room was relatively well lit compared to the rest of the building.

"I have to get out of these wet clothes," Elaine said. She opened a desk drawer and pulled out sweats and a towel with which she fluffed her boyish hair. "Mind turning around?"

"I've seen you naked," I said.

She tilted her head to one side to let me know that privilege had been revoked.

I reached into my pocket for a cigarette. They were soaked beyond smoking. I chucked the soggy pack onto the floor.

"You can use the towel when I'm done," she said, waiting for me to face the other way.

I stared out the window at the Campanile, listening to the slap of her wet clothes on the back of a chair. Now that I was up on the third floor, the clock tower's Plexiglas gave off less of a reflection and vague shapes were visible behind it. A flash of lightening penetrated the semi-transparent barrier, momentarily illuminating Cantwell who waved down at the building across the road from us.

"Do you have a weapon?" I asked.

Wearing blue sweats she squeezed next to me and looked out the window. "What?"

"A knife or anything?"

"No."

"Lock the door—push the table, desk, everything you can against it," I said. "I'll be right back."

"Not a chance," she said.

"I'm just going down to the basement to get the fire axe."

"An axe? In your condition?"

"We don't have time to argue," I said, going out the doorway.

She caught up to me at the stairs. "I'll go in front, in case you stumble."

"No. I want to be between you and whatever's down there," I said, already beginning my descent.

Elaine stayed close behind me.

Adrenaline had mercifully kicked back in and I didn't need to hold onto the railing. I forced myself to picture the basement I'd been in the week before. Without any windows, it would be even darker than on the stairs. The axe was in the main hall, but locating it would be like blindly groping through a maze. First, the basement stair landing was walled off on all sides. We could get so turned around simply trying to find the exit, we'd be likely to go the wrong way after coming out the door and get trapped in a corner under the stairwell. Then, once we'd gotten into the auxiliary hall off the stairwell, several stub walls would present themselves. In the light, walking around them was automatic. But mistake one of those walls and we could easily find ourselves wandering down the wrong hallway.

We came to the bottom of the stairwell and exited the landing, turning back toward the basement stairs. Gray light filtered through the glass front doors of Wheeler, faltering halfway to the back of the large rectangular room. About thirty feet away a match flared in the dim foyer.

"You're early," Milan said. He held the match over his watch. "About eleven minutes."

"Eleven minutes?" I said.

"Your fellow officers will appear on the outside stairs," he said. "When they hear the shot they'll wait just long enough for me to get out the back door. You'll be arrested for the murder of the two women killed today by your gun."

Wiki was the first and Elaine would be the second.

He took several deep drags off his cigarette and used its ember to read his watch again. The high-ceilinged lobby began to quake as the helicopter once again lowered above the road out front. Milan looked surprised as its searchlight swept up the outside stairs and through the glass doors, filling the hall with a blinding glare. I grabbed Elaine's hand and pulled her toward the back of the building. In the few seconds it would take for Milan to see again, we might be able to disappear into the darkness at the back of the foyer.

A gunshot's steely echo penetrated the helicopter's low rumble. From its high-pitched ping I gauged that the shot had hit in front of us, on the corner of the wall that led to the basement's stairwell. When the searchlight rotated away, we were safely in the darkness of the passageway that led to the stairs. Milan's angle was all wrong to put a bullet into that narrow space. We arrived at the stairs without his firing another round.

A spasm shot up my right side as I pivoted to lower myself onto the first step. Bending my right leg to carry my body's weight, the pain became crippling. I'd only be able to put my full weight on my left foot and take the stairs one at a time.

"Go first," I whispered, grabbing Elaine's hand and guiding her around me.

"But—"

"Turn around at the bottom. Look for the door on your right. Hurry!"

Milan would reach the top of the stairs before I'd be able to get down to the safety of the landing. The stairwell was only four feet wide, and even firing blindly into the dark, he could find me with three well-angled shots. And I was sure that despite the pulse of the copter's rotors his hearing was keen enough to pick up even the slightest scuff of my feet descending the stairs. I'd have bet that over the sound of his own charging boots he'd heard Elaine's footfalls on the steps. But could he have actually discerned that it was only one set of feet? Or had he naturally assumed that we were both already down in the basement?

Staying put on the top stair, I lay back against the wall. Milan's footsteps halted just shy of the stairwell. Then nothing; I had no idea where he was. The copter's rotating searchlight invaded the lobby again, reflecting off walls and onto Milan's forearm, extended with the gun pointed down the stairwell. I grabbed and pulled. As his weight rolled forward, he tried to stop his downhill tumble by holding onto me. I threw my arms around him, and locked to one another we bumped against the railing. Somehow managing to keep on our feet we spun like ballroom dancers down several steps. I heard the clank of the pistol bounce down the stairs. On our third twirl, with my back against the wall, I pushed off with my foot and held onto Milan as he landed on his back.

We sledded down the stairs head first, Milan's skull bouncing off the edge of each step before we hit the floor of the landing and his arms went limp. I literally saw stars shoot through the near-total darkness, but at least I was conscious. Breathless, I climbed onto my hands and knees. Crawling over Milan I began to search for the .38, feeling around the bottom few steps and sweeping my arm across the floor, working my way toward the doorway.

Then came the gun blast—deafening in the small confines of that landing. Had Milan fallen on the pistol? I couldn't waste time thinking about how he'd regained consciousness and found my .38. Crawling out the landing's doorway, I was even more short of breath than before. From sheer terror? The bullet had split the air above my head. Milan had heard me and known exactly where I was, but he'd shot at what he thought was a standing target.

Yet the bullet might as well have penetrated my side, the way I felt when I tried to get to my feet. I couldn't catch a breath. I'd have to stay on my hands and knees. Hopefully Milan didn't know the layout of the basement and I'd still have the advantage of darkness. The important thing was not to let the pain interfere with my thinking. I had to focus on the path I'd laid out in mind.

Where was Elaine? I wondered, as I bumped into the second stub wall and crawled around it into the main hallway. About five feet up I'd cross an intersecting hallway and have no wall to feel my way along. I hoped I'd do better on my hands and knees staying on a straight course than I would have on my feet. If I veered, I might end up crawling down the wrong hall. When it seemed I'd gone too far, I realized I must have angled off to the right, otherwise I'd have hit the wall of the transverse hallway. Angling to the left I looked for a guidepost.

The first object I came to did not feel at all familiar. Rubber, canvas and strings. Elaine's foot? Sliding my hands higher, my fingers gripped legs that didn't move a muscle. She knew better than to make a sound. We were still too close to Milan. I rose onto my knees and slid my hands along her body, over hips and breasts, until I had hold of her upper arms. She put her hands under my elbows and lifted me. Rising with the weight of my body against hers, my breaths were quick and shallow.

After several seconds on my feet, I felt as though something had readjusted in my rib cage. The pain diminished and my breathing came slower and easier. With my body still pressed against Elaine's, we edged along the wall toward the fire axe, sliding in and out of three doorways. After we'd gone about twenty paces, I figured that even if Milan had found his way out of the landing, he couldn't pinpoint our location by the sound of our whispers echoing down a long hallway.

"I think I'm okay on my own now," I said, pulling away.

She gently rotated my shoulders so that my back was against the wall, then rubbed a finger across my lips. I could feel the blood's warm lubricant. She put an ear to my chest. "You've punctured your lung. I can hear the air leaking out. If it collapses you might only have a few minutes of consciousness."

"I need that axe," I said, continuing to edge toward it.

Keeping my back against the wall for support, I slid in and out of the next three doorways. Elaine walked sideways in front of me. From time to time I felt the touch of her fingers, waiting to catch me if I passed out. I stopped at the fire box. Everything was silent for a second. Then I thought I heard a footstep at the other end of the hall.

Somehow Elaine knew I'd begun removing my jacket. Her thumbs hooked the lapels. I turned around so she could slide it off and faced her again. She laid the jacket over my arm. I touched her cheek to say thank you and nudged her around to the far side of the box, in case Milan aimed for it.

I pressed down on her shoulders. She supported me as we both dropped to our knees. I wrapped the jacket around my fist and broke the glass on the front panel of the fire box. In rapid order, the bullet pinged shy of us and then we heard the gun's explosion. While I was tying the jacket around my waist, Elaine moved so silently I didn't know she'd gotten up and taken down the axe. She lifted my right hand and put it on the handle, which I used to pull myself to my feet. I was hardly aware of any pain, although my breathing was still short and shallow.

I moved my cheek across hers to find her ear and whispered, "Stay here."

She rubbed her forehead against mine to let me know she was shaking her head.

"Please," I said, touching my lips to hers as I withdrew.

I couldn't drag the axe; the sound of its metal head sliding along the floor would have given away my location, the direction I was heading and my speed. I held it up in front of me, the grip in my right hand and the throat in my left. If carrying the weight caused my body harm, I couldn't feel it. I guessed Milan was near the intersecting hallway. That's where I'd seen the flash of the gun's muzzle. I didn't think he'd have moved from there. It was a good defensive position, giving him a wall to duck behind. Besides, eventually we'd have to come to him; there was no other way out.

He must have heard my footsteps as I followed along the wall. But he held his fire. Why give away his location until I was on top of him and he'd be sure of hitting me? About ten feet from his estimated position, I laid my jacket on the floor. Although the fabric made a slight rustling sound, I didn't think he'd be able to figure out what I was doing. I stepped onto the jacket to silence my footsteps as I angled across to the opposite side of the hall.

Leaning against the wall to steady myself, I laid down the axe head, making sure the hickory handle protruding through the steel eye touched the floor first. No metal clink that way. I lowered my hand into my pants pocket, just above change and keys, to avoid a rattle. Pinching a corner of the yellow star, I slid it out, with the tin-can top still inserted. The metal-weighted fabric would make a sound closer to flesh and bone than something purely metallic like coins or a cigarette lighter. I tossed Sarah's star within a few feet of Milan and watched for the muzzle flash. The shot was so loud, I felt as though I was at the center of a thunderclap. The bolt of lightning that immediately followed seared into my mind the image of the man I wanted to destroy.

I lifted the axe above my head as I took two long strides, and brought down the blade. Thunk—the sound of tendon and bone. Clunk—the pistol landing on the floor. Milan's wail was like nothing I'd ever heard before—as close to the sound of a wild animal as a person could make. I pulled back the axe, summoning a slightly altered picture of the assassin in my mind. He'd have bent over at the initial pain of the blow, but have risen again, arms and chest out like an enraged bear. I'd be aiming for his neck.

I swung the axe like a baseball bat looking for a waist-high pitch. I heard him duck at the sound of the blade coming through the air. The weight of the axe head flew out of control, twisting me off balance. I felt Milan's right hand grasp the handle. Rather than let loose, I allowed myself to be pulled down by the axe. Now it was my turn to make animal sounds, as flames licked the insides of my ribs.

Like wrestlers at the beginning of a bout, I was on my hands and knees, with Milan draped over me, breathing down my neck. His right hand was still on the axe handle, just above mine. His left hand hung limply by my side. That's what I'd hit. As long as he kept his one functioning hand on the axe, I thought he had nothing to fight with. But when he began yanking the axe away, his right hand seemed almost as powerful as his left. And I'd lost control of my searing stomach muscles. I wasn't going to be able to hold on. There was only one move left.

I couldn't fall directly onto my ruptured stomach, nor did I dare land on my broken ribs. Keeping my right hand on the axe, I rolled onto my left hip and let my torso follow. It worked. I fell on my good side and Milan's weight pressed down on his bad hand. He groaned as he tumbled away and let loose of the axe. I used the handle to help me to my knees. This time I'd bring the blade straight down; even if Milan had risen to his knees it should split open his head.

I heard footfalls and voices upstairs. Police? I raised the axe over my head anyway. The lights went on. Milan was on his feet, looking down at me. Now that he could see, I had no advantage at all. I'd be much too slow trying to swing an axe from my knees. The best I could do was use the handle to block his blow. Milan leaned left as if he was going to kick me with his right foot. It really didn't matter that it was a feint; I could not even lift the axe to defend myself. I watched helplessly as he switched weight onto his right leg. I think he knew my ribs were fractured and a well-placed kick could be as lethal as a bullet. He pulled back his left foot, winding up to give me the full benefit of his steel-toed boot.

For a moment I thought the sound of thunder came from my mind snapping in anticipation of the pain. The impact of the bullet altered Milan's kick just enough that it landed high, under my armpit. In the split second it took for me to register the pain, I watched all passion and desire drain from him. His face looked like a mask whose maker lacked the imagination to give it expression. He stumbled forward, exposing Elaine, who stood behind him clutching my .38 in both hands. My vision became blurred by a muscle-wrenching pain that traveled to every part of my body.

Milan hit the ground first. I was just conscious enough to land on top of him so that he cushioned my fall.

CHAPTER FORTY-FOUR

"Simon, Simon," Elaine said, shaking me until my eyes opened.

My head was lying on Milan's lifeless body.

"Where are they?" I asked.

"They'll find the stairs and be down here any minute."

"Help me up," I said.

When Elaine lifted my shoulders a few inches, I felt as though I was about to pass out.

"We have to get you to a hospital," she said.

Something wet and warm was sticking to my hair and neck. I touched it with my fingers. Blood. Was it mine? I saw the gun lying on the floor, out of reach.

"Get me off him first," I said.

Supporting my shoulders, Elaine slid me onto the floor, exposing the bullet wound in Milan's back. That's where the blood had come from. My head had been lying in it. I reached over, picked up my .38 and lifted it onto my stomach. Clutching the grip in my right hand, I laid my bloody fingerprints over hers.

"It's not that easy, Simon."

"His killing will never be investigated," I said.

I didn't think she'd heard me. Her eyes were filled with a dark silence I knew only too well. No words could resurrect the men whose lives she'd taken. No apologies make up for the loss—not to the world at large, which would be happier without them—but to her inner world, where every life no matter how derelict was integrated into the wholeness of mankind.

Richard and Fanelli came downstairs. They halted just outside the door to the stair landing, surveying the situation. Milan lay face down, the circle of blood spreading across his back. I lay next to him, gripping my .38 Special, the pistol that had killed him. Elaine looked ashen, slumped against the wall, head on her knees.

"Shit," Fanelli said. "I'll call for an ambulance."

"Don't you want me to do that while you question them?" Richard asked his boss.

Fanelli stood silently for a second. "No. I think we all know what happened."

Richard looked puzzled.

I wasn't. The lieutenant was going upstairs to find out exactly what it was we all knew.

"My wife's with Dr. Meyers' daughter upstairs," Richard said. "Maybe a squad car could take them home?"

Fanelli nodded and left.

"He attacked me," I said. "I shot him."

Richard looked at Elaine, then Milan and at me again. "In the back?"

"It was dark. He was turned around. Didn't know where I was."

"The shot came several seconds after the power was turned on," Richard said.

I knew it sounded absurd that a trained killer like Milan would have remained with his back to an opponent who was holding a gun, when he would have had plenty of time to turn around after the hallway was lit. And I was fairly certain that Richard had guessed who had really killed him.

Forty-five minutes later I was carried out on a gurney. It had stopped raining, although the clouds still looked threatening. About fifty police guarded the road in front of Wheeler Hall where an ambulance was waiting for me. Cantwell and his wife were on top of the stairs with the chief standing at attention by their side. The congressman was addressing the press:

"And here comes the inspector now—our own brave officer who disarmed and killed the communist terrorist that is responsible for today's regrettable events and the tragic death of that lovely coed."

Flashbulbs went off in my face. TV cameras waited for me at the bottom of the stairs. Richard rushed over and pushed away the reporters. "Give the inspector some room, for Christ's sake." He grabbed the gurney away from the attending medic, who said he'd meet us at the ambulance.

"You killed a communist terrorist!" Richard said when we were alone.

"Cantwell, the chief, Fanelli, they're all saying I shot him," I said. "It's got to be true."

"Shit, you'll probably even get a fucking commendation," he said with a smile. "Something ain't right."

"No, it isn't," I said as Richard stopped the gurney at the ambulance.

The medic loaded me into the back and left me alone while he took care of some last-minute business.

Mrs. Cantwell poked her head in.

"Good work, Inspector, you're a hero," she said, taking off her sunglasses.

"I think you know better," I said.

"I'm no different than anyone else. I only know what I'm told. Listen, you don't have to worry about Allen anymore." She crinkled up her nose. "He likes things just the way they are."

Fanelli walked past with one arm around Elaine and the other around Nikki, leading mother and daughter to a squad car.

"I'm not worried," I said.

"Good, then we have a marriage made in heaven, or wherever." She waved her sunglasses across the sky, allowing them to eventually fall in Elaine's direction. "You'll keep silent to protect her and she'll do the same for you."

"How long did it take you and your husband to learn the fine art of compromise?" I asked, lifting my head to watch Nikki climb into the squad car.

A wind kicked up. With a gloved hand Mrs. Cantwell pulled down one side of the hat's floppy black brim, hiding an irrepressible blue eye. She gave a classic Dietrich smile—the beautiful woman who knew she was trapped in outward appearances.

Fanelli held open the back door of the squad car. Before getting in, Elaine turned to me. She had the perplexed look of somebody who'd spotted a familiar face in a crowd, but couldn't remember where she'd seen it before.

ACKNOWLEDGEMENTS

I am deeply grateful to the many people who have helped me with the writing of this novel. More people than I am able to remember have added their insight and wisdom to these pages. I have been working on *Prague Spring* for ten years and I apologize to anyone whose input I have overlooked or forgotten. First of all I would like to thank the members of my writing group who have patiently helped me shape this work, Trai Cartwright, Eileen Austen, Teresa Rhyne, Lorna Freeman, Chris Kern, Julia Erlich and Stacy McDaniel. I also owe a debt of gratitude to Todd Goldberg, in whose UCLA writing class most of us met, and to members of his various classes I attended whose names I have forgotten. I cannot forget Joe Bratcher, Judy Farrell and the entire Twin Bridges Salon who worked with me over many years as I developed the basic story idea. I must also mention the members of my poetry group who suffered through my lengthy chapter readings in place of pleasantly short poems: Mary Armstrong, Jacquie Tchakalian, Sherman Pearl and Nan Hunt. I have had several close readers who have counseled me through innumerable drafts. My sister Rafaella Del Bourgo has offered so many story ideas I can no longer remember which are hers and which mine. Her husband Carlos Runng helped me to keep the action real. Ed Stanton combed each sentence of every major draft to rid them of clichés, cacophonies and cheap poetic sentiment; if any remain they are due to my stubbornness rather than his efforts. Ruth Jaeger provided me with psychological insight into my characters and helped me give them depth. Her husband Steve Wolf, who grew up in San Francisco and went to U.C. Berkeley, offered his memories of the Bay Area in the late Sixties. Larry Rosenberg, who has worked in various government positions in the Bay Area, helped me with descriptive period details, as well as giving me insight into the operation of law enforcement. Dewayne Tully of the San Francisco Police Department gave me invaluable insight into the workings of the SFPD. Brett Borah, who has practiced law in the Bay Area, helped me with an understanding of their court system. Matt Bogaard of the San Marino Police Department explained the psychology of police departments and law enforcement. Norm Levine, who owned a pharmacy in the Sixties, reached into his memory for details about that world back then. I would also like to acknowledge the Squaw Writers Community and the encouragement of their instructors. And to give thanks to Leda Shapiro for proof reading. Also many of my non-writer friends read the book in various stages to give me the positive feedback and support I needed to keep going; they include, Miriam Bamberger, Pam Ross, Celeste Zellin, Steve Robman, Lynne Kaufman, Peter Kakkavas, Anne Bennis, Lesley Heaton, Susan Rodwig, Miriam Sidanius, Cindy Burg, Gail Boyle, Bruce Haga, Pete Ulyatt and Mike Berg. I must not forget the hard work of my agent, Irene Kraas of the Kraas Literary Agency, who supported me through the ups and downs of getting this book to print. Most importantly I owe a debt of gratitude to my wife Judy Bamberger without whose love and support this book would have never been completed.

ABOUT THE AUTHOR

David Del Bourgo attended U.C. Berkeley in the mid-Sixties as an English major. He now lives in the Los Angeles Area with his wife Judy. David paints as well as writes. He has published three books of poetry. *Prague Spring* is his first published novel.